SCOTTY
— AND —
ELVIS

★

SCOTTY AND ELVIS

ABOARD THE MYSTERY TRAIN

★ ─────── ★ ─────── ★

SCOTTY MOORE
WITH JAMES L. DICKERSON

UNIVERSITY PRESS OF MISSISSIPPI ★ JACKSON

www.upress.state.ms.us

The University Press of Mississippi is a member of the Association of American University Presses.

Manufactured in the United States of America

First printing 2013

∞

Library of Congress Cataloging-in-Publication Data

Moore, Scotty.
Scotty and Elvis : aboard the mystery train / Scotty Moore, with James L. Dickerson.
pages cm. — (American made music series)
Includes bibliographical references, discography, and index.
ISBN 978-1-61703-791-7 (cloth : alk. paper) — ISBN 978-1-61703-818-1 (pbk. : alk. paper) — ISBN 978-1-61703-815-0 (ebook) 1. Moore, Scotty. 2. Guitarists—United States—Biography. 3. Presley, Elvis, 1935–1977. I. Dickerson, James. II. Title.
ML419.M665A3 2013
787.87′166092—dc23
[B]   2012045265

British Library Cataloging-in-Publication Data available

To Bill Black

(1926–1965)

CONTENTS

SCOTTY
— AND —
ELVIS

★ 1 ★

DIGGING UP WEST TENNESSEE ROOTS

When I came into the world two days after Christmas 1931, the same year that George Jones and Skeeter Davis were born, Rudy Vallee and his Connecticut Yankees were all the rage, even in rural West Tennessee, where my mother gave birth to me at home on the family farm. That year Louis Armstrong had a hit with "Lazy River" and Bud and Joe Billings had a country hit with "When Your Hair Has Turned to Silver." Also on the charts that year were Ted Lewis with "Just a Gigolo" and Duke Ellington with "Mood Indigo." It was a very good year for music, but obviously I came along too late in the year to appreciate it. That was just as well.

I hate to admit it, but my existence was pretty much a mistake.

Three years earlier, my sister Mildred Lee, the only daughter in a family of three sons, came down with pneumonia and died at the tender age of fourteen, throwing my mother, Mattie Moore, into a deep depression. My father, Winfield Scott Moore Jr., was equally devastated, but he had an emotional release that Mother did not possess—music. A natural-born musician, he'd learned to play the fiddle and banjo at an early age; in turn, he taught his sons, Carney, Ralph, and Edwin, to play the guitar. In the evenings after work and on Sunday afternoons, they sat on the porch and performed for each other, their music wafting a sunset tinged with honeysuckle.

Mostly, it was a guy thing. Mother and Mildred Lee watched from the sidelines.

In those days, during the decade before the Great Depression, most families, especially those that lived on farms, had to entertain themselves. There was no television. No Internet. No movie theater within a half day's drive. Tennessee didn't have a radio station until 1921—and it was located on the other side of the state in Knoxville. Not until the Grand Ole Opry went on the air in the mid-1920s on WSM in Nashville did we have reliable, Southern-friendly entertainment that traveled the airwaves into every home.

3

The men of the family were fine with entertaining themselves. But Mother didn't have an acceptable release for her grief and there was no slot in the family band for her (women in our community didn't do such things at that time). What Mother needed was another daughter to fill the void left by Mildred's death. By 1930 Mother and Father decided to have another child. Mother was 38 and Father was 40. In those days, it was considered scandalous to have a child at that age.

They knew the neighbors would talk if she got pregnant again, but, by god, they wanted a daughter—and a daughter they would have. Sure enough, Mother got pregnant. No doubt her pregnancy was an embarrassment to her sons, by then fourteen, seventeen, and twenty years of age, but she was headstrong and knew what she wanted out of life. By the time she went into labor, she was convinced that she would give birth to another daughter. There was no doubt in her mind that the first sounds out of her new baby's mouth would have a girlish ring to them.

Oh, boy, did I ever fool her!

She must have asked the midwife several times if she was absolutely certain that I was a boy. "Just check one more time . . . please!" There was no way they could hold me up to the light and twist and turn me and not see that I was of the male gender. Resigned to the reality of a fourth son, they named me Winfield Scott Moore, III. I never knew what name they had chosen for me had I been a girl. Was I destined to be known as Winnie? That wasn't something they ever discussed in front of me. To their credit, they never let on that they felt my birth was a mistake, at least not in my presence. I figured that out for myself. They raised me with the same love and affection they gave their other children.

Because of the age difference, I grew up in relative isolation from my siblings. Carney, my oldest brother, left home two years before I was born to work for the Piggly Wiggly grocery chain in Memphis. Piggly Wiggly would go on to receive fame as the first supermarket chain in America, but we didn't know that then; we were just grateful that Carney had a good job. My second oldest brother, Edwin, joined the Navy when I was two. Ralph, the brother closest in age to me, joined the Navy when I was five. As a farewell gift he gave me his guitar and showed me how to play it. I think it was a Gene Autry model that Sears was selling at the time. It was a bright, arch-top guitar, a lot prettier than the one that Father had given me. He said, "Here, you take mine and I'll keep yours." Later he mailed me a miniature sailor's suit, which I wore with great pride.

★ ★ ★

At the turn of the century, when Mother and Father were coming of age, agriculture was the economic mainstay of rural West Tennessee. Everything revolved around farming. Courtship and family were not undertaken for entertainment or for fulfillment of some vague inner quest for self-identity; economic survival required a successful courtship, followed by successful child rearing. A man who aspired to success as a farmer also aspired to success as a family man. The two went hand in hand. Sons were a lot cheaper than hired hands.

Winfield Scott Moore, Jr., a strapping six-footer, had met Mattie Priscilla Hefley the year before, probably at a school or church picnic. By January 1908 he was wooing her with a passion and devotion to duty that was typical of the times. Couples didn't court by telephone or automobile in those days because there were none. They sent postcards. Depending on where you lived on the postman's route, your musing would be delivered the next day or possibly the same day if you were one of the postman's first stops.

One of the surviving postcards that Father sent Mother was done in pastels. "Go Woman!" read the caption; then beneath it, a quote from the poet Milton: "Fairest of creation, last and best!" There was a drawing of a beautiful woman, reclined as if in sleep. Whispering into her ear was a blond cherub. On the reverse side, written in bold script, was the address—Miss Mattie Hefley, Route 10, Humboldt, Tenn.—and a message.

"Hello, Mattie: How are you this cold morning? This little token sent by me to bring best wishes dear to thee."

The postcard, postmarked January 10, 1908, was unsigned, but sixteen-year-old Mattie knew who the card was from. It was from my father, Winfield Scott Moore, Jr., an eighteen-year-old farmer's son who lived up the road, also on Route 10.

In the beginning, Mattie was reserved in her responses to Scott. She followed up his "Go Woman!" card with a standoffish view of Confederate Park in Memphis.

Hello Scott,
*   Will you allow me to drop you a postal? I received your card OK after so long a time. It was cute. How are you by now? OK, I hope. I don't never see you. Do you stay at home all the time? Your friend,*
Mattie

Scott stepped up his postcard attack. As the weeks passed, the cards became more intimate. Once he sent a card that bore a photographic image of a woman with her arms lovingly placed around a man's neck. The caption suggestively read: "Your kiss is love supreme."

Mattie sent a card with a romantic image of a well dressed couple and a cryptic message that read: "Listen, Scott, I will be at Kate's Saturday night, if I am still alive . . . you ought to see me now."

Then on February 25 Scott sent the following card:

> Hello Mattie,
>   How are you by this time? OK, I hope. Would like to see you. When you are sad and lonely and think of the past, just know that I am your friend as long as life shall last.
>   Your friend,
>   Scott

By then Mattie was head over heels in love. She sent Scott a card with roses on it. In her message, she was complimentary of the days they had spent together and she looked to future days spent together. She ended her note by saying, with un-enigmatic boldness, "I hope to spend them all with you."

Scott and Mattie were married on August 7, 1910. They settled on a 150-acre farm located in a sparsely populated section of Crockett County about five miles from Gadsden and five miles from Humboldt. Memphis was 70 miles to the southwest and Nashville was 120 miles to the northeast. On the gently sloping farmland they planted cotton and corn, and raised cows for milk and hogs for slaughter. And, of course, they started a family. Their first child, born August 31, 1911, was a son. They named him Carney. Then along came a daughter, Mildred Lee, born August 14, 1913. Two additional sons followed—Edwin, born January 24, 1915, and Ralph, born May 2, 1917.

As Mr. Scott, as he was called by family and friends alike, and Mattie worked to establish their farm during the 1920s, the ground rules followed by their parents and their parents before them seemed to have less and less meaning. For generations, cotton had been the main cash crop in West Tennessee; but by the 1920s the crop had come under relentless attack from a tenacious new enemy—the boll weevil, a cotton-hungry insect that'd been unknown to Scott and Mattie's parents. By the end of the 1920s farm life had become progressively more difficult because of the devastation caused by *Anthonomus grandis*, more commonly known as the boll weevil.

To make matters worse, the Great Depression loomed ahead, a dark shadow that danced menacingly across the graves of their ancestors and threatened to move underfoot to trip up their best laid plans. Mother and Father were hit hard by the Depression. There were a couple of years when they couldn't afford to make the payments on land they rented for farming. When the bottom fell out of the cotton market, Father looked for other ways to supplement his income. One way was to use his horse and mule teams to haul logs out of the lowlands. For that he was paid twenty dollars a day, very good pay for the times. Another way was to perform at square dances and parties whenever his sons could get home.

I wasn't old enough to play, but I can barely remember going to a function or two when they were all playing. My daddy was old enough to where he wasn't interested anymore. I'm sure his hands were starting to get stiff on him. I remember he showed me one chord on my guitar, and I thought that was the most beautiful chord I ever heard. I used to just sit there and play that one chord over and over again.

It was around that time that I became friends with my next door neighbor, James Lewis, who was four years my senior. Our friendship was cemented in later years when James's half-sister, Louise, married my brother Ralph. Her most vivid memory of those days is when we all rode to school in her father's wagon. "I was older and I drove the old horse," she recalls. "My brother and [Winfield] would make racket and that poor old horse would just run and run."

James's first recollection of me was when the Moore family came over on Saturdays to perform. I was just a toddler. "Back in those days they had ice cream suppers, and the only entertainment was family bands," says James. "The Moores would come over to our house. That was what inspired me to play guitar. His whole family was musically inclined and they had a family band. His dad played the banjo and one of his brothers played the fiddle and the others played guitars."

Everyone in our community, it seemed, played a musical instrument. The same year I got my first guitar, a neighbor, an old man by the name of Rip Brown, taught James to play his first tune, "Little Brown Jug," on a Sears, Roebuck guitar that his parents had purchased for him. Recalls James: "I learned to play well enough, they later bought me a Gibson. I remember they paid $80 for it and that was a pile of money back then."

James and I used to meet at Rip Brown's house (he lived on the farm between ours) and pick up pointers from him. But the neighbor who probably taught us the most was Oscar Tinsley, who lived in a log house about a mile up the road. Oscar was the most serious guitarist in that part of the country. He dreamed of playing on the Grand Ole Opry, and he sometimes bought time on the nearest radio station so that he could perform in hopes of being discovered by a scout from the Opry. Recalls James: "He was a pretty good country guitarist. He showed us some chords, and finally we got to playing together." In later years, being called an "Oscar Tinsley" was the equivalent of being branded a hopeless dreamer. All us kids wanted to play like Oscar, but no one wanted *to be* like him.

What I wanted most was to play with the family band, but I was too young and inexperienced to keep up with them musically. Still, the rejection stung. I couldn't understand why, if I was a member of the family, I wasn't allowed to perform with them. That exclusion was made even worse by the neighborhood boys who all looked up to my father.

"Mr. Scott was one of the best bass singers I have ever heard," says James. "Us boys would all line up behind him at church and imitate him singing bass. He was good, and he wasn't bashful at all. Of course, at the Church of Christ, they sang a cappella."

Because of our devotion to music we gained a reputation for eccentricity. Sometimes, instead of working in the fields with the neighbors, we sat out on the porch and played music. "We'd go by on our way to the fields and Mr. Scott and the boys would all be sitting out on the porch playing guitars," says James. "We made fun of them because they did that. It wasn't meant as criticism. People just talked about them because they sat out on the porch and played."

When James and I weren't learning new songs, we were getting into trouble. "There were a bunch of families around that had kids our age," recalls James. "What we did for entertainment was to wander the fields and hunt possums. This one particular day, we found a half-pint bottle full of whiskey. There were three or four of us boys, Winfield included. We all took us a drink. Winfield was afraid to go home. He was afraid his mother, Miss Mattie, would smell it on his breath, so he ate him a bunch of wild onions to cover the odor on his breath. Of course, when he got home smelling like an onion patch, his mother knew something was wrong. From that, we named him Onion Seed, which was one of his nicknames. I had an uncle who called him Wimpy, after J. Wellington Wimpy from Popeye."

James had his own nickname, the "Chicken."

Onion Seed and Chicken were the closest thing to outlaws that part of the country had.

I escaped detection that day, but I was not so lucky the next time. I was nabbed stealing communion wine in church. This time I got my butt whipped just as soon as Father got me outside the church. My family always observed Sunday as a special day, but rarely celebrated holidays such as Christmas. My whole family more or less saw Christmas as just another day. You had to feed the hogs and do all that good stuff. I guess I've always been that way.

I remember Mother as being more serious than Father. Since my brothers were so much older, they would never tell me any dirt on him, but there were indications he was pretty tough in his earlier days. But when Miss Mattie got a hold of him, she straightened him out pretty good. He was very jovial. I can't remember ever seeing him completely lose his temper. He would make up his mind about something, and that was it. He would go ahead on. My mother spent most of her time chasing me, usually with a stick of stove wood in her hand.

One of the things I did that irritated her was to play with the black children who lived on the farm as sharecroppers. We played baseball in the pasture, using the typical bases—piles of cow manure—but because there weren't always enough white kids to make up a team, we invited the black kids to join in. "Scotty's mother didn't approve of him playing with them," recalls James. "She objected to him playing with 'niggers,' though it wasn't a derogatory name at that time, it was just another word."

I started school at the age of five at a one-room schoolhouse in Coxville. Before the year was out, I was transferred to a larger school in Humboldt. Some things about school I liked, some I didn't. When it came to schoolwork, I guess I was average. Some things I didn't get as good a grade as others, like math, but I loved geography, prose, and poetry. English and math were probably my worst subjects.

One hot summer afternoon James and I decided to walk home from school instead of riding the bus. As we meandered along the road from town, we were passed by a slow-moving pickup truck towing a trailer. The temptation was too much to ignore. On impulse, we swung up onto the trailer to hitch a ride. I was eight at the time, but remember it as if it were yesterday.

We were ambling along at a steady pace, when James said, "'When it slows down for the bridge, just hang off the end and drop off.'"

I did as I was told, but the truck didn't slow down when it crossed the bridge. I fell to the ground, bumping my head against the gravel road. The accident left me with a knot on my head and a swollen right eye. Mother gave me hell for being careless, and I stayed home from school the next day to nurse my wounds. I had received a BB gun the previous Christmas and I went out back to play with it. Nestled among the farmyard debris I found a rusted barrel that was pocked with holes. In an attempt to fire BBs into the rusted barrel I aligned the barrel of the gun with the holes. As I was shooting the gun, one of the BBs ricocheted back into my face, striking me in my left eye. They say you can't remember pain. Bull. I still remember that.

Mother and Father took me to a specialist in Jackson, but there was nothing the doctor could do to save my sight. Ever since the accident, I have been legally blind in one eye. Needless to say, the BB gun got chucked. My daddy took care of that.

★ ★ ★

The Depression gnawed away at the West Tennessee economy, but life went on. My family, like most families in the region, was able to survive because we grew our own vegetables and raised hogs, the mainstay of protein in the South. The average Southerner in those days consumed two entire hogs a year. Traditionally the hogs were slaughtered during the first cold snap and the hams, shoulders, and sides of bacon were cured in smokehouses. Properly salted and cured the meat lasted indefinitely. Usually, it was fried or boiled with vegetables such as green beans, sweet potatoes, butter beans, or turnip greens and served with well-buttered cornbread and fresh strawberries for dessert when they were in season. The exception to that routine usually occurred on Saturday when Mother and Father went to town to do shopping for the entire week. Mother did not cook lunch on those days. Instead, she served store-bought baloney on white bread, a meal that I recall being absolutely a treat.

Most of the plowing was done with mules, an animal as unpredictable in its behavior as it was dependable in its labor. Sometimes the mules on the Lewis place would break free and make a dash to Mother's flower bed. No matter what the hour—traditionally 3 a.m. was the time favored by the mules—Mother called the Lewises and demanded that they remove their mules from her prized flower bed. The Lewis retaliated in later years by selling their mules to my family. "They'd get out and then they'd come back home and we'd get the pleasure of calling Miss Mattie and telling her to come get her mules," laughs James Lewis.

Seventy miles away in Memphis, Carney Moore carved a niche for himself in the business world. The unemployment rate seemed to double each year. When Carney arrived in Memphis in 1930, there were fewer than 4,000 unemployed, but within two years it had climbed to 17,000. Carney had the good luck, or the good sense, to find work with the most progressive and visionary food market chain in America, Piggly Wiggly.

Clarence Saunders opened his first Piggly Wiggly store in Memphis in 1916. By 1923 there were 2,600 stores nationwide, bringing in more than $180 million a year. Saunders invented the concept of the supermarket, and his marketing techniques revolutionized the American grocery business. Stable work conditions at Piggly Wiggly enabled Carney to support himself and his wife, Auzella, until he could find employment more to his liking. Eventually he took a job with Model Laundry and Cleaners, working as a route man until he could afford to open his own laundry and cleaners, which he named University Park Cleaners. It was located in midtown on North McLean Street near the zoo.

When my brother Ralph was discharged from the Navy, he gravitated to Memphis and worked for Carney at the cleaning plant as a spotter. The entry of America into World War II threw Ralph's life into a tailspin. Although he already had served a stint in the Navy, he was drafted to serve another tour of duty. He took the news with characteristic aplomb: "They were short of men, and I guess they needed me."

The Navy trained Edwin to be a machinist. One day he fell from one deck to another and busted his ankle, earning a medical discharge. He used his newly acquired skills to get work as a machinist at a shipyard in Mobile. From there he was transferred to Huntsville, Alabama, where he earned a reputation as a top-of-the-line tool and die maker for America's space program.

On November 27, 1944, when I was 12, the Chicago Bridge and Iron Company shipyard at Seneca, Illinois, launched a 329-foot cargo ship that was christened the U.S.S. LST-855. With appropriate ceremony, the ship, with its crew of nine officers and 104 enlisted men, was turned over to a ferry crew, whose job it was to get the ship to New Orleans by way of the Mississippi River. On December 10, the LST-855 left Seneca on the Illinois River and made its way to the Mississippi River, passing through West Tennessee and then Memphis about mid-December before arriving in New Orleans on December 20. The LST, the letters of which stood for Landing Ship Tank, was placed in full commission and turned over to its military crew, who prepared it for its voyage to San Diego by way of the Panama Canal.

At the time the LST-855 passed Memphis, I was in the eighth grade and still riding to school on a horse. Tramping around the countryside were bluesmen Sleepy John Estes and Hammie Nixon, who were born in nearby Brownsville. Twenty miles to the south, rockabilly legend Carl Perkins, who was four months my junior, traveled the same countryside, taking in the same experiences. About 25 miles to the west at Nutbush, Annie Mae Bullock, who later changed her name to Tina Turner, was coming of age. For a time, Tina, Carl, Sleepy John, Hammie and I traveled the same roads, popped in and out of the same country stores, and sweated under the same sun—all without ever meeting.

As James and I advanced through the school system, we continued to get in trouble on a regular basis. As a youth I was slender and introspective, happiest when I could avoid being the center of attention. Recalls James laughingly: "Being older and meaner than a snake, I was a bad influence on him. But he was respectful of his parents. Actually, he was a little afraid of his mother. Back then, corporal punishment was in style. If you didn't do right, you'd get your butt paddled."

One day James and I decided to become chemists. We acquired some sulfur and used it to start a fire in the house. Things went from bad to worse and we ran out of the house with the fumes chasing after us. I'm not sure, but I think we were going to invent something. Whether it was the acrid smell of burning sulfur, or the stinging we felt in the seat of our pants after we were punished, neither of us ever again aspired to be chemists.

From that point on, I confined my experiments to music.

Looking back on it, what James Lewis remembers most about my guitar playing was this inner drive I had to do something else with a song. James liked to play the music slow, the way it was written; I wanted to go fast. He wanted to play music you could dance to. It was as if there was some, yet undefined, inner rhythm simmering inside me, something wild and raw trying to break out into the light of day. Sometimes we argued over the right way to play the music. In the end, I usually offered my version of compromise: "You do it the way you hear it, and I'll do it the way I hear it."

In those days James and I were inseparable. We worked together, went to church together, and played music together. Usually we went to school together. "There was a man who hauled us to school in the back of a pickup truck," recalls James. "It had this tarpaulin over the sideboards. He was a cow buyer and he didn't always manage to wash out the truck before he took us to school. Sometimes we rode to school in a truck that smelled like cow shit."

That got old with me. By 1944 I had my own horse to ride to school.

Because my maternal aunt lived directly across from the school, Father built a stable on her property and bought me a horse, which I named Roy. The horse soon became a source of lively debate around the house when Mother decided to display her equestrian talents. It made me furious, and I called out: "Mother you're going to hurt yourself on that horse. You're too old to be doing that." But Mother, who was 53 at the time, didn't think she was too old. She threw a saddle on Roy and rode off down the road, western style, leaving me behind to fret over her headstrong ways.

One day after school, I saddled up Roy and headed back to the farm. Earlier that afternoon a thunderstorm had dumped enough rain to soak the fields. When I reached a 30-foot-wide drainage ditch that I had often forded on the horse, I saw that the water level had risen considerably because of the rain, but I decided to cross anyway. The current was stronger than I realized, and I was pulled from the saddle. Somehow I managed to hang onto the horse and we both made it to the other side. That little horse took me on across. I told him when we got up on the bank, we won't do this anymore.

I was an average student, but by the time I finished the ninth grade I was thoroughly bored with school. I had no close friends at school, and I hadn't started dating yet. If you saw a girl, it would be at a school function or something. I can't remember ever taking anyone to a movie on Saturday. Distance was the big deal, living out in the country and not having a car.

I asked my father if I could quit school and work on the farm. He agreed to let me do that and paid me an acre of cotton for my labor. That year's work netted me a bale of cotton, which I sold, using the money to buy my first professional guitar, a big, black jumbo Gibson that had a sunburst on the front, along with a noticeable crack. I didn't care, though.

Our house was built on a slight incline just off the main thoroughfare, a dirt road that connected all the farms in the area. Later the road would be graveled and then eventually paved. Today it is called Tinsley Road, a tribute to Oscar the Dreamer, who never made it on the Opry but at least got his name on a road sign.

My bedroom was in the back of the house, just off the living room and the kitchen. Mother and Father's bedroom was in the front of the house. To the side of the house was a large oak, with a second oak providing shade not far from my bedroom. Even at midday the room was shadowy and dimly lit, a natural-built haven for young dreams and secret fantasies. From my vantage point in the bedroom, I could pick on my guitar and see everything that was happening in the house, with the exception of Mother and Father's bedroom.

If my guitar picking interfered with Mother's work in the kitchen, I was asked to go outside to the barn or beneath the oak trees. Also out back was the toilet, called an outhouse, and a large, No. 2 galvanized washtub which was allowed to fill with rainwater. The best time to bathe was at the end of the day, after the sun had heated the water.

Tired of my life as a sunup-to-sundown farmer, I returned to school the next year and entered the tenth grade. But school still wasn't for me. I had had a taste of independence and I felt restricted by all the rules that I had to follow at school. The defining moment of my young adulthood probably occurred when James married his sweetheart, Evelyn.

On their wedding day, I went to visit James with guitar in hand; but not until I arrived did I realize something important had changed. All of a sudden, or so it seemed, he turned up married. I was over there trying to get him to play guitar on the night of his honeymoon and that didn't go over too well. James laughs when he remembers that night: "He really didn't know what girls were all about."

James and Evelyn consummated their marriage, but no thanks to my interruptions. Two or three nights a week I went over to James's house and played guitar with him, usually until midnight. Later, when Evelyn was pregnant, my father tactfully warned me that I was going to "run into a party over there" if I didn't stay away. The fact that my best friend had a sex life never occurred to me. Luckily, Evelyn was forgiving of my ill-timed intrusions.

"She tolerated our music making, you know what I'm saying?" says James. "She still tolerates my picking. It's embarrassing to her, I reckon. She calls me 'Oscar Tinsley.' We had this one tune we were pretty good on—at least we thought we were—the 'Hillbilly Boogie.' Evelyn would say,

'Ya'll just play it one more time before you quit.'" James laughs. "She didn't mean it. She was being sarcastic."

Fifty years later, Evelyn still has an opinion about our guitar picking. "It was tough on me," she says. "I had to do all the cooking and tend the children when he was picking and grinning with Winfield. His mother used to call him home and he would usually stay another hour after that.'"

James always described our guitar playing as an "obsession."

Evelyn smiles when she talks about me back then, thank goodness. "He was a pretty good boy," she says. "He was at home when he came to our house. He used to say, 'I'm going to quit and go home after I play this one.' Then he'd finish and start all over again."

Midway through the tenth grade, I awoke one morning feeling I was at a dead end. School wasn't for me. James and Evelyn were forging a new life that, despite their hospitality, I knew did not include me, all of which deepened the sense of isolation that I'd felt my entire life. Everyone seemed to have a purpose but me. Music was the dominant force in my life, but no one, not even I, considered it a potential vocation.

"It was something we did for entertainment," says James. "I don't think Winfield had any inkling of ever becoming a professional musician."

By January 1948 I had made a decision. I would do as Ralph and Edwin had done before me. I'd join the U.S. Navy and see the world. I just had ants in my pants. I had tried farming, and I thought, 'I'm not digging this.' I didn't dig school. I think my brothers had something to do with it. I wanted to do everything they did. But before I could enlist in the Navy, there was an obstacle to overcome. The minimum age was eighteen—or seventeen, with a parent's permission. I was only sixteen. For me to enlist there would have to be a major conspiracy between me and my parents. I went to Jackson, Tennessee, and enlisted. A buddy of mine, a great big ole boy, a six footer, named Sonny Evans went with me. He was older than I was by a couple of years.

The way I had it figured, my friend by association would make me appear older and bigger. After I signed on the dotted line, swearing up and down to the recruiting officer that I was seventeen and had my father's permission, the Navy recruiter, perhaps suspicious of my slender build and youthful face, told me that he would need proof of my age.

The only lie I know my daddy ever told was when he wrote a false birthday in the family Bible. The recruiter came out to the house to check with my daddy and there it was, right there in the family Bible, proof that

Winfield Scott Moore III was seventeen years of age. Who was going to question the veracity of a family Bible? Certainly not the U.S. Navy.

Satisfied that I was of age, the navy recruiter sent me to Nashville for my preliminary physical. Despite being legally blind in one eye, I was referred to Chicago for additional processing. From there, we took a train across the Rockies to San Francisco. Then we went south to San Diego. Almost overnight, I was as deep into the Navy as a man could go, and a long, long way from my West Tennessee roots. The first thing that changed was my name.

Back home they called me Winfield.

In the navy I became Scotty.

★ 2 ★

SLOW BOAT OUT OF CHINA

By the time I entered the Navy in 1948, the number of enlisted personnel had dropped from 2.9 million in 1945 to a little more than 300,000. I could have been sent to boot camp at one of three training centers: Baltimore, Maryland; Waukegan, Illinois; or San Diego, California. By the luck of the draw, I got San Diego, also the training site for the U.S. Marines.

San Diego was more than half a continent away from West Tennessee, but, for all its cultural and geographical differences, it might as well have been on the other side of the world. Standing five feet nine inches—and weighing 136 pounds—I presented myself for eight weeks of rigorous boot-camp training, a slender, square-shouldered teenager away from home for the first time in my life.

No sooner did I arrive than they slapped me down into a barber's chair and shaved my head. Then the medical technicians prodded and poked my body in all the usual places, asking the most personal questions imaginable. After completing my second physical, I was called into the doctor's office. I was terrified I had been found out. I was sixteen, and I looked my age. Maybe that trick with the family Bible hadn't fooled the Navy after all. Maybe they were smarter than I thought. Maybe I was in a big mess of trouble.

The doctor told me to have a seat.

"Do you think you'll like the Navy?" he asked.

I squirmed. "Yes sir."

"Legally I can't pass you," said the doctor. "Because of your eye."

"Yes sir."

The doctor gave me a penetrating gaze, as if he were searching for some semblance of truth or honor or courage. He must have liked what he saw. "I tell you what—I'm going to leave it up to you," the doctor said.

"Yes sir."

"If you want to go home, we'll let you go," he said. "Or, if you want to stay, you can stay."

"I'll stay."

At the time I went into the Navy, blacks had not yet been fully integrated into the armed forces. They had been allowed into previously all-white programs on an experimental basis since the end of World War II; but, for the most part, they were still assigned to duties as cooks.

While I was in boot camp, I got into a fistfight with another recruit, a white sailor from another company. It was one of those situations where the whole damned company is following you and egging you on as you are slugging it out. Just like in the movies. We were going over bunks, throwing each other down the stairs. The whole nine yards. We fought all up and down the barracks. We were about the same size, but I ended up getting the best of the guy.

After the fight, I went to take a shower. Standing under the water, I sensed that someone was watching me. I turned and saw I had a visitor. This big ole black guy from the other boy's company comes in and just slaps the dog shit out of me. Apparently, he didn't like the way the fight turned out. He was taking up for the other white guy.

I suddenly found myself in a new world that only days before would have been beyond the comprehension of any sixteen-year-old from West Tennessee. Not only was I away from home for the first time, I was standing buck naked in a shower with a black man who slapped the shit out of me. I took the beating like a man and chalked it up to experience.

Don't ask me how, but I somehow survived boot camp. Before being assigned to a ship I was given leave to go home. On the way back to Tennessee I was involved in a bus accident in Texas. There was a hill and a curve, and this big truck came down the hill and went over the line. The bus driver pulled to the right, trying to get on the shoulder, and the truck hit the back of the bus and cut it clean off at the wheels. It killed a couple of people. Just ten minutes before that I had been sitting on the back seat. For some reason I got up and walked to the front.

Although I'd only been gone three months, my family and friends saw a pronounced change in me. To the surprise of James Lewis, I tried to renew an affair with a married woman while I was home on leave. It was a woman I had a crush on before I went into the Navy. She was only a couple of years older than me.

"Do you know she's married?" James asked.

"Yes," I said. "But I don't care."

Looking back on it, James still marvels at his friend's boldness. "You just didn't do things like that back then," James says. "He had it pretty bad for her." But if I shocked my friend by chasing after a married woman, talking about racial integration, and showing off scars of fistfights, it would not be the last time. There were more surprises to come.

★ ★ ★

On the day I enlisted, the lead story in *The Commercial Appeal* bore the headline: "Britain Denounces Reds/Moves To Create Bloc/Halt 'Ruthless' March." The story quoted the British Foreign Secretary as accusing the Russian Kremlin of propelling the world toward global war through its efforts to "dominate" Europe. Halfway across the world, nasty words had become nasty deeds. The National Government of China, under the leadership of Generalissimo Chiang Kai-shek, had come under increased attack from revolutionaries allied with the Chinese Communist Party. The struggle had been going on for years, long before the Japanese attacked Pearl Harbor. U.S. President Franklin D. Roosevelt had tried to align China with the Allies during World War II, but Chiang Kai-shek, who had two potent enemies at that time—the Japanese and the Communists—limited his support of the United States to logistical contributions. Americans were allowed to use China to establish bases from which to fight its war with Japan. That's as far as the Generalissimo would go.

By January 1948 it was clear the Communists were gaining the upper hand. Fearful for the safety of Americans in China, Secretary of State George Marshall ordered officials at the American embassy in Nanking to prepare for evacuation. Marshall suggested that all nonessential personnel from interior points north of the Yangtze River and east of Sian be withdrawn while commercial air facilities remained operational.

American naval officers stationed in China were not happy with that decision. After the end of the war in 1945, more than 130 American naval vessels had been transferred to China, along with 50,000 Marines who were put ashore at Tientsin and Tsingtao. The Navy ferried Chiang's troops north to fight the Communists, clearly a violation of the United States' public policy of neutrality in the Chinese war. Any suggestion of a possible withdrawal was greeted with derision by naval officers. The Navy wanted to stand and fight.

Panic set in as the Red Army chalked up one victory after another. *Life* magazine published a photograph in late January 1948 of terrified citizens in Shanghai struggling to get into a government bank to exchange paper money for gold. Refugees poured into Shanghai, Tsingtao, and Tientsin. Inflation reached such exaggerated proportions, beggars would not accept anything less than a ten-thousand-dollar bill. Officials on the cruiser *Los Angeles* became accustomed to treating sailors wounded in knife fights on the streets of Shanghai and treating them for exotic new strains of venereal disease.

As I was leaving boot camp on leave for my visit to Tennessee, Chinese Communists captured four American Marine fliers after their plane made a forced landing in Tsingtao. It was the third time the Communists had captured American soldiers. Eight days earlier the Communists had released four Marines they had held for three months.

When I returned to San Diego, I was pumped up over my visit to Tennessee. I had experienced about as much fun as a sixteen-year-old could have. Within two months of my sixteenth birthday, I had thrown my first drunk, had my first fight, been slapped naked by a black man in the shower, dated a married woman, and scammed, by virtue of my forged birth date, the most powerful government in the world—in short, I had become a man. Now I was ready to flex a little muscle. On my return to the naval base, I was assigned to the U.S.S. LST-855. Destination: Shanghai. I was flown in a seaplane to San Francisco, where I caught a transport to Hawaii, then on to Guam and, finally, to Tsingtao, where the LST-855 was based.

Since it had passed through Memphis in 1944, the U.S.S. LST-855 had an interesting, if undistinguished, war record. Scheduled to be part of the Okinawa invasion, it developed problems and was dry-docked for repairs. In July 1945 it was sent to Pearl Harbor, from which it ferried troops and supplies to Guam. In 1946 the LST-855 was assigned to duty in Tsingtao, China, where one of its first actions was to evacuate Marines from the city of 2.7 million. It was a strategically important city because it was located on the Hai Ho River, which meandered to within a few miles of Peking. A contingent of Marines was left at the American consulate in Peking, as was customary for all foreign diplomatic outposts. The departure of the Marines from Tientsin had little effect on the American civilians who remained. The Navy still had a strong presence in the area. The LST-855 made frequent trips from China to the Philippines during 1947, and made a regular run between Tientsin and the coastal cities of Tsingtao and Shanghai.

I reported for duty on the ship in June or July 1948. If I thought the shocks that I had undergone at boot camp were over, I was mistaken. No sooner had I put away my gear than I was told by the other men that the ship had just experienced a scandalous court martial. Two men aboard the ship, I was told in hushed tones, had been convicted of sodomy. I was warned to be on the lookout in the shower for homosexuals. After what had happened in the shower with the black soldier at boot camp, I was put on guard. Sodomy—the idea that a man would do that to another man—had never crossed my mind growing up in Crockett County, Tennessee.

As if to further emphasize the changing times, President Truman signed executive order number 9981 in July, ordering an end to racial segregation in the armed forces. That was a huge deal at the time. Thus I became a member of the nation's first fully racially integrated armed forces. My rank was fireman III, one grade below third-class petty officer. I was assigned below deck to monitor the ballast tanks, the generators, and the pumps, all of which were run by diesel engines. The petty officer who had held the job previously had just retired. When his hitch was up, they said to me, "We're going to put you there." I was a one-person division on that ship. They never got another chief or petty officer.

Once I learned the ropes, I made friends with a 20-year-old electrician, Merle Parise. "Scotty was still wet behind the ears, just a kid," recalls Merle. "We all knew he had fudged on his age to get into the Navy."

Apart from my age, I stood out from the others because I played guitar. Usually, I played below deck, but sometimes I found a private spot on the stern. During those moments of quiet reflection, I allowed my guitar to express the inner turmoil I felt at being the odd-man-out my entire life. When I played songs the way they were written, they somehow came out different—faster, more energetic. On the outside, I was cool and collected, a shy country boy. On the inside, I was bubbling with some serious emotions that bubbled up from only Lord knows where. Music was my passion. No one had ever heard music the way I heard it. No one had ever felt it the same way I felt it. I was convinced of that.

I was never an instrumentalist. There's not a song that I could sit down and play you the melody all the way through. Most of the stuff I heard I would try to do my own way and capture the feel of it. I never tried to copy a song note for note. People ask, "How did you come up with that lick?" I tell them I was stretching, out on a limb, and that's what came out.

Throughout the summer of 1948, the LST-855 carried cargo up and down the Yellow River, the Wang Po, and the Hai Ho. Usually the ship would load at Shanghai. "Our job was to supply the missionaries," says Merle. "We'd deliver rice, mail, food, anything that would help sustain their livelihood in the back country. As the war got worse for the Chinese republic, our trips became more frequent. It got to where we were hauling tons and tons of rice from Shanghai into Tsingtao. They would off-load the rice, and then send it to the front lines for the troops of the Nationalist government. We even hauled coal to supply the steam trains on the coast."

By the end of the summer Merle and I were best friends. We did everything together. We especially liked to get drunk together when we got shore leave. "Scotty had him a White Russian girlfriend in Shanghai," says Merle. "Once we went to the French Quarter of Shanghai to visit her in a Catholic hospital. She had appendicitis. They were pretty close. If the law had allowed, I think they would have gotten married."

As the Nationalist army disintegrated in the face of Communist opposition, the seaport towns resembled Wild West frontiers more than they did the ancient cities of Chinese lore. Nationalist soldiers jammed into the cities, along with refugees from the countryside, shedding their uniforms as they deserted, breaking into stores, when necessary, to get civilian clothing. Amid the chaos, I roamed the streets with Merle and a new friend, John Bankson.

There were certain sections you had to stay in. It was a dangerous place, but there was also an upside. If you had a carton of cigarettes, you could sell it for $25. You'd see the captain get off the ship with his pockets bulging with cigarettes.

That fall it became clear that the Communists would be victorious. The Truman administration had two options: It could send in American combat troops on a large scale and try to prop up the Nationalist government; or it could give the order to pull out. Truman decided to cut his losses. To the dismay of the Navy, he gave the order to evacuate American embassy personnel and dependents. The long-standing conflict between the Navy and the State Department over China policy snowballed into unseemly confusion as senior officials argued over who was in charge of the evacuation. If the evacuation was not handled correctly, warned the ambassador, it would result in violence against American citizens and embassy personnel.

Incredibly, the evacuation became a free-for-all. On October 23, 1948, the ambassador told the consulates in Peking and Tientsin to issue a formal evacuation warning to all American citizens in the cities. On that same day, the consul general at Tientsin requested help in evacuating the American citizens who remained. He specifically requested Navy LSTs for the operation. He estimated that there were 177 Americans left in Tientsin.

Three days later, Edmund Clubb, the consul general at Peking, cabled the Secretary of State advising that December 15 would be the last date possible to take personnel out of Peking by river. Noting that LSTs draw 13 feet of water, he said that the river now stood at 15 feet. Tientsin harbor normally froze solid by mid-December. Time was running out. Clubb had an additional problem. An American newspaper correspondent based in Peking had found out about the evacuation order. Clubb advised the Secretary of State that the reporter was being cooperative, but he couldn't hold off the reporter much longer.

By the time LST-855 arrived in Tientsin, the Communists and the Nationalists had squared off against each other along the river. As the ship made its way up the narrow Hai Ho channel, I recall shells flying overhead. They did most of their firing at night. They'd fire from one side to the other. They weren't firing at us, but you could hear the shells and see them exploding. Making our way up and down the river was like running a gauntlet. We were watching a movie one night and had to quit because it got so noisy with all that shelling going on. It was an antsy time. You could see the bloated bodies washed up on the bank of the river. You'd see bodies everywhere you went. There was no guarantee that one of the shells from either side would not land right in your lap and dump you into the river with the rest of the casualties. The only ships that got fired on deliberately, recalls Merle, were British. "They put a good sized hole in the side of the *London*," he recalls. "When she came up the river, she came right by us."

By the end of November, Shanghai had become the last American stronghold in China. John Cabot, in charge of the Shanghai consulate, notified the Secretary of State that he had asked the female members of the staff to remain on duty in defiance of the authorization that had come for them to be transferred to Manila. Cabot ordered that American businessmen be given priority over women and children for evacuation.

About one week later, Vice Admiral Oscar Badger notified the chief of naval operations that there were about 2,500 United States nationals left in Shanghai. He had seven ships left in his command, including a cruiser and an LST. My ship made several trips upriver to Tientsin pick up evacuees, but on December 15, we picked up our last load, meeting Clubb's deadline to the day. There were hundreds of people on the main deck. It was loaded to the gills.

It was during this final trip that I made a miscalculation on one of the valves below deck. I mistakenly overfilled the ballast tanks, dumping water onto the deck and down into the passageways. When I heard screams, I ran into the engine room to see what had happened. The exec said that everyone was screaming because they thought the boat was sinking.

"It scared the passengers to death," says Merle. "We all thought we were sinking. I was standing watch over the generators at the time. When I heard the commotion, I went up the hallway and there was water all over the place. I wasn't too scared. If we were sinking, we were sinking. When I found out who was involved, I started laughing like hell."

That December, as the fighting centered around Tientsin, I turned seventeen. Unknown to me or to my family, who had absolutely no idea where I was, our mission had attracted the attention of the *New York Times*. A story in the December 22nd edition reported that Communist troops had converged on the suburbs, cutting the city's rail and water routes. To the northwest, those Peking residents who had not left aboard LST-855 knew it was now too late to escape. My ship had been their last chance for freedom.

Two days later, the *Times* reported that "summary arrests and executions under the guise of 'discipline supervision'" were being carried out in Peking by the national government as a means of keeping the population in line: "Mobile 'courts' in trucks, carrying their own judges and executioners, were established six days ago to investigate cases reported to military headquarters. They are authorized . . . to try cases and mete out punishment on the spot."

Stateside, word of the atrocities in China filtered down to the sailors' wives. Bankson's wife, Analee, was terrified by the stories she heard. Finally, when she could stand the waiting no longer, she demanded an explanation from the Navy. "When I asked them, they said, 'Don't worry. They're probably anchored out in the harbor.'"

With the remaining Americans and their dependents gathered at Shanghai, my ship, along with the remaining ships in the fleet, continued to carry out missions in the Yellow Sea and the East China Sea, taking supplies in and out of Shanghai. By January 8, 1949 (the day on which Elvis Presley celebrated his thirteenth birthday), fighting was fierce in the streets of Tientsin. In a page one story, the *Times* described fighting taking place around the campus of the university. Quoting a foreign diplomat who had remained in the city, the story said that huge flames could be seen rising from the campus.

On January 15, 1949, Tientsin fell to the Communists. Shanghai was still under government control, but Mao Tse-Tung had encircled Peking with his troops. Shanghai businessmen complained to the American embassy that General Tang En-po, the national defense commander, was "putting the squeeze" on the city for protection money. By late spring the

Communists were within 35 miles of Shanghai. On April 25 Communist troops in nearby Nanking entered the U.S. embassy and awakened Ambassador Stuart. They took the 72-year-old diplomat out of his bed and questioned him for "his own safety."

For two weeks Nationalist and Communist forces fought for control of Shanghai. Counsul-general Cabot sent an urgent telegram to the Secretary of State asking for permission to arm embassy guards with 45-cailber pistols. Soldiers were going into the homes of embassy workers while they were at work and going through their belongings. On May 25 the Communists broke through Nationalist defenses and took control of the city. The city's 6 million Chinese and one thousand foreigners were allowed to go about their business as usual, but more than six hundred Marines stationed in Shanghai were transferred to Pearl Harbor, and the fleet's remaining vessels, including my LST, were kept a respectable distance offshore. Throughout the summer and into the fall, my LST meandered about in the Yellow and East China seas, keeping a sharp eye out for Nationalist "mistakes." We were safe from the Communist navy, because the Communists had no navy, but the Nationalists still controlled a fleet of about 100 ships.

Throughout it all I continued to play my guitar. The guitar style of the day dictated two types of performance: rhythmical strumming and cleanly fingered "picking" that stressed the resonance of individual notes. Something inside me led me to "pick" with rhythms instead of individual notes. I never realized it was a radical concept. I played that way because I felt the music that way. I just went with the flow that I felt in the music.

With the Chinese ports now off limits to American servicemen, shore leave was confined to ports in Formosa and Hong Kong. Our main assignment was to stand ready for a final evacuation of Shanghai. When we were out at sea, the only recreation that we had was on the ship itself. "The bow doors on the ship were closed at sea, but it was a free flooding area," recalls Merle. "There were a lot of ladders. As the ship pitched up into the air, we would go down and hang onto the ladders and let the water come rushing up in there. It was a good way to go swimming without going overboard."

By December it was obvious that China was a lost cause. The Communists were firmly in control. The Navy was ordered to take out one last load of refugees and then to head home. My LST was dispatched to Tientsin, where American officials estimated there was only one month's supply of food left. When we pulled into Tientsin, fighting in the streets was still vicious. Two supply ships, the *Butterfield* and the *Swire*, had been machine-gunned as they entered the harbor. A number of bullets hit the bridge of the ships, but no one was injured in the attack.

Everyone aboard LST-855 was on edge. The Associated Press filed a dispatch on December 15, stating that LST-855 had loaded 90 percent of the remaining 400 people waiting for evacuation. Most of them had come down the river to Tientsin from Peking. As our ship pulled out of the harbor, the Communists cut the Peking-Tientsin railroad behind us.

We went to Shanghai, picking up one final load of evacuees before heading for the open seas. Merle, who eventually retired a lieutenant commander in 1970, said the LST-855 was the last Navy ship to leave China. As we left Chinese waters life aboard LST-855 quickly returned to normal. With the sun setting on an old way of life in China, I pulled out my guitar and strummed furiously, creating, I realize now, the first driving guitar licks of rock 'n' roll.

★ ★ ★

After stops in Formosa and Japan, LST-855 was sent to the Aleutian Islands to rid Attu and some of the other small islands of large deposits of live ammunition and bombs left over from World War II. The ammunition was taken out to sea and dumped in deep water.

From there, we went to Bremerton, Washington, for decommission. Located across Puget Sound from Seattle, Bremerton offered yet another cultural shock. As I waited for the decommission to proceed—a process that took about six weeks—Bankson and I formed a band that we named the Happy Valley Boys. Bankson died twenty-nine years later of cancer contracted after he boarded a ship that had been used in the testing of hydrogen bombs in the Pacific in the 1950s, but his widow, Analee Bankson, recalls the Happy Valley Boys with bemused fondness. "I told them they didn't have any talent," she says with a laugh. "I'll never live that down. But they would never play anything all the way through, and that irritated me to no end. They would start something, and then go into something else."

While I awaited my next assignment, I formed a new band, recruiting a steel guitar player named Johnny and a vocalist/guitarist named Sparky. We were good enough to get our own weekly, fifteen-minute show on radio station KPRO in Bremerton. We did a live show, two or three songs and that was it. I don't recall what kind of music we played. Probably country. We probably didn't play very well, but we were about as good as anyone else around, so it didn't matter. Sometimes we performed off-base at nightclubs and private parties. It was at one of those parties that I met a striking five-foot-four brunette named Mary Durkee. That January we started dating. She was eighteen, out of work, and still living at home with her parents.

I got the impression early on that she wanted to get serious, but I was in no hurry. I just didn't feel that I was ready for that. I had never really dated anyone, at least not in the traditional sense. I didn't date before I joined the Navy because I didn't have a car. Once I was in the Navy my experiences with women were confined to the married woman I went out with during my first leave home and the women I met in the various ports we visited.

Years later, Mary was asked how she changed my mind. "I started flirting with his buddy Johnny, and he got jealous and said he didn't want me to go with anyone else," she candidly recalled. "Music was his life. He loved music. That's why he didn't think going with me would be good because music was his first love. It was his life."

Mary remembers me at that age as being very concerned about my appearance. I had a wave in my hair in the front and it drove me crazy because I couldn't do anything with it. One day Mary talked me into getting a home permanent on the grounds it would make the wave go away. I didn't much care for that experience. The chemicals had different odors, all very distinctive, but when they combined they smelled like rotten eggs.

I got my next assignment during the first month of my relationship with Mary. I was attached to the U.S.S. *Valley Forge*, an aircraft carrier that, because of its huge size, was one of the most impressive vessels in the Navy's fleet. Knowing that I was going to be shipped out soon, I proposed to Mary and we were married on March 12, 1950.

"My stepdad wasn't too keen on the idea," recalls Mary. "My mother wouldn't buy my outfit until the night of the wedding. She didn't think I was really going to get married."

We spent our wedding night at her mother's house. On the second night, we later discovered, she got pregnant. After a few days at her parents' we went to live with my friend Johnny. Years later, Mary laughed about it. "We slept in the same bed with Johnny," she explained. "There wasn't much hanky-panky going on then."

Shortly after we got our own apartment, I received my orders. On May 1 the *Valley Forge* shipped out for deployment in the Far East. Bankson also was assigned to the carrier. Merle was transferred to a submarine and Johnny was sent to San Diego. Incredibly, Merle's 19-year-old brother

Frank, whom I'd never met, was assigned to the *Valley Forge*. Asked about their meeting, Merle said: "Scotty was standing in the chow line—and they had 2,000 or 3,000 men on that ship—and he had on one of my old dungaree shirts with my name on the back. This guy tapped him on the shoulder and said, 'What do you mean wearing my brother's shirt?' It was my brother Frank."

After that, Frank and I became inseparable friends. I was assigned below deck, where I helped take care of the auxiliary motors and engines. I had numerous opportunities to obtain a higher rank, but turned them down because I expected to be discharged in a few months. Frank was a yeoman in the engineering office. "We went ashore together a lot in Japan," says Frank. "And San Diego. Once we decided to get a hotel room because we didn't want to sleep on the ship. We bought some scotch. I had never tasted scotch before. We had some water glasses and we drank the scotch out of the water glasses."

On June 25, 1950, the *Valley Forge* was anchored in Hong Kong harbor when it received the electrifying news that North Korea had sent troops across the 38th parallel into South Korea. The next day the carrier steamed southeast to Subic Bay, where it took on provisions and headed straight for Korea. Late in the day on June 30, President Truman authorized the commitment of American troops to defend South Korea. For the second time in my brief naval career, I was headed for a war zone. My length of service was extended another full year.

Eight days after being notified of the North Korean attack, the *Valley Forge* launched the first carrier air strike of the Korean conflict. As outnumbered South Korean troops fought to repel the invaders, wave after wave of Skyraiders, Panthers, and Corsairs from the deck of the *Valley Forge* slammed the North Korean rail yards, airfields, and fuel storage depots.

Between July 3 and November 19, when the *Valley Forge* headed back to San Diego, the carrier sent over 5,000 combat sorties into Korea. It was during this time that a training exercise got out of hand. Frank and I listened with amusement to the ship's public address announcement that the *Valley Forge* had been sunk by an enemy torpedo. The "sinking" was part of a training exercise, but back in Bremerton, the sinking was reported as fact.

"I was working for this woman, cleaning up her house, when I heard about it on the news," says Mary. "It knocked me over. I thought I had lost him. I thought I was a widow—a pregnant widow."

Below deck, life went on as usual. I played my guitar, channeling my emotions into my music. Frank played harmonica and for a time he and I, along with a black serviceman who had a talent for singing, formed a band to amuse ourselves. Recalls Frank: "One evening we got together in the radio shack, and the three of us recorded a song. It was probably the first recording Scotty ever made. I can remember Scotty played 'Double Eagle' on the guitar. He was fantastic." Frank laughs when he thinks about the recording: "I wish I had kept it."

The *Valley Forge* arrived in San Diego on December 1, 1950, only to be ordered back to Korea. The Chinese Communists had entered the war, sending a wave of troops that sent United Nations forces reeling to the south. *Oh, no*, I thought. *Not those guys again.* On December 16, shortly after I returned to the war zone, a little more than a week before my nineteenth birthday, Mary gave birth to our first child, a seven-pound girl we named Linda. Mary gave up our apartment in Bremerton and moved to San Diego to live with Johnny and his wife. When that didn't work out—they got into an argument, the substance of which no one remembers—she and the baby went to live with a couple who employed her as a baby-sitter.

Meanwhile, the Chinese sent a blitzkrieg into South Korea that leveled everything in its path. Over the next three months, the *Valley Forge* fought back with some 2,580 air sorties against North Korean targets. By the end of January, the Communists were pushed back north of the 38th parallel. On March 29 the *Valley Forge* headed back to San Diego for repairs.

When we arrived in San Diego, I was transferred to the second carrier in the Seventh Fleet, the *Boxer*, but after 30 days aboard that ship, I was assigned to the San Diego naval base when the carrier received orders to go to sea. Considered a short-timer at that point—my enlistment was up in January—the Navy didn't want to ship me out on another long engagement.

I don't recall my time on the *Boxer* nor my time on the base at San Diego with much fondness. When you're a short-timer you're the dregs of the crew. A guy on the base told me, with that short time left, go find yourself a file folder and fill it up and just keep walking. I did and it worked. Just look busy. That's the secret to government service.

Since I couldn't live with Mary and the baby, and my discharge was only months away, we decided it would be best if Mary and the baby went to Tennessee to live with my family until I was discharged. I took her to

Los Angeles to catch a plane to Memphis. When we arrived at the airport, we were given the unsettling news that the plane she was to board had crashed on its way to Los Angeles. We spent the night in Los Angeles, and the next day I put Mary and the baby on a different plane for Memphis. Mary still remembers the flight with a certain amount of horror.

"The plane had no heater, and it was cold, and we stopped at every airport along the way," she says. She had a really bad feeling about the plane. She was afraid something bad was going to happen. She couldn't get the plane crash out of her mind. When the plane stopped in Kansas City to take on passengers, Mary and the baby got off and bought a train ticket to West Memphis, Arkansas. There, she was met at the train station by my brother Carney, who lived in Memphis, and my father, who had driven down from Gadsden to pick up his new daughter-in-law and granddaughter. Mary does not remember the experience with great relish.

"He was chewing tobacco," Mary says of her first meeting with my father. "He kissed me with tobacco on his mouth. Ugh, that didn't make a very good impression." Back at the farm, Mary underwent culture shock. As Christmas approached, she learned not everyone felt the same way she did about the holiday. "His family was a lot different from my family," she says. "They didn't believe in a lot of things my family believed in—like Christmas."

On January 4, 1952, I was discharged from the Navy. I boarded a bus in San Diego and headed east to Memphis with my duffel bag and two medals, a Korean Service Medal and a China Service Medal. I was free at last to follow my dreams. All I needed was a singer.

DOING THE MEMPHIS *THANG*

During the four years I had sailed the Pacific, experiencing the horrors of war, the sensual and sometimes bizarre pleasures of foreign cultures, and the mind-numbing boredom of life as a below-the-deck seaman, the America I left behind had undergone radical changes. On the day of my discharge, the federal government conducted the largest drug bust in history. In a nationwide effort that targeted every major American city, federal agents made more than 500 arrests, including eight in Tennessee. The Tennessee drug bust was the lead story in the January 5, 1952, edition of the Nashville *Tennessean*. The newspaper made a big deal out of the men arrested as being black or Mexican and the women arrested as being white. Nashville residents were shocked and outraged to learn that drug dealers had infiltrated the city.

Tennessee had been transformed in my absence.

There were no parades to greet me when I returned to Crockett County. For the first time, I was faced with the day-to-day tedium of life as a married man. I had a wife and a daughter to support. I had served with honor in the China and Korea campaigns; now it was time to find a job and get on with the rest of my life.

I renewed my friendship with James Lewis, but we both had changed in four years. James had become a serious farmer and husband, and me . . . well, I hadn't. "He wasn't the Winfield I knew," recalled James. "I had never seen him like that. He had discovered women. He and Mary couldn't keep their hands off each other. I remember my wife and I talked about how lovey-dovey they were together."

We jammed on our guitars, but it just wasn't the same. Something was missing. James had a pretty good idea what it was. "His guitar playing had improved. He had left me behind. I had gotten busy trying to make a living."

With no opportunities for employment in Crockett County, I took my job search to Memphis. One of the first places I went was the Greyhound bus terminal, where I hawked my naval experience with diesel engines. The boss said he'd hire me because they used the same kind of engines I worked on in the Navy. The only difference, he said, was that theirs were air cooled and the ones I worked on were water cooled.

"Come over here," he said. "Let me show you something."

We walked out into the garage. There was this guy taking a big ole tire off a bus. The tire was almost as big as he was. Said the boss: "I'm not gonna kid you, that's what you'll be doing for six months before we can get you on the engines."

I said, thank you very much—but no thanks.

One day Mary and I went to Memphis together to look for work. James and Evelyn offered to babysit Linda. "We kept her one night," says James. "I remember trying to rock the child to sleep and she was screaming bloody murder. She was just learning to talk. She kept saying, 'bed, bed,' and I put her in bed and she went right to sleep."

Mary had a hard time adjusting to life on the farm. Southerners had their own way of doing things, she discovered; things that were obvious to them were incomprehensible to her. "She was strictly not country like we were," says James. "She was a different type person. She was nice, but she was not our kind of people, if you know what I'm saying. She wasn't country like we were." Forty years later, James pondered that remembrance a moment, and then laughed in a self-effacing way that made it apparent why we were such close friends.

"We were all rednecks," he said with a grin.

My parents had a similar reaction. Although they made it clear they would love Mary like a daughter, they did question my judgment in choosing her.

"What'd you marry a Yankee for?" they asked, genuinely perplexed.

At times, I felt like a referee. She was used to going out dancing on Saturday nights and so forth. As far as my mother and daddy were concerned, that was a sin. The Church of Christ had no music and didn't allow for dancing.

Eventually, I found work in Memphis at an engine repair shop, overhauling and rebuilding small engines. To Mary's relief, we left the farm and found an apartment in the city. For the first time, after two years of marriage, we lived together alone as husband and wife. It wasn't an easy adjustment for either of us.

Four years in the Navy had convinced me that a certain degree of regimentation was the best way to deal with life on a day-to-day basis. People said I was a neat freak. I folded my shirts a certain way. I rolled my socks a certain way. I placed my clothes a certain way in the dresser drawers so their usage could be rotated. I had a system that worked for me. The Navy way.

Mary was just the opposite. For two years, she had the freedom, as a married woman, to do as she pleased. When I was at sea she conferred with me by letter on the small matters of married life, but when I was in port, we didn't waste a lot of time talking about mundane matters: We made love. Now, almost overnight, everything changed. She was no longer free to do as she pleased. To her dismay, she discovered that I wanted her to do things *my* way. Her system was that she had no system.

"He didn't like me wearing pants or shorts," complained Mary. "He liked me dressed up in heels and I didn't like that. I didn't like to wear heels. I liked jeans and shorts and he didn't like those things. Scotty wanted everything perfect. Everything had to be clean and spotless. He used to put my clothes out, what I had to wear. He was very finicky and fussy. He was different from anyone I knew."

My job at the engine shop didn't last very long. I was offered a job on a tugboat on the Mississippi River, but it would have required me to be gone for six weeks at a time, so I turned it down to look for something closer to home. Finally, I decided to take a job with my brother Carney at the dry cleaners until something better came along. I was made the official hatter. My job was to dissemble the hats for cleaning—that is, remove the band and the lining—then put the pieces back together after cleaning and block them into their original shape.

I also learned how to make hats from scratch. They came in big cones that looked like dunce caps. You would take the fabric you wanted in whatever size you wanted; then you would steam it and block it. Some places made them with machinery, but we did it by hand. You would work the fabric, making it pliable, then you would add the flange, which was the brim—and we had all different types of brims—then you would put the brim over the top and work it out on the flange. When you got to the point where you had it stretched out pretty good, you would cut off the excess. If they wanted a binding on it, you would do that with a sewing machine. Then you would put the lining inside and attach a sweat band—and you were finished. I made all kinds of hats. I even made women's hats out of the scraps from the men's hats.

Once I had settled into a routine at the dry-cleaning shop, I turned my attention back to music. I don't recall what happened to the guitar I had in the Navy—actually I bought several inexpensive Japanese models over the years; most had frets made from aluminum beer cans—but by the time I set up housekeeping in Memphis I no longer owned a guitar. As soon as I could afford one, I purchased a Fender Esquire guitar and a Fender Champ Deluxe amplifier. Knowing how I felt about music, Carney told me that I could practice during my lunch break at the shop. Soon I got into a routine of doing my work with the hats, and then taking a break to play guitar, finishing up my day's work, and going home to pick up where I'd left off on my guitar.

University Park Cleaners was in a prime midtown neighborhood. Located at 613 North McLean Street, north of Poplar Avenue, it was near the city zoo and Snowden Elementary School. The neighborhood contained a mixture of small businesses and residential buildings, both single-family dwelling and apartments.

The sidewalk outside the dry cleaners was usually busy. People came and went all day. One of the people who passed by on a regular basis was nine-year-old Emily Evans, who stopped by the market next door to the University Park Cleaners and bought a dill pickle to eat on the way home from school. I sometimes stood in the doorway to the cleaners, watching the traffic go by. Emily smiled at me as she passed the building and we exchanged polite greetings. Fifteen years later, when she had matured into a striking redhead, we would become better acquainted, but for now I was a regular part of her after-school routine.

Poplar Avenue was one of three east-west thoroughfares that connected downtown Memphis with more densely populated East Memphis. Union Avenue was south of Poplar and Summer Avenue was to the north. Most of the black population was centered in an area south of Union, with some pockets of black residences north of Poplar and Summer. About a mile southwest of University Park Cleaners, in a neighborhood beyond the white mainstream, Elvis Presley and his parents lived in a federally funded housing project called Lauderdale Courts.

That summer, as I adjusted to my new life as a hatter, Elvis tried to adjust to being a teenager. He had another year to go at Humes High before graduation. He had no idea what he wanted to do with his life. For a while, he talked about being a famous singer and driving Cadillacs, but his friends laughed at him, so he stopped being so free with his talk. That summer he entered his "zoot suit" phase.

Jimmy Denson, whose family lived at the Courts, told Michael Donahue for *Mid-South Magazine* that almost overnight Elvis underwent a transformation from a skinny kid to a decked-out fashion hound. "This was his version of what the 1942 zoot-suiters had been, only he was ten years behind the zoot suiters," said Denson. "His hair was very short until the zoot suit. Then he started putting that greasy Brilliantine on it. It was greasy and dirty-looking and long with ducktails in the back. . . . Apparently, he read an old magazine and would see old people of the zoot suit era. He liked that."

Johnny Black, brother to Bill Black, knew Elvis at that time and sometimes went to house parties with him. The women were impressed by Elvis's zoot-suit phase, recalls Black, but the men were not. Says Black: "All these guys with crew cuts and muscles resented a pretty boy."

Elvis began showing up at Ellis Auditorium, located downtown at the west end of Poplar, to attend gospel concerts by the Blackwood Brothers Quartet, a local group with a national following. The Blackwoods attended the same church as the Presley family and Elvis had gotten to know several of them quite well. He also began attending the East Trigg Baptist Church, a black congregation led by Reverend W. Herbert Brewster, who also directed a radio show, the *Gospel Treasure Hour*. B.B. King attended services during this time, so it is likely they were sometimes in church at the same time. Elvis was testing the waters. Of what, exactly, he wasn't sure.

If Mary thought she finally had her husband settled into a job and a family way of life, she was sadly mistaken. I formed another band that summer. Actually, it was sort of a moveable band, with a membership that changed as the demands of the job changed. I'm not sure if the band even had a name. How I met the people I started playing with, I don't know. I'd do a Saturday night here and there. Back then I can only remember one or two groups in town in which the players were always the same. The rest of the bands were all little, make-up groups. You'd have all kinds of combinations of instruments. We had to play country, R&B, pop, whatever was popular. You had to play stuff people could dance to. It was a mixture. People just called it honky-tonk. Some days we might have an accordion and a trumpet and a guitar, most any kind of combination you could think of.

Soon I realized that there was no future in being a floating musician. I had played a few gigs with Bill Black and we had become close friends, so I talked him into joining a more stable group I was putting together. Acting as our manager, I began booking the band. We played a few club dates. Sometimes we played out of town. I remember one fall we almost froze to death playing on the rooftop of a drive-in theater. There was frost on the ground.

If Elvis and I had crossed paths in 1952, I probably would have been appalled by Elvis's outlandish appearance. If you think about it, it is not surprising that we never met until that fateful day in July. As a family man with a day job in a nice part of town, I traveled in circles not open to Elvis. As a musician I performed in honky-tonks that would not have admitted Elvis because of his age. I occasionally went to church, but I didn't share Elvis's bent for gospel concerts. I shared Elvis's appreciation of the blues, but there were no blues clubs in Memphis at that time open to whites. In 1952 Beale Street was only a shell of its former self. It was seedy and rundown, primarily a gathering place for unemployed laborers attracted to its garish history. Elvis liked to hang out there, especially at Lansky's, a clothing store that specialized in outrageous clothing. I would not have been caught dead there.

Toward the end of the summer, my band started playing at Shadow Lawn, a honky-tonk in Laconia, Tennessee. Sometime that fall Bobbie Walls went into the club with her two sisters, Janie and Alice. She lived in Memphis, but often went to Somerville to visit her parents and sisters. The club was just a joint, a bottle club where men and women could meet and dance, but it was the only nightspot for miles around and it was *the* place to go if you were young and single. Bobbie and her sisters were regulars at the club.

"One night Bill Black came into the club," recalls Bobbie. "He had his bass in the car and said he wanted to sit in with Scotty. He was sort of a clown, always cutting up and carrying on, hollering *sueee* and things like that. He was a card."

Bobbie noticed me, but that's as far as it went.

"The first time I saw Scotty, he didn't strike me much," she says bluntly. "After about the fourth time, I started to wonder about him. He didn't seem to associate with too many people."

One night she noticed that I arrived with a date. No one remembers for certain, but my "date" that night may have been Mary. In the early months, Mary accompanied me on many of my gigs. That enabled her to get out of the house, but it did little to alleviate her homesickness or her inability to adjust to life in the South. She started working part-time in the dry cleaners selling head bands, but that, too, became a source of contention when she complained that Carney did not pay her as much as he paid the black employees. "We had a fight, so Scotty wouldn't let me go with him anymore when he played music," she says.

As my marriage disintegrated, I turned inward, looking to music as a release for emotions I little understood. Mary was correct: music was becoming my life, though I never admitted that to myself or anyone else. I never dreamed of obtaining worldly riches, but I did dream of having control over my life. When I played music, I had that control, if only for the moment.

One day Mary accused me of seeing another woman. We had a big fight and she blamed our troubles on my music. She felt that honky-tonks were no place for a married man. To make matters worse, she had gotten pregnant that spring. The baby was due in December. She took out her frustration on what she saw as the source of our marital discord—my guitar. One day she lost her cool and lashed out at me by striking my Fender Esquire in a fit of anger.

"That was a no-no," she says.

That guitar was more than an instrument of wood and metal. It was my life. I lost my cool and responded by slapping her across the face. Normally, I am reserved and soft-spoken. Mary had never once seen me angry. Neither had she ever seen me take a drink. That was important to her because both her mother and father were alcoholics. She had grown up in an atmosphere of alcoholism, with all the sudden mood swings that entails. In me, she had found the opposite—or so she thought. The fight over the guitar frightened her. She did what young women often do when things go awry in a marriage: She called her mother, who sent money for a ticket back to Bremerton. "I was a mama's girl and I was homesick," she says. "The people were different there, and I didn't know anybody."

Mary took the gamble of her life. She packed up the baby and headed back to Bremington. Despite the fight, I think she still loved me. I don't think it was her intention to end the marriage. She wanted to get me away from the source of what she'd decided was our problem—my music, and, of course, the other woman.

After she returned to Bremington, she gave birth on December 16, 1952, to a son she named Donald. Incredibly, both of our children shared the same birth date. She was certain that I would come to be at her side. My response was not what she expected: I filed for divorce.

"I was shocked," she says, looking back to the day it occurred. Even after all this time her voice, emotional and tinged with regret, betrays her pain. "Scotty's a sweet guy. I always thought we would get back together again." She pauses, sifting through nearly fifty years of memories. "If we had more time together, we might have made it," she says wistfully. "We had a crazy marriage, but I loved him and always will."

★ ★ ★

One night Bobbie was in Shadow Lawn with her sisters when one of the guys in the band, Bud Deckelman, came over to their table and talked to Bobbie's sister. "I asked him about Scotty," Bobbie says. "He said, 'Do you want to meet him?' He brought him over and introduced us. Scotty rode back to Memphis with us that night. I didn't think I would see him again for a while, but the next night my sister and I were driving down Getwell toward the VA hospital and we stopped at the light and there Scotty sat with Bud Deckelman. They had been playing at the VA hospital. They hollered at us and we went on Park Avenue to Berretta's, a drive-in, and got together. It seemed, after that, we were together almost every night."

As I was getting my romantic life in order, Elvis concentrated on graduating from high school. On a parallel course with me, he experimented with his musical talents, trying to find a place to fit in. He learned to play guitar, though not very well. It was as much a prop as anything, something to hold onto while he sang. Jimmy Denson remembers how Elvis would sit on the steps at night and perform for his friends. Invariably, he reached a point where his singing outran his guitar playing. If he lost his way, he threw up his hands in exasperation and said with a sheepish grin, "I forgot the chords." When he saw that got a laugh, he started doing it even when he knew the chords. Anything for a laugh. Music was a means to an end. Attention was what he really wanted.

In the fall of 1952, Elvis and a friend, Ronald Smith, sang and played guitars in an amateur show at South Side High School. That December Elvis sang the dog-lover's tearjerker, "Old Shep," at a Christmas concert at Humes.[1] January was an emotional month for him. First came Hank Williams's sudden death. Then he and his parents moved from Lauderdale Courts to an apartment at 398 Cypress Street, and then to a house at 462 Alabama Street, located just across the street from the Courts. In the spring of 1953, as Elvis was approaching graduation, he sang in the Humes High Annual Minstrel Show and with the choir at East Trigg Baptist Church.

---

1. Elvis subsequently recorded the song and included it in his 1956 album, *Elvis*. It marked the first time he accompanied himself on piano on a recording.

In March, the big news, musically, was that Sam Phillips had recorded a hit record in his tiny studio on Union Avenue. The record, "Bear Cat," was a takeoff on Big Mama Thornton's "Hound Dog." Recorded by Rufus Thomas, a popular black disc jockey on radio station WDIA, the song gave Phillips the momentum he needed to get Sun Records off the ground.

Later in the year, Phillips followed that success with a song called "Just Walkin' in the Rain." It was recorded by five inmates from the Tennessee State Penitentiary in Nashville who called themselves the Prisonaires. Phillips talked the prison warden into allowing the inmates to come to his studio in Memphis under armed guard to make the recording. The session attracted the attention of the afternoon newspaper, the *Memphis Press-Scimitar*, which reported on the session as though it was a major event. Tennessee Governor Frank Clement was so impressed by the success of the song that he pardoned some of the inmates, proving that crime, when spiced with a dash of celebrity, could be made to pay.

In June, Elvis was graduated from Humes High. He got a job as a truck driver at Crown Electric Company, but it didn't pay enough for him to leave home and get a place of his own. While he technically wasn't of age—in Tennessee the age of majority was 21—he was in the eyes of most adults, himself included, now a man.

Instead of parading up and down Beale Street, his ducktails plastered into place, he sought refuge in the neighborhood movie theaters. Others have written that Elvis sampled the nightlife inside the clubs on Beale, sometimes sitting in with Johnny and Dorsey Burnette, two brothers he had met in the projects, but I never heard Elvis or the Burnette brothers talk about doing that. I performed with the Burnette brothers during that period, but I don't recall ever hearing Elvis's name mentioned. Once, when I was two players short for a booking at the Shadow Lawn, I asked the Burnette brothers to perform with me. In those days, Johnny played bass and Dorsey played steel guitar. Before playing the date, I rehearsed with them at the dry cleaners. Musically, they clicked, so I was confident everything would go smoothly.

Was I ever wrong!

Shadow Lawn wasn't what you would call a high-gloss supper club. It was a roadhouse located on the side of the road off Highway 64 in the middle of nowhere between Memphis and Somerville. Most of the patrons were farmers and blue-collar workers who partied as hard on the weekends as they worked during the week. They liked their music hard driving one minute, and crying-in-your-beer, hold-your-honey-tight sweet the next.

The roadhouses in and around Memphis were all identical. There was usually a front room that contained a bar (you had to bring your own hard liquor since by-the-drink sales were still illegal) and a back room where the band performed. Some were more freshly painted than others, but for the most part they all looked alike. The lights were always turned down low and you couldn't see a thing once you walked in the door.

That night there was a mixed crowd since several carloads of people had driven in from Memphis. For most of the evening, everything went smoothly. Then, for reasons no one recalls, all hell broke loose in the club. Johnny and Dorsey were notorious fighters. Both were Golden Gloves in Memphis. They were banned from all the Cotton Carnivals. That night we were playing and someone got into it and they emptied that place. I don't know how many the two of them were fighting, but it was a bunch. Dorsey got stuck in the thigh with a knife. It wasn't a huge cut, but I'm sure it smarted a bit. I decided right then, 'Well, boys, I don't think we can book you again around here.'"

If Elvis ever heard my band, there is no record of it. We didn't move in the same circles. When I wasn't working at the dry cleaners—or playing in honky-tonks—I spent all my time practicing on my guitar. It was about this time that I traded in my Fender Esquire for a Gibson ES 295, a cello-shaped, semi-acoustic jazz guitar. The streamlined Fender just didn't feel right when I played it. It probably had something to do with its shape. The Gibson was more feminine. I could make out with the Gibson. I couldn't get it on with a Fender.

In June 1953 Bobbie and I were married by a justice of the peace across the state line in Mississippi, where there was less paperwork associated with marriage. Unlike Mary, Bobbie was a born-and-bred Southerner—and she owned a car. Bobbie didn't like to wear dresses and high heels any more than Mary did, but I never pressed the issue with her. One thing Bobbie did differently was to encourage me in my dream of becoming a professional musician.

"I knew he didn't want to do anything else," says Bobbie. "He hated working nine to five. Of course, if you marry a musician, you know you are going to be separated a lot, but I wanted to see him do well. Scotty tried to teach me how to play the guitar, but I didn't have an ear for it. I guess opposites attract."

Bobbie felt the excitement of the music. She sat and watched me prac-tice for hours at a time. "I liked what he played," she says. "Today, I can even tell if he's playing on a record. I got to know his style of playing, I guess. He admired people like Chet Atkins and Les Paul. He tried to be like them. He was playing country music at the time, but he didn't really like it. He wanted to play something else. He just didn't think he was good enough."

Growing tired of my work as a hatter—and seeing little future as a Saturday night, honky-tonk guitar picker—I got serious about putting to-gether a first-rate band. "He was looking for someone who would go on the road," says Bobbie. "Family men, like the ones he was playing with, didn't want to give up their jobs to go on the road. Scotty didn't have a good job, like at Firestone or something like that. He thought that he could record and maybe make a living at it."

What I needed were musicians who had the time and dedication to make the Big Time. Married men were fine—if they were like me and had an understanding wife—but single men were preferable, especially if they were hungry for success. It was during that period when I was beating the bushes to put together a band that Elvis strolled into Sam Phillips's studio to make a record for his mother's birthday. Marion Keisker, the secretary, told him it would cost $3.98, plus tax, to make a two-sided acetate. While he waited to make the record, he engaged Marion in conversation. "If you know anyone that needs a singer . . ."

"What kind of a singer are you?" she asked.

"I sing all kinds."

"Who do you sound like?"

"I don't sound like nobody."

Elvis recorded two songs, "My Happiness" and "That's When Your Heartache Begins." He wasn't too pleased with the way he sounded, but Marion was impressed enough to ask him for his name and phone num-ber in case Sam ever needed a singer and wanted to get in touch with him. Elvis took his time leaving the studio, and Marion surmised it was because he thought Sam might come out from the back to speak to him. After schmoozing with Marion for a while, Elvis stuck the acetate under his arm and left.

Convinced she'd made a musical discovery, she told Sam about Elvis. Sam brushed her comments aside, which is not surprising. No self-re-specting studio owner of that era would have entertained recommenda-tions from a mere secretary.

In later years, as Sam began to take more credit for discovering Elvis, Marion wrote a letter to Elvis biographer Jerry Hopkins in which she complained about Sam's version of events. The way Sam tells it, he was searching for a way to merge black and white music when Elvis walked in the door. He worked with Elvis for several months, and then introduced him to me.

In her letter, Marion took exception to Sam's version. She sent Hopkins a copy of an interview Sam did with a Memphis newspaper. "I can only say this ain't the way I remember the first visit of EP to our small shop," she wrote. "Perhaps he is actually recalling a later visit. Elvis did come by several times in the months between his first record and the time Sam actually started to work with him. I know that he came by at least once when I was out of the office, because—as I think I told you—I found a note in Sam's handwriting on my desk saying: 'Elvis Presley—good ballad singer, Save.' So I guess you just take your choice of authentic, genuine first-hand versions of what happened. I still have not seen the great SCP (Sam Phillips). I understand he has bought a weekend place on Pickwick and spends a lot of time there. As for being 'disappointed' by him—well, Jerry, it's like eating at a restaurant where the service is consistently poor and the food always unpalatable. If you keep going back, you forfeit the right to complain."

I must admit I also am mystified by the "official" version that has come to be accepted as fact. Sam may have been talking about merging black and white music in those days, but he never talked about it to me. Marion's version, that Elvis came in to do the vanity recording, then kept in touch with her over the next few months, is the version I heard at the time. I was shocked in later years when Sam told interviewers he had worked with Elvis prior to the landmark July 1954 session. That just doesn't jive. When we went into the studio, Elvis acted like it was the first time he'd ever met Sam. I have often wondered why Sam, if he had worked with Elvis before, never mentioned it at the time.

In the ten months or so that elapsed between the time he first went into Sam's studio and did the July 5 audition with Bill and me, nothing seemed to go right for Elvis. Various clubs in Memphis and across the river in West Memphis allowed him to take the stage on amateur night or during intermission, but, for the most part, his efforts to become a singer were ignored. He seriously considered a career as a gospel singer.

The Blackwood Brothers Quartet allowed him to hang out with them backstage and they encouraged him with his singing. On occasion they allowed him to sing, backing up his struggling solos with their own polished harmonies. When Cecil Blackwood, a cousin of the founding member of the quartet, formed a group called the Songfellows, Elvis tried out for a slot left by a departing member. Unfortunately, the departing member changed his mind about leaving the group and Elvis did not get the job.

Elvis kept in touch with Marion, who obviously had become smitten with his gentlemanly mannerisms and youthful good looks. "He always called me Marion, which was queer, because anybody two years older was mister or missus," she says. "Here is a young man so pure, so sweet, so wonderful, that he's unbelievable."

For his part, Elvis must have been impressed with Marion's glamorous good looks and her reputation as "Miss Radio of Memphis." Before going to work for Sam, the former child actress had her own program called *Meet Kitty Kelly.* The fifteen-minute show aired daily at 2 p.m. on WREC. The thirty-something Marion had a flair for the dramatic and that would have been exotically attractive to Elvis, who was himself experimenting with alternative personas.

The only thing going right for Elvis during that time was his personal life. He started dating Dixie Locke, a pretty, 15-year-old high school sophomore. She became his first serious girlfriend, and despite their age difference—and her father's opposition to his daughter dating an 18-year-old truck driver—they toyed with the idea of living together forever and forever, amen.

Memphis was a hotbed of musical activity that fall and winter. Sam was scoring with his black artists. Memphis was becoming a secondary recording center—however small—to New York and Los Angeles. Black entertainers were making records in vacant rooms all over town. Black radio was vibrant, shaking the city to its foundations.

Caught up in the excitement of it all, I put together my first real band, the Starlite Wranglers. To front the group and sing lead vocals, I asked Doug Poindexter, a baker who had a Hank Williams type of voice. I added Bill Black on bass, Millard Yow on steel guitar, Clyde Rush on guitar, and Thomas Sealy on fiddle.

To cement the relationship, I had a lawyer draw up an ironclad contract that designated me as the personal manager of the group. Such contracts were rare in Memphis at that time. Each member of the group would receive 16-2/3 percent of the net proceeds, except for me who, as manager, would receive an additional 10 percent.

Under the terms of the contract, I would make all the business decisions and collect the money. The signees agreed to "abide by" my directions and to "carry out all engagements, appearances, and performances,
faithfully and unless prevented by illness or good cause" and to appear "at
all times promptly and faithfully for rehearsals under the direction of the
manager."

In the five years that had elapsed since I left the farm to join the Navy,
I had become savvy to the ways of the world. The Starlite Wranglers contract offers a revealing glimpse of my state of mind at that time. I wanted
success—and all the trappings of success—but more than that I wanted
control of my destiny. The best way to do that, in my mind, was to find
people who were agreeable to "fronting" for my ambitions. I was most
comfortable when I was behind the scenes, pulling the strings that made
the show work. The Starlite Wranglers was my creation and everyone understood that. What did I care if people thought Doug Poindexter was
calling the shots? More than glory, I wanted anonymity.

I booked the group at Shadow Lawn and then got bookings at various
nightclubs around Memphis, including the Bon Air. Then I got the group
on radio station KWEM in West Memphis. I dressed everyone in matching hats and shirts, and I constructed a large star out of Christmas lights
and used it to illuminate the band's name. Once I had all the pieces in
place, I prepared for the final step. I knew that to get better jobs, we had
to put a record out. You had to have a record to get radio play and you had
to have radio play to get bookings. I had that much figured out.

At that time, there were two record labels in town. Modern/RPM, a
west coast label that had a branch office in Memphis, was operated by
the Bihari brothers and specialized in blues recordings. Sun Records, a
Memphis owned label, was housed in Sam Phillips's Memphis Recording
Service. Although both labels targeted blues performers, I focused my
attention on Sun Records. As Elvis was going in one door of the Union
Avenue studio, I must have been going out another. We never met during
that time, but we were wooing Sam and Marion at about the same time.
It took a while, but I finally talked Sam into giving the Starlite Wranglers
a chance. Sam either came out to a nightclub and saw us perform, or we
went down to audition. I don't recall which. After hearing us, he finally
agreed to put a record out on us.

The Starlite Wranglers went into the studio in May and recorded two
sides, both written by me. The A-side was titled "My Kind of Carryin' On."
I gave songwriters' credit for one song to Poindexter because he was the

singer and I gave one-third to my brother, Carney, because he wrote out the lead sheet for us. The song was released in June. It got a little airplay, but not enough to generate sales. Of course, we didn't get paid anything to do the record.

Discouraged by the record's failure, but encouraged by the fact that I had broken the recording barrier, I stopped by every day after work to talk to Sam. I had been to China and back, with a detour to the waters off Korea, so I had more past than most people my age, but all I could think about was the future. Don't ask me how I knew that Sam would figure into that future. I just knew. It was just a gut feeling that I had.

★ 4 ★

THE SUN RISES ON THE BLUE MOON BOYS

If you have ever been in Memphis in July, you know that the heat is unbearable. On most days the temperature hits one hundred degrees. Drive ten miles in any direction, out into the rich farmland of north Mississippi, east Arkansas or west Tennessee, and the temperature drops noticeably. Whether Memphis is a thermal hot spot because of the tons of concrete that surround it or because rising moisture from the Mississippi River envelopes the city in a suffocating cover of humidity—or simply because the gods bear a grudge for some unpardonable sin anchored in the city's past—is really beside the point: July is the month Memphians dread the most, a make-or-break month in which temperatures and passions run the highest.

For most of the previous century, Memphis was known as the "murder capital of America." In mid-2012, the FBI designated it as the "most dangerous" city in the country. What would you expect in a sun-baked city in which blistering heat is the norm? Some folks considered killing someone to be a way of cooling off.

On the afternoon of July 3, 1954, I stopped by Memphis Recording Service to chat with Sam Phillips. It was hot as all get out. My clothes stuck to the seat covers in the car. It had been two months since the release of "My Kind of Carrying On." I wasn't wedded to the music of the Starlite Wranglers, though the country band was my own creation. It bore Poindexter's name only because of my desire to stay in the background. I liked to be in control of my surroundings, but I didn't like the spotlight. If the term, "front man," had not been in existence at that time, I might have invented it. I was happiest when I had an alter ego, someone to take the credit for my actions. It is a characteristic that has stayed with me all my life.

I wasn't sure my future was in country music. I also liked to play blues and jazz. I made it clear to Sam that I was open to new musical styles.

I am a detail man. Give me a problem and I will solve it. Sam was also a detail man, although he approached problem solving from a different angle. He didn't always know what was wrong with a song. He didn't possess the musical expertise for that. But he usually knew when something was right.

Sam had opened his recording studio in 1950, five years after moving to Memphis from Alabama to work at WREC, an AM radio station at 600 on the dial. Sam kept his job at the radio station while he worked to get his recording studio off the ground. Most of his business was vanity related—weddings, funerals, ordinary people who wanted to find out how they sounded singing their favorite songs—but he had some success with African American entertainers, whose recordings he was able to sell to record labels in Chicago and Los Angeles.

In 1951 Ike Turner recorded a song in Sam's studio that went to No. 1 on the national R&B charts. The song, "Rocket 88," featured Jackie Brenston, Turner's saxophonist, as the vocalist. Because it gave Chicago-based Chess Records its first No. 1 hit, it resulted in stiff competition for black talent in the Memphis area.

In the early fifties, Sam discovered a number of major black artists, such as Chester Burnett, better known as Howlin' Wolf, but he couldn't hold on to them. After brief stints with Sam, they usually left for greener pastures up north. Race relations were not good in Memphis in 1954. All the public facilities were segregated. There were signs everywhere that read "whites" and "colored." It was illegal for blacks to go into the public library, unless they had been invited there to do janitorial or repair work. That July, race relations worsened when five black students sought enrollment at Memphis State College, the largest state-supported institution of higher learning in West Tennessee. The state board of education in Nashville rejected their applications, but in the eyes of many whites the city of Memphis compensated for that by erecting a 30-foot memorial to Tom Lee, a black man who had saved the lives of 32 whites following a riverboat disaster in 1925. The memorial was built in the shape of a giant shaft, the symbolism of which was not lost on black residents.

On that July 3 the heat was suffocating. Since it was Saturday, many people sought refuge in the air-conditioned movie theaters. Memphis had dozens of theaters in those days. On that particular day, you could see Gary Cooper and Susan Hayward in *Garden of Evil*, Elizabeth Taylor and Dana Andrews in *Elephant Walk*, or if your tastes were more exotic, Lana Turner in *Flame and the Flesh*. The hottest movie in town would not be shown until after dark, when the Sunset Drive-In ran the steamy *Naughty New Orleans*, an uncensored look at New Orleans strippers.

Memphis Recording Service, home of the fledging Sun Records, was located at 706 Union Avenue, just a few blocks from the busy downtown district. Union Avenue was one of the main thoroughfares in the city. If the street today seems a little gritty, the result of urban wear and tear, sixty years ago it sparkled with promise as a major street in the Mid-South's largest city. In keeping with the custom of the day, I put on a clean, neatly ironed short-sleeved shirt and wore my good shoes to go downtown to do business.

Memphis Recording Service was a five-room building, with an entrance at which Marion Keisker sat at her desk and took care of the day-to-day business. Beyond the entrance and the studio was a partitioned control room. At the rear of the control room was a bathroom. Past that were two additional rooms, which no longer exist, that contained a warehouse and a room for the equipment used to cut acetates. The studio was not air-conditioned. The window units popular at that time were too noisy for use in a studio, and quietly efficient central air-conditioning systems were a rarity. On most days Sam would wear a necktie and dress shirt, and sometimes a sports coat, to work, depending on how hot it was outside; Marion usually wore a dress, her well-groomed hair sometimes set off by large earrings. It was a time when ambitious go-getters dressed up, not down, for success.

For weeks I had been talking to Sam, trying to figure out where he was headed with his studio. Finally, after it became clear that my subtle probes were getting nowhere, I asked Sam outright the question that had been tormenting me:

"What exactly are you looking for?"

Sam said he wasn't sure. He would know it when he heard it. All he knew was that it wasn't the same-old, same-old, everybody else was recording. Sam had a feel for music, but little technical understanding. He wasn't a professional musician. His experience was limited to what he had picked up on the tuba and the drums in his high school band.

At that point, Marion joined in the conversation. "Sam, you remember that boy who came in to record that song for his mother's birthday about a year ago?'

"Yeah, I remember him," said Sam. "A dark haired boy."

"Well, you said you thought he had a pretty good voice. Why don't you get him to come in and try it?"

"Yeah, I'll probably do that."

That was all I needed to hear. For two weeks, I worried Sam to death with the same question: "Have you called that boy yet?"

When I arrived at the studio on Saturday, July 3, there were no customers, so the three of us went next door to Taylor's cafe for a cup of coffee. We had no sooner been seated than I got right to the point: "You called that boy yet?"

Finally, Sam gave in. He told Marion to dig out the boy's name and phone number and give it to me. Later, when she gave me his name, I was taken aback. "What kind of a name is this?" I read the name over a second time—Elvis Presley.

"I don't know," answered Sam. "It's his name. Give him a call. Ask him to come over to your house and see what you think."

By the time I got home it was late in the afternoon. I called Elvis that evening after dinner. Gladys Presley, his mother, said that he had gone to a movie. I told her that I represented Sun Records and wanted to talk to Elvis about an audition. Gladys was polite. She said she would make sure Elvis returned my call.

At that time Bobbie and I were setting up house at 983 Belz Street in north Memphis. We had moved into the four-unit house in June after our friends, Bill and Evelyn Black, who lived down the street, told us it was for rent. At night and on weekends, Bill played bass with the Starlite Wranglers; during the day he worked a few blocks away at Firestone Tire Company.

Belz was a quiet, family-friendly, residential dead-end street. Children played in the streets and swung on the young trees that showed promise of one day becoming shade-bearing giants. The front door of our house opened into the living room. Past the living room was a hallway that led into the kitchen on the left and the bathroom on the right. The kitchen was large and had an adjoining dining area that opened into the bedroom.

When we got married in June 1953, Bobbie moved in with me at my boarding house for a month or so; then we stayed with family members until we found the house on Belz. Although this was my second marriage, it was Bobbie's first, and she worked hard to make the house into a home. At twenty-two, she had been out on her own for several years, but she had met no one special until I came along. She was a tall, leggy brunette who wore her hair cut fashionably short.

Dresses were still the accepted fashion of the day, but Bobbie liked to wear pants, especially "pedal pushers," tight fitting slacks that ended past mid-calf. She didn't know it in 1954, but she was only three years away from turning prematurely gray. She was much more outgoing than I was and she was very attractive, a quality high on my wish list when it came to women. Bobbie had just cleared away the dinner dishes when the phone rang.

"My name's Elvis Presley," the caller said. "I'm returning your call."

I explained that I worked for Sam Phillips, helping him look for talent for Sun Records. Technically, that wasn't true since I was not on the payroll; but in this instance it was true in the sense that Sam had given me a task to perform. I asked if he would be interested in coming over to the house for an informal audition.

"Well, I guess so," said Elvis.

"How about tomorrow?" I asked. It was a holiday, the Fourth of July, but I was never much for celebrations. Besides, I was eager to hear the youngster, because if it worked out it would be my ticket back into Sam's studio.

"All right," said Elvis.

I gave him directions to the house.

On Sunday, July 4, 1954, the temperature peaked at 100 degrees at 3:20 p.m. and didn't dip below ninety until 8 p.m. The humidity hung fast at 92 percent. The Fairgrounds Amusement Park opened at 2 p.m., offering cold watermelon and a concert by Slim Rhodes. There would be no fireworks on the Fourth that year—it would be sacrilegious to do that on Sunday—but the following day the skies over the fairgrounds would be ablaze with rockets' red glare.

Elvis arrived shortly after noon.

Bobbie saw him coming up the sidewalk. White, lacy shirt. Pink pants with a black stripe down the legs. White buck shoes. He was carrying a guitar.

"Is this the right place?" he asked when Bobbie answered the door.

"Yeah, it's the right place." She didn't bother to ask his name. If he wasn't Elvis, his outlandish dress alone was enough to earn him an audition, at least to her way of thinking.

"Come on in."

Bobbie left Elvis in the living room and went into the bedroom where I was playing my guitar, not aware that someone had arrived.

"That guy's here," she said.

"What guy?" I asked.

"You know—the guy you invited over."

"Oh, that guy."

After Elvis and I exchanged pleasantries, Bobbie offered Elvis a Coke. "They sat around for a while talking," recalls Bobbie. "Then they started playing. Scotty asked me to go and ask Bill Black to come down and I did."

Bill's bass was already there, propped in the corner of the living room. He kept it at my house because with two children he didn't have room for it at his own place.

As we went through Elvis's song list, Bill arrived and quietly sat down to listen. When he had heard enough, he got up and went home without saying much, an unusual occurrence for him. I guess what impressed me the most was how uncanny it was that Elvis knew so many songs—everything from Eddie Arnold to Billy Ekstine, just about every damn song in the world.

An hour or two later, Bobbie returned. "Elvis had his audience then," she recalls. "He was doing a lot of slow ballads. Everything had the word 'because' in it—'Because of You,' 'I Love You Because,' 'Because You Think You're So Pretty'—I don't think anyone was real impressed. He had a good voice and he could sing, but the type of stuff he was singing, he was just like everybody else."

Bobbie was impressed even less by his appearance. "He was still kind of a pimply faced kid, you know," she says. "He had his duck-tail hair pulled back. He was kind of odd for that time."

When we ran out of songs to do, we put the guitars aside.

I told Elvis that I'd talk to Sam and we'd be in touch. It was my first time to use the "we'll be in touch" line, but it wouldn't be the last.

We tried our best to chat each other up, but there were lots of long silences.

Finally, Elvis said goodbye and left, nodding his head in that self-effacing way he had as he made his exit, and Bill came back to help critique the audition.

"What did you think?' I asked.

"Well, he didn't impress me too damned much," said Bill. "How about you?"

"I thought he had good timing. A good voice. Nothing different jumped out from the material he was doing."

After Bill left, I called Sam to give him a report. I was upbeat but not gushing in my assessment of Elvis's talents. I mentioned that I was surprised that Elvis knew so many rhythm and blues songs. Sam asked if I thought it would be worthwhile to audition him in the studio.

"Sure," I said.

Sam called Elvis and set up an audition for Monday night at the studio.

Bobbie and I suffered through another stifling night. The temperature never went below 85 degrees. By the time we left for work Monday morning—me to the dry cleaners and Bobbie to her job in the billing department at Sears—the temperature was already pushing 90 degrees. As usual, I took my guitar with me to work. I now played a Gibson ES 295, a wider-bodied instrument that had a more impressive appearance and a more intricate sound than my Fender Esquire. Most days I practiced during lunch hour. This day was no different.

In and out of the dry cleaners that day, as she was all summer, was 12-year-old Mississippi transplant Wynette Pugh. Years later she would change her name to Tammy Wynette and become a superstar of country music, but for now she was like most girls her age and curious about the world around her. Since her mother worked in the office of the dry cleaners, she often stopped by to hang out—and to listen to my guitar picking. She was fascinated with guitars. Her father, William Hollis Pugh, who died when she was an infant, was a well-known guitarist in northern Mississippi. As a result, she had grown up in a home filled with musical instruments.

Nearly forty years later, Tammy Wynette recalled the experience with relish. "Oh, yes. I watched Scotty many times," she says. "There was this old black guy who worked in the back and Scotty would go back there with his guitar, and this old black man and him would talk back and forth about guitar licks."

As the summer of '54 wore on, she was drawn inextricably to a series of practice sessions held upstairs over the dry cleaners—and to the mystery of the boy named Elvis.

I didn't mind the young girl's curiosity. I had two children of my own from a previous marriage. Besides, I knew what it was like to be drawn to the sound of music. Perhaps I was a little more focused than usual on this day. It would be my second trip into the studio with Sam. I knew as well as anyone that the music business didn't always abide by the three-strikes-you're-out rule. Sometimes you got only two strikes. If I struck out, it wouldn't be because I was caught flat-footed at the plate. I was determined to make it as a guitarist.

That night we all showed up at the studio around seven o'clock. I had offered to bring the entire band, but Sam didn't want to make a big deal out of it. The idea was to see what Elvis could do, not to make a record.

Me on guitar and Bill on bass would be enough. Sam wanted to keep it as simple as possible.

That was fine with me, but it put added pressure on me. On most nights the Starlite Wranglers were a six-piece group, with a fiddle, a standup bass, and three guitars, and, of course, the vocalist Doug Poindexter. With all those instruments in the fray, I could play a little lead or play a little rhythm or simply fade into the background. Tonight, for all practical purposes, I was the entire band.

First came the small talk. Complaints about the heat (the temperature was still hovering around 90 degrees). Then the inevitable, "what songs do you know?" Then, "what songs do you know that I know?"

Finally, for starters, we picked "Harbor Lights," a song that had been a hit for Bing Crosby several years back. Then we did one of Elvis's "because" numbers. "I Love You Because" had been a hit for Ernest Tubb on the country charts. We did both songs just like they had been recorded. When it became obvious they were not going to outshine the work Tubb and Crosby had done on their own songs, we moved on to something else.

We did one ballad after another. Musically, ballads were easier to play than up-tempo numbers, but that wasn't where my heart lay, especially with the musical setup we had in the studio. I preferred up-tempo tunes. With only three pieces, everything we did sounded naked to me. During all of this, Sam sat in the control room, pressing the record button, and then rewinding the tape to start over again on the next tune. As the night wore on it became obvious we were going nowhere fast. Of course, no one wanted to give up, least of all me.

Around midnight we took a break. It was late and we all had to go to work the next day. Maybe it was time to wrap it up. We could try again tomorrow. We had sort of lulled ourselves into a post-session stupor when Elvis suddenly jumped up and started playing his guitar. Actually, as I remember it, he beat the hell out of the guitar. He started singing a blues song that had been recorded by Arthur "Big Boy" Crudup in 1940, "That's All Right, Mama."

At the time, Bill was sitting on his bass. When Elvis started singing, he leaped to his feet and began playing. Then I joined in. The up-tempo tune hit home with me. Fast music was what I liked. For years I had been making up guitar licks for up-tempo music, a combination of finger slides and bent-string pauses, but I had found nowhere to put them. It wasn't until Elvis was flailing away at his guitar that I suddenly knew where those licks belonged.

While we were playing, I saw Sam's head perk up on the other side of the glass. He looked at us for a moment and then stuck his head out of the control room door.

"What are ya'll doing?" he asked.

"Just foolin' around," I said, making excuses in advance of criticism.

But Sam surprised me.

"Well, it didn't sound too bad through the doors," he said. "Try it again. Let me get in there and turn the mics on."

We played it several times, with Sam making some technical suggestions, telling Elvis to move closer to the microphone or further away from it. Throughout it all, Elvis looked confident and terrified at the same time, his energy level revved to the max. He broadcast dual images. He seemed not to care what anyone thought. Then, with the blink of an eye, he seemed to care what *everyone* thought. Finally, Sam thought we were ready to run the tape. We played it through again, with the tape machine on; then Sam ran it back for us to listen to. No one said anything for a moment.

"Man's, that's good," he said, finally. "It's different. What is it?"

We looked at each other. That was a damn good question.

"Well, you said you were looking for something different," I said.

"Damn, if we get that played, they might run us out of town," Bill said.

"Okay, we've got to get a back side," said Sam. "I just can't take one song down to the disc jockey."

Exhausted, we called it a night at two o'clock in the morning. When I got home Bobbie was waiting up for me. I told her all about the session. I said that we were tired and worn out but planned to return to the studio that night to pick up where we left off. I told her all about "That's All Right, Mama." About how Sam finally heard something that he liked.

When we went to sleep that night, we had no way of knowing that the session had launched a revolution in American music.[2] All we knew was that it had been a good day.

Unknown to me, I had become a father that night. It would be six years before I would learn that Frankie Tucker, an aspiring nightclub singer I'd

---

2. Two months later, Michigan-born guitarist Bill Haley made the Top 20 with a rhythm and blues song, "Shake, Rattle and Roll," following that up in 1955 with his only No. 1 hit, "Rock Around the Clock," an upbeat bop song he'd recorded in April 1954. He had been on the fringes of rock 'n' roll since 1951, when he recorded a cover version of Ike Turner's "Rocket 88," an upbeat R&B song that possessed some of the characteristics of what would become rock 'n' roll.

met in West Memphis three months into my marriage with Bobbie, had given birth to my child, a bright-eyed girl she named Vikki.

★ ★ ★

On the evening of July 6, 1954, Elvis, Bill, and I returned to Memphis Recording Service to pick up where we'd left off after recording "That's All Right, Mama." We were pumped. Sam Phillips himself had told us we had a record. Well, half a record. All we had to do to have a record was come up with a B-side. Sam said he'd take care of the rest. He could be very convincing when he took charge.

When we faced off in the tiny 18-by-32-foot studio, we weren't sure what to expect. "That's All Right, Mama" had been a fluke—and we understood that. No one had to explain to us how the song had conjured itself out of nothing. We were there when it happened. It was a little bit like being in the center of a tornado. But if Sam thought we could do it again, then we probably could conjure up another musical apparition. At least, we convinced ourselves of that. There was still an hour's daylight left when we began and the studio was stifling hot. We ran through a number of songs, including Billy Eckstine's 1949 hit, "Blue Moon."

Nothing clicked. It was one disappointment after another.

We were all below-average musicians. Elvis didn't know all that many chords, but he had a great sense of rhythm. Sam used that. I don't think he did it deliberately, but he treated Elvis as another instrument and he kept his voice closer to the music than was the norm at that time. If you listen to the records that were being played then, the singer's voice was way out front. If he left Elvis's voice way out front, it would have sounded empty because we only had three instruments. Elvis had great rhythm in his voice. He could do just about anything he wanted to. Sam took his voice and brought it back closer to the music like it was an instrument.

After a series of duds, Sam suggested we take a couple of days off and then try again. He was upbeat. He told us that he knew that we could do it. What Sam's secretary, Marion, remembers most about the first week was how much fun everyone had. "One session had run on and on," she recalls. "Bill was on the floor and we couldn't get him up. Finally everybody else dropped [to the floor]. Suddenly, Bill leaped to his feet and said, 'Where's everybody? Where's everybody?' Sometimes Elvis would just roll on the floor, kicking his heels."

Despite his assurances that we would be able to get a B-side, there seemed to be some doubt in Sam's mind as to whether we actually could.

That night after everyone left, he called a local disc jockey, Dewey Phillips. The two men weren't related, but, over the years, they got into the habit of not correcting people who jumped to the conclusion that they were.

Dewey had a daily nine-to-midnight show on radio station WHBQ, which broadcast from the downtown Hotel Chisca. In 1954, Dewey was easily the most popular white disc jockey in Memphis, though none of his listeners, if pressed, would be able to explain exactly why. He was in the vanguard of America's shock-jock tradition, sort of a southern-fried Howard Stern. A moon-faced country boy from West Tennessee, he was decidedly unschooled in the radio tradition. He taunted his listeners with nonsensical exuberance and language that did not endear him to the parents of teenagers. For example, he once called people he didn't like "piss ants" on the air until the station manager made him stop. For those of you new to Southern vernacular, a piss ant is someone so insignificant as to be worthy of being pissed on. Dewey's comment was his way of pissing on listeners who did not agree with him.

Sam told Dewey he had something he needed to hear. After he put the wraps on his *Red, Hot and Blue* show that night, he stopped off at Sam's studio on his way home. Sam had a racket going with Dewey. He would give Dewey copies of tapes or acetates before they were released as records. If Dewey liked them—and played them on his show—Sam could judge by audience reaction how many records to press.

That night Sam played "That's All Right, Mama" for Dewey. For nearly two hours, they drank beer and listened to that one record. Sam played it over and over again. Dewey sat and listened stone faced. He left the studio without ever commenting on the record.

Early the next morning he called Sam and told him it was the damnedest record he had ever heard. He asked for a copy to play on *Red, Hot and Blue*. Later that day, Sam made an acetate and left it for Dewey at the radio station. Then he called Elvis and told him to be sure to listen to Dewey's show that night.

Elvis told Gladys and Vernon about the show, but he ducked out of the house and went to a movie before it aired. As expected, Dewey debuted "That's All Right, Mama." He played it and he played and he played it. When he liked a song he played it over and over again, back to back, without a break. Some say he played Elvis's song seven, ten, fourteen times in a row—then took a break, whooping it up, screaming this hoodoo jive he had made up himself—and started playing the record all over again. The phones rang off the hook.

"That's All Right, Mama" was an instant hit. Dewey got Elvis's phone number from Sam and called him at home. Gladys said he had gone to the movies. Dewey told her to get her cotton-pickin' son down to the station.

Within minutes Gladys and Vernon rounded up Elvis and got him to the station. He was so nervous, he shook all over like a wet puppy. In one of the last interviews before his death in 1968, Dewey told writer Stanley Booth that Elvis told him: "Mister Phillips, I don't know nothing about being interviewed." Dewey's advice was simple and to the point: "Just don't say nothin' dirty."

The notion that Elvis would say anything dirty—even think about saying anything dirty—struck Marion as absurd. "He's never said a wrong thing," she says. "He's been misquoted, but he's an innately fine person. It's not in him to do anything or say anything malicious. He didn't smoke. He didn't drink. I never even heard him say 'damn.'"

When the three of us returned to the studio on Thursday we were local celebrities, at least among Dewey Phillips's hip radio listeners. Sam had let the cat out of the bag. He really did have to get a B-side now.

"The reaction was fantastic," says Marion. "We were back-ordered 5,000 records on this brand new artist, this brand new type of thing, before we could get our mastering done. It was that immediate."

Over the next few days we had our work cut out for us. Not only did we have to come up with a B-side, the group had to have a name, Marion had to draw up contracts for Sun Records, and Elvis, as the vocalist, had to find a manager. Marion did the Sun Records contracts herself, a fact that later became a source of contention between Sam and herself. "While our advisors thought it was perfectly legal, I don't think Sam had much trust in it," she recalls.

Since Elvis, at nineteen, was legally a minor, Vernon signed as his guardian. The contract was for three years. To our surprise, Bill and I were not asked to sign contracts. We were told to make our own deal with Elvis. We agreed on a 50-25-25 split, with Elvis getting 50 percent since he was the vocalist. Nothing was ever put in writing.

★ ★ ★

By the end of that first week it seemed like the world had been turned upside down. Within the space of four days, Elvis, Bill, and I had recorded "That's All Right, Mama," Dewey Phillips had played it on the radio, creating a stampede to the stores—which placed orders for more than 5,000 records—and Sam had slapped a recording contract down in front of Elvis. Add to that my need to get a contract drawn up between myself and Elvis, and you understand how hectic it all became. In the midst of all that chaos was Sam's voice: "Don't feel pressured or anything, but we got to have a B-side by tomorrow."

Twenty-four years after the fact, Sam looked back to that week, telling a reporter for *The Commercial Appeal* that he thought one of the key ingredients for the success that followed was a spirit of teamwork.

> *I think my biggest contribution was to let these people [the musicians] know that I wasn't a record executive. Never was and never would be . . . so instead of a big producer behind the glass window, looking onto a group of people in the [studio], saying "Man, you got to do this, you got to do that," I was one of them. We all had the same goal in mind. . . . At that time, I did not see one person in there thinking in terms of, "Man, I'm gonna be a superstar." It was "Isn't there some way we can say what we want to say through music?"*

If the trio had a weakness, it was our inability to compose original songs. There wasn't a penny's worth of songwriting talent among us. That meant we had to work our magic with songs written by other people. That's what happened with "That's All Right, Mama." What we tried to do over that three-day period—Friday, Saturday, and Sunday—was find another song we could breathe fire into. Sam made suggestions. So did the three of us. We went through song after song, just running through them. I don't think any of them were ever put on tape.

Nothing we tried seemed to work out.

Then we got lucky again. "Blue Moon of Kentucky" was a beautiful waltz that Bill Monroe had scored a hit with in 1946. Since then it had become a classic country tune, revered by the Grand Ole Opry and handled with kid gloves by country and bluegrass musicians, who had anointed it with magical properties. No one told Bill the song wasn't fair game.

Bill jumped up and grabbed his bass and started slapping it, singing "Blue Moon of Kentucky" in a high falsetto voice. It was Bill doing what Bill did best. The song was recorded as a ballad, but Bill sang it up-tempo, his bass lines thumping at a feverish pace. Elvis loved it. He jumped up and started singing along with Bill. I joined in right behind them.

Suddenly, Sam stuck his head out the door. "Hey, that's the one!" he shouted. On the final take, Sam was jubilant: "Hell, that's fine. That's different. That's a pop song now."

With "That's All Right, Mama," Elvis took a blues song and sang it white. With "Blue Moon of Kentucky" he did the opposite: He took a country song and gave it a bluesy spin. On paper it probably wouldn't have worked, but in the laid-back, anything-goes atmosphere of Sam's studio it seemed perfect. It had the same sort of feel as "That's All Right, Mama." After that, we sort of had our direction.

Sam didn't need a direction. He was running straight ahead as fast as he could. Over the weekend, he made two-sided dubs of the songs and distributed them to all the disc jockeys in Memphis. Dewey Phillips had lost his exclusive. Getting acetates this go-around were Bob Neal, a popular early-morning country DJ at WMPS, Dick Stuart at KWEM in West Memphis, and Sleepy Eyed John, a country announcer at WHHM. By Monday both songs were getting airplay. As Dewey was going crazy over "That's All Right, Mama," Sleepy Eyed John, who had a country band of his own and booked bands for the Eagle's Nest, was talking up "Blue Moon of Kentucky."

Jack Clement remembers hearing "Blue Moon of Kentucky" on Sleepy Eyed John's show. Jack went on to become Sam Phillips's engineer—and right-hand man—and a highly regarded songwriter and producer in his own right, but at that time he was trying to get his own band off the ground. Sleepy Eyed John had booked Jack's band at the Eagle's Nest, and whether out of a sense of loyalty or a desire to monitor his bosses' musical tastes, Jack listened to his show on a regular basis. One morning Jack awoke and turned on the radio by his bed. Sleepy Eyed John was doing his regular country show. As Jack rubbed the sleep from his eyes, Sleepy Eyed John said, "Here's the record everyone is screaming about." Then he played "Blue Moon of Kentucky." The song left Clement dazed. He had never heard anything like it. No one had.

By today's standards, "That's All Right, Mama" and "Blue Moon of Kentucky" seem more like country music than rock 'n' roll, but that's because, over the years, country music has changed, incorporating many of the chord changes and rhythms introduced by rock 'n' roll in its infancy. At the time they were released, "That's All Right, Mama" and "Blue Moon of Kentucky" were raw, irreverent, and bristling with energy. Those were the elements that made it rock 'n' roll.

The elements that define rock music today—the blistering electric guitar solos, the pounding drums, the omnipotent bass—were added in later years by musicians to duplicate electronically what we accomplished with little more than raw talent.

"Blue Moon of Kentucky" gave us more than a B-side, it ultimately gave us a name: the Blue Moon Boys. On the first two records, we were identified simply as Elvis, Scotty, and Bill. By the third record, we had started going by the name Elvis and the Blue Moon Boys, an outgrowth of my Navy band, the Happy Valley Boys.

In the beginning, we were a band. We thought as one, created as one, performed as one. David Briggs, a prominent Nashville producer—who, as a member of the Muscle Shoals rhythm section, opened for the Beatles when they first came to America—views the Blue Moon Boys as a band that succeeded not just because of Elvis's star power, but because of our ability to work together as a unit. "Everyone gives the Beatles credit for being the first group to make history," says Briggs. "My point is that they weren't the first white group. The first was Bill, Scotty, and Elvis. Although Elvis was the star and eventually outshone them, they were a group. They were the first [group] to make number one records."

★ ★ ★

At some point during those first few weeks, we were sitting around the studio, throwing out "what if's." Someone (I don't remember who) asked what we were going to do if some jerk of a disc jockey or wannabe booker pressured Elvis into signing a management contract. Unsigned, Elvis was a target for unscrupulous disc jockeys and bookers who might demand a piece of the action in return for playing his records. The best way to avoid those problems was to get Elvis locked into a contract with a "safe" manager. Sam and I decided it would be to everyone's advantage if I became Elvis's personal manager.

The contract between Elvis and myself was similar to the contract I had drawn up for the Starlite Wranglers; but it was done by a lawyer, not Marion. Sam was several years my senior, but it was the sailor from Shanghai who, at age twenty-two, better understood the machinations of an imperfect world. Over the years I found it advantageous to assume the role of the shy, quiet second-fiddle, the farm boy who made good. If Sam, Elvis, or anyone else wanted to take credit for something that I did, that was fine with me. All I asked in return was that the spotlight not shine on me, which was fine with them.

On July 12, 1954, one week to the day after our first session, I got the managerial contract back from my lawyer. It identified W. S. Moore III as a "band leader and a booking agent" and Elvis Presley as a "singer of reputation and renown" who possessed "bright promises of large success." The agreement allowed me to "take over the complete management of the professional affairs of the said Elvis Presley, book him professionally for all appearances that can be secured for him, and to promote him, generally, in his professional endeavors." As compensation, I was to receive ten percent of "all earnings from engagements, appearances, and bookings made by him." The agreement prohibited Elvis from signing any other contract pertaining to his professional work for a period of one year.

That day I took the contract to Vernon and Gladys Presley to sign as Elvis's guardians. With my short, neatly trimmed hair and boyish personality I made a good impression. Elvis didn't smoke, drink, or use profanity. He went to church and had a deep spiritual center. Vernon and Gladys wouldn't sign their son over to just anyone. They didn't know much about me (Elvis had only known me for little over a week), but I *looked* like a nice clean-cut young man and they knew all about Sam Phillips because his name was in the newspapers and Elvis had been talking about him for about a year. If Sam said I was all right, then I must be all right. The four of us signed the contract and dated it. After the signing, Gladys told me she expected me to look after her son. It was an obligation I took seriously.

As Sam got ready for the record's release, I got busy being Elvis's manager. Since we only had one record with two sides to play, the best way to introduce us to the public, I figured, was to incorporate Elvis and Bill into the Starlite Wranglers as "special guests." Since the band was booked that weekend at the Bon Air Club, a bar on the outer rim of the city limits, I asked Sam to bring Elvis to the club that night to sit in with the band.

The next step for Elvis and the Blue Moon Boys was for us to learn enough songs to perform on our own. Carney told me that I could use the room up over the dry cleaners as a practice hall. Late in the afternoon or early in the evening, or whenever we could all three get off work together, we met at the dry cleaners to build up a playlist.

Tammy Wynette remembers the rehearsals with fondness. Just getting to the dry cleaners from her house or from school was always an adventure in itself. Since the zoo was located nearby, she often was greeted by a cacophony of grunts, groans, and hair-raising bellows from the always hungry, caged animals. The noise frightened her sometimes, but once she got to the dry cleaners, she always had fun. Carney, Auzella, and I would take turns pushing her around the shop in a clothes cart. Of course, when the Blue Moon Boys were upstairs, rocking and rolling, there was no better place in the world to be.

"The day I remember the most, was the one when they were coming down the stairs and Auzella looked up and said, 'My, my, my. Look at the stars,'" says Tammy. "Elvis was nothing then, but he looked at her with that little smile of his and he said, 'Auzella, one of these days I'll wrap you up in hundred dollar bills.'"

★ ★ ★

That Saturday night Sam took Elvis to the Bon Air as planned. When the time came, the Starlite Wranglers, with the exception of Bill and me, stepped down—and Elvis took the stage. We performed our two songs and Elvis sat down. The reaction was polite but not wildly enthusiastic. Elvis felt dejected. Sam agreed it wasn't a great reception, but he told Elvis that he had given a solid performance. He told him better days were ahead.

After Sam and Elvis left I realized that all was not well with the Starlite Wranglers. Doug Poindexter considered himself a local star of serious magnitude. He and the others were miffed that Bill and I had not included them on the recording session with Elvis. Quickly, it became apparent to me that my idea of making the Blue Moon Boys part of the Starlite Wranglers show was not going to work. Egos aside, there was a contractual problem. The Starlite Wranglers contract clearly stated that "any and all compositions and songs, or productions, composed or written by any member of the group, or in conjunction with, or with the aid of any member or members of the group, will be considered by all parties as community property, owned by the group, and any and all monies received from sales, recordings, or royalties, from said compositions, shall be community property and divided among the members."

Where did the Starlite Wranglers end and the Blue Moon Boys begin? The Starlite Wranglers wanted answers. Were they entitled to a share of the earnings from the Blue Moon Boys? My earlier desire to control the destiny of the Starlite Wranglers came back to haunt me. That tightly drawn contract now had the potential to control me. Was that the reason Sam did not include Bill and me in his contract with Elvis? No one seems to remember today, but it is interesting that Doug Poindexter was asked to play guitar on a couple of tracks with Elvis.

On one song, "Just Because," Poindexter put paper through his guitar strings and made it sound like a washboard. The paper is just threaded between the strings. That way you don't have to make chords. You just strum the guitar. I did a similar thing by tucking a handkerchief in under the back of the strings to make the guitar sound like a banjo. On another song, "I Don't Care If the Sun Don't Shine," guitarist Buddy Cunningham was in the studio. "Wait a minute," he says, and goes into the back room. He returns with two or three different sized boxes, which he tapes together into a bongo drum configuration. His box-playing rhythms can clearly be heard on the record.

On top of the loyalty issue, Elvis's exotic appearance did not go over well with the more conservative Starlite Wranglers. They didn't like the way he looked. They didn't like his attitude. They didn't like anything about him. After that night it was obvious that while its contract ran until March 1955, the Starlite Wranglers were finished as a group. We parted on good terms, and Bill and I gave our full attention to the Blue Moon Boys.

On Monday, July 19, Sam released "That's All Right, Mama" and "Blue Moon of Kentucky." By that time the record had already generated over 6,000 orders from local record stores. Sam's radio blitz was paying off.

After the disappointing showing at the Bon Air, Sam called disc jockey Bob Neal, who was putting together a hillbilly show for later that month at the Overton Park Shell, an amphitheater located adjacent to the city zoo. Sam asked Neal if he would book Elvis for the show. The headliner was Slim Whitman. Sam thought the family-oriented audience he would attract would be more receptive to Elvis than the hard-drinking crowd at the Bon Air. Neal agreed to add Elvis to the bill on the condition that Sam get Elvis and the Blue Moon Boys signed up with the local musicians union.

I continued to hustle club bookings for the group. I asked Sleepy Eyed John to book us at the Eagle's Nest as the floor show with the eight-piece swing band fronted by Jack Clement.

"I had to bring him on and then I had to follow him," says Clement. "When he came on—just the three of them, with Scotty on electric guitar and Bill slapping that bass—it was magic."

We performed at the Eagle's Nest three weekends in a row, with the club packed each night. On July 27, three days before the concert at the Shell, Sam asked Marion to take Elvis to the newsroom of the *Memphis Press-Scimitar* for an interview with entertainment writer Edwin Howard. They went during Elvis's lunch-hour break at Crown Electric. It was Elvis's first newspaper interview and he was scared to death. Howard later wrote about that first meeting:[3]

---

3. Howard, Edwin, *Seeing Stars: Memoirs of a Celebrity-Seeker.*

Except for the pre-tied bow-tie [sic] nestling just below his adams'
apple, he looked like he might be an assembly line worker himself. His
shirt and pants and gray leisure jacket didn't quite go together. His
plastered-down, growing out, flat-top haircut with ducktail looked
as if it had been administered by a lawn mower. His pimply face and
long, scraggly sideburns stirred not a ripple among the women in the
office. And yet there was something about him. You could imagine
young girls being intrigued by his slumberous eyes and curly, almost
surly, mouth.

Howard tried to interview him, but all he could get were "Yes, sirs" and "no, sirs." Marion did all of the talking. "The odd thing about it," Marion said in the interview, "is that both sides seem to be equally popular on pop, folk, and race record programs. This boy has something that seems to appeal to everybody."

Howard's story, which ran the next day, touted the record as showing promise of becoming "the biggest hit Sun has ever pressed." He dutifully plugged Elvis's upcoming appearance at the Shell. Interestingly, he never quoted Elvis in the story—with his "yes, sirs" and "no, sirs" he surely must have been the toughest subject he had ever interviewed—and he never mentioned the Blue Moon Boys or myself and Bill. Whenever Sam booked us or promoted the record, it was always as "Elvis." When I did the bookings and promotions, it was always as Elvis and the Blue Moon Boys. The records themselves gave us equal billing, identifying us as "Elvis Presley, Scotty and Bill."

On July 30, the day of our scheduled performance at the Shell, we realized that we had forgotten to join the musicians union. Amid the hurly-burly surrounding our first big public performance, we scraped together the money we needed and completed the necessary paperwork to become members of the American Federation of Musicians, Local No. 71. It was not the largest chapter in the country, but it was on its way to becoming one of the most important. In time, its membership read like a Who's Who of American music. Bluesman B.B. King joined in the early 1950s and is today still a member in good standing, as am I.

That night, when the show began at 8 o'clock, Elvis was a nervous wreck. He was so jumpy I was surprised he couldn't hear his knees knocking. The stars of the show, Slim Whitman and Billy Walker, had a loyal fan base. Elvis wasn't sure they would like him. Sam, who was there with

Marion and Elvis's girlfriend, Dixie, reassured him: "You're going to be great."

When the time came, Bob Neal did the introduction. From the audience the stage at the Shell doesn't appear all that large, but, if you are on the stage, looking out at the audience, it seems enormous. When we heard our names, we took the stage, facing row after row of waiting fans who had no idea what to expect. We felt dwarfed by the conical shape of the backdrop.

We were scared to death. All those people—and us with these three little funky musical instruments. We started out with "That's All Right, Mama." Elvis was so nervous that he raised up on the balls of his feet and shook his leg in time with the music, a move he sometimes used in the studio. To his shock—and horror—the young girls in the audience went crazy, yelling and applauding. He couldn't see what the audience saw.

Because he was wearing baggy pants that were pleated in the front, his attempt to keep time with the music created a wild gyrating effect with his pants' legs. From the audience's angle those movements seemed exaggerated against the backdrop of the Shell, which had a tendency to amplify whatever was on stage, visually as well as acoustically. We didn't know what was going on when all those people started screaming and hollering. We followed "That's All Right, Mama" with "Blue Moon of Kentucky." When we got off stage, Elvis asked why people were yelling at him. Someone told him it was because he was shaking his leg.

Later in the show, we returned to the stage and repeated the same two songs. Marion remembers that we also did a new song they were working on, "I'll Never Let You Go (Little Darlin')." Elvis looked at her when he sang it. "Now I'm a restrained person, in public anyway, and I heard somebody screaming, and I discovered it was me—the staid mother of a young son," Marion says. "I was standing out there screeching like I'd lost my total stupid mind. The rest of the audience reacted the same way."

Sam couldn't believe what he was seeing—and hearing. He suddenly felt like the luckiest son of a bitch in the world. In August, he loaded up his car with records and hit the road, preaching the gospel of Elvis to every promoter, local distributor, and disc jockey in the South. Many nights he slept in his car. He ate in cafes when he could find them. When he couldn't he ate out of a can. As Sam was taking care of business, spreading the word about Elvis, I continued to book us in every Memphis venue I could find.

In early September, we performed at a Katz Drug Store opening. The store was located in a shopping center at 2256 Lamar Avenue. We set up on the back of a flatbed truck that was parked in front of the store. Attending that performance was Johnny Cash, a newcomer to Memphis, and John Evans, who later achieved fame as the keyboardist on the first Memphis pop record to go to No. 1: the Box Tops' "The Letter."

Evans was a Dewey Phillips fan and had been listening to him plug "That's All Right, Mama." "My dad had wired our house so that we had an intercom running through the house," explains Evans. "That way the radio could be heard throughout the house. We listened to Dewey Phillips that way. He played that song all the time. Those were magic moments in broadcasting history."

When Evans, who was about six, and his brother heard on the radio that Elvis would be performing at the shopping center, they went to watch since it was just a short distance from their home. "People came from all over the neighborhood and swarmed down on the place," he says. "My brother held me up to where I could see. I remember they were dressed like real weird country musicians. Elvis was wearing pink and gray. I was struck by that. They had a big string bass and the guy would twirl it around. There was only one amp and it was sitting on a chair. There was a little guy playing a big guitar."

Encouraged by his reception at the Shell, Elvis repeated his leg shaking movements at the shopping center. He just started adding a little more to it and made it into a fine art. But it was a natural thing for him to do.

Ralph Moore, supportive of my sudden success, was also at the shopping center that day. What struck him was the fact that it was a racially mixed audience. "The coloreds were dancing and they'd get up on these barrels and they would fall off," he says. That was the first time that he met Elvis, and he walked away that day carrying an impression of the man that stuck with him over the years. "He was a plain ole country boy—very polite. It was 'yes, sir' and 'yes, ma'am.'"

★ ★ ★

In September, we returned to the studio. We were solid hits in Memphis, but we hadn't broken out of the city, with the exception of a *Billboard* review that had praised our single in the magazine's "Spotlight" section. It was beginning to dawn on us—Elvis, Sam, and I were all Capricorns—that we were on the verge of something. Of what, we weren't sure.

Bill and my feelings were, "Hey, this guy is going to be big," but none of us felt it was going to be as big as it was as fast as it was. We weren't in any rush. It busted loose so fast we didn't really have time to think about it.

In the studio Sam gently nudged us as he had done before.

He was like one of the guys. He would have made a great preacher. You can get him started on any subject. Sometimes we'd get to drinking and he would get off on a tangent. Him and me would argue like you would not believe—really get into each other's face—but we were having fun with it. He had his own set of beliefs on everything. He was a taskmaster when we were working, pushing everybody to the limit—and he was right on a lot of it. "Let's do it one more time," he would say. He couldn't tell you what he wanted, but he would suggest you try something. He wanted it loose. He didn't know what he wanted, but thank goodness he recognized it when he heard it.

Performing with Elvis was a joy; but working with him in the studio was sometimes difficult because he never came prepared. Choosing the songs we recorded was a trial-and-error process. In later years Sam would see the value in having a publishing company and recording original material, but in the early days of Elvis's career no one brought original material to the sessions. It was during this time that I developed the style that stayed with me the rest of my life. Although a song might be like something we did before, it made no sense to play what I played earlier. I tried to come up with something different. I tried to play around the singer. If Elvis was singing a song a certain way, there was no point in me trying to top him on what he was doing. The idea was to play something that went the other way—a counterpoint. Sometimes it got pretty rough. A few times it was just pure anger and I got frustrated. Sam treated Elvis's voice like it was a musical instrument and I came to view it the same way. If you are a musician you don't try to play over the lead instrument, you play around it. B.B. King is a good example of a singer/musician who followed that philosophy. You never see him playing while he is singing. As the lead guitarist of his own band, he plays around his own voice.

We recorded a number of songs during the September session, but the two that made the next single were "Good Rockin' Tonight" and "I Don't Care If the Sun Don't Shine." Marion took a special interest in the latter.

Elvis came up with just one verse—that's all he knew. So we took a break and I wrote the second one. We recorded it and Sam took the only dub to a record convention. He called back and says, "Everybody loves it . . . taking orders like mad." Then I got a call from New York, from a music firm, and they said we understand you're releasing a record of "I Don't Care If the Sun Don't Shine." They said, well, Mack David wrote that song and he's very particular about what you do with his songs and he reserves the right to hear the material before you release it.

Marion told Sam and he sent the record airmail to the publisher the next day. When Marion heard back from the publisher, he was ecstatic. David walked into his office while he was playing the record. "He thinks it's great—go ahead," said the publisher. "But I noticed you added a verse and I'm sending you some disclaimers that say whoever wrote the verse can't put their name on the label, can't collect any royalties and so on."

"I said, okay," recalls Marion. "I just wanted to get the record out . . . (but) every time I turned the radio on, I'd hear [Elvis] singing my lyrics."

"Good Rockin' Tonight" and "I Don't Care If the Sun Don't Shine" were released in late September. By that time Elvis was becoming a regular visitor at the Moore household. One day Bobbie and I were home alone when I decided to go to the store to get some cigarettes. I left the front door unlocked. Bobbie was standing in the bathroom combing her hair, when she heard the front door open. She assumed it was me. She heard footsteps in the living room. Then she looked up and saw Elvis standing in the bathroom door looking over her shoulder.

"Where's Scotty?" he asked matter-of-factly.

Startled, Bobbie told him I had gone out for cigarettes.

"He'll be back in a minute," she said. "You can wait, if you like."

"Uh, I'll be back," Elvis mumbled, and left.

When I returned home, Bobbie told me about the unexpected visit. Although Elvis said he would return, he did not. We never did find out why he stopped by the house. He was unpredictable in some ways, but in other ways we always knew what to expect.

"He liked to walk, walk, walk," says Bobbie of his nervous energy. "He paced the floor. He couldn't be still." Sometimes he roamed nonstop through the house, "looking in the refrigerator . . . making himself at home."

Once, after we came in late from a performance or rehearsal, Elvis decided to spend the night. Bobbie was shocked. "He had said something about his mother never going to sleep until he got home, and I wondered if she was going to sleep that night," says Bobbie.

Our sofa made into a bed, so we flipped it out for Elvis and gave him some clean sheets. The next morning, while Bobbie was cooking breakfast, I told her Elvis liked his eggs fried real hard. She cooked them to specifications and put them on Elvis's plate.

"He looked at me and said, 'Could you cook this a little more?' and I put them back in the skillet and cooked them some more." Bobbie laughs when she thinks about it. "He still didn't eat but a couple of bites. He ate the bacon and toast. I like mine well done, too, but . . ."

Elvis was still dating Dixie at that time and they often "double dated" with Bobbie and me. One of the places we went was a drive-in on Park Avenue where we could sit outside and eat watermelon. Invariably, Elvis and I ended up in a watermelon seed spitting contest. After shows, we often went out together to eat. Usually Bobbie was the only one who had any money. Her nine-to-five at Sears wasn't glamorous, but it did pay on a regular basis. "When they played at the Eagle's Nest, they didn't get paid until they went to the union," she says. "Elvis never had any money. We'd go out to eat and we had to buy his burger and milkshake. One night he wanted another milkshake. He asked Scotty if he could have one. Scotty said he would have to ask me. I was the only one who got paid."

Once Elvis cleaned his plate, he had a tendency to munch off the plates of those around him. It was Evelyn Black who discovered, quite by accident, the secret to protecting her meal from Elvis's wandering fingers. "We stopped once to get a sandwich and some French fries, and I put ketchup on my potatoes—you know so I could dip them," says Evelyn. "Elvis would get a potato off of my plate, and I noticed he always got one that didn't have ketchup on it. From then on, I learned to put ketchup on my fries or else Elvis would eat them all."

Besides his voracious appetite for burgers and shakes, one of the things that Bobbie remembers most about their outings with Elvis was his refusal to dance with her. She kidded him about it. The more she urged him to dance with her, the more adamant he became not to dance. Bobbie was mystified. "He danced on stage, but he never danced on the floor," she says.

Once she asked him to autograph a photograph. On the back he wrote: "No, I will never dance." He signed it "Elvis Q-Ball Presley."

★ ★ ★

In August, Sam Phillips called Jim Denny, manager of the *Grand Ole Opry*, and talked to him about booking Elvis for the show. Denny told him that he had heard the record and—while it wasn't exactly his cup of tea—he would keep an open mind and if there was ever an opening he would give him a call. Meanwhile, Nashville buzzed over "Blue Moon of Kentucky." Record executives weren't sure they liked it, but they were sure of one thing: it was a hit.

Sam pressured Denny until he finally agreed to let us play the *Opry*. But there were conditions: We couldn't do an entire segment, but we could do *one* song—"Blue Moon of Kentucky"—during Hank Snow's segment.

Sam was elated. So were we. In those days, playing the *Opry* was the pinnacle of success; there just wasn't anything bigger. On Saturday, October 2, we loaded up Sam's big, black Cadillac, strapping Bill's bass to the roof, and drove the 200 miles to Nashville. Marion closed the studio and took a bus. Elvis didn't own a suitcase, so Marion loaned him hers. He packed most of his wardrobe into the suitcase.

When we arrived, Elvis wandered about the Ryman Auditorium. It was unpainted and had a homey feel to it. It smelled like old wood. Elvis was disappointed. He expected it to look a little fancier. "You mean this is what I've been dreaming about all these years?" Elvis asked Marion. The disappointment was mutual.

When Denny saw us walk in he was shocked.

"I wanted the full band that's on the record," he said, counting a singer and two musicians. "Our agreement was we were gonna have the performance just like it is on the record."

Denny expected a big band to go along with the big sound he heard on the record. We explained that it was only the three of us on the record. He was amazed. He sent us backstage to get ready for the show.

Marion sat out in the audience.

"Who'd you come to see?" she asked a woman next to her.

"Marty Robbins," the woman said. "I never miss Marty Robbins. Who'd you come to hear?"

"Elvis Presley," Marion said.

"Who?"

"After this show, you won't ask me again," she told the woman.

Unknown to Bill and me, our wives had disobeyed orders to stay at home. "After they left Memphis, Evelyn came by the house and said, 'Let's go,'" says Bobbie. "We didn't get there until about eight o'clock, but we got some good seats down front. Bill stuck his head out from backstage and saw us and they took us backstage. Scotty was kind of mad, but he got over it."

Before they went on stage, Hank Snow turned to Elvis and asked him his name.

"Elvis Presley."

"I mean, what's the name you sing under?" he asked.

Elvis looked at him like he thought he was crazy.

"My name's Elvis Presley."

When we took the stage we didn't know what to expect. We played the song exactly the way we had recorded it. The audience applauded, but they didn't go wild. There wasn't any booing or hissing. Just polite applause. It wasn't as bad as people have written it up to be. It was after we did the song and went off stage that Jim Denny, according to Sam and Elvis, made the comment, 'You'd better keep driving the truck.'"

Afterward Bobbie and I both heard accounts that Elvis cried after the show. Neither of us saw that happen. "He seemed pretty happy to me," says Bobbie. The fact that the audience was polite—and not wildly enthusiastic like they were in Memphis—was disappointing, but not ego shattering. It didn't take long to get over it.

Bobbie and Evelyn drove back to Memphis with us that night. Since Sam wanted to listen to a piano player who had been recommended to him, he got rooms at a motel for himself, Marion, and Elvis so they could spend the night. Elvis went into the club with them to hear the piano player, but quickly turned around and went back outside. Marion followed after him and asked why he had left. He told her it wasn't the type of place his parents would want him to be. He told them to go ahead and have a good time. He would wait outside on the sidewalk.

On the way back to Memphis the next day, Elvis took Marion's suitcase into a service station bathroom to change clothes. Not until they got home did they realize he had left the suitcase at the service station. It took three or four stress-filled days for them to retrieve the suitcase, which contained Elvis's entire wardrobe.

That November, Bob Neal took Sam aside and asked him if he could take over Elvis's management contract. Sam told him they couldn't make any changes right then—my contract with Elvis still had five months to go—but he authorized Neal to arrange bookings for the band. Everyone, including myself, liked Neal. He was a good man, straight as an arrow.

The squeeze play was on for me, but I didn't realize it at the time. We were all much too busy in the present to worry about the future. By the end of 1954, Sun Records had released four records of Elvis and the Blue Moon Boys. Sales were brisk, but since I wasn't under contract—and, in fact, was receiving nothing from record sales—my only income from music was from performance fees. My share of that was twenty-five percent. Tax records show that my total income for 1954, from all sources, including my job at the dry cleaners, was $2,249.49. Of that, only $139.25 was derived from my performances with Elvis.

★ 5 ★

HITTING PAY DIRT

Sam sparred with the *Louisiana Hayride* for several weeks over booking Elvis for its weekly, Saturday-night radio program. Broadcast on KWKH, a 50,000-watt station in Shreveport, it was second only to the *Opry* in influence with country-music audiences. In some ways the six-year-old program had eclipsed the *Opry* in importance, especially in the area of discovering new talent. While the *Opry* boosted the careers of big-name artists, the *Hayride*, perhaps feeling it had more to gain by banking on long shots, took a chance on new talent such as Hank Williams, Jim Reeves, Kitty Wells, and Faron Young.

Pappy Covington, the booking agent for the *Hayride*, had heard "That's All Right, Mama" and "Blue Moon of Kentucky." In the latter part of September 1954, he told Sam he wanted to book Elvis and the Blue Moon Boys for the show. Sam put him off, saying he didn't want to make any commitments until after the *Opry* performance. Since he thought Elvis would be a sensation at the *Opry*, he didn't want to do anything contractually that would limit his ability to make Elvis available for future performances at the Ryman. The smattering of polite applause we received from the *Opry* audience brought Sam back to reality. The day after we returned to Memphis, Sam got Covington on the telephone . . . *yes, yes, Elvis will be delighted to perform at the Hayride.* The first performance was booked for October 16.

A couple of days before the show, D. J. Fontana was asked by management to stop by the office to listen to Elvis's records. On weekdays, D. J. played drums on the cocktail and strip-joint circuit with Hoot and Curley's, a popular Shreveport trio. On Saturday nights he was the staff drummer at the *Hayride.* That meant that D. J. was called upon whenever visiting artists wanted to beef up their act with drums. He always played behind the curtain, so he could not be seen by the audience. In those days, country music fans considered drums a musical sacrilege.

"Good Rockin' Tonight" had been released in September and was doing well in Arkansas, Mississippi, and Alabama. That day in the office D. J. listened to the record with great interest. He commented on the echo effect. He had never heard anything quite like it. "That's a good record. How many musicians they got? Five? Six?"

When told there were only three people in the band, it floored him. "I've never heard anything like that. Boy, that's good."

Early Saturday morning, after we wrapped up our Friday night gig at the Eagle's Nest, we loaded up two cars and struck out for Shreveport, a drive of about seven hours. It was our second big road trip. Awaiting us was the *Louisiana Hayride*, broadcast each Saturday night from the Shreveport Municipal Auditorium. The sturdy, brick-and-concrete building, located at Grand Avenue and Milam Street, on the fringe of the city's business district, boasted a large stage and a seating capacity of 3,800. The three-hour *Hayride* was broadcast in its entirety over a 28-state area. Curtain time was 8 p.m.

When we arrived at the auditorium, we went backstage to meet with the announcer, Frank Page, D. J., and others on the *Hayride* staff. Page gave us a rundown on how the show operated. "They all seemed nervous, being on a big show like this," says Page. "They knew how many people had become stars by being on the *Hayride*. I talked to Elvis. He was a little discouraged by the things that had happened so far, about being turned down by the *Opry*, about not getting kick started like he wanted to be. I encouraged him and told him to just do his thing."

After the meeting, we went to the dressing room so D. J. could listen to the records again. We'd never performed with a drummer and were looking forward to it, particularly after our reception at the *Opry*. D. J. listened to the songs, asking questions about what we wanted him to do, offering his ideas. "I figured the best thing for these guys was to stay out of the way," says D. J. "Why would I clutter it up with cymbals? I'll just play the back beat and stay out of their way. They already had the good sound."

Not only did D. J. have good instincts for music, when to push the beat and when to pull back, he also had a knack for sizing up people. Right away he figured out that Elvis looked to me for guidance. As he explained in an interview with my co-author, "Scotty was acting road manager and took care of the business end. Elvis would agree to anything. If someone said, 'Would you work this free?' he'd say, 'Well, yeah.' Rather than Elvis being the bad guy, it was Scotty. He'd just say, 'We can't do it.'"

That night Page introduced us as we stood on stage in front of the backdrop, a thin curtain on which was painted a barn, a wagon, trees, and moss. Page tried to engage Elvis in conversation. "Well, I'd like to say how happy we are to be here," said Elvis. "It's a real honor for us to get a chance to appear on the *Louisiana Hayride*. And we're going to do a song for you."

Self-consciously, Elvis ended his onstage banter with Page with a pregnant pause, followed by a question. "You got anything else to say, sir?"

"No, I'm ready," said Page, who knew he had squeezed every ounce of conversation he could out of Elvis. He turned the show over to him and left the stage.

With D. J. hidden behind the curtain, Elvis launched into "That's All Right, Mama." Elvis didn't have a monitor, so he couldn't hear himself, only the music. D. J. couldn't see any of the other players. Standing offstage, Page noticed how nervous we all looked. Elvis seemed ill at ease and I struggled with my guitar solo. The audience was polite, but there was no screaming or dancing in the aisles. We did two songs, and then left the stage.

We were scheduled to return later in the show to repeat the first set. Backstage, Sam gave Elvis a pep talk. He told him to just relax and do it the way he did it in Memphis. If these people didn't like that . . . *well, to hell with them.* That was language Elvis could understand.

During the first performance, Page watched with interest. "The audience was a little shocked," he later recalled. "Scotty's guitar, of course, was different and had a unique sound the audience was not quite ready for at the time."

When we returned for the second set, the audience had changed somewhat. There were more students in the crowd. As we repeated the same two songs, Sam, who sat in the audience, noticed a marked difference in the crowd's reaction. This time the students were shouting and clapping. While it wasn't exactly on the level Sam had grown accustomed to in Memphis, it confirmed his belief that Elvis was on the right track.

The *Hayride* management felt the same way. They invited us back for a return engagement. "Elvis didn't really take off until two or three weeks after that," says Page. "The young ladies started showing up. Elvis wiggled his leg a bit, snarled a bit, and let his hair hang down. The audience changed as the demeanor of the act changed."

Three weeks later, Elvis returned to Shreveport with his parents to sign a 12-month contract with the Hayride. We would be paid basic union scale—$18 to Elvis as the band leader, and $12 each to me and Bill. We were expected to perform for 52 consecutive weeks, with occasional absences permitted with adequate notice.

★ ★ ★

That November, after Sam gave Bob Neal permission to do bookings for Elvis, it became obvious that Bill and I were in a precarious contractual position. Neither of us had a contract with Sam. The *Hayride* contract included us only if Elvis took us along as his musicians. I was Elvis's manager, but it was an uncompensated position: I never received a penny for being his manager. I had always been ambivalent about the contract, but now, with Neal usurping some of my responsibilities as manager, I put extra effort into trying to get bookings with big-time promoters. One of the promoters I approached, Colonel Tom Parker, was based in Madison, Tennessee, but had an office in Chicago that operated under the name Jamboree Attractions. The company's slogan was "We cover the nation."

I thought that had a nice ring to it. I wrote the office in Chicago, asking if they could book us in or around Chicago. Maybe I wasn't crazy about being Elvis's manager, but neither did I want the contract snatched away either because that piece of paper was the only legal connection I had to the music that we had created as a group. If I could be the first to book a big-time performance outside of the South, I knew my value to the group would increase. It took a while for Jamboree Attractions to respond, but on January 13, 1955, Parker's assistant, Tom Diskin, sent me a letter that curtly informed me that there were few outlets for "hillbilly" entertainers in Chicago. Wrote Diskin: "While we are a booking and promotion agency I don't have anything at present where I could place your artist."

★ ★ ★

One evening Elvis and I sat out on the steps of Elvis's house on Alabama Street and talked about the future. Elvis could see that Bill and I were being squeezed out of the picture. That troubled him. Under our agreement, there was a 50-25-25 split, with expenses coming off the top, but that was for performances only. Bill and I didn't make a penny off the records. Further highlighting those inequities was the fact that our touring car, a '54 Bel Air Chevy, had been purchased by Bobbie, who alone was making the payments and taking care of repairs.

Elvis told me that he thought it was only fair that the record royalties should be split among us the same way we split performance fees. I told him that wouldn't work. If we do that, you'll start resenting that later when you learn more about the business.

"But you guys need to share in this."

Elvis was adamant we needed to do something. We talked about it a while longer. Finally, seeing that Elvis was determined to find a solution, I offered an alternative that he thought was fair. Give Bill and I each one-quarter of one percent.

I knew Elvis was getting three percent. That would have cut him to two and a half. In my mind, that was fair. From what I knew about the business, I knew it would turn sour down the road if we did it his way. He said, "OK, fine—I understand." We left it at that; nothing was ever put down in writing. There was no need to. We trusted each other.

In December we returned to the studio in between performances at the *Hayride* and an occasional appearance at the Eagle's Nest. We recorded "Milkcow Blues Boogie" and "You're A Heartbreaker," which were released in January 1955. With Bob Neal doing more of the booking, we started performing in Texas, Arkansas, Alabama, and Mississippi. Sometime in January, Neal officially took over Elvis's management. No lawyers were involved in the transfer. Neal took a 15 percent commission and set up an office across the street from the Peabody Hotel.

I began the New Year with high hopes, not paying particular attention to the fact that I had relinquished all contractual ties to Elvis and Sun Records. From that point on, Bill and I would remain members of the team only at the pleasure of management. I reminded Neal of Elvis's offer to include Bill and me in the royalties received from record sales.

"Oh, yeah, we need to do that," said Neal.

Today, in retrospect, I wish I had been more aggressive in pursuing the matter. I should have gone the next day and gotten it drawn up and signed, but I kept putting it off. Whether Elvis talked to Neal or his mama or daddy, or later to Parker, I don't have any idea. I told Bobbie about it, and Bill, and I can almost hear me telling Sam. There were just the three of us. We were a group. Elvis was the main guy and I said the main guy always gets paid more, but that doesn't keep the main man from helping out the other guys a little bit. I didn't want to make a big deal of it. The band was just getting off the ground. I didn't want to cause trouble. Elvis said he would cut us in on record royalties, and I had no reason to doubt him.

On February 6, 1955, a meeting took place that sealed the fate of the band. After a Sunday performance at Ellis Auditorium in Memphis, Elvis, Bill, and I went across the street to a cafe, where we met Sam and Neal.

Also there was Colonel Tom Parker and his assistant Tom Diskin. In his new capacity as manager, Neal had set up the meeting to introduce us to Parker, who had recently taken over the management of Hank Snow, one of the *Grand Ole Opry*'s most popular members. Parker's booking agency, which had been formed in partnership with Snow, was making a name for itself at the national level. As a country music disc jockey, Neal knew how important a good booking and promotions man could be to an artist's career.

After a few minutes of banter, Bill got up and returned to the auditorium. I had only received the letter from Diskin the week before informing me that Jamboree Attractions was not interested in booking a hillbilly performer like Elvis in Chicago. Now Diskin and Parker were making a spiel to Elvis and Sam about how much they could help Elvis's career. I didn't say anything about the letter. Mostly, I sat and listened, watching the show.

Parker and Neal could not have been more different. Neal was an affable man who didn't have an enemy in the world. In his mid-forties, he had a son about Elvis's age, and perhaps because of that he developed a paternal approach to dealing with us. We all liked Bob. He was a big ole, bear-like guy—real easygoing.

Parker was equally gregarious, also in his mid-forties, but there was something about his demeanor that bothered me. At the time, I couldn't put my finger on it. The more Parker talked, the less I trusted him. On paper, Parker seemed just what we needed to get us over the hump. He had what we needed most: *connections*. In addition to Snow, he was booking Minnie Pearl, Mother Maybelle and the Carter Sisters, and Slim Whitman. I didn't know enough about Parker to dislike him. My reaction to him was purely instinctive, colored perhaps by my dealings with club owners and by my experiences in the Navy.

No one knew it at the time, but Parker was an illegal alien. Born Andreas Cornelius van Kuijk in Holland, he had entered the United States under mysterious circumstances in the late 1920s. For twenty years, he worked as a carnie, learning the trade as an advance man and two-bit huckster. In the mid-1940s he found a home in country music by becoming the personal manager of Eddie Arnold, a new RCA artist who was quickly making a name for himself. It was because of that association that he picked up the title of "Colonel."

In the South at that time it was customary for governors to anoint their campaign supporters with the honorary title of "colonel." It was used as a signal to law-enforcement officials, particularly highway patrolmen, that the bearer had once done a favor for the governor. Parker received his title from Louisiana Governor Jimmie Davis, himself a former country-music performer. The Colonel, as he liked to be called, was a boisterous, cigar-chomping braggart, and he rubbed Sam and me the wrong way; but Neal had known him since the mid-1940s, when he first came to town with Eddie Arnold—and, if he said the Colonel was the real thing, we felt we had to respect his judgment.

When the meeting ended, Parker agreed to put us on the bill with Hank Snow. We knew enough to know that was a major break for us, but I left the meeting with a sinking feeling in the pit of my stomach. Elvis, Scotty, and Bill—as a band—were about to become history.

With the last single doing poorly on the charts, we returned to the studio to record "Baby, Let's Play House." Before we could nail anything down for the B-side, we went back out on the road, with performances booked by Neal in New Mexico and Texas. On February 16 we joined the Hank Snow jamboree in Odessa, Texas. Also on the bill were Hank's 19-year-old son, Jimmie Rodgers Snow, and Whitey Ford, a popular comedian who performed under the name, the Duke of Paducah. It was the first stop on a five-day tour.

To Snow's displeasure, the audiences, one by one, began to show a vociferous preference for Elvis. Snow may have been the star, but it was the youngster from Memphis who made the crowds scream for more. I felt sorry for Hank. It didn't matter whether Elvis was on first or last on the stage the reaction was always the same. In towns where we had radio exposure from KWKH in Shreveport the audience reaction was always frenzied, with the girls jumping up and down, screaming and sometimes passing out. The more excited the girls became, the more their dates resented us.

In the midst of all the excitement over our first tour, I noticed things going on behind the scenes. The Colonel started sabotaging Neal's relationship with Elvis. Bob tried to go on the road with us, but it took a toll on him. He got tired, especially under the stress of the other Elvis stuff coming along. With Neal wavering under the pressure of a heavy touring schedule, Parker promoted himself with Elvis, telling him he deserved better than what he was getting from Neal. Once he felt he had Elvis's confidence, he took aim at his next target: the Blue Moon Boys. I got the news from Hank Snow's band. They told me that Parker had approached them about backing Elvis. Parker told them he wanted to ditch Bill and me.

Elvis absolutely refused. Hank's band didn't want it either. They blew up when they heard about it. Hank had a great band, but they didn't play the type music we played. Most of them were older. We knew from day one the Colonel didn't want us around. It became more obvious as it went along. I had Elvis's ear, and he didn't like Elvis's friends being around.

After completing the tour with Snow, we drove to Cleveland, Ohio, to perform on a country show broadcast from the Circle Theater by radio station WERE. It was our first trip out of the South. Neal went along because he thought it would be helpful if he did promotions with the radio stations. When we returned to Memphis, we went back into the studio to do the B-side for "Baby, Let's Play House." We chose a song co-written by Memphians Bill Taylor and Stan Kesler, a steel guitarist who had been hanging around Sam's studio trying to do what he could to break into the business. The song, "I'm Left, You're Right, She's Gone," was Sam's first attempt to tap into the local songwriters' talent pool.

With a bluesy introduction borrowed from the Mississippi Delta and cutesy lyrics of the type that were popular with country fans, the song gave Elvis an opportunity to do a vocal that ran counter to my guitar. It also gave Sam an opportunity to add a new element to our sound: drums. For that, he used a local drummer, a high-school student by the name of James Lott.

As Sam prepared "Baby, Let's Play House" for an April release, Neal took us to New York to audition for a popular television show, *Arthur Godfrey's Talent Scouts*. Neal had been to New York before, but none of us ever had. The trip took on added significance when it was learned that neither Bill nor Elvis had ever flown. Neal had to scrape together the money for the trip, but he was convinced television was the key to breaking us with a national audience.

Once we arrived, we took in the sights; then, with Bill acting the clown, cracking jokes, making faces, and poking fun at the bustling crowds of city folks around us, we rode the subway to the television studio, where we performed live for the show's talent scouts. The reaction was not what we had hoped for.

"Don't call us, we'll call you," we were told.

Elvis didn't take the rejection well. A new side to his personality was beginning to emerge. The youthful, super-polite teenager we had started out with was beginning to display signs of developing an ego. He was still playful and self-effacing, but for the first time it was becoming apparent that he really did care what people thought about him.

I wasn't as bothered by the rejection. I wasn't too impressed with any of it, to tell you the truth. None of us ever liked television. That electronic eye is so unforgiving.

Back in Memphis, we awaited the release of our next single and got ready to go back out on the road. With its odometer spun around three times, Bobbie's '54 Chevy had made its last trip with the band. Elvis bought a 1951 Lincoln for us to tour in and painted the words "Elvis Presley—Sun Records" on the door. Over the years, it would be a source of mystery—and consternation—to Bobbie as to why Elvis never replaced the car she had purchased and freely loaned to the band for our road trips. In later years, when she read stories about Elvis giving new cars to perfect strangers, she wondered if he would remember to replace her 1954 Chevy. He never did.

★ ★ ★

Bill and I sat in the lobby of the Shreveport hotel. Since we couldn't afford more than one room on what we were being paid to perform on the *Hayride*, we rented a room with two beds and tried to stay out of each other's way as much as possible. That night Elvis used the room to have sex with a girl he had met earlier in the day. The more I think about it today, the more convinced I am that it was Elvis's first time to have sex.

Time spent waiting in a hotel lobby, especially at two or three in the morning, is never time well spent—not when you're waiting for someone who is in the process of losing his virginity. We were the only people in the lobby, aside from the desk clerk. Finally, after what seemed like hours but was probably only minutes, I looked up and saw Elvis coming down the stairs with the girl at his side, wild-eyed and clinging to his hand. After a moment of confusion and indecision, he left her at one end of the lobby with assurances that he would return and he walked over to where we were sitting. We could tell from his face that something was wrong.

Elvis walked up to us and stood there a minute before speaking, collecting his thoughts. Finally, he said matter-of-factly, "The rubber busted. What do I do now?"

Bill laughed. "I think you had better marry her—or get the hell out of town."

Realizing that I didn't have a follow-up to Bill's comment, I simply shook my head. Neither of us had any pearls of wisdom to offer, so we went upstairs to the room and went to sleep, leaving Elvis and the girl in the lobby to deal with the problem. Before he had sex with her we cautioned him about disease and getting girls pregnant. Short of putting the condom on him and monitoring its condition during the experience, what more could we have done?

The next morning we asked Elvis how he had handled the crisis.

"Oh, I took her to the emergency room at the hospital," he said nonchalantly.

"The emergency room!"

We had both had condoms break. It'd never occurred to us that it was a matter for the emergency room. "So what happened?" I was really curious.

"Yeah, I got them to give her a douche."

I looked at Bill. "I didn't know they did that."

"Me either."

Elvis was certainly an original thinker.

We returned to Memphis with our horizons expanded. We had to give the boy credit. It took balls to take a girl to the emergency room for treatment from a busted condom.

After that experience, whenever I went by to pick up Elvis for a road trip, Gladys always took me aside and admonished me to "take care of my boy." *Had he told his mother about the busted condom? Surely not!* Regardless of what spooked Gladys about out road trips, it was an assignment I took seriously. Although I had brothers, they were so much older than I was that I never had the day-to-day experience of being someone's brother. Out on the road Elvis became the younger brother I never had. In time Elvis started calling me "The Old Man," a reference not only to my paternal attitude, but to my penchant for tidiness.

In the beginning, we shared our rooms the same way we split the paycheck: Elvis took one bed; Bill and I took the other. I was appalled at Elvis's grooming habits. We had to ease him into more hygienic methods of living. It was the way he was raised. People didn't take a bath every day back then. We all sweated like hogs. We had to coach him, without being insulting, you know, to take a bath. Later his buddies would say he would get home and when you opened his suitcase all his dirty clothes would just be piled in there and would be all smelly. At home he probably threw his dirty socks into the corner and his mama picked them up. I had been in the Navy, and you couldn't do that. As time went by, he got more and more in tune with the norm. He just wasn't used to being closed up with other people. He didn't stink to high heaven, but in a closed car, any odor—however slight—gets blown out of proportion. In the Navy, you learned those things pretty quick.

Marshall Grant, who traveled with us on occasion while working as Johnny Cash's bass player, noticed the lifestyle differences between Elvis and me with amusement. Watching us pack our suitcases was always entertaining. Elvis tossed his things into his suitcase and slammed the lid shut. Observed Grant: "Scotty would take a shirt, and he would straighten the collar and he would take the sleeve and he would work with it and he would take the other sleeve and do the same thing. When he got through folding his shirts, they looked just like they came out of the laundry."

I paid the same attention to detail when I was loading the car. My amplifier was the first thing that went into the trunk. Once I had it in place, I padded it with foam rubber, and then I loaded my guitar into the car. I was consistent. I didn't pack the car with reckless abandon and I didn't play guitar with reckless abandon. I packed and played with purpose.

"Scotty was one of those immaculate types of people. He treated everything with kid gloves," says Grant. "When they got to the next stage, his amplifier would always work. It was a delicate piece of machinery and it was only because of the care he gave it that he could make it work. Everyone else would throw theirs into the trunk and when they got down the road the next day, they wouldn't work."

Bill and I decided that the best way to get Elvis to take better care of himself was to make a joke out of it. Some mornings we would rise before Elvis and threaten to throw water on him if he didn't get up and hit the shower. Once, while driving along in the car, we smelled an awful odor. We pulled off the road and made a big deal out of searching for the source of the bad odor. It turned out to be Elvis's shoes, which he had taken off and slid beneath the seat. We got back in the car, but when we passed over the next bridge we grabbed his shoes and threw them into the river. After that, it got to be a game. Without warning, Elvis would throw our clothing, or the car keys, out the window, all of us laughing like maniacs.

Elvis liked to do pranks—just kid stuff. We used to do all kinds of silly stuff out of boredom. Sometimes we'd get into arguments and be ready to kill each other. It might be me and Elvis, or me and Bill, any combination. We'd jump out of the car, running around, chasing each other with clenched fists—just normal stuff, when you're cooped up like that.

Actually, it was our game of throwing things out the car window that evolved into Elvis's habit in later years of throwing scarves to the audience. We'd be playing something and Bill would walk over to Elvis and whisper in his ear and say something like, "Take off your belt and throw it out into the audience"—and he would do it. We did that for several weeks.

He would do it to me, too. I would be taking a solo and he would take my belt off or my tie off and throw it out into the audience. Then one day in Texarkana, Elvis took off his shoe and threw it out into the audience and it hit some old lady in the head. After that, we figured we'd better stop before somebody got hurt.

To combat boredom on the road, we developed a game in which a tap on the forehead was used as a signal. It was just this silly thing we did. Whoever was talking or doing something, someone else would reach over and tap him on the forehead. Then you automatically did a 180 on whatever you were saying or doing. Sometimes we did that on stage. Bill would walk over and tap Elvis on the forehead and he would stop whatever he was doing and start doing something else. Kid stuff, sure, but it helped with the monotony—and it helped channel Elvis's nervous energy. He was always keyed up. There was many a night when we would stop 50 miles down the road from leaving a town and either Bill or I would get out and start walking Elvis around, trying to get him calmed down so we would be able to sleep to get to where we were going. It was Elvis's hyperactivity, not his sexual exploits, that was the main reason we started getting two rooms as soon as we could afford it. We would want to go to sleep. Elvis was so full of energy he wanted to stay up and talk all night.

In the early days, Elvis was like a young stud at a rodeo when it came to girls. I didn't blame him for trying. I think he later came to think that was expected of him. If he didn't give her a peck on the cheek, show some kind of interest, then people would be disappointed—it was part of the act. But I've always told people, put yourself in his shoes. You've got all these girls chasing you and they aren't camp followers. They're all nice girls, well-scrubbed, well-dressed. They weren't groupies. Who could hold up under that? I once read where someone wrote that Bill and I had pillows in the back of the car and would run the girls in one side and out the other. That's a bunch of bull. Never happened.

Rumors in later years that Elvis was bisexual or homosexual astound me. That's a bunch of horseshit. They could have nicknamed him Man-O-War. He'd have been the first one to lay someone out if a man made an advance on him, I can tell you that. If he was prejudiced about anything, that was it. I attribute the rumors of homosexuality to the fact that Elvis wore eye makeup. Let's face it, the man was damned near too pretty to be a man. He had those Roman chiseled features. He found out by watching movies that Tony Curtis wore mascara so that when they took pictures his eyes would be more defined, so he started doing it when he performed.

Later on, he got to where he just wore it all the time. Why not? Every time he stuck his head out the door, someone took his picture. Actors have been wearing makeup for as long as there have been actors. I didn't see anything wrong with it.

Once a day—sometimes twice a day—Elvis would want to stop so that he could call his mother. He kept her updated on where we were going and what we were doing. He called his girlfriend, Dixie, a lot, too, in the beginning. As his roving eye kept getting bigger, those calls ended. Dixie was a nice little gal. I liked her. He wasn't prepared for all that was happening and she wasn't either—all that adoration. Looking back, he stayed in trouble all the time.

★ ★ ★

Lovesick fans and busted condoms weren't the biggest problems we faced on the road. Automobile accidents became our constant—and most unwelcome—companion. Only a month or so after Elvis purchased the Lincoln, we loaded up the car in Memphis, with Bill's bass strapped to the roof, and headed out for a performance in Texas.

With Bill at the wheel, somewhere near Carlisle, Arkansas, a truck pulled out in front of us from a side road. Bill slammed on the brakes and hit the tail end of the truck, sending his bass careening off the car into the dark. As we assessed the damage to the car, Bill went to look for his bass. Soon the *thump, thump, thump* rhythm of the bass filtered out of the darkness, back up to the accident site. It had landed perfectly. It didn't hurt it one bit.

Later in the year, while in the 1955 Cadillac Elvis purchased to replace the Lincoln, we were leaving New Orleans for Texarkana, when a pickup truck turned in front of us. This time I was at the wheel. We were late, as usual, heading north. The law was that if you made a left turn, you had to pull off on the shoulder, stop, and make sure the traffic was clear before you turned. Well, this guy made the signal and pulled over, but he immediately turned in front of us.

Damage to the Cadillac was estimated at $1,000, and the accident made news because I picked up a speeding ticket. Subsequent published stories that Elvis was the driver, with me and Bill traveling in a separate car, were untrue.

Not all of our road difficulties were the result of accidents. Sometimes we were waylaid by mechanical troubles. Once our car broke down in Forest City, Arkansas, just outside Memphis. We called Bobbie and asked her to come pick us up. Elvis rode back with us. We put him in the back seat. He sat there leaning over the seat, talking to us. He liked to talk, that's for sure. Bobbie, who was wearing shorts, later commented on Elvis being so friendly. I knew the reason why Elvis was leaning over the seat talking so much.

"He's just looking at your legs," I explained.

"Do you think?" she asked.

"Oh, yeah."

In the years after Elvis's death, journalists wrote stories galore about the eccentricities of his living habits, creating minor mysteries for the faithful to ponder. Many of those stories have left me scratching my head. The one, for example, about Elvis carrying his own knife and fork out on the road so that he would not have to use restaurant utensils. If he did, he was the quickest sleight of hand person I have ever seen. I never saw him do that. I don't understand why people would say that. All the time that we spent together, I think I would have noticed it.

Then there is the matter of Elvis's sleepwalking. A number of his close associates, including his former wife, Priscilla, have made a big deal of Elvis's sleepwalking. I never saw him do that. I never even heard it discussed. His mother never mentioned anything about him sleepwalking. You would think she would have if he was that bad. She always called me over to the side and said, "Take care of my boy and make sure he gets his rest." She never said a word about sleepwalking and he never did it when I was around him. I don't know which bothers me more: The fact that people would make up stories like that or the possibility that he was a sleepwalker and no one told me. I was supposed to be the father protector. I would have felt terrible if the boy had walked out of the room into the highway and stepped in front of a car.

As the excitement built over the spring and summer, Bobbie and Evelyn got more involved, doing what they could to promote the records, traveling with us whenever possible. Once Bobbie and her sister, Alice, loaded up the battered 1954 Chevy with records and drove to Biloxi, Mississippi, a distance of about 300 miles, to work the radio station there.

"The disc jockey took us back in the office and played both sides and asked us a lot of questions," Bobbie recalls. "He did like the record. It was interesting to watch the reactions of people to the records." Before heading back to Memphis, they circled around through New Orleans and stopped at a radio station there. The reaction wasn't as hospitable. "The guy there took the record and kind of pushed the door shut on us."

Bobbie always got a kick out of watching the way the young girls reacted to Elvis. "After shows, they would come backstage and they'd go back to the dressing room with him," she says. "Elvis would come out, saying, 'It's dark back there. I'm not sure who I'm kissing.'" Sometimes he would talk to Bobbie about certain girls. "When he'd see a girl, he'd say, 'She's fine,' or 'Oh, she don't show me much.'"

The irony wasn't lost on Bobbie, especially when she and I were out with Elvis and Dixie. Bobbie noticed that Elvis pouted when he didn't get his way. She later recalled: "One night Elvis and Dixie were arguing about something in the back seat. Someone had seen her with another guy, in a park or something. She thought he was probably going with other girls. He said, 'That guy's too old for you anyway.' She answered, 'What am I supposed to do?' I guess he expected her to just wait for him." Of course, to keep Elvis's relationship with Dixie in perspective, it should be remembered that she was only fifteen—not yet old enough for a driver's license.

What Evelyn remembers most about traveling with us was how crazy the fans sometimes got. "They were as wild as can be," she says. "One time Bobbie and I were sitting on the steps that led to the dressing room. I had never seen so many kids. This guy said, 'When they hit that last note, you had better scatter because they're coming down these steps.' Boy, we liked not to have gotten down the steps in time. We were lucky to find an open place where we could get out of the way. You had to be careful or they would run over you. They were just wild—out of their head. I never got scared for my own safety. It was fun."

One time that was not so much fun was when Evelyn and Bobbie went with us on a tour that took us through North Carolina. We had reservations at the Robert E. Lee Hotel, a decent place to stay, but there was a convention in town and when we didn't claim our rooms before midnight the hotel gave them to someone else. The only place we could find rooms was at a three-dollar-a-night hotel named the Ambassador.

"It was a flea bag hotel," recalls Bobbie.

We were assigned rooms on the second floor, but to get there we had to dodge a phalanx of winos wandering the hallway. There was one bathroom for the whole floor, and I don't think any of us used it. Not long after we went to sleep, Bobbie and I were awakened by a loud bang. It came from across the hall, where Bill and Evelyn were staying. I hurried to the door and peered out into the hallway. Just as I did, Bill cracked open his door.

"Damn," said Bill, looking embarrassed. "The bed fell down."

Bobbie and I went back to sleep. There was no need to ask why the bed fell down. Without asking, we had a pretty good idea why. Bill and Evelyn didn't go to sleep, neither did they resume whatever it was they were doing when the bed collapsed. "After the bed broke, we went out to the car," says Evelyn. "We couldn't stand the smell of the room."

Early that morning, about five o'clock, Bobbie and I hopped up, washed in the sink that was in our room, and left before anyone could see us. Neither of us had enough nerve to visit the bathroom. Some things seen are difficult to forget. To our surprise, Bill and Evelyn were already waiting for us in the car when we walked out of the hotel. It would be forty years before I learned they had spent the night in the car rather than sleep in the hotel. "It was a place to stay, but that was about all," said Bobbie. "I'll never forget the name of that hotel."

By 1955 Bill and Evelyn had been married nine years. At age twenty-eight, Bill already had a good sense of who he was and what he wanted out of life. They had met in her home state of Virginia when she was fifteen. Her father and brother had a country band that played for the USO. She sometimes performed with them, singing duets with her brother.

Once, when they showed up for a USO show, they discovered they were short a bass player. Bill, who was stationed with the Army in Virginia, volunteered to sit in with them. Sparks didn't fly musically that day, but it was love at first sight for Bill and Evelyn. They were married the next year, when she turned sixteen. After his discharge later that year, Bill returned to Memphis alone.

"I didn't want to leave home," explains Evelyn. It was her brother who finally convinced her she should join her husband in Memphis. "He said, 'I'll just go down there with you.' We went down on a Greyhound bus and got off somewhere on the other side of Nashville. We were sitting there, eating, when a bus pulled up that had Richmond written on it. We both got on that bus and went back home. Bill had a hissy. He didn't know where we were. I finally had to break down and move to Memphis."

Sometimes the trajectory of Elvis and the Blue Moon Boys carried us through Crockett County. A couple of times we spent the night with my parents at their 150-acre farm. Mattie was proud of her youngest son, a fact made evident by the publicity photographs of us that adorned her bedroom wall. After a home-cooked meal, she'd send us on our way.

I didn't see much of my parents after the wild ride with Elvis began. My father died of leukemia in 1963, thirteen days before his seventy-third birthday. I wasn't there when it happened, but my friend James Lewis did what he could to make the old man comfortable.

"I remember him getting on the floor and being unable to get back up on the bed," says James. "We had to roll him back up on the sheet and two or three of us picked him up on the sheet. He was in so much pain he couldn't bear for anyone to touch him."

"James, is there bugs crawling on me?" he asked.

"No, Mr. Scott, it's just the medicine they're giving you."

James thought nothing about being there for Scott Moore's passing.

"You try to help your neighbors," says James, reflecting a generations-old custom, still strong at that time in Crockett County, of maintaining deathbed vigils for friends and neighbors.

★ 6 ★

ON THE ROAD WITH ELVIS

The summer of 1955 was in many ways the most eventful year of our career. It began with us further honing our skills as stage performers and experiencing the first wave of fan hysteria. As the summer progressed, it became even more hectic. Back in Memphis after a 21-day tour with the Hank Snow jamboree that had taken us across the Southeast—and spawned a pattern of fan reaction that would at times leave Elvis shaken and stripped of some of his clothes—we played dates in Arkansas and Mississippi and got ready for another session in Sam's studio that July. We had no way of knowing it would be our last session for Sun Records.

On July 7, four days before the session was scheduled to begin, I traded in my Gibson ES 295 for a Gibson L5. In May I had purchased a new amplifier that would duplicate the echo effect heard on our records. I first heard the amplifier, called an Echosonic, on one of Chet Atkins's records. I investigated and found out that it had been custom built by a radio repairman named Ray Butts, who operated a music store in Cairo, Illinois.

I tracked Butts down and gave him a call. He agreed to make an amplifier for me, but would not let me buy it on an installment plan (the only way I could afford the $495 price tag). We worked out a deal in which the Houck Piano Company in Memphis bought the amplifier from Ray and then sold it to me on an installment plan. I got a $65 trade-in allowance for my Fender Champ Deluxe amplifier, made a down payment of $25 and agreed to pay Houck $26.54 a month until the Echosonic was paid for. Any analysis of the development of rock 'n' roll would have to include Ray's Echosonic. His amplifier defined the fledging art form by allowing it to project a raw, full-bodied sound that set it apart from any other music being created at the time.[4] Ray was an important person early in my career and we remained friends until his death in 2004.

---

4. Scotty sold the original amplifier in 2008.

Bob Neal was getting offers for Elvis's contract on a regular basis. He told Elvis about some of them; others he kept to himself for whatever reason. Sam Phillips put out word that he would consider selling his contract if the price—and the buyer—suited him, but to the best of my knowledge he never sat down and talked seriously with anyone about it. If he did, he kept it a secret.

The July session was no different than the others, except that Sam had asked Johnny Bernero, a local drummer, to be there in case he was needed. The first song was "I Forgot to Remember to Forget," another Stan Kesler composition. Elvis didn't particularly like the song at first, but we experimented with the drums, adding a rim shot on the offbeat and—by the time we finished—Elvis was high on the song. Next we tried a song that Little Junior Parker and the Blue Flames had recorded for Sam two years earlier. "Mystery Train" was the same type of blues number that had brought us our first success. We started playing around with the song without the drummer, much as we had done with "That's All Right, Mama," when we suddenly discovered the defining lick in the song.

The rhythm of Elvis's voice fed an extra bar of rhythm into the song that I was able to duplicate on my guitar. I don't think I could do it again, but at the time it just fell into place. I got caught up in the moment. With him singing the way he did, it just felt natural to play it the way I did. We wrapped up the session with "Trying to Get to You," a rhythm and blues tune that we had failed to nail down earlier in the year. This time we got it. For the next single release, Sam paired "Mystery Train" with "I Forgot to Remember to Forget." It was released in August.

With "Mystery Train" my style of guitar playing was cemented into place. My idea of using the guitar to provide counterpoint to the vocalist was a radical concept in popular recording at that time, especially when I used that same counterpoint rhythm as a foundation for my sparse solos that people later said cried out with a voice of their own. Intuitively, my guitar became the anti-Elvis component of the music. It was like we were doing a ballroom dance with each other. I tried to match him step for step, always playing counterpoint.

Before heading out on the road again, we took a few days off to relax. Elvis used the time to visit with Dixie and to be seen about town in local clubs. Colonel Tom Parker used the time to politick with Vernon and Gladys Presley. Bill and I liked the way the drummers had worked out on the last couple of sessions. Now that our records included a drummer, we wondered if the touring band shouldn't also have one. I was in favor of it because it helped fill out the sound. Just how much music could one guitar produce?

In the late 1990s, when Nashville producer David Briggs revisited our early material, he was amazed at the sound we had created. He was especially generous to me. "Scotty was the whole deal," he said. "He made it all work. Listen to it. It's all guitar. People still try to copy what he played 40 years ago."

When Bill and I suggested to Elvis that we needed a drummer, he agreed with us, but said that he couldn't afford to hire one. Bill and I talked it over. If Elvis would hire D. J. to tour with us, we would share the cost of his $100-a-week salary. D. J. already was performing with us every week at the *Hayride* (after the first time, he was allowed to come out from behind the curtain and be seen by the audience), and we all liked him. Elvis and management finally agreed. That August, D. J. officially joined the band, although he didn't get paid until December.

Bill and I were elated. We didn't mind helping with D. J.'s salary. The music was the important thing . . . *you know, the music was everything*. Unfortunately, our excitement was short-lived. That same month, after a conference with Elvis, Bob Neal told us that it had been decided that our old verbal agreement, whereby Elvis received 50 percent and Bill and I each received 25 percent, was no longer acceptable. Neal explained it this way: "It became obvious this wasn't fair, because Elvis was the star, regardless of the fact they contributed largely to it. So we had a crisis and I had to handle that, announcing to Scotty and Bill we were no longer going to operate like that, but that they would receive a fee we would all agree on."

Bill and I were devastated. It was the end of the Blue Moon Boys. We had begun with Elvis as partners. Now we were nothing more than salaried sidemen. We never had a written contract, so we didn't have a legal leg to stand on. We threatened to quit, in a quiet sort of way, but Neal was adamant: Take it or leave it. Bill and I both blamed it on Parker, but Neal told us it was not Parker's doing, a story he stuck to over the years. Despite Neal's protestations that it was not Parker—and evidence that the decision was indeed made by Elvis—to this day I refuse to believe Elvis would betray me. It just wasn't in his nature.

Bill and I agreed to go on salary. Henceforth, we would receive weekly paychecks of $200 if we were working and $100 if we were not working. It looked like we would make at least as much as if we were blocking hats or making tires. It was a bird-in-the-hand situation. That may not have been a decent salary for what we were doing, but at that time it was for the guy on the street. The problem was the guy on the street didn't have all the responsibilities we had. We bought our own food and our own clothes, plus paid all the incidentals. Elvis didn't know about money. I think his daddy looked at it like the guy on the street. He was probably thinking: "Those guys are making $200 a week. I never made over $30 or $50." I can understand that mindset. But that still doesn't make it right.

Neal was clearly uncomfortable about what happened, but he viewed it as part of his job. "My contract was with Elvis, not with Scotty and Bill," he explained later about the fairness of that decision. "They weren't contracted to me—or to Sun." I hated it every time they reminded us of that sobering fact. We were expendable.

Later that month, Bill and I got more bad news. Parker, having convinced Vernon and Gladys that he—and only he—could navigate Elvis's career through the musical minefield ahead, took over his contract from Neal. Oddly, Neal turned it over without a whimper. Just as things were beginning to happen for us, he stepped aside, keeping nothing for himself. Strange things were beginning to happen in Elvis's career.

Parker was now top dog. Bill and I knew what that meant. He didn't want us around, he had made that clear. Elvis was being brainwashed. We'd be traveling together in the same car, and Elvis would bring up something—"The Colonel said so and so."

I'd respond, "Elvis, you have to stand up and speak your mind. There's nothing wrong with you arguing with him about something."

He'd say, "Ah, well, I made a deal with him—I'd do the singing and he'd take care of the business."

He'd mumble and grumble about it for a day or two and that'd be it. He'd go ahead and do whatever it was he didn't want to do. I tried to be the big brother, I really did.

Parker didn't have many conversations with Elvis in front of us or anyone else. If he ever came to a recording session, he'd stay back in the control room. Elvis had control of the sessions. But it bothered us the way Elvis was being manipulated by Parker behind the scenes. We had heard in the very early days, probably from Hank Snow's band, that he was really here illegally. Of course, we never paid any attention to it. It was never any deep, deep secret. In later years, when Parker wouldn't let Elvis tour Europe, we wondered if there wasn't more to the story. Why, after Elvis got so big—and this is the part that puzzles me—wouldn't he go to Germany? I believe they had enough pull they could have gotten Parker a waiver of some kind. The Tennessee senators would probably have done something for him. So I maintain there is something even more mysterious about why he wouldn't leave the country. It's not logical. He tried to beat Elvis down on European tours. He told him all kinds of stuff, except the truth that he didn't want Elvis to leave the country because he couldn't go with him.

Before we went out on tour again—this time with D. J.—Parker got in another dig at the former Blue Moon Boys. From the beginning, Bill had been in charge of the group's concessions, which at that time were confined to photographs. Bill was selling pictures for twenty-five and fifty cents and keeping a nickel for himself and doing well. That was when a nickel was worth something. As soon as Parker got control, he took away the concessions. He offered Bill some pittance so he could keep selling the pictures, but Bill turned it down and I don't blame him.

As bad as things were getting, we didn't dwell on our troubles. We had shows to do, and regardless of what was happening with Elvis and his management, we were too busy to be distracted for long by Parker's not-so-subtle machinations. The Colonel's biggest coup of all was in the works, but we knew nothing about that when we set out from Memphis in August for performances in Texas and beyond. D. J. didn't have the same Memphis cultural nexus shared by Bill, Elvis, and me, but his Louisiana bayou ways endeared him to us and allowed him to slip right into the Memphis groove.

The addition of D. J. also meant that we had another driver. In those days, we took turns behind the wheel. That usually worked out fine, except when Elvis was driving. He was a good driver, but he didn't pay attention to where he was going. We were afraid to go to sleep when he was driving because, without someone acting as navigator, Elvis was certain to miss the scheduled turn-offs. Sometimes his oversights would take us miles out of our way. Several times we went 100 miles out of the way and had to double back because he took a wrong turn.

If Elvis was behind the wheel, the only way that we could be certain of getting to our destination was to stay awake and watch his every move. "We'd let him drive during daylight hours," says D. J. "They'd let me drive if it was a straight shot to El Paso or something." The driving thing got to be a big joke with us.

Late one night, as we were driving through St. Louis, I pulled off the road and gave the wheel to D. J. The loop was new at that time and signs were not yet in place. Confident that we were in good hands, the rest of us curled up best we could on the car seats and went to sleep. Hours later, I was awakened at sunrise as the car filled with sunlight.

"Where are we?" I asked.

I raised up and looked around.

The car was pulled off on the side of the road.

My question was the one that D. J. had dreaded the most.

"Where are we?"

"Hell, we're still in St. Louis," D. J. said.

I looked at him in disbelief.

"How can we still be in St. Louis?"

"I got lost," D. J. said. He explained that he had been driving in circles for hours trying to find a way out of St. Louis. "I didn't want to wake you up."

I was refreshed after a good night's sleep so I told him not to worry about it. I got behind the wheel and drove to the next stop. In retrospect, D. J. figures he should have awakened us, but when you're the new guy, you naturally want to make as few waves as possible. Besides, he felt he would get us out of there any second.

Life on the road for our band bore little resemblance to today's mammoth undertakings. A typical Rolling Stones or Bruce Springsteen concert requires a caravan of trucks, hundreds of support personnel, and a logistical organization capable of dealing with mind-boggling detail. For Elvis and the Blue Moon Boys, it was a matter of loading up the car, piling in on top of each other, and striking out for the next town. The trick was to keep the floorboard clear of soft drink and beer bottles, and to keep unwrapped candy bars off the seat.

In the beginning, Elvis was filled with questions. He had never been out of Memphis. He wanted to know what was out there. I had been all over the Far East. Elvis asked me lots of questions about the Navy, about where I had been and what I had seen. Pretty soon he knew more than you did, or at least he thought so. But he had a good mind. He was fresh out of high school, so he was inquisitive—mainly about girls. You let him out the chute, and there he went. We might be going down the road after a show and he would say, "What did you think of so and so?" They were the same type of questions he asked Bobbie. Girls were new to him. How could he possibly know what *he thought* until he knew what others thought? He approached dating like he approached buying a new car. How much mileage does it get? How fast does it go? What will she show me the first time I take her out?

I tried my best to get the others to hold rehearsals while we were on the road. They all told me what a good idea it was, but we always found excuses not to do it. I was always wanting to work up something new or different; I hated playing the same songs every night. I guess that's one of the things I feel cheated about—well, not really cheated, but when I started playing with Elvis I was extremely interested in learning to play other things. Once we got on the road and got into a rut, doing all those one-nighters, I was too tired to think about it. Everything becomes very focused. You play the same things day in and day out, then you go into the studio and cut some more, which I really loved doing, then you start all over again, except then you have some new material. But then you get in another rut again until you get back in the studio.

Food was a constant problem on the road. Because of the hours we kept—if we had asked the promoter the name of the nearest caterer, we would have been slapped silly—finding a decent restaurant that would fry up a late-night order of burger and fries was always a challenge. Since fast food restaurants had not yet been invented, we learned to rely on truck stops. In those days truck stops had higher standards than they have today. Now they are into selling souvenirs of all kinds, while back then it was not magazines or T-shirts they sold, but food. The fans wanted something to eat—and getting it to them fast was the vendors' top priority. Sometimes we would get lucky and the local promoter would take us home for a meal with his family. One of them that I recall quite well was Tom Perryman and his wife, Billie, who lived in Tyler, Texas. If it were not for the kindness of strangers—and the "all for one" and "one for all" attitude we honed into a loosely defined brotherhood—we would never have survived the rigors of life on the road. There was nothing "fun" about long trips and long hours. What made it fun was what we did once we stepped up on the stage.

Suddenly, amid the screams and shouts of fans, we were transformed from road-warrior vagabonds into cheerleaders for a phenomenon we neither recognized nor understood. We knew *something* important was happening, but we were far too busy acting it out to spend time thinking about what it was. When we first started out, our shows lasted only ten or fifteen minutes. Concerts in those days were multi-entertainment programs, with each act performing only their own records. The music business was built on singles—albums didn't come along until much later—and most recording acts were lucky if they had released enough singles to fill fifteen minutes on stage.

For several months, "That's All Right, Mama" and "Blue Moon of Kentucky" were our only hits. I remember working up several songs recorded by other artists so that we they would have enough music to fill fifteen minutes. We worked up a couple of Chuck Berry's songs. And we did "Tweedle Dee"—six, eight, maybe ten songs like that—up-tempo things that fit the rhythm of the first two songs we cut. As soon as we cut more songs, we'd drop the others off.

Looking back on those early performances, I am amazed at what we were able to do under such primitive conditions. Usually we had only two microphones: one for Elvis and one for Bill's bass. My amplifier rested on a chair behind me. I usually stood to Elvis's right, with Bill on his left and D. J. directly behind him. The only time we could hear Elvis's voice was when he was announcing a song. Once the music began—and the cheering from the audience reached a fever pitch—we played by sight alone. Everything else was just a continuous roar. The only way I could describe the sound is that it was like, you know, if you dive into a swimming pool— that rush of noise that you get. In audio terms, it would be like phasing— phew!—it would be so loud that all you could hear in your ears was that roaring sound.

Since Elvis didn't have a monitor, he couldn't hear himself or the music. Once we started a song, we all watched Elvis, measuring the progress of the song by his movements. Says D. J.: "Elvis would never miss, even though he couldn't hear. I never saw him break meter. He always came right back in there. How he didn't get lost is beyond me. Scotty, Bill, and I just used eye movements to communicate with each other. We could tell by Elvis's arm and leg movements which part of the song he was in."

I once told a reporter that we were the only band in the world directed by an ass. I thought that poor guy was going to faint—he took it literally.

Marshall Grant watched a lot of those shows. "Bill and Elvis were the show," he says. "All Scotty did was stand alongside Elvis and play his guitar. He duplicated what you heard on the record. He's a perfectionist. He let Bill and Elvis do their thing, and he just did what he did best—play his guitar."

Elvis and Bill had a regular act. For years, it was standard practice in country music for the bass player to be the comedian. Bill was a natural at it and he incorporated that element of country music into our act. He taunted Elvis. He yelled at him, He cracked jokes.

Grant recalls one of their routines:

Bill walks over to Elvis's microphone.

"Roses are red and violets are pink," Bill says.

"No—roses are red and violets are blue," Elvis corrected.

"No, no, man. Roses are red and violets are pink."

"Naw, you're wrong, Bill."

"I know Violet's are pink," he says, at which point he yanks a pair of pink panties from his back pocket and holds them up for the crowd to see. "I know Violet's are pink 'cause I got them right here."

I occasionally participated in the skits. Bill would say something about me playing checkers. Elvis would say, 'He doesn't play checkers.' Then Bill would say, 'No, I was out in the parking lot and I heard someone say to him, 'No, it's your move'—so he must be playing checkers."

Looking back, it is clear to me that Bill deserves a lot of credit for our early success. Elvis wasn't a great MC—I think everyone agrees on that. If it hadn't been for Bill, there were a bunch of shows where we would have died on the vine. Elvis picked up a few corny lines that he would use in between songs. All he wanted to do was go out there and sing.

Sometimes our comedy routine was upstaged by acts that preceded us. June Carter, who as a member of the Carter Sisters was also managed by Colonel Parker, sometimes found herself on the same bill with Elvis. Recalled June: "I used to do a little comedy act in the beginning and do my little set and then they would go on." Before and after the shows, they would sometimes all go to a cafe. She remembers Elvis playing Johnny Cash's record, "Cry, Cry, Cry" on the juke boxes. Often Elvis used Cash's song to tune his guitar. Continued June: "Red West [a Humes High senior who later became one of Elvis's bodyguards] was with him at the time and that was about the only way we could get Elvis's guitar tuned [using 'Cry, Cry, Cry']. Red and I used to sit backstage and try to change those strings because Elvis kept breaking them all the time. We spent all our time stringing that guitar and keeping it in tune."

★ ★ ★

On November 21, 1955, Sam announced that he'd sold Elvis's recording contract to RCA Records. With great ceremony, Elvis, Sam, Colonel Parker, Hank Snow, and representatives from RCA gathered at the studio to sign the contracts.

Bill and I were stunned.

D. J. was so new to the group he didn't know what to think.

While we were out on the road that November, Sam Phillips was wheeling and dealing, expanding his financial base in a business partnership with Kemmons Wilson, a successful Memphis entrepreneur who would soon launch a hotel chain named Holiday Inns. The previous month, with $25,000 borrowed from Wilson, Sam made history by starting up the nation's first all-female radio station. He gave it the call letters WHER. The deal called for Wilson to become a 50/50 partner once Sam repaid the loan.[5]

After conducting secret auditions that fall at Memphis Recording Service, Sam hired a female broadcaster, Dotty Abbott, to run the station. Next he hired his wife, Becky, with whom he had worked at a radio station in Alabama, as an announcer. Marion Keisker was the next hired. Sam moved her from her all-important post at the studio—she was in many ways the foundation of the business end of Sun Records—and put her on the air at WHER as an announcer and news reporter. Marion cleaned out her desk at the studio and moved over to the radio station office, located in a Holiday Inn on Third Street south of Crump Boulevard.

With Marion gone, Jack Clement became Sam's right-hand man in the studio. Even though he was signing new artists to Sun Records—Johnny Cash had already released "Cry, Cry, Cry"; Jerry Lee Lewis was cutting some hot tracks; and Carl Perkins was only a couple of months away from recording "Blue Suede Shoes," Sun's first record to break the Top 10 on the pop charts—Sam was building radio stations and looking and talking more like a businessman than a record executive.

The deal with RCA Records was Colonel Parker's biggest coup to date. The agreement called for Sam to receive $35,000 and Elvis to receive a signing bonus of $5,000. Later, when asked why he had sold Elvis's contract, Sam said it was an offer he couldn't refuse. Still later he explained his decision by saying he was having financial difficulties and needed the money. It was a curious explanation, then and now. Kemmons Wilson maintained that he advised Sam to accept RCA's offer so that he could spend money to promote Carl Perkins's new single, "Blue Suede Shoes."[6] The oft-repeated story that Sam sold Elvis's contract so that he could purchase Holiday Inn stock is a stretch. The first Holiday Inn was built in 1953, but public stock for the hotel chain was not offered until 1957.

Despite the politics of the contract sale, the music continued.

5. This account of the partnership is from Kemmons Wilson's autobiography, *Half Luck and Half Brains: The Kemmons Wilson Holiday Inn Story.*

6. Wilson, Kemmons. *Half Luck and Half Brains: The Kemmons Wilson Holiday Inn Story.* In the 1960s Kemmons and Sam operated a recording studio and record label called Holiday Inn Records.

"Mystery Train," released that August, went to No. 1 on the country charts, giving us our first chart-topper. Our records were selling like gangbusters. Bill, D. J., and I were excited about the success of our records, but that excitement was tempered by the fact that we received no performance or mechanical royalties from record sales. On top of the success being enjoyed by Sun, Sam's new partnership with Wilson had put him on a financial fast-track. Everyone associated with Elvis was raking in money except for us. Our sole income came from concerts. The more records that Sun Records sold, the more concert bookings we received. It was an early version of trickle-down economics.

Apart from sentiment for the tiny studio itself, Bill and I had no reason to want Elvis to remain with Sun Records. There was nothing in it for us. Since Elvis had only recently severed our partnership as equal band members, putting us on salary, there was now a ceiling on our expectations. No matter how successful Elvis became, no matter how many hit records we recorded with him, we were nothing more than employees. Of course, we had every reason to think we would benefit in some way. We figured our cut would increase as we went along. If he made more, we would be compensated more. I never begrudged him his success. In fact I told him so, that he should make more because he was the star, but I always figured I would share in it somehow.

Sam told the *Press-Scimitar* he thought Elvis was one of the most talented "youngsters" in the country: "By releasing his contract to RCA-Victor we will give him the opportunity of entering the largest organization of its kind in the world, so his talents can be given the fullest opportunity." As Sam was stepping out of Elvis's life, others were stepping into his life. On that same day, Parker and Bob Neal agreed to evenly split their combined 40 percent commission on Elvis's earnings until March 15, 1956, at which time Neal would step out of the picture and Parker would become Elvis's sole manager.

Marion Keisker kept quiet at the time, but years later she was not hesitant about expressing her unhappiness over Parker's relationship with Elvis. "Colonel Tom had been working on the family at least a year—in the most polished and Machiavellian way," she says. "You couldn't believe it. Mrs. Presley, God rest her soul, she was just a mother, was what she was, you know. The Colonel'd go to her and say, 'You got the finest boy in the world and it's terrible the way they're making him work.' Sam might deny this, but I think it's the only thing Elvis ever did against the advice of Sam."

For his part, Bob Neal was content to move out of Parker's way. "My contract was going to expire, and I simply let it go," he says. "I [didn't] ask for anything and [didn't] try to negotiate anything. I could have, but I didn't try to." Realizing he was no match for Parker, he opened a record store on Main Street in Memphis and extended his management arm by becoming Johnny Cash's manager.

D. J. had watched Parker long enough to know he didn't want to get any closer to the man than he had to. "Oh, yeah, you had to watch him," says D. J. "He didn't want us as the band. He'd say, 'Don't pay the boys, they'll just want more money. We can get more guys.' That was his theory. I didn't let him bother me. We'd all get mad at him, but we didn't have to deal with him. Elvis paid us. We didn't care what the Colonel thought."

With RCA Records stepping into the breach, I knew the pace was going to pick up—and fast. Our first session was scheduled for January. Our new producer, Steve Sholes, was lined up to work with us at the RCA studio in Nashville. At year's end, my financial situation had improved. My income for the year from Elvis amounted to $8,052.24. I figured it would skyrocket from there. I didn't know it at the time, and I'm glad I didn't know, but it was the second best year I'd ever have with Elvis.

That Christmas, as Bobbie and I celebrated our apparent good fortune, Auzella Moore asked 13-year-old Tammy Wynette if she wanted to go with her to take some Christmas presents by Elvis's house. That April Elvis had purchased a three-bedroom house at 1034 Audubon Drive in Memphis for himself and his parents. After Gladys started hanging her wash out on a clothesline, neighbors put together a petition and asked the Presleys to move. In March 1956 they did move—to Graceland. After visiting the Audubon Drive home, Tammy thought she had died and gone to heaven. When she returned home, she couldn't wait to tell her mother about the visit. "I said, 'Mother, that rug that you walk on, it comes up around your ankles'—it was white carpet."

★ 7 ★

SCRIPTING THE MOVIE YEARS

Our first recording session with RCA Records took place on January 10, 1956. By the time we arrived in Nashville the record label already had released our previous records under its own imprint. Overnight, it was as if Sun Records had never existed in Elvis's career. That should have been a lesson to the remnants of the Blue Moon Boys, but we were much too busy making music to devote much time to reading tea leaves.

RCA's first release was the last single issued by Sun Records, "I Forgot to Remember to Forget." It stayed on the country charts for weeks, but did not make it onto the pop charts. Four additional singles from the Sun Records sessions were re-released two weeks before the Nashville session began. RCA didn't expect the earlier singles to reappear on the charts. They re-released the earlier singles so that they would have records with their imprint to cover back orders, and to "brand" their new artist with the RCA logo as a means of severing ties with Sun in the minds of radio DJs and retailers. For his part, Colonel Parker printed up new souvenir booklets that proclaimed Elvis to be RCA's "sensational, new singing star." In small print, the booklet announced, with no special emphasis, that he was performing with the Blue Moon Boys.

Within weeks, RCA dropped the band's name from its materials, and Colonel Parker soon followed—although Elvis and others continued to use the name when introducing us. The interesting thing about the new booklet and all the others that followed is that they did not contain photographs of the band members. It was a transparent ploy by Colonel Parker to disassociate Elvis from Bill, D. J., and myself.

In the months that followed, as fan magazines clamored to turn out special issues on Elvis, Parker monitored the reportage with an iron hand. Under no circumstances, he told the magazines, were they to publish photographs of Bill and I. Most of the magazines did as they were told. Those who ignored Parker's instructions experienced the wrath of the Colonel, who was not shy about administering tongue lashings.

Typical of the special Elvis publications flooding the newsstands in 1956 was one titled *The Amazing Elvis Presley*. It contained fifty pages of text and photographs, including four shots of a teddy bear collection said to belong to Elvis: but there were no photographs in the magazine of me and only one of Bill (a long shot in which his hand covers his face). However, Elvis did mention us in the text in a Q&A in which he was asked about us by a reporter.

For the Nashville session, Steve Sholes decided to augment the sound that had been successful at Sun. Sholes was more than just a producer at RCA. As head of A&R, he also served as the label's top Nashville executive. That meant that he often made decisions of a political nature. In addition to Bill, D. J., and me, he booked Floyd Cramer on piano and Chet Atkins on guitar. At that time, Atkins was already a guitar legend, with many hit records to his credit. But he was more than that to RCA, which had hired him as a staff guitarist and consultant; he was the foundation upon which the label would build its roster in the late 1950s and early 1960s. Sholes put Atkins in charge of the session.

When Atkins asked Elvis who he wanted for background singers, he chose the Jordanaires, a popular gospel quartet that had been touring with Eddy Arnold. Elvis had met them in Memphis at Ellis Auditorium at one of the many gospel concerts he attended. RCA had just signed a new gospel quartet called the Speer Family. For Elvis's session, Atkins constructed a trio of his own making. He asked two members of the Speer Family—Ben and Brock Speer—and he added Gordon Stoker of the Jordanaires. Stoker didn't much like the idea of performing without the other members of his group, but Atkins told him he couldn't use the entire quartet and needed to use some of the Speers since they were new to the label. Stoker was taken aback by Atkins's attitude toward Elvis. Recalls Stoker: "He didn't think Elvis would be around long. He said, 'You know, we've signed this kid from Memphis, but—you know—he's a passing fad.'"

When we arrived at the studio, none of us had any idea that Atkins had reservations about Elvis's talent, nor did we know that Sholes was antsy about RCA's investment in Elvis. It was the first time RCA had ever bought out a contract, along with previously produced masters.

Sholes's job was on the line, and he knew it.

The session itself went smoothly enough, although it took us a while to adjust to the more structured Nashville way of doing things. Instead of Sam sticking his head out the control room door, yelling "Hey, how about doing it again," we had a seasoned engineer, Bob Ferris, calling out take numbers. I felt the pressure, but I was excited about working with one of my heroes, Chet Atkins. I knew Chet was there to do what he could to help.

At one point, I was working on a guitar part and paused to ask Chet what he thought about what I was playing. Chet, who was also working on a guitar part, looked up at me and smiled. "Man, I'm just playing rhythm," he said. "Just keep doing what you've been doing."

Elvis was unhappy that Atkins had not booked the Jordanaires, but he did not make a big deal out of it. Instead, he called Stoker aside and told him that he would see to it that all four Jordanaires were at the next session.

Over a two-day period, we cut five songs—Ray Charles's "I've Got a Woman," "I Was the One," "Money Honey," "I'm Counting on You," and "Heartbreak Hotel," a song co-written by Mae Axton, a Floridian who did promotional work for Colonel Parker. Years later, when asked about the session, Stoker recalled me being "cool and collected." I appreciate the compliment, but despite my calm exterior my insides were churning inside.

One of the things that amused me about the session was the lengths to which Ferris and Atkins went to copy the echo effect Sam had captured in Memphis. For "Heartbreak Hotel," they added slapback—or delay as it is called today—to Elvis's vocal and then recorded the song in a hallway of the studio. They had a speaker set up at one end of this long hallway and a microphone at the other end. They had a sign on the door that said, "Don't open the door when the red light is on."

After the session we returned to Memphis, and then left for Shreveport to perform our weekly show at the *Hayride*. From there we went to Texas for a series of one-nighters; at the end of the month, it was on to New York for our first appearance on the nationally broadcast television program, *Stage Show*. While we were out on the road, Sholes took the five cuts to New York to play for his bosses at RCA. To his horror, they hated all five. They told him to head straight back to Nashville and record something that sounded like what Elvis had recorded in Memphis for Sun Records. Sholes told them it had taken him two days to get those five songs and he didn't think it would do any good to rush back into the studio to do more. Apparently it never occurred to him that the music sounded different because additional musicians were involved. Of course it sounded different from what we recorded in Memphis. Because Elvis was going to be in New York at the end of the month to do the television show, Sholes suggested, why not do more recordings in New York? The RCA executives agreed to set up a session for the week following our appearance on *Stage Show*.

★ ★ ★

Despite the rejection from the Arthur Godfrey show, Colonel Parker felt Elvis was perfect for television. The contract with RCA gave him added ammunition, for it helped dispel criticism that Elvis was nothing more than a regional success. Finally, his efforts paid off when Jack Philbin, executive producer of *Stage Show*, saw a picture of Elvis and commented, "This kid is a guitar-playing Marlon Brando." Elvis was booked for four consecutive performances on the weekly, Saturday-night show, beginning January 28. He was paid $1,250 per show.

Stage Show was a musician's dream. Produced by Jackie Gleason, it was hosted by Tommy and Jimmy Dorsey, two of the biggest names in big band music. The contract was dutifully reported in the *Press-Scimitar* by television reporter Robert Johnson: "Events are spinning faster than his records for the Memphis youngster," he wrote, concluding with a bit of advice: "Don't let your head spin with them, Elvis!"

Three days before we flew to New York to do the show, I purchased a pair of tuxedo trousers for $21.12 from Wolf the Tailor in Memphis. The Blue Moon Boys had come a long way since the days of matching western shirts. We had only a vague idea of what the Big Time was all about, but everyone seemed to think that it was a good thing, so we embraced it.

The executives at RCA in New York weren't sure about the material that we had recorded in Nashville, but they decided it would be foolish not to release a single to coincide with Elvis's appearance on *Stage Show*. On January 27, the day before the show, they released "Heartbreak Hotel," with "I Was the One" on the flip side. Steve Sholes went to New York, so that he would be there the following Monday to begin production on the second recording session. If things didn't work out, he knew his career with RCA was probably over. He had the uneasy feeling that "Heartbreak Hotel" could be his swan song. All of which shows you how subjective music really is. How could he and the RCA executive not know that it would be a hit?

Stage Show was broadcast from CBS's Studio 50, a theater located between 53rd and 54th Streets. When Elvis was introduced, he ran out on stage like he'd been shot out of a cannon; then with barely a glance at us he launched into a song we had not yet recorded, "Shake, Rattle and Roll." Elvis would eventually play our new RCA single, "Heartbreak Hotel," on his third appearance on the show, but the performance would be marred somewhat by a trumpet solo from the Dorsey Brothers band. The solo was solid musically, but ran counter to the guitar sound we had developed for the song. Even so, we were happy with the treatment that we received. They were super nice to us. They had such a great band. Louie Bellson played drums and D. J. was a big fan of his and they got to be pals. I don't remember any problems with Tommy or Jimmy, either one. I'm sure they were looking down their noses at what we were doing. Our three pieces sounded so empty out there on their stage. They tried to do things with us—like adding a big crescendo ending—but the sound was bad in that theater and the engineers didn't know how the record was cut and therefore did not know how to duplicate the sound.

All the television executives cared about, recalls D. J., was how the band looked. "We were just out there," he says. "But those guys had a good band, and the Dorsey brothers were nice guys. I knew Louie Bellson, the drummer, from way back. He sounded like thunder back then, with those bass drums. They knew they had a job to do. They played chasers and stingers for us. That was what they got paid for."

Back home, Memphis watched in awe and held its breath.

★ ★ ★

The week after the first *Stage Show*, we gathered at the RCA studios on East 24th Street. Steve Sholes hired Shorty Long, a honky-tonk piano player who specialized in Broadway musicals, to sit in with the band. To Elvis's disappointment, the Jordanaires were not booked for the session. Elvis was polite, but distant. He said "no, sir," and "yes, sir." Non-Southerners don't understand that when a Southerner says "yes sir" and "no sir," it is not always a sign of politeness. Coming from a Southerner those words sometimes mean "I don't like you much—keep your distance." Sholes wasn't connecting with him and he sensed it. For our first song, Sholes chose Carl Perkins's "Blue Suede Shoes," the latest single from Sun Records. The song was going great guns up the charts. As a courtesy, Sholes called Sam Phillips and told him we were recording the song. He promised Sam it wouldn't be released as a single.

After more than a dozen takes of "Blue Suede Shoes," Elvis begged off, saying he really didn't think they could improve on the original. After all, it *was* Carl's song. Elvis wanted to record "My Baby Left Me," a blues song written by Arthur Crudup, who had penned his first hit, "That's All Right, Mama." It was the type of music that Elvis preferred.

Perhaps because it was the music that we *felt*, the song went effortlessly to tape. For the first time since the addition of D. J. on drums, we clicked as a band. Sholes was afraid that our raw, energetic music wasn't the pop sound his bosses wanted to hear. By trying to make Elvis conform to his vision of what he thought RCA wanted to hear, Sholes was making a classic mistake: He was *thinking* the music, instead of *feeling* it. For all his success as a music executive, he didn't seem to understand that Southern boys invented new music better than they copied it.

Elvis recorded another Crudup number, "So Glad You're Mine," and Sholes persuaded him to do one of the honky-tonk numbers he brought, "One Sided Love Affair." It went back and forth like that all week. Sholes wanted to get enough songs so that RCA could release an album. He didn't come right out and say, "If you do one of mine, I'll do one of yours," but that is what it amounted to. There was a lot of horse trading going on. Elvis was young and inexperienced but he knew what he wanted to record and what he didn't want to record. Much of what Elvis felt was instinctive, but he did have a broad understanding of music.

When we had time off, Elvis went sightseeing, but we hung close to the Warwick Hotel, where we were staying. When we got paid, we took the cash across the street to a bar. Says D. J.: "We had a couple of hundred dollars apiece, and we'd spread it out across the table, like a big deal. We got to know the bartender. We said, 'When this runs out, throw us out.' The bartender bought us drinks. We bought him drinks. I think the name of the place was Jerry's Bar. When we were in New York, that's where we stayed. We had a good time there."

We wrapped up the session that week, did the second *Stage Show*, and then hit the road. "Heartbreak Hotel" was soaring on the charts, but we had no idea how well it was doing. We didn't have time to read newspapers and the only time we were near a radio was late at night when we were traveling. Even at that early stage in our careers we lived in a cocoon.

In those days few radio stations broadcast after midnight and the ones that did tended to play old standards. For the next several weeks, we stayed on the road, returning to New York each weekend to appear on *Stage Show*. The original four performances were extended to six, with the last show scheduled for March 24. After four consecutive shows, we took time off to meet our Saturday night obligations to the *Hayride*.

As March began, "Heartbreak Hotel" hit No. 14 on the pop charts. It was the first time Elvis had broken the Top 20 on the pop charts. Just ahead of "Heartbreak Hotel" at No. 13 was Carl Perkins's "Blue Suede

Shoes." Fiercely competitive, Sam Phillips arranged for Perkins to receive a gold record on the *Perry Como Show*, which aired opposite *Stage Show*.

Sam was just one dance step away from proving that his decision to sell Elvis's contact was a flash of brilliance. The problem was that his dance partner tripped and fell.

On the way to New York, Perkins and his band were involved in an automobile accident in Delaware. Perkins was seriously injured and missed the show. We heard about the accident on the radio as we drove to New York to do *Stage Show*. When we passed through Delaware, we stopped by the hospital to visit Perkins. Elvis was already in New York, but he sent a telegram to Perkins wishing him a quick recovery.

"It was in the wee hours of the morning," Perkins later said of the visit. "That was one of my darkest hours . . . and I remember so well when I looked up and saw them."

Ironically, as Perkins languished in the hospital, "Heartbreak Hotel" overtook "Blue Suede Shoes" on the charts. By May, Elvis's song would be No. 1 and Perkin's song had stalled at No. 3. Perkins recovered from his injuries, but his career never fully recovered from the bad timing of the accident. For the rest of his life, Carl wondered how different his career might have been had he received that gold record and the exposure the *Perry Como Show* would have brought.

On March 13 Elvis's first LP was released. It contained seven songs recorded in January in New York and Nashville, and five previously unreleased songs gleaned from the Sun Records masters. With "Heartbreak Hotel" racing to the top of the charts, there was little suspense about how the self-titled album would do. By March 1, RCA already had received 362,000 advance orders.

Bob Neal watched from the sidelines. Colonel Parker had been running things for months. When Neal's contract formally ran out on March 14, he quietly stepped out of the picture. One of the first things Parker did as Elvis's manager was to get him out of his contract with the *Hayride*. A country-music venue was hardly appropriate for the nation's new king of pop. To get him out of the contract, according to Neal, Parker allowed Elvis to do a benefit at the Shreveport Coliseum, with the proceeds going to the *Hayride*.

Elvis's next television appearance was for April 3 on the *Milton Berle Show*. It was scheduled to be broadcast from the deck of the aircraft carrier U.S.S. *Hancock*, which was docked in San Diego. We arrived several days early so that Elvis could do a screen test with movie producer Hal Wallis. The test went well and Wallis, who was famous for films such as *Casablanca* and *The Maltese Falcon*, was impressed enough to offer Elvis a role in an upcoming movie named *The Rainmaker*. However, Parker would not allow him to accept that role. He asked Wallis to find Elvis another movie. By the end of the week, Elvis had signed a seven-year, three-picture contract with Paramount.

The *Milton Berle Show* was vintage slapstick. Berle played the part of "Melvin," Elvis Presley's twin brother. Elvis sang three songs, including "Heartbreak Hotel"—and perhaps with his thoughts on his fledging movie career, didn't protest playing opposite "Melvin." I felt right at home on the carrier deck. I was the only member of the entourage who had been on a ship.

We had a ball. Uncle Miltie was great. He did the wig thing with Elvis and busted up a guitar. He did all kinds of goofy stuff. It was funny. For two nights following the Berle show we performed at the San Diego Arena, drawing 11,250 screaming fans to each show. Back in San Diego for the first time since my release from the Navy, I tracked down John Bankson, who was still in the Navy. Luckily, he was still in port.

Analee recalls me phoning when I got to town. "He invited my husband down to see the first performance," says Analee. "He was backstage with Elvis and Scotty. When he got home, he told me he had helped Elvis tune his guitar. I said, 'Oh, you did.' Of course, we didn't know who Elvis was at that time. Scotty came out to the house and they played until one or two in the morning. I went to bed. That was the last time I saw Scotty."

A decade later, Bankson saw service in the Mekong Delta in Vietnam before succumbing to the cancer caused by his exposure to radiation during the nuclear testing that took place during the 1950s. "If he had lived, he would really have loved all this with Scotty," says Analee. "He really thought a lot of Scotty."

With that trip to San Diego I closed the door on my Navy past. I had to reinvent myself when I left West Tennessee to join the Navy. Once I left the Navy and moved to Memphis I had to reinvent myself once again. Reinvention would soon become a way of life for me.

While we were on the West Coast, Parker booked us for a two-week engagement at the New Frontier Hotel in Las Vegas. It was a gamble to book us in a venue accustomed to older, less frolicsome entertainers, but Parker was on a roll. Every time he threw the dice, he won. Before going to Vegas, we worked in more concerts; then we headed for Nashville on April 14, where we were booked for another recording session. Because we were behind schedule, we chartered a twin-engine plane in Wichita Falls, Texas. The flight plan called for us to stop in Little Rock to refuel, and then proceed straight to Nashville.

While we were still en route to Little Rock, the pilot realized the plane was running low on fuel. He explained the situation to us and asked us to help him look for landmarks. When we spotted an emergency landing strip near Hot Springs, he took the plane down and landed so that he could refuel. Daylight was just breaking. A police car drove up and the officer asked us who we were and why we had landed. When we told him, he took us to an all-night diner so that we could get something to eat while the attendant filled the gas tanks.

After dinner we returned to the airport. This time I got into the co-pilot's seat for takeoff. The plane ascended to 1,500 or 2,000 feet and leveled off. After a while, the pilot turned to me and said, "Here, hold the wheel while I get the maps out from under the seat."

I said, "I don't know how to fly a plane."

"Just hold it a minute," he said.

Just as I put my hands on the wheel, both engines sputtered and quit. As soon as that happened the pilot reached over and threw a switch, and then took over the wheel. Both engines restarted, but it was enough to shake everybody a little bit. The only thing that I can figure is that he forgot to switch back to the main tanks after we took off. After we crossed the Mississippi River, we hit a bunch of turbulence. Bill turned white and put his coat over his head. I think he would have jumped if he could have gotten out. When we got to Nashville, Elvis eased up to us and whispered, "We're through with this guy."

When we arrived at the studio, Elvis saw that the entire Jordanaires quartet had not been hired as he had requested. He was presented with the same configuration—two Speers and one Jordanaire. Hired to play piano was Marvin Hughes. The music didn't sound right to Elvis. We ended up recording only one song, a ballad titled "I Want You, I Need You, I Love You." It was a song that Sholes had brought to the session.

Elvis was polite, as were the rest of us, but it was apparent that Sholes just didn't get it. The song he had not wanted to do at the last Nashville session, "Heartbreak Hotel," had gone to No. 1 on the pop charts. Why didn't he understand that the best way to get records out of us was simply to turn us loose and let us play what we felt? After the session we returned to Memphis that same day. This time we took a regularly scheduled commercial flight.

★ ★ ★

The flyer for the New Frontier Hotel advertised Freddy Martin and his orchestra, who were scheduled to do a stage show version of the Broadway musical *Oklahoma*. Also on the bill were comedian Shecky Greene—and added attraction the "Atomic Power Singer," Elvis Presley. Since Nevada was the site of atomic testing, Parker thought the name would be catchy. What Parker hadn't figured on was how an older, more sedate nightclub crowd would react to Elvis.

After the first performance, at which the audience politely applauded, but showed none of the wild enthusiasm to which we were accustomed, we all knew we were in for a long two weeks. Says D. J.: "I don't think the people there were ready for Elvis. He was mostly for teenagers, kids. We worked with [Freddie Martin's orchestra] on *Oklahoma*, and here we were three little pieces making all that noise, and they [the audience] were eating $50 and $60 steaks. We tried everything we knew. Usually Elvis could get them on his side. It didn't work that time. The Colonel did a show for teenagers on Saturday, and it was just jam-packed, with everybody screaming and hollering."

In our off hours, we did pretty much what we did in any town. We hung out in the bar. None of us were interested in the casinos. One night we all went to check out the other acts on the strip. Performing at the Sahara lounge were Freddie Bell and the Bellboys. They had a hit in 1953 with a song, titled "Hound Dog," that also had been a hit for rhythm and blues singer Big Mama Thornton. When we heard them perform that night, we thought the song would be a good one for us to do as comic relief when we were on stage.

We loved the way they did it. They had a piano player who stood up and played—and the way he did his legs, they looked like rubber bands bending back and forth. Jerry Leiber and Mike Stoller wrote the song for Big Mama Thornton, but Freddie and the Bellboys had a different set of lyrics. Elvis got his lyrics from those guys. He knew the original lyrics, but he didn't use them.

Somehow we survived our two-week stint in Vegas. When it ended, we returned to Memphis and took a couple of weeks off before heading out on the road again. At a concert at the Municipal Auditorium Arena in Kansas City, Missouri, we performed in the round surrounded by the audience. When we started playing, the crowd surged forward, as every-one tried to get closer to the stage. Twenty minutes into the set, the crowd broke past the police barricade and stormed the stage.

Elvis took off. I remember I just turned around with my back to the crowd and turned my guitar up out of the way. We looked out into the crowd and saw Bill's bass going across the room, and then D. J.'s bass drum. We thought people were trying to steal them, but it was the peo-ple who worked there trying to help us get the stuff off the stage. They were holding the instruments up over their heads and it looked like the bass was just floating out of the room. Same thing for the drums. I don't think we ever played another concert in the round until the 1968 televi-sion special.

Whatever momentum we lost in Vegas, we picked up in the heartland, drawing record crowds. In June we returned to Los Angeles to appear on Milton Berle's last show of the season. With the Jordanaires backing him, Elvis did a sedate performance of "I Want You, I Need You, I Love You." Then, perhaps inspired by Berle's patented turned-foot walk, Elvis shocked a national television audience by gyrating with wild abandon as he sang our newly worked up version of "Hound Dog." In the days that fol-lowed, the network was bombarded with protests from people who called Elvis's performance obscene and vulgar. Elvis's unrepentant response was to the point: "You have to give them a show, something to talk about."

By the time we arrived in New York on July 1 for a performance on television's *Steve Allen Show*, the host was gunning for him. Several weeks earlier, Allen told his audience that he had received requests to cancel Elvis Presley's upcoming visit as a result of the protests that followed his performance on the *Milton Berle Show*. Explained Allen: "As of now he is still booked . . . but I have not come to a final decision on his appearance. If he does appear, you can rest assured that I will not allow him to do any-thing that will offend anyone."

Allen's solution was to have Elvis, dressed in a tuxedo, sing "Hound Dog" to a basset hound. The way Allen figured it, Elvis could hardly gy-rate his pelvis if his audience was a dog. Elvis gamely went along, giving what certainly had to be one of the most excruciating performances of his career. Later in the summer, Allen came to Elvis's defense in an interview with *TV Guide:* "Opinions may vary as to the scope of his talent and the duration of his popularity, but I happen to think that he is a very solid performer, and will be around a lot longer than his detractors think."

After his performance on the *Steve Allen Show*, Elvis went backstage for a live interview with Hy Gardner, who had his own show on a local television station. Gardner asked him if he bore any animosity toward critics who criticized his style of "gyrating."

"Well, not really," answered Elvis. "Those people have a job to do and they do it."

"Do you think you have learned anything from the criticism leveled at you?" Gardner asked.

"No, I haven't. Because I don't feel I'm doing anything wrong."

"Do you read the reviews or comments concerning you?"

"Not if I can help it."

The next day we went to the RCA studio for our second New York session. We had been playing "Hound Dog" for weeks in our live performance, so we felt that we pretty well had it nailed down. It was the first time we had ever gone into a session with a song we knew we would record. Also, it was the first time that all four Jordanaires were booked for a session with us. Unfortunately, our familiarity with "Hound Dog" did not make it an easy song for us to record. For some reason, we couldn't get the song down on tape the way we performed it live. We did take after take. Sometimes D. J.'s drums were off beat. Sometimes I was off on my solo, my notes wandering off to nowhere. At one point, Shorty Long, who was playing piano, had to leave to keep another appointment. He was replaced on piano by Gordon Stoker.

Finally, on the twenty-sixth take, Sholes said he thought we had it. Not satisfied with the track, Elvis said he thought we could do better. Not until the thirty-first take[7] did we get a keeper. One of my favorite parts of the song was my guitar solo. Looking back on it today, I can see that it was the result of frustration over the way the session had been going. To me, the final cut was an angry song. People used to ask me if I was mad at someone. I'd say, "Yeah, I was." It was a rough, grunting song and that's what I tried to portray.

For our second song, we chose one sent by Elvis's publisher, Hill and Range. The publisher had sent a stack of demos with lead sheets and Elvis had listened to them, one by one, as Sholes played them over the studio speaker. When Elvis heard, "Don't Be Cruel," he asked Sholes to play it again. It was written by Otis "Bumps" Blackwell, a rhythm and blues singer.

---

7. We did not play the song through 31 times; many of the takes were simply false starts.

Elvis was hooked. The song had a Memphis feel to it.

For me, the song was a breeze. I played the intro, but didn't hit another note until the end, when I played the last chord. It just didn't need more, not with the Jordanaires doing the rhythm behind it. I learned a lot from that day's session. I squirreled away that knowledge and used it later as a producer. It used to be that a producer hired seven or eight guys for a session. He wanted to look out into the studio and see all of them playing all of the time, which was dumb. You hire a guy to play a certain instrument. If he's a good musician, he'll usually come up with something neat. The difference between a good studio musician and a good concert musician is that the good studio musician plays only when he thinks he can make a difference. A good musician will walk in and out of the song when he thinks it will make a difference.

When we left New York the next day on the train to Memphis, we left with more than just a pair of hit singles. We left with a definite idea of how we wanted to structure our future sessions. Over the years, we pretty much stuck to that format. Typically, Elvis would stand with his back to the wall, facing the band. The Jordanaires would stand next to him. He wasn't overly concerned about mistakes, unless he made them in a vocal. If the band made a mistake—and the music still *felt* right—he would leave it in. How each musician played was up to the individual, but Elvis would sometimes make suggestions by asking, "Can you do this?" If the answer was no, he would say, "Do the best you can."

"Scotty did a lot of creating on the session," said Gordon Stoker. "All those guitar licks, like on 'Heartbreak Hotel,' that was all Scotty and D. J. working things out together. When we started doing backgrounds with Elvis, we found out he wanted suggestions. We would come up with all kinds of ideas and ninety percent of the time he would keep them."

When sidemen were hired for sessions, Elvis was usually more reserved in the studio. "If there was a strange musician there, he wouldn't talk as much," says Gordon. Unless he knew you, says Neal Matthews, Elvis wouldn't let his hair down: "He was very shy. He couldn't look you straight in the eye. Most of the time he looked down when he talked to you."

What Gordon noticed most about Elvis and me together in the studio was the way we related to each other and to the others in the room. "I never heard Scotty be rude to a singer or musician on a session, and Elvis was the same way," he says.

In Ray Walker's eyes, I was more protective of Elvis than the Colonel was:

*It was like Scotty was a speedboat and Elvis skied in the smooth wa-
ter behind the speedboat. That's the way it had to be. Elvis trusted
him for that. The first thing I heard about Scotty was that they had
nicknamed him the "old man." Scotty told me they didn't do that
for nothing. Scotty would meet the challenge and Elvis wouldn't.
Elvis would let people walk right through him at times, but Scotty
wouldn't. He knew where to draw the line. You can go a little way, but
don't step or spit across the line. Scotty would cut people short because he could recognize someone who was going to take advantage
quicker than Elvis could. Even when Elvis recognized it, he didn't
have the heart to do anything about it.*

Back in Memphis, we did a benefit concert for the *Press-Scimitar*'s annual milk-fund event. We performed "Hound Dog," with Elvis announcing to the outdoor crowd of 6,100 that the song would be our next single.
After the show, he told us that he was going to take the remainder of July
off so he could indulge himself with a little rest and relaxation. I was sorry
to hear that because it meant that my salary dropped from $200 a week
to $100 a week.

The next day sheriff's deputies showed up at my home at 1716
Tutwiler and took me off to jail. They had a warrant sworn out by my ex-
wife, Mary—she had since married an Air Force officer named Vernon
Cortez—that accused me of being delinquent in my child-support payments for my two children. The deputies allowed me to call my lawyer
before they took me downtown, but it was a humiliating experience. The
warrant accused me of being six payments—or $240—delinquent.

Obviously, Mary had seen me on television and convinced herself that
anyone who was touring with Elvis Presley and appearing on network
television certainly had the money to pay his child support. What neither
Mary nor anyone else knew was that I and the other band members were
not sharing in the wealth. As a result of the child-support incident, I went
by O. K. Houck Piano Company on July 15 and asked if they would refi-
nance my guitar and amplifier. With an unpaid balance of $445.20, they
agreed to lower my monthly payments to $34.60.

In those days, being a rock musician was not all that it was cracked up
to be.

★ ★ ★

After cooling my heels in Memphis for nearly a month, my salary reduced to $100 a week during the down time, I headed to Florida the first week in August with Elvis. Our first stop was Miami, where Elvis told reporters he was tired of being called the "Pelvis." He had picked up the hip-slinging moniker earlier in the summer from Pinckney Keel, a reporter with the *Clarion-Ledger*, a Jackson, Mississippi, morning newspaper. Keel had done a 15-minute interview with Elvis and was headed back to the newsroom when the phrase, "Elvis the Pelvis," popped in his mind. To Elvis's displeasure, the tag stuck.

Everyone in the show was on edge, but just how much did not become evident until we moved on to a concert in Daytona. We arrived at the hotel after driving all night. It was one of those godawful, all-night rides and everyone was ill and in a mad mood. We came in at three or four in the morning—and they didn't have any rooms ready for us or we didn't have any reservations, I don't remember which. We went to two or three different motels and there were no rooms. Bill popped off something and we went to blows and had a fistfight right there in the parking lot. All I remember is that it had *something* to do with a motel. Whatever the cause of the fight, it pushed my button.

The Jordanaires were traveling with us. "It was a pretty good fight," recalls Neal Matthews. "It didn't last very long. Scotty was a pretty good fighter."

"Yeah," says Gordon Stoker. "And Bill was bigger than Scotty. A whole lot bigger."

We moved on to Jacksonville, where we were scheduled to play six shows over a two-day period at the Florida Theatre. When we arrived we were greeted by unsigned warrants prepared by Juvenile Court Judge Marion Gooding. The warrants charged Elvis with impairing the morals of minors. The judge told us that he was upset over what had happened during our last visit (hysterical fans nearly ripped Elvis's clothes off) and he wanted to prevent a reoccurrence. If Elvis did those hip-gyrating movements for which he was famous, Gooding warned, he would sign the warrants and Elvis would be taken straight to jail.

In the days before our arrival, Gooding used the threat as if it were a platform in a political campaign. He was photographed at the Optimist Club, holding up a magazine with Elvis's image on the cover. He wanted voters to know that he was taking a stand against the evils of rock 'n' roll. He treated Elvis like he was a terrorist who had invaded the homeland.

When we did the concerts, the police were out in force, armed with movie cameras. Elvis did as he was told, but all that hip-swinging, nervous energy had to come out in some way. That's where the curled lip and the little finger thing really got started. He stood there flat-footed and did the whole show. The judge was delighted with the performance, which was a huge relief for us. None of us liked the idea of our families reading about us being busted for obscenity.

Later, Elvis told reporters he was unhappy about the controversy.

"I don't do no dirty body movements," he told a reporter.

I was surprised by the criticism. We weren't doing anything compared to what was going on five years later. We were clean cut. We wore jackets and ties on stage and had neat haircuts. We took baths. I never understood what people were upset about.

After Alan Freed was credited with coining the phrase "rock 'n' roll," there was a raging controversy among religious fundamentalists over use of the term. That didn't surprise me. Any homegrown Southerner knew the phrase had been used by blacks for years as a code phrase for sexual intercourse. Blues singers used the phrase long before Alan Freed ever did.

I got tickled when some of the preachers got up and made statements about "This rock 'n' roll has got to go." What were they saying? Did they even know what it meant?

Looking back on it now, the odd thing to me is that despite all the hoopla over Elvis's stage movements, it failed to generate a single new dance step among the fans. When the fans danced at their concerts, they did the jitterbug, the dance perfected by their parents. The girls all wore those big skirts with oxford shoes and socks. The guys all wore slacks and nice shirts. T-shirts were not allowed. Chubby Checker came up with the Twist later, but, with all that commotion over our music, the kids were dancing just like their parents did.

After a concert in New Orleans and a couple of days rest in Memphis we converged on Hollywood. Elvis had accepted a role in the David Weisbart movie *Love Me Tender*. Costarring with Elvis were Richard Eagan and Debra Paget. Although Elvis had signed with Hal Wallis at Paramount, they had a loan-out agreement with Twentieth Century-Fox, which was producing *Love Me Tender*. Since Steve Sholes wanted to use that opportunity to get more recordings for RCA, we all assumed we would have plenty of work. Initially, Elvis was told he wouldn't be asked to sing in the movie. After several songs were added to the script, the other band members and I were taken over to Twentieth Century-Fox to audition. They took us out into a little bungalow. No one told us it was going to be a western movie with hillbilly songs. Elvis didn't know either. So we did our regular act. They said, "No, that's not what we're looking for." But it was all politics. They were going through the motions to pacify Elvis.

I was furious, not because we were turned down, but because no one told us at the audition they wanted country music. Bill and I had been charter members of the Starlite Wranglers. We had been weaned on country music. It had been a setup from the beginning. Ken Darby, the movie's musical director, had his own singing trio and musicians he wanted to use. He never had any intention of using the Blue Moon Boys. Colonel Parker was tickled pink. His boy would record with these new pickers and Elvis would see for himself that he didn't really need the Blue Moon Boys. Elvis told me that he was sorry, but for us not to worry about it. He would see to it that we were involved with his next motion picture.

It was sometime around this time that Arlene Camacho of Pleasant Hill, California, started up the first Scotty Moore fan club. "Hi. I would like to start a fan club for the coolest of the guitar players, Scotty Moore," she explained to would-be members in a small magazine advertisement. "For those who don't know, Scotty is the 'git' man with Elvis Presley. If you would like to join, make with the pencils and pens." I was never informed about the fan club. In fact, it was not until 1996, when the ad was brought to my attention, that I learned of its existence. I have no idea how many fans she garnered, if any.

While Elvis was shooting the movie, Sholes booked time at Radio Recorders, an independent recording studio, so that we could record new sides for RCA when Elvis had time off from the movie. "Don't Be Cruel"/"Hound Dog" was on its way that month to No. 1 on the charts. Once it got there on August 18, it would remain there for eleven weeks. RCA needed a follow-up single, plus material for a new album. We recorded a number of songs, including "Love Me," "Old Shep," "Too Much," and "Anyplace is Paradise." RCA earmarked "Love Me Tender" for upcoming release as a single.

"Too Much" gave us fits in the studio. It was in A-flat, an unusual key for us to play. We did several takes, but on this particular song, I just got lost for some reason. I just kept chunking away. I didn't make any mistakes, but it wasn't the same solo I played on the other takes. Somehow I came out of it exactly where I was supposed to be.

When the song was over, Elvis raised his hand—his method of calling for a playback. As he listened, he leaned over on the speaker with his head down so that the sound was hitting him full blast. When the guitar solo came on, he twisted his head and looked at me with a shit-eating grin that told me that he knew I had gotten lost but he loved the way it turned out. When the song ended, he raised up and said, "That's it," and he did it for damned meanness. He knew I had gotten lost and he knew damned well I would have to live with it.

In between working on the album—and sitting on our backsides while Elvis filmed the movie—Bill, D. J., and I made a September 9 appearance with him on the *Ed Sullivan Show*. It was Sullivan's premiere show of the season, but he did not host the show because he was recuperating from an automobile accident. That night the guest host was actor Charles Laughton. The show was broadcast from New York, but we performed our segment from the CBS studio in Los Angeles. We opened with "Don't Be Cruel," then did "Love Me Tender," which Elvis explained was from his upcoming movie. Elvis was paid $50,000 for three appearances on the show; Bill, D. J., and I each received $78.23 per show from Sullivan.

We followed Elvis back to Memphis and then performed in Tupelo, Mississippi. From there we went to Texas where we did a few concerts. Tensions were still running high between Elvis and the band. We were happy to get the session work, but union scale at that time amounted to just $75 per three-hour session. That meant we could go to California for two weeks with Elvis, play eight or ten concerts coming and going, record a song or two, and our income for the two weeks would be less than $600—and out of that had to come our living expenses. From that we had to deduct money to send back to our families for their living expenses. For the same work, Elvis literally received hundreds of thousands of dollars. We discussed the situation among themselves, but never with Elvis. Money was not something he was comfortable discussing with us. Even so, I am certain that he began to feel the tension, however subtle.

During one of the *Love Me Tender* down times, I went out on the road with Jerry Lee Lewis for a two-week tour of Arkansas and Texas. Lewis hadn't yet scored a hit for Sun Records, but his career was in high gear at that point. Everything went smoothly until we reached New Orleans. It was our last stop on the tour. That night we sat around my hotel room, drinking.

Suddenly, Lewis jumped up on the bed and started preaching a blue streak. We were having a normal conversation about something, and then all of a sudden he flipped over into hellfire and brimstone recitation.

"I don't want to hear that," I told him, but he went on and on.

We were fixing to get with it, but his daddy-in-law got him quieted down. I made up my mind then about Jerry Lee. There's the old saying, "Cold ass me—and you is through."[8]

In October, Elvis pulled into a Memphis service station to get gas for his new Mark II Continental. He politely asked the manager, Ed Hopper, to check his gas tank for leaks. As his car was being serviced, a crowd gathered. Elvis took time to sign autographs and chat with his fans. When he finished servicing the car, Hopper told Elvis that his fans were blocking traffic and he asked him to leave. Elvis said he would do that, but he continued signing autographs. Hopper impatiently slapped Elvis across the back of head with an admonition to "move on." It was the type of disrespectful slap that'd been used for generations by whites to get the attention of blacks perceived to be non-obedient.

Recognizing the disrespect, Elvis leaped out of the car and punched Hopper in the head, inflicting a half-inch gash at the corner of his left eye. When one of Hopper's employees, a six-four, 220-pound man, ran out of the office to help Hopper, he also was punched by Elvis after he pulled a knife. Before the fight could escalate further, it was broken up by a cop and a bystander.

"I'll take ridicule and slander, but when a guy hits me, that's too much," Elvis told the cop. When the arresting officer asked him his name, he jokingly said, "Well, maybe you'd better put down Carl Perkins."

When the case went to court the following week, Elvis went without an attorney and answered all the judge's questions with a "yes, sir" or "no, sir." After hearing all the evidence, the judge dismissed all charges against Elvis and the service station attendants were fined $25 and $15. The judge's decision was greeted with applause by the packed courtroom.

On October 26 we went with Elvis by train from Memphis to New York for our second appearance on the *Ed Sullivan Show*. The trip took two days. This time Sullivan was there and engaged in onstage banter with Elvis. The next day, RCA Records announced they had concluded a new, long-term contact with Elvis. *Variety* declared him a millionaire, and RCA proudly announced he had sold well over ten million singles. That translated to an income from records of about a half-million dollars for Elvis. I couldn't help but fantasize about what my and Bill's share would be if Elvis had stood by his offer to give us a percentage of the royalties.

---

8. A takeoff on the expression, "Give me the cold shoulder and we're through."

After taking a few weeks off, we went out on a four-day tour that began in Louisville, Kentucky, and then moved on to Toledo, Ohio, where we did two shows in the Sports Arena. After the show, we went to the bar of the Commodore Perry Hotel to relax. As we sat around talking (Elvis, Bill, D. J., me, and Oscar Davis, Colonel Parker's assistant) we were accosted by a nineteen-year-old man, who said he was angry because his wife carried a picture of Elvis in her wallet. He drew back like he was going to throw a shot at Elvis and I jumped on his back. There was a railing there—one of those things they put besides steps—and he tried to roll me over his back onto the railing. He actually threw me over the railing. But by that time, Elvis was absolutely using him as a punching bag. Elvis was real fast. Quick as lightning with his hands. He would have made a good fighter, but that would have messed up his face.

When the police arrived to break up the fight, six teenage girls who had been watching from the lobby rushed up and gave their names as witnesses. The police officers took the man off to jail and didn't file charges against Elvis or me. Contacted later by a newspaper reporter, one of the police officers said, "Presley's no slouch. He was really working that guy over."

Damn right. Memphis boys know how to take care of themselves.

Later the man told reporters that he was hired by Elvis to stage the fight. He said Elvis still owed him his $200. "I read where Presley takes $16,000 out of Toledo for them two shows at the arena," he said. "Sixteen grand and he is too cheap to pay me my lousy $200."

When he was asked if the fight had been staged, Colonel Parker screamed out angry denials at reporters, then—after thinking about it a while—he calmed down and said, "Anyway, they've got Elvis's name spelled right." If the man was hired to start a fight it wasn't by Elvis—and it damn sure wasn't me.

As the November 16 release date for *Love Me Tender* drew near, Elvis took time off to go to Las Vegas for a mini vacation. "Love Me Tender," the song, had gone to No. 1, with "Don't Be Cruel"/"Hound Dog" in the No. 2 slot. For the first time since *Billboard* began compiling its charts, the No. 1 and No. 2 positions were held by the same artist. "Love Me Tender" also had another distinction: It was the first song Elvis recorded that didn't include the Blue Moon Boys.

When *Love Me Tender* was released, it set a record with the release of 550 prints by Twentieth Century-Fox, the largest release of a film ever. As

Elvis basked in the glow of having both hit records and a hit Hollywood movie, I was back in Memphis on $100-a-week down time, taking stock of the year. In 1956, I had earned $8,193.58 from my work with Elvis. That was a decent enough income for a working stiff—it sure beat being a hatter—but, with all my expenses, I was quickly going into debt.

★ ★ ★

On January 4, 1957, after Elvis completed his pre-induction physical at the Selective Service headquarters in Memphis, we boarded a train with him for New York, where we were scheduled to do our third—and final—appearance on the *Ed Sullivan Show*. It was a long trip, with a train switch in Washington, D.C. The possibility of Elvis being drafted had never entered my mind. I had been too busy picking my guitar to think about a lot of "what ifs." In the beginning, Elvis had asked me lots of questions about the Navy. I had answered in terms of my own experiences, without thinking about it being something Elvis would ever have to face.

On the train to New York, I thought about it a lot, both in terms of what Elvis would have to go through—for all my frustrations over the money issue, Elvis was like a brother to me, and I felt protective toward him—and in terms of what it would mean for my career as a musician. The more I thought about it, the more I convinced myself that Parker would never allow "his boy" to be drafted. All it took to beat the draft was a little of what Southerners called "pull," a commodity Parker had acquired an ample supply of in recent months.

We arrived in New York early Saturday morning and went by the Maxine Elliot Theater later in the day for a rehearsal. Years later, the theater would be refurbished for *The Late Show with David Letterman*. We returned to the theater the next day for another rehearsal before show time.

That night, during the actual show, Sullivan pulled out all the stops. In three separate appearances, we performed seven songs, including "Heartbreak Hotel," "Love Me Tender," and "Too Much," our latest single. To accommodate critics, cameramen had orders to provide shots of Elvis from the waist up whenever it appeared he might swivel his hips and shake his leg. Also on the show that day was comedienne Carol Burnett, who was just beginning her career.

Watching the show back in Crockett County were James and Evelyn Lewis. "There's Winfield!" James shouted out whenever the camera got a shot of his old friend. He couldn't pass up the opportunity to kid his wife,

Evelyn: "See, if you had encouraged me, I would be picking somewhere, too, making lots of money [like Scotty]."

When we returned to Memphis, I contacted Chicago Musical Instrument Company in Chicago and made arrangements to trade in my Gibson L5 for a Gibson S 400, the so-called "blond" model with which I am most identified. The guitar and a case were shipped to O. K. Houck Piano Company in Memphis and sold to me on the installment plan for $735 ($675 for the guitar and $60 for the case).

Things were going pretty much as usual during our first week back. Then the draft board announced a shocker: Elvis had passed his physical and would be classified 1-A. The board told reporters it was just a matter of time before Elvis received his draft notice. That was an unsettling prospect for us to consider. Contacted by the same reporters, Elvis said he would be honored to serve his country. What else could he say?

By mid-January, we were back in Hollywood. First, to do another recording session for RCA Records, and then to start filming on Elvis's next movie. Critics had panned Elvis's performance in *Love Me Tender*. Elvis was devastated by the criticism. He told friends he thought he had done a terrible job of acting. He'd lost his self-confidence.

Steve Sholes was greatly relieved to get Elvis in the studio again. He had been begging Colonel Parker for months for studio time. Parker had deliberately held him at arm's length. Parker would keep Elvis on the road, anything to keep him out of the studio. He didn't want them to get a backlog of material. It was a supply-and-demand issue. He milked it as close as he possibly could. Too little Elvis was more profitable than too much Elvis.

Parker begrudgingly gave Sholes two weekends at Radio Recorders, but there was a condition attached: If the movie studio decided to alter its start-up date, then Sholes would be out of luck. Elvis was somewhat distracted during the sessions. He found it difficult to stay focused. Who could blame him? But despite that handicap Sholes was able to get two No. 1 singles, "All Shook Up" and "Teddy Bear," plus additional material to squirrel away for the next album.

True to his word, Elvis got us hired for the next movie. *Loving You* was a departure from the first movie in that it cast Elvis as a singer out on the road trying to make it to the Big Time. Elvis would have plenty of dramatic scenes, but he also would sing and . . . well, be *Elvis*. Bill, D. J., and I were hired to play on the soundtrack and to play the roles of his band members in the movie. We were paid $285 a week by Paramount.

For Paramount's first picture with Elvis, Hal Wallis chose a director that he thought would be perfect. Hal Kanter had never directed a movie, but he was from Savannah, Georgia, and had written the screenplay for Tennessee Williams's *Rose Tattoo*. Perhaps Kanter could talk to Elvis in his own language. Before we started filming, Kanter went to Memphis to get acquainted with Elvis. He even went with him to Shreveport for his farewell "benefit" performance for the *Hayride*.

Unfortunately for Kanter, the visit didn't have the desired effect. Elvis told friends that he thought Kanter was a little strange. But they got along well enough. "I found him to be a very pleasant young man," Kanter told my co-author. "I enjoyed his sense of humor and his appreciation of films. He seemed to be a student of the cinema. He wanted to a good job in anything he attempted. I had the impression that if he was a truck driver, he wanted to be the best truck driver around. If he was a singer, he wanted to be the best singer around."

Elvis was relaxed and enthusiastic when we began shooting the movie. It was all new to me, so it was a learning experience. What Bill, D. J., and I didn't like was the waiting that is required to make a movie. You might wait around all day and then it would take thirty minutes for you to do what they wanted. I was always more interested in the audio side of it. I would go into the control room and watch as they did their thing with the knobs and dials. It amazed me how different everything sounded in the control room.

After we began work, we were told that we would be paid as extras, not as actors. Since the pay for extras was only about $100 a day, we knew we could expect only a day or two of work a week, if that much. Because we knew that we were going to be out there four or five weeks, we approached Wallis on the set and told him we were going home because we weren't getting paid enough. Wallis was over a barrel—and he knew it. We already had appeared in several scenes with Elvis; if we went home, Wallis would have to reshoot the scenes. His money guy told him we could work so many weeks as actors on the musicians' card, so he let us do that. That was damned good, considering what Elvis was paying us. At least we would have enough to send something back home.

★ ★ ★

We didn't have any elaborate dance segments in *Loving You*. Most of choreographer Charles O'Curran's efforts were directed toward the extras in the crowd scenes, when they had to be instructed on how to sway and clap, and on the actor musicians who had to be taught moves to do on stage while Elvis was singing and the music was playing. Charlie also decided which songs Elvis did his dance moves to while he sang.

I have always been irritated at the way dancers in Broadway plays or movies use exaggerated movements when they dance to country music. It's so hokey. It's like they think everyone down South does a buck dance. In later years the television show *Hee-Haw* offered that kind of dancing, but it was done in a joking way and everyone understood that it was a joke, at least in the South. It is to Charlie's credit that no one was asked to do dances like that in *Loving You.*

Because I had a lot of down time on the set, while they set up scenes and shot scenes that did not involve me, I took my guitar and amplifier with me each day. Elvis got the electricians to get power for my amp so in between takes we could jam. It made the director mad because the crew gathered around to listen and sometimes didn't pay attention to their work.

Wallis didn't want me and the others in the band playing on the soundtrack, but Elvis insisted and we were allowed to play, although Charles O'Curran hired a piano player, Dudley Brooks, and a second guitarist, "Tiny" Timbrell, to work on the session with us. We tried to record the songs on the Paramount sound stage, but we all felt uncomfortable there and couldn't really get into a groove. We were used to recording in smaller rooms.

The studio tried to accommodate us by putting up 15- or 20-foot baffles around us, in effect creating a smaller separate room on the sound stage. When that didn't work, we packed up and went to Radio Recorders so we could do our recordings in a more comfortable atmosphere. Accompanying us was the union representative for the studio.

Everyone, including Elvis, was happier at Radio Recorders, where we worked with Thorn Nogar, the chief mixer, and his backup engineer, Bones Howe. What we couldn't get used to was the union representative, who stood up every hour on the hour and clapped his hands—a signal that it was time for us to take a ten-minute break. It didn't matter to the union man whether the band was in a groove or not. Rules were rules. Every hour on the hour: clap, clap, clap.

I could see that it was really beginning to irritate Elvis. Finally, we were in the middle of something—I mean, we just about had it nailed—and we stopped to listen to the playback. Elvis said, "Let's try it one more time." At that precise moment, there it came: clap, clap, clap. Elvis turned around and looked at everybody. You could see by the look on his face that he had enough. He told the control room, "Roll it." He just ignored the union man. The guy never said another word. He was a nice, old gentleman; his job was to hire the orchestra and be the timekeeper. He was into a different thing, and we were, too—but he got the message.

Two or three weeks into the filming, Gladys and Vernon Presley arrived in Hollywood for a visit. Elvis showed them around the set and took them to a movie theater to see one of the biggest hits of the year, *The Ten Commandments*. During that time, my wife Bobbie decided that she, too, wanted a glimpse of my glamorous new world.

"I wanted to see as much as I could," Bobbie says. "Scotty tried to talk me out of it. He said, 'Why don't you wait and we'll come back out by ourselves.' I said, 'No, it'll never happen. I'm going. I may not see you, but I'm going.'"

After Bobbie arrived, Elvis asked me if I would mind taking Gladys and Vernon to Burbank to see the *Tennessee Ernie Ford Show*. With me at the wheel, driving Elvis's new white Cadillac, we took Gladys and Vernon to the show. Afterward, we went backstage and met Tennessee Ernie Ford.

That March, when we all returned to Memphis, I received a nice letter from Kanter, addressed to my home address at 1716 Tutwiler, which Bobbie and I shared with her three sisters and a brother-in-law. Wrote Kanter: "I want to take this opportunity to thank you for your cooperation during your period of employment, and also thank you for your valuable contribution to the project."

Elvis bought a present for his parents and for himself. The two-story mansion, named Graceland, had a $100,000 price tag, and was the most conspicuous symbol yet of Elvis's growing wealth. The *Press-Scimitar* sent a reporter out to interview them. Elvis told the reporter he was going to put a "hi-fi" in every room. "I want the darkest blue there is for my room, with a mirror that will cover one side of the room," he explained.

"We will have a lot more privacy, and a lot more room to put some of the things we have accumulated over the last few years," said Gladys. Vernon impressed the reporter as being a little "skittish" about the purchase. "Moving is going to be a problem," Vernon grumbled. "Although a moving company has said they will move us free of charge. We just had the old place fixed up like we wanted it. Now we have to start all over again."

The trappings of success were piling up around Elvis, but there were indications he was feeling the pressure of being a star. One day, shortly after he had purchased Graceland, he went out on his motorcycle dressed as a cop: black leather jacket, vest, helmet, sunglasses. He stopped by Sun Studio, but Sam wasn't there. He was hardly ever there anymore.

Jack Clement was in the studio that day.

"Me and my ole buddy were back in the control room shooting craps and in walks this motorcycle guy who looked like a cop," says Clement. "It was Elvis. He scared us."

One day Elvis was cruising on Parkway Avenue when he saw Betty McMahan, one of his girlfriends from the projects. He pulled her over to the side of the road. Betty didn't recognize him at first. When she saw that it was Elvis she was surprised at how bad he looked. "His face looked pitiful," she told a reporter for *The Commercial Appeal.* "He had bumps [pimples] even on his shoulders."

★ ★ ★

By the time we arrived in Hollywood with Elvis on April 13 to begin work on his new movie, *Jailhouse Rock*, our last single, "All Shook Up," had been No. 1 for eight weeks. In 1957 stars just didn't come any bigger than Elvis Presley. We checked into the upscale Beverly Wilshire, but Bill and I weren't comfortable there and moved to the less opulent Knickerbocker. It was written later that the backup men were moved out of the hotel on Parker's orders, but that's not the way it happened. We were the ones who instigated it. We didn't want to get tied in with the crowds. We wanted to get out and walk up and down the street and look in the windows.

By this point RCA Records felt it was slightly ahead of the curve. They had "Teddy Bear" in the can for upcoming release and they knew they could count on *Jailhouse Rock* to spawn a hit or two. For the first time, they saw the benefits of merging Elvis's recording career with his movie career. Steve Sholes could do no wrong in the eyes of RCA. He was moved from Nashville and put in charge of the pop division in New York. Whatever his private thoughts about the direction Elvis's music was taking, his lack of aggressiveness demonstrated that he didn't want to rock the boat.

Jerry Leiber and Mike Stoller, the songwriting team who had penned "Hound Dog," were hired to write songs for the *Jailhouse Rock* soundtrack. They were given a script and pretty much told to write songs that would fit in certain scenes. As usual, they laid down the tracks at Radio Recorders. When the song "Jailhouse Rock" was explained to us, we talked about how we could generate a jailhouse sound. It would have been nice if we had a big sledgehammer and could have done a sound effect, but we didn't have a sledgehammer, so we did it musically. We took that intro—when I'm doing a half-step drag and D. J. is doing a beat on the drums to imply a rock pile—and tried to repeat it in one way or another on all the songs.

The *Jailhouse Rock* sessions were the first at which I noticed that Elvis's heart was no longer in the music. One day Elvis once spent five or six hours doing gospel songs with the Jordanaires as a means of escaping the work at hand. Some of that movie stuff was impossible. That's the reason why he would play the piano and sing with the Jordanaires, to psyche himself up. Once he got started on the movie again, he would do the best he could. Once, when a studio executive complained Elvis was wasting time with the Jordanaires, Elvis walked out of the studio and didn't return until the next day. Whenever Elvis criticized a song, he was told how much money it would earn for everyone. He didn't want to let anyone down, so he did the songs.

Bill, D. J., and I were written into a number of scenes, but we had to buy our own clothes since we were not provided with a wardrobe. I had two new sports coats that I purchased for $58.50 from Lawrence Douglas Clothes on the corner of Santa Monica and Vine and a pair of shoes I bought for $15.95 from Regal Shoe Shop on Hollywood Boulevard.

When we filmed the swimming pool scene, I was in the background, playing my guitar. Portions of the scene were filmed early in the day; other portions were done later in the day. As a result, when the movie was released, I noticed that some of the cut-away, close-up shots showed me wearing sunglasses, whiles others that showed me from a distance did not. That glitch somehow slipped past the continuity person and the film editors.

I was also on the set when Elvis did the famous dance sequence. What they ended up with was not what they started out with. Choreographer Charles O'Curran initially designed an elaborate dance sequence for professional dancers. What impressed me about Charlie was that when that didn't work out too well, he retreated and watched footage of Elvis doing his live show. Then he staged that entire dance sequence around Elvis's natural moves. Elvis had to follow a routine, but those were his own moves. It was what he did on the stage all the time when we were playing concerts. Elvis would probably still be out there working on that scene if they had asked him to do something they had made up. I always enjoyed working with Charlie. He went out of his way to think of things that Elvis could do well.

★ ★ ★

In early April, we did two shows at the Sports Arena in Philadelphia. Before the first show, Elvis met with a small group of high school reporters. Dressed in black, but wearing "spotless" white shoes, he showed up for the interview with five bodyguards. One of the students asked him what he thought of his movie, *Love Me Tender*.

"It was pretty horrible," answered Elvis. "Acting's not something you learn overnight. I knew that picture was bad when it was completed. I am my own worst critic. But my next picture is different."

Another student asked him when he would be drafted.

"Everyone thinks I've been drafted already, but I haven't," he said. "I've only passed the physical. But I'm not definitely going in."

From mid-April to late August, Elvis stayed off the road, vegetating in Memphis. Mostly, he tinkered with his new toys at Graceland. Of course, that meant that we were knocked back down to our $100-a-week salary for the duration. If food stamps had been invented in 1957, we would have qualified for benefits. Luckily for me, Bobbie had a good job and was able to bring home a paycheck. At one point I applied for unemployment, but that lasted only a week or so before I found work.

Finally, we got word that Elvis had more work for us. In late August we drove to Spokane, where we were to begin a five-city tour of the Northwest, after which we would go to Los Angeles to do another recording session for RCA Records.

The first concert in Spokane was sheer madness, with over 12,500 screaming teenagers, mostly women, testing the resourcefulness of the 100 police officers there to keep order. The next stop was Vancouver, British Columbia. It was one of the few foreign concerts Colonel Parker ever booked for Elvis. That may have been because Canadian border officials did not require passports and visas for entry from the United States. Parker could go to Canada without having his citizenship challenged.

When we walked out onto the stage with Elvis, we faced 26,500 screaming fans, the largest audience to date. The stage was constructed on the back of two flatbed trucks parked at the north end of the stadium. A fence was put up around the stage, and between the stage and the audience was nearly one hundred yards of football field. When the music began, the crowd surged past the police officers onto the field and sat down in front of the stage.

We must have looked like ants to them back where they were sitting. All they wanted to do was to get closer. They didn't care whether they had seats or not. At one point, stadium officials stopped the show and told the crowd it would not continue until they got back off the field. D. J. remembers how defiant the crowd was. Stadium officials couldn't budge them. "They tried and they tried, and they wouldn't move, so we finally started the show," says D. J.

Frightened by the surging fans, Parker told Elvis to cut the show short. When Elvis abruptly left the stage and made a dash for his waiting car, we were left on stage to face the fans alone. The kids all ran up on the stage and the platform tilted to one side. By the time we got our instruments loaded into the car, we were surrounded by fans. "They shook the car a little bit, thinking he was in there with us," says D. J. "But, finally, they let us go. It took about two hours for us to get out. It usually took us about two hours to get out of all the buildings."

The media later called it a riot, but it wasn't really that bad. The fans were just trying to get closer to the stage to see, that's all. If they wanted to see a *real* riot, they should spend some time in a Chinese war zone.

After two additional shows in Washington State, we went to Hollywood the first week in September for the scheduled recording session at Radio Recorders. Steve Sholes wanted to get some new singles, but he was mostly interested in trying to put together a Christmas album. *Jailhouse Rock*, the movie, was scheduled for release in a few weeks, along with the single, and he had a single in the can, "I Beg of You," that had been recorded the previous February.

We were especially eager for this session. Elvis had been talking to us for months about doing an album of instrumentals on which he would play piano. The project was his idea. Financially, we were getting desperate. Every time we put something together that would allow us to make extra money or receive items in exchange for endorsements, Colonel Parker shot it down. Earlier in the year, while we were headed out of Hollywood back to Memphis in Elvis's bright yellow limo, we were flagged down on the street by a couple of men from a local Chrysler dealership. They introduced themselves, saying they were with the biggest Chrysler dealership in town. They asked us to go to a restaurant and have a cup of coffee. They told us, "Look, we know Elvis is into Cadillacs, but we will give you boys a brand new Chrysler every year and all Elvis has to do is say, 'My band members drive Chryslers.'"

I thought that was a great idea. Finally, someone had offered *us* something—and it wouldn't cost the Colonel a penny. Of course, when we asked Parker about it he said, no way. He said he would never approve anything like that. We received the same type of endorsement offer from the appliance division of RCA. That was fantastic! They were going to give us stoves, refrigerators, whatever. But Parker shot that down, too. To him the world was one big con.

While we were making *Loving You* he showed up on the set with an armload of homemade sausages. He handed them out to people on the set, except to us, of course, but when he approached Kanter, he pulled the sausages close to his chest and offered to sell him one. It was an honor to be lumped in the same group with Kanter. Later I heard that when he learned that Kanter had written the script for *Loving You* he had the audacity to ask him to write his biography for him, explaining that he had the perfect title, *How Much Does It Cost If It's Free?* That may have been directed toward the band, as if to say that any free perks given to us would end up costing him money in some unforeseen way. He was obsessed with money.

Parker had it written into Elvis movie contracts that Parker would be paid for being a technical advisor and would be provided with a suite of rooms. Now what's a technical advisor on an Elvis film, you tell me? He had it written into the contract that they got an extra $25,000 if Elvis ever used any of his own clothes in a scene. One day Parker saw that Elvis was wearing his watch in one of the scenes and he made the movie company pay him $25,000. That's the kind of crap he was always pulling. He kept the people he dealt with always looking over their shoulder. I think that Parker's stunts had a lot to do with Elvis not being given a chance to come out from under the musical stuff in the movie parts.

After we completed work on the singles and Christmas album, we got ready to record the album of instrumentals. We had even picked the name out for the group: the Continentals. Elvis booked studio time for us. We even rehearsed some songs for the album. But before we got started, Parker found out about it and shut us down.

As a result, there was an awkward scene in the studio in which Elvis physically backed away from Bill and me and disappeared behind the protective wall of his entourage. Bill was furious. He slammed his electric bass into its carrying case. I was more disappointed than angry. I just couldn't bring myself to believe that Elvis would treat us that way. Financially, I was desperate. Just how desperate can be ascertained by a look at my tax records. Because Elvis had cut back on his touring schedule, my income from Elvis in 1957 had dropped to $6,656.65. My total income, before taxes, from Elvis for three and a half years amounted to only $23,041.72.

Elvis had become a millionaire. Compared to the incredible wealth Elvis was amassing, $23,041.72 wasn't much to show for three and a half years' work. When we started out, we were Elvis and the Blue Moon Boys, the musical equivalent of the Three Musketeers: all for one, and one for all. Now Bill and I were struggling to make a living wage. It would have helped if Parker had allowed us to make endorsements, but he would not even consider it.

The album of instrumentals would have given us an opportunity to make royalties from our music. All those hit records with Elvis and we never made a penny in royalties. When the instrumental session was scrapped, I—perhaps for the first time—saw things as they really were. There was never going to be any sharing of the wealth, as Elvis had promised. I was a salaried employee, nothing more. My salary of $200 week, when I traveled with Elvis, was about the same salary he paid the members of his entourage—the Memphis Mafia, as they later were called—except the members of his entourage also received free automobiles and expensive gifts. Elvis never once purchased cars for Bill or me. Sometimes when I think about it, it just seems so crazy I can't wrap my head around it.

★ ★ ★

When we returned to Memphis, we sat down with our wives for a heart to heart. We had to do something drastic. We couldn't continue the way we were going. Before leaving California, we had tried to talk to Elvis about our situation, but we couldn't get through to him. Finally, out of frustration, we agreed—with the support of our wives—to write out letters of resignation. We called D. J. and asked him to write a letter as well, but he told us that he was in a different situation. He had been hired as a salaried employee from the beginning. He had no reason to expect more from Elvis. In later years, D. J. was more supportive of our decision. "I don't blame them one bit," he explained in an interview for this book. "They should have left before that. It was Scotty and Bill and Elvis who started out. They had a legitimate reason to complain. I told them, 'If I'd have started like you guys, I'd be right with you.'"

Elvis was still in Hollywood when he received the special delivery letters on September 7. First, he was shocked, passing the letters around for everyone to see. Then he became angry and accused us of being disloyal to him. Colonel Parker had us right where he wanted us. He knew the best thing he could do to help things along was to stand aside and not get involved. Steve Sholes told Elvis not to worry, that he would find him better musicians than us. By the time Elvis returned to Memphis on September 11, the local media was on the story.

"I don't believe Scotty and I could raise more than 50 bucks between us," Bill Black told *The Commercial Appeal* in story the newspaper ran on the front page. "I'm still living day to day."

I was equally blunt in a newspaper interview, saying, "He promised us that the more he made the more we would make. But it hasn't worked out that way."

Bill said he had started working in the service department of Ace Appliance Company to help make ends meet. He said he was "embarrassed" over the way things had turned out. "We'd be put up in a big hotel, and certain things were expected of us because we were with Elvis. Like picking up a check for coffee, and tipping and things like that. We'd go out to eat where we could get it cheaper . . . We're not jealous of anyone, but we found out other people were laughing at us. Even the guys selling souvenir books were making more money than we were."

I received a phone call from Elvis when I returned to Memphis. Elvis asked me what I wanted. I suggested a $50 raise and a flat payment of $10,000 so that I could pay off the debts I had acquired while touring with him. Elvis said he would have to think about it.

We did some thinking of our own. From day one, we had subsisted on dreams and promises. We didn't want to quit Elvis. All we wanted was something to show for our efforts. We would stand by our resignations if we had to, but in our hearts we just knew Elvis would come around. He would see what Parker was doing to him. Once he understood, he would reward us for their loyalty. Surely, he would see the truth.

In a way it was like Elvis had been kidnapped and taken off into a sideshow of a circus. The thing that got me, the thing that wasn't right about it, was that Elvis didn't keep his word. If I had instigated the idea of Bill and me receiving royalties, and had tried to get royalties from him, that would be one thing. But I didn't. It was all his idea. I tried to make it as palatable as possible. There were other things he could have done to compensate us. The endorsements, the deals for new cars—especially the album of instrumentals, that would have made a tremendous difference in our lives. Those things would have mattered.

After conferring with Parker and others for several days, Elvis responded to my request for a $50 raise. This time he didn't call to talk it over with me. He went public. In an interview with Bill Burk of the *Press-Scimitar*, Elvis issued an "open letter" to Bill and me: "Scotty, I hope you fellows have good luck. I will give you fellows good recommendations. If you had come to me, we would have worked things out. I would have always taken care of you. But you went to the papers and tried to make me look bad, instead of coming to me so we could work things out. All I can say to you is good luck."

Elvis told the reporter that it was a mystery to him why we hadn't come to him to talk over our problems. "We've had our problems before—even some arguments—but we always settled them," Elvis said. "Every time they ever came to me and asked for something, they got it, no matter what. Had they come to me, we would have worked it out and they would have got more money."

With his next performance scheduled for the Tupelo Fair on September 27, Elvis said he would start auditioning new guitar players immediately. "It may take a while," he said, "but it's not impossible to find replacements."

When we read the newspaper story, we knew it was all over. Despite his statements to the press, I still refused to blame Elvis for what happened. Parker was behind it all. Parker had not told Elvis about our many requests over the years. Elvis didn't know. He never understood. It was Parker's doing. I tried not to be around him any more than I had to. I had heard stuff about him from other people when he first appeared on the scene and I was leery of him. Frankly, he was just a con man. I could see what he did with Bob Neal. He whittled away at getting rid of him. He wanted to get rid of the band. He wanted to get rid of anyone who was pre-Parker.

On September 18, 1957, Vernon Presley sent me a brief, one-paragraph letter:

> *This is to advise that, pursuant to your notice of September 7, 1957, we are accepting your resignation from our employment effective September 21, 1957, and, accordingly, enclose herewith notice of separation and your final salary check in the amount of $86.25, representing payment in full for all services rendered for us by you prior to September 21.*

★ 8 ★

TRAGEDY IS A REVOLVING DOOR

Once I was officially unemployed, I wasted no time looking for work. I booked Bill and me for a sixteen-day engagement at the Texas State Fair. As it turned out, it was the most lucrative booking of our career. We were asked to play four shows a day from October 5 through October 20. We were paid $1,600 plus expenses. It was double what we made working for Elvis. Not a bad deal.

As I read the newspaper accounts of our resignation—and Elvis's comments to reporters about Bill and myself—I realized that Elvis just didn't get it. It wasn't about recognition, as Elvis told reporters. Neither of us cared about fame. We certainly didn't begrudge Elvis his success. We just wanted some perks, so we could stick a few bucks in the bank. It was a fantasy thing for us. Working for Elvis, at the pay he was giving us, was better than digging ditches, but we felt we deserved better than that. We just wanted more money. Later, people wrote that it was Bill who talked me into resigning. That wasn't the way it happened. Bill was always more vocal about it than I was, but we were both pretty adamant about it.

We looked back over the past few years with more than a little self-loathing over our reluctance to stand up for ourselves. My advice to musicians is to stand up for yourself because it is a certainty that no one else will. When Elvis signed with RCA Records, we could have fought to keep using the name, Blue Moon Boys, but we didn't want to rock the boat. Unlike us, the Jordanaires insisted on keeping their name and identity. As a result, many people thought we were members of the Jordanaires.

When we looked at the situation, we knew we had brought a lot of our troubles on ourselves by not speaking up sooner. In many ways Elvis was like a child. How could we blame him? We knew that our problems all originated with management, with Parker, who had masterfully used our silence as a weapon against us.

When Bill and I quit, I'm sure he just rolled over and ha-ha'ed. We didn't want to be around him anymore than we had to. I never called him

Colonel unless it was a slip of the tongue—and that would piss him off. Later on, I got an honorary title of my own from Tennessee Governor Winfield Dunn, so he didn't outrank me after all.

As Bill and I got ready for our two-week engagement at the Texas State Fair, Elvis prepared for a homecoming performance at the Mississippi-Alabama Dairy Show and Fair in Tupelo. It would be his first performance without us. From all accounts, he took our resignation hard. He told people he felt betrayed, let down. It never occurred to him to blame Parker.

One day during this time, Elvis went by Sun Records to see Sam and Marion. Unknown to Elvis, Marion and Sam had had a fight and she had stomped out of the studio and joined the Air Force. His visit to the studio only served to confirm his increasing suspicion that the world was an unfriendly place. He couldn't understand why everyone was fighting with each other.

For the Tupelo show, Elvis hired two Nashville session players to replace us—Hank Garland, another of my heroes and a great jazz guitarist, and Chuck Wiginton on bass. Chuck was close friends with both D. J. and myself. When the Jordanaires arrived at the venue, they were shocked to learn that we had quit. They hadn't heard a word about it. Says Neal Matthews: "I didn't know for two weeks that they had left."

After the show, Elvis told D. J. that it just wasn't the same without us.

"Elvis was very upset, I assure you," Jordanaire Gordon Stoker said in an interview for this book. "He loved both of those guys."

When we returned from Texas we received a telephone call from Tom Diskin, Colonel Parker's assistant. Elvis had four concerts scheduled for San Francisco and Los Angeles for October 26 through October 29. Diskin told me that if we rejoined the group, Elvis would pay us $1,000 each, or $250 per show. We agreed to rejoin the band on those terms, with the understanding that any future bookings would be on a per diem basis.

"Just send us some contracts," I said, getting some satisfaction from knowing how the phone call must have made Parker cringe. Later, we learned that the phone call had been made at Elvis's insistence.

On October 17, the day after we returned from Texas, Diskin sent the contracts. In his letter, Diskin asked me to send the contracts special delivery to the Sahara Hotel in Las Vegas. The letter, which was formal and to the point, said that we could travel from Memphis to California with D. J. in Elvis's limousine at no extra charge, but then added—with a characteristic Parker jab—"Should you decide to travel by some other method that would be of course at your own expense."

We took the limo. The drive took a day and a half. We met Elvis at the San Francisco Civic Auditorium and he acted as if nothing had happened. Nothing was said that I can remember. We laughed and went on and did the show like we used to do. There weren't any hard feelings visible with anyone. We didn't go there with a chip on our shoulder. I don't think that our resignations were even brought up.

From San Francisco, we went across the bay to Oakland for a concert the second night, then it was on to Los Angeles, where we were booked for two nights at the Pan Pacific Auditorium. Elvis and his entourage checked into the Beverly Wilshire Hotel. We checked into the more economical Hollywood Knickerbocker Hotel, where we got rooms for seven dollars a night. According to one review of the first concert, the auditorium was "packed to the rafters" with 9,000 cheering, screaming fans who threatened to "break loose in a riot at every hip flip by Presley."

We closed the show with "Hound Dog," with me doing my special guitar riff and Elvis rolling on the floor of the stage with a plaster dog critics later concluded was the RCA Records trademark. It was like old times. Elvis was at his best when he let the child in him come out and play. We were among the few people in Elvis's life who knew the child.

A few days after we returned to Memphis, we had a contract for two days of concerts in Hawaii. Elvis went by ship, traveling on the U.S.S. *Matsonia*; but we took a United Air Lines flight. This time we would break tradition and stay in the same hotel with Elvis, who had reserved the entire fourteenth floor of the Hawaiian Village Hotel. My $12-a-night room was plusher than I usually got on the road.

The two concerts at the Honolulu Stadium attracted nearly 15,000 fans, bringing in more than $32,000 to the promoters. The second day we performed for 10,000 civilians and military personnel from Schofield Barracks Army Base near Pearl Harbor. I was happy to be back on stage again with Elvis, but with Elvis facing the draft, questions about our future lingered.

★ ★ ★

On December 19, 1957, Elvis received word from the draft board that his induction notice was ready. He was told he could drop by the draft board office, if he wished, and pick up the notice himself. That way there would be less likelihood the news would be leaked to the media. That sounded like a good idea to Elvis. Following their suggestion, he drove to the draft board office and picked up the notice. The following day, Elvis stopped by

Sun Records studio to show off his letter of greeting from Uncle Sam. Jack Clement was there when he walked in.

"Jack," said Elvis, "I got drafted."

"We got to talking," says Jack, who had served with honor in the Marines. In music circles Jack was sort of famous because of a photograph *Life* magazine published showing him as part of the Marine honor guard protecting Queen Elizabeth during one of her visits to America. "I got the distinct feeling he was happy about being drafted. He said, 'Well, might as well have fun.' I think he probably did. He seemed kind of excited, like it was going to be an adventure."

No one knows for sure what was going through Elvis's mind at that time, but certainly all those stories about Shanghai wenches, floating bodies, and exploding rockets that I had shared with him out on the road were not far from his thoughts. I had survived military service. So had Jack. Elvis, too, would survive. At issue was whether his career would survive.

That month "Jailhouse Rock" was the No. 1 record on the charts, but closing in quickly was Jerry Lee Lewis's "Great Balls of Fire." With production scheduled to begin in January on Elvis's next movie, *King Creole*, Paramount studio wrote the draft board and asked for a sixty-day deferment, citing the enormous pre-production costs they had invested in the movie. The draft board responded that it would consider such a request, but it would have to come from the inductee himself. Elvis promptly wrote the board a letter requesting a deferment, to which the board responded in the affirmative. Elvis was given until the end of March to finish the movie.

On January 10, 1958, we checked into the Hollywood Knickerbocker. As usual, we planned to work on the soundtrack at Radio Recorders before filming began. Elation over the reconciliation with Elvis was short lived. The Memphis draft board had thrown a wrench into my long-term career goals. Would Elvis put me and the others on some sort of salary during the two years he would be gone? Would Elvis even have a career when he got out of the Army?

Songwriters Jerry Leiber and Mike Stoller were again put in charge of the session. They turned out a respectable slate of four songs for the movie, including "King Creole," "Crawfish," and "Trouble," but their hearts were not in the project. Seasoned session players were brought in to give the soundtrack a Dixieland feel. Paramount had given up trying to get Elvis to record on the soundstage. Not only did Elvis not like the size of the soundstage, he hated the engineering process we went through to get recordings. In a studio, you'd say, "OK, let's do a take" and reach over and turn on the tape recorder and start singing. But on the soundstage we had to wait for all this stuff to get locked up. The engineer up in the control booth would tell the people down below, "OK roll." Everything had a number and a countdown and you had a guy on the soundstage and he had to do something. You're talking about two or three minutes before everything was locked up and ready to go. Reminded me of the Navy.

When filming began, we played the part of Elvis's movie band. This time we were given a few lines to deliver. When Elvis sang "King Creole," we stood behind him on the stage. At one point during the song, Elvis pretended to play a guitar solo. He can be seen looking back over his shoulder at me, a sly grin on his face. That grin wasn't in the script; it was a private joke between us. With his eyes, he was asking me if he was doing his fingers correctly on the solo. When they wanted to shoot the close-up of his hands, I put on Elvis's shirt and played the solo for the camera. At one point, I was handed a banjo to play. It was a prop and didn't have real strings on it. I had never played a banjo, but pretended to play it for the scene. The more I thought about it, the more I realized that everything Elvis was doing had a "pretend" air about it. Before we headed back to Memphis, we did two recording sessions for RCA. Elvis was distracted and the sessions didn't go well. We did get two hits—"Hard Headed Woman," which went to No. 1 in July, and "Wear My Ring Around Your Neck," which peaked at No. 2 in April.

When doomsday arrived it did so with barely a ripple. On March 24, Elvis reported to the induction center in Memphis and then boarded a train for his basic training. As he left for exile into the Army, his biggest musical competitor, Jerry Lee Lewis, scored a Top 20 hit with "Breathless." Elvis must have wondered if the Killer was going to leave anything for him. What he could not possibly have guessed was that "Breathless" would be the last Top 20 pop hit Lewis would have, his career destroyed by his marriage to his teenage cousin.

The week before he left, Elvis answered all the lingering questions about what would happen to his "boys" in his absence. They were simply let go. He called me and Bill to say goodbye. His attitude was like, "So long, see you when I get out." Before leaving, he bought his girlfriend, Anita Wood, a new car. I couldn't believe it. It was like a dream—or a nightmare. Why would Elvis buy his girlfriend a car and not buy one for Bobbie? They had their differences, sure, but Elvis had turned Bill and me out to pasture like broken-down mules, without a penny. We were supposed to be the King's men. In reality, we were the court jesters. People only laughed at us.

★ ★ ★

After Elvis received his physical at Kennedy Veterans Hospital in Memphis, he was sent to Fort Chafee, Arkansas, and then on to Fort Hood, Texas, where he was allowed to rent a home in nearby Killeen for his parents. Despite his statements that he just wanted to be treated like any other soldier, Elvis was given special treatment by the Army. He was allowed to have a sports car, which he drove to visit his parents. Gladys cooked for him, but she was clearly not in good health. They had been told Elvis would be stationed in Germany. Vernon and Gladys planned on relocating in Germany to be near their son, but Gladys had reservations about going overseas.

When Elvis completed basic training on May 31, he was given a furlough, which allowed him to return to Memphis for more than a week. On June 10 he went to Nashville where, at Steve Sholes's frantic pleadings, a recording session had been arranged. We were not invited to the two-day session. We were replaced by Hank Garland on guitar and Bob Moore on bass. D. J. was invited, but not as the main drummer. A number of sides were recorded at the session, including "I Got Stung" and "A Fool Such As I," which Bill and I might well have adopted as our theme songs.

When his furlough was up, Elvis returned to Fort Hood. In August, as his training was coming to an end, he put his parents on the train to Memphis. The day after they arrived, Gladys was admitted to the hospital. When the physician saw that it was serious, he telephoned Elvis, who was given a leave to fly to Memphis. Gladys had an advanced hepatitis infection, but she was conscious and conversed with her son, reassuring him that everything would be all right. While at the hospital, Elvis ran into his old girlfriend from the projects, Betty McMahan, who was employed at the hospital. "He had on his uniform," she recalled. "He just grabbed me, hugged me just like he always did. Just a good friend."

After visiting his mother, Elvis went to Graceland, leaving his father in the hospital with Gladys. The next morning Elvis returned to the hospital and stayed several hours. Early the following morning, Elvis was called back to the hospital: Gladys was dead. When Elvis received the news, he was overcome with grief. At the funeral, nearly three thousand mourners filed past the casket. Four hundred people crammed into the chapel, which had seating for only three hundred. Outside, sixty-five police officers were on duty to control the crowd that had gathered to get a glimpse of the mourners and the celebrities who had arrived for the services.

Noticeably absent from the services were Bill and me. Later it was rumored that we had not attended because we could not afford suits. That explanation was only partially true. I had a couple of relatively new jackets I had purchased to wear in his movie scenes, so I did have something to wear if I wanted to go. What I could not afford were groceries. My total income for the year amounted to only $2,322, all of which resulted from my work on *King Creole*. I had received no income from Elvis since the concert in Hawaii.

When Elvis had an opportunity to give me work again—but didn't—during the recording session in June, it stung. Had Elvis forgotten what it was like to live day to day? I felt the pain Elvis experienced over Gladys's death. I knew what Elvis was going through because I knew how devoted he was to his mother. What I couldn't bring myself to do was to share that pain in a public way. People could damned well think what they wanted to think.

★ ★ ★

After Elvis went overseas, Bill and I went our separate ways, though we stayed in close contact and occasionally worked together on recording projects. With the newly formed Memphis label, Hi Records, just getting off the ground, Bill started spending time at the label's headquarters, a recording studio named Royal Recording. While doing session work with guitarist Reggie Young, he often expressed resentment about the treatment he had received from Elvis. He told Reggie that toward the end of their association with Elvis, he and I were asked not to speak directly to Elvis, except on stage.

For the first week after Elvis left, I drew unemployment. Then I entered into a partnership with Ronald "Slim" Wallace, the truck driver with whom Jack Clement had built a garage studio named Fernwood. Slim had two or three microphones and a little mono tape recorder. I took a few pieces of gear out and we started recording this and that.

One day, Thomas Wayne Perkins, my former paperboy at my old Belz Street address, asked if he could stop by the house and audition for me. Perkins's brother, Luther, was the guitarist in the Johnny Cash band, so I thought it was worth a listen. Musical talent sometimes seems to run in families. The youngster, still a senior in high school, was so nervous when he arrived at my house that he sat on Bobbie's glass-topped coffee table and broke it into little pieces. She was not too happy about that. When he finally got around to singing for me, I liked what I heard, broken glass and all.

I worked with Perkins at Fernwood, but our first demos attracted no interest from the major labels. At one point Wallace and I thought that Mercury Records was interested in Perkins, but for some reason a deal never materialized. The music business is like that. One day everything is in place for a deal. The next day the deal evaporates.

Without Bobbie's job at Sears, we would have been destitute that summer. I certainly wasn't bringing in any money. I don't remember if Bill had a day job or not, but we were both scratching to stay afloat. My work at Fernwood wasn't bringing in much money, but it helped me to keep the faith. I felt that sooner or later something would break in my favor.

One day I was walking along the street when I ran into Gerald Nelson, a disc jockey from Kentucky. We had met some time back at a concert. Gerald told me that he and Fred Burch, a college student, had written a song titled "Tragedy." Fred had snatched the title from a course he was taking on Aristotelian tragedies.

Gerald said he had played the song for Chet Atkins, who had told him it sounded like a hit, but was not a song he could do anything with in Nashville because it wasn't country enough. Encouraged by Atkins's assessment of the song's potential, they had driven to Memphis, to the very cradle of rock 'n' roll.

"We played it for Sam Phillips," says Gerald, "but he said he couldn't use it either."

As I stood on the sidewalk and listened, Gerald sang the song to me, playing the music on his ukulele. I loved it. I told Gerald that I knew just the guy to sing it: Thomas Wayne Perkins. Fred and Gerald felt so encouraged by my reaction that they moved to Memphis to begin new careers as songwriters.

Unhappy with the technical limitations of Fernwood's garage studio, I looked for a better place to record the songs. In exchange for studio time at Hi Records' studio, Gerald sang background on one of their sessions. When we went in to record Thomas Wayne's session, we discovered the studio had installed new equipment; the studio was going to use us as guinea pigs to test the new machine. Thomas Wayne brought three girls from his high school—his girlfriend and her two friends—to sing background. Bill and I were the only musicians.

"It was the first time [the tape machine] was used," says Fred Burch, laughing. "They couldn't get it to work. Finally, someone kicked it and got it going. They cut the song three times and ended up using the first cut. There was no echo in the studio, so they took the tape to WMPS radio, where they had two Ampex machines."

Using the technique I learned from Sam for adding "slapback" to a record, I recorded a simultaneous dub on a master tape at the radio station. This time, instead of offering it to a major label, we put the record out on Fernwood Records. The A-side was an up-tempo song written by Nelson-Burch titled "Saturday Date." The B-side was "Tragedy."

When "Saturday Date" was released in September, it had little impact on radio. But because I believed in the record, I kept pushing it well into the spring of 1959. Finally, lightning struck. A disc jockey in Kentucky flipped the record and started playing the B-side in heavy rotation. As a result, phone requests for "Tragedy" started flooding into the radio station. Before I knew what had happened, I had a hit record.

With its understated instrumentation and lush background vocals, Thomas Wayne's macho-breathless baritone carried the song. "Tragedy" was one of those fifties-type ballads that never failed to get dancers hot and bothered. It was a Memphis thing: A song written by novices barely old enough to vote, sung by the producer's former paperboy, with background vocals provided by high-school girls, and recorded on bartered studio time. It was the stuff of which Memphis music magic was made.

It was like it happened overnight. We didn't have a dime to promote it. As the orders started coming in, we hired a national promotion man, Steve Brodie of Buffalo, New York, to push the record. He said, "I can make this a big hit," so we paid him a nickel a record.

Because we needed an infusion of capital, Wallace and I added a third partner, Memphis attorney Robert Buckalew. Our most immediate problem was getting large orders of records pressed. Working together, Buckalew and Brodie persuaded record pressing plants to give us sixty days' credit because we knew it would be at least that long before the money started trickling in. Once that happened, Brodie started working the song on radio, beginning with his hometown of Buffalo. As it climbed the charts there he focused his attention on larger markets.

By March, "Tragedy" had risen to No. 8 on the national charts, making it a million-seller. Ironically, without trying to compete with Sun Records, I had stolen its thunder. Before "Tragedy" hit, only three records recorded in Memphis had ever scored higher on the pop charts and they were all

Sun Records releases: Jerry Lee Lewis's "Great Balls of Fire" and "Whole Lot of Shakin' Going On" and Carl Perkins's "Blue Suede Shoes."

Trying only to stay afloat, I had made history and a few bucks in the process. We grossed about $600,000. Of course, when the money started coming in and I sat down and started writing checks, it went pretty fast. I remember writing one check for $150,000 to the pressing plants. Oh, that hurt.

After the record hit, I sent a copy to Colonel Parker, who responded on April 2 with a letter. "Have just returned from a promotion trip on Elvis [sic] latest release and LP," he wrote. "Thought it only proper to congratulate you on the fine work you have been doing with Mr. Thomas Wayne. My best wishes are with you and him for a big future." He signed the letter "Colonel."

I paid myself a salary from the record company with the agreement of the two other partners, but most of the money was funneled back into Fernwood Records. We rented an office downtown in the same building where our attorney (and new partner) was located. Later we rented a building on North Main Street and installed a fully equipped studio. It was located next door to a delicatessen that specialized in corned beef. What I remember most about the studio is the plentiful supply of food. I've never eaten so much corned beef in my life.

That spring and summer, I was on top of the world. I had a hit record. I had my own recording studio. It was another one of those rags-to-riches stories of which the music industry is so fond. In March I purchased a C-5 Classic Gibson guitar for $85 from Chicago Musical Instrument Company and I bought a black El Dorado Cadillac with a red interior.

To promote Thomas Wayne's record, I organized a touring band made of myself, Bill, D. J. Fontana, and Reggie Young. I was coming and going so fast, I sometimes lost my sense of direction. Reggie remembers one night when we returned to Memphis at three o'clock in the morning. "We pulled up in front of Scotty's house, stopping out in the middle of the street," recalls Reggie. "He just got out, left the car running, and went into the house and went to bed. Bill or someone slid over and took us home."

I often booked Reggie for sessions at Fernwood. We got to be good friends and usually wound up the sessions by sitting on the curb to drink cheap wine. Reggie went on to become one of the premier session guitarists in the country, working in Memphis with literally hundreds of artists including Neil Diamond, Wilson Pickett, and Dionne Warwick, and later in Nashville with Willie Nelson, Waylon Jennings, and Johnny Cash, going on tour with them when they added Kris Kristofferson to form the Highwaymen. But in those days he was just finding himself as a musician; the Blue Moon Boys were among his heroes.

"That whole deal of Scotty, Bill, and Elvis was unique," Reggie said in an interview for this book. "Scotty and Bill were as much a part of Elvis's music as he was. No one sounded like that. You always copy records you can play the parts to. Scotty's parts, they weren't real easy to play, but they were playable. They weren't something you couldn't figure out. I'm sure a lot of would-be guitar players sat down with Elvis's records and copied Scotty's licks. He was the first one to make people want to do that."

Fernwood followed up "Tragedy" with a number of Thomas Wayne recordings, including: "Scandalizing My Name," "Girl Next Door," "Just Beyond," and "Guilty of Love," some of which were written by Burch and Nelson. One Thomas Wayne release, "This Time," was penned by a newcomer to Memphis, a young Georgian named Chips Moman.[9] Unfortunately, none of Thomas Wayne's subsequent releases achieved the success of "Tragedy."

In the aftermath of "Tragedy," Sharri Paullus, a songwriter whose physician husband had started a record label named Rave Records, took two promising instrumental ideas to Fernwood. For that project, I asked Bill to play bass and saxophonist Ace Cannon to do the horn work. The finished product, with its gritty, hypnotic groove, is remarkably similar to records later recorded by the Bill Black Combo. The songs, "The Gambler" and "It's Not Fun Loving You," were released on Rave Records.

As the year ended, I reported my highest income to date—$13,547.64—but the money from Thomas Wayne's hit was quickly petering out at Fernwood.

★ ★ ★

Elvis stayed on the charts in 1959 with songs recorded in Nashville before he left the country. He adjusted to the Army better than he, or anyone else, thought, but it was clear after he arrived at his station outside Friedberg, Germany, that he was going to receive special privileges. Originally the Army said he would be assigned to the crew of a medium Patton tank. However, after he arrived in Germany in October 1958, it was announced that he would serve sixteen months as a scout Jeep driver. His

9. Moman went on to become one of the most successful record producers in Memphis. His 1969 sessions with Elvis Presley produced a number of hits, including "Suspicious Minds" and "In the Ghetto."

father and grandmother arrived four days later and Elvis was given a pass to visit them at a luxurious spa several miles outside Friedberg.

Elvis rented a two-story house for his father and grandmother; then he was given permission to move in with them. The Army allowed him to commute to the base. If I had any concerns about my friend's personal safety in the Army, they quickly dissipated when I read press accounts of Elvis's special treatment. *It's sure not like it was in the old days*, I thought. *Hell, he's missing half the fun.*

In November, Elvis's social life improved considerably when he was introduced to 14-year-old Priscilla Beaulieu at an Army party. Priscilla was the daughter of an Air Force captain stationed in Wiesbaden. He dated her several times, taking her to movies or for a drive in his BMW. He must have chuckled to himself over his involvement with her. Jerry Lee Lewis had married a girl only a year younger than Priscilla and he was roasted by the press. When a reporter asked Elvis about Lewis's marriage, he said, "I'd rather not talk about his marriage, except that if he really loves her, I guess it's all right."

Elvis was not as understanding of May-December romances when his father started dating a young married woman, Dee Stanley,[10] only a year after his mother's death. The same month he met Priscilla, he hired a South African fitness instructor to give him massages. He paid him $15,000, roughly the equivalent of the total salary he paid me for the first three years we worked together.

Before his discharge from the Army in March 1960, it was announced that his next movie would be *G.I. Blues*. Colonel Parker was delighted to be getting him back in circulation. Elvis's income had dropped to only $2 million in 1958, Parker told Nashville reporters. On the day before he left Germany, the Army held a huge press conference for him at a gym in Bad Nauheim. He walked in the door flanked by MPs and wearing red stripes and a gold braid. Standing near the door was Marion Keisker, by then a captain in the Women's Air Force.

"Hi, hon," said Marion.

Elvis was shocked when he saw her. "What do I do? Kiss you or salute you?"

Marion flung her arms around him.

The Army officer in charge was outraged. He accused Marion of staging the event. He ordered her to leave, but she refused, citing her position

---

10. Vernon Presley married Dee Stanley on July 3, 1960 at the home of her brother. Elvis did not attend the ceremony.

as assistant manager of Armed Forces television. For Elvis, it couldn't have been a better sendoff.

★ ★ ★

Elvis's first stop in the United States was at Fort Dix, New Jersey. His plane landed in a blinding snowstorm. Knowing Elvis, it was probably white-knuckle for him all the way. An Army major told assembled reporters Elvis had "behaved himself in a manner so as to cast great credit on the Army." For two hours Elvis answered reporters' questions, announcing that he had seven movies lined up and he was scheduled for a television appearance with Frank Sinatra. So that people would not get the wrong impression, Colonel Parker told reporters that although Elvis had a $1.6 million income in 1959, 91 percent of that went for income taxes.

When Elvis returned to Memphis he discovered the city's musical balance of power had altered considerably. Jerry Lee Lewis had fallen from grace and was in the midst of a steep nosedive into obscurity. Sun Records hadn't had a Top 20 hit on the pop charts since Johnny Cash's "Guess Things Happen That Way" in July 1958. The biggest hit makers in the city were those two former members of the Blue Moon Boys: Bill and myself. I had scored my Top 10 hit with Thomas Wayne and Bill had cracked the Top 20 with "Smokie (Parts 1 & 2)," recorded by the newly formed Bill Black Combo.

Even as Elvis unpacked his bags at Graceland, Bill had another hit zooming up the charts, an instrumental titled "White Silver Sands." In April, "White Silver Sands" was No. 13 on the charts and Elvis's "Stuck On You" was No. 11. The Bill Black Combo evolved from the Hi Records session band that Bill had organized with Reggie Young. An executive from London Records, which had the distribution rights for Hi, was in the studio one day and heard them playing. He suggested that they form a band. They didn't need much encouragement. They named the group the Bill Black Combo. "We were equal owners of the group," says Reggie. "We tried to figure who to name it after. It was either Bill or me. I had been working at the *Louisiana Hayride* with Johnny Horton, so I had some name recognition. But Bill had been with Elvis and knew more disc jockeys than I did."

With Bill on bass, Reggie on guitar, Carl McAvoy on piano, Jerry Arnold on drums, and Martin Wills on sax, the Bill Black Combo popularized a whole new genre of groove-based instrumentals. "I tuned my guitar down a couple of steps, where it was real low, and I played rhythm with a pencil as a pick—that's how that shuffle kind of came about," explains Reggie.

As "Smokie (Parts 1 & 2)" peaked on the charts, Reggie received his draft notice. He left the group for two years, but when he returned he picked up where he had left off. Bill and I remained friends, and helped each other on projects whenever we could, but I had my own thing going and never considered becoming a member of Bill's group. In my heart, I still felt everything would work out with Elvis. I believed in Elvis, perhaps more than Elvis believed in himself.

As expected, Elvis contacted Bill and me when he returned to Memphis. He had a recording session scheduled in Nashville on March 21 and a television special with Frank Sinatra set the following week in Miami. Would we be able to hit the road again with him? I said yes, but Bill declined, citing his responsibilities to the Bill Black Combo.

In 1960 Bill Black was easily the most famous bass player in America. A headline in the *Press-Scimitar* proclaimed "Bill Black Getting the Top Breaks." The story, written by Robert Johnson to announce an upcoming appearance of the combo on the *Ed Sullivan Show*, said: "Things are breaking wide open for Bill Black, the Memphis musician who started out with Elvis, went with him all the way to the big time, then got lost for a time in the backwash."

Even without the success of the combo, it is doubtful Bill would have signed on with Elvis again. "Bill was upset because of the way they treated him" says his wife, Evelyn, in an interview for this book. "If it hadn't have been for him and Scotty and D. J., Elvis would never have been as popular as he was. He thought a lot of Elvis and he missed playing with him. He wasn't mad. It was more like he was disappointed. He would have liked to have stayed with Elvis until he died."

I went out to Graceland to meet with Elvis. I hadn't seen him in nearly two years, but it was like old times. Elvis didn't say anything to me about me not going to Gladys's funeral. I didn't say anything to Elvis about being left high and dry. We talked about the upcoming recording session and the Sinatra show.

Elvis told me that RCA had offered to build him a studio at Graceland so that he could record whenever he felt like it. He asked me if I would be interested in taking care of the studio for him. I said that would be great, although we never talked about a salary.

Elvis complained about how ragged his Gibson J-200 looked. Because I had obtained an endorsement deal from Gibson several years back I offered to send Elvis's guitar to the Chicago Musical Instrument Company to have it refinished and repaired, and to have his name inlaid on the fingerboard. I wrote a letter to O. K. Houck Piano Company and asked them to ship Elvis's guitar to Chicago Instrument. In a separate letter to Chicago Instrument, I wrote, "I would like for you to do some extra inlay work on the front, nothing too elaborate, something a little different possibly that he would like very much. I will leave the design of this to your discretion."

Since Elvis wanted the guitar to use at the session in Nashville, Chicago Musical Instrument shipped it air express to me in care of Chet Atkins at RCA in Nashville. The guitar arrived in time for the session. It looked great. Elvis was pleased with the work. Not until years later, when I began work on this book, did I compare the serial number of the guitar I had shipped to Chicago with the serial number of the guitar that arrived in Nashville. I discovered that the serial numbers did not match. Instead of repairing Elvis's old guitar, they had shipped a brand new guitar. I was never able to find out what happened to the original guitar or get an explanation for the substitution.

March was a pivotal month, not only in my relationship with Elvis but in my relationship with Bobbie. Before I left for the Nashville session, Bobbie got pregnant with our first—and only—child, a girl we named Andrea, who was born on November 25, 1960.

Elvis showed up at the Nashville studio wearing his Army uniform and using the name Sivle Yelserp (Elvis Presley spelled backward). He was becoming more and more eccentric, but in a playful way. Humor was his way of connecting with people.

After recording two ballads, "Stuck on You" and "Fame and Fortune," Elvis and the band boarded a train in Nashville and headed south to Miami. I remember seeing people lining the tracks along the way. The trip was supposed to be secret, but Parker, in an effort to get publicity, called every small-town newspaper along the way. At some stops, Parker got Elvis to stand on the back platform, like he had seen presidents do, and wave to the cheering crowds.

When we reached Miami, we checked into the Hotel Fontainebleau. The television special was scheduled to be taped in the grand ballroom of the hotel and aired at a later date. Elvis was backed by the Nelson Riddle Orchestra, which was augmented with D. J., myself, and the Jordanaires. Two weeks before we arrived there was a news story in which the show's co-producer, noted songwriter Sammy Cahn, had complained about Elvis's expensive fee. Out of a total budget of $250,000 Elvis was paid

$150,000. Complained Cahn: "That means after we pay Presley, we have $100,000 to pay for Sinatra, Sammy Davis, Joey Bishop, Peter Lawford . . . and Nelson Riddle and his forty-two musicians." Asked to explain, he said, "That's Sinatra. He wants to do what he wants to do."

It was fun going to Miami, but musically it was a far cry from the good old days when our music was raw and bristling with energy—and needless to say, D. J. and I didn't receive a big cut of the bounty. Of course, we were used to that by then. The news story mentioned the Tom Hansen Dancers, whoever they were, but there was no mention of D. J. or myself.

In April there were more recording sessions in Nashville for an album, *Elvis Is Back*—two singles, "It's Now or Never" and "Are You Lonesome Tonight," went to No. 1 later in the year—and additional sessions for the soundtrack for *G.I. Blues*. When filming began in May, D. J. and I were hired as extras. They had us wear these Bavarian outfits with short britches. We had to get out there at five or six in the morning, when it was cool, and had to get leg makeup. All that trouble and you couldn't even see our legs in the movie.

By the start of summer, I began to suspect that my earlier optimism might have been misplaced. No one was talking about going out on tour. The session work was nice and it paid well, but it wasn't enough to support a family. My involvement in the movies was regressing. Elvis was back, but my income was plummeting. The money that had rolled in from "Tragedy" was gone now, spent on new ventures at Fernwood. More to the point, Elvis never again mentioned his offer of hiring me to run a studio at Graceland. It was yet another promise that never materialized. Sometimes he got very excited about things and then just moved on to something else to get excited about.

★ ★ ★

With Fernwood Records in dire straits—I had sold my share later in the year—I started looking around for a day job. I went by to talk to Sam, who told me that in addition to the new studio he was building on Madison he was buying out a studio in Nashville. He needed someone to oversee both studios. I hadn't had a regular job since my days as a hatter at the dry cleaners, but working for Sam seemed like a good idea. I would no longer be playing for thousands of screaming fans, but I would still be in the music business and I would have a regular income.

In June 1960 the "Sun-Liners," a newsletter put out by Sun Records, announced the title of Johnny Cash's latest album, *So Doggone Lonesome*, along with a release from newcomer Bobbie Jean titled "You Burned the Bridges." Also, in the newsletter was an announcement that I had joined the staff of Sam C. Phillips Enterprises as production manager. In that capacity I would supervise all aspects of studio operation, including sessions, mastering, and new artist acquisition. "His will be a full-time job with Sun PI, et al., but he may get together with his old buddies, Elvis Presley and Bill Black, for a gig now and then," said the newsletter. "Persons wishing to utilize Sam C. Phillips Recording facilities for recording may reach Scotty in Memphis at Jackson 7-8233."

My photograph was prominently displayed in a *Press-Scimitar* feature that heralded the opening of the new studio at 639 Madison. Sam Phillips told the reporter, Edwin Howard, that he had invested $750,000 in the new facility in an effort to stay competitive.

"Woodshed recordings have had it," Sam said. "You've got to have latitude today—all the electronic devices, built-in high and low frequency equalization and attenuation, echoes, and metering on everything."

The new studio, on a site formerly occupied by the Midas Muffler Shop, had all that and more. Howard asked if there was a possibility Elvis Presley might use the new facilities. "I don't know," said Sam. "Of course, RCA has its own studio in Nashville, and Elvis has been cutting there. But Ed Hinds of RCA's Nashville office is coming over for our opening. Something might develop eventually." I knew there was fat chance of that: I knew Colonel Parker would never allow Elvis to record again in a studio owned by Sam Phillips.

Nineteen-sixty was a watershed year for me. At age twenty-nine, with a child on the way, I had come to terms with my life. For six years, I had been waiting for the economic situation with Elvis to change. Whenever I thought about it, it gave me a sinking feeling.

In my heart I knew that Elvis was not responsible for all the things that had gone wrong in my life, but somewhere, deep inside I could not help but think that Elvis could have eased the pain I felt on a daily basis. I don't know if you, the reader, have ever had a hit record. But it is a seductive event that changes your perspective on life.

Why can I not have what I had before?

It is one of those questions for which there is no answer.

Shortly after I settled into my new routine at the studio, I received a telephone call from someone from my past. Frankie Tucker had seen my photograph in the newspaper. She reminded me of our liaison in West Memphis in 1953. Then she dropped a bombshell. She had had my child six years ago, a little girl she had named Vikki. Would I like to see my daughter?

Who could say no to that? That news had come at a low point in my life, but I couldn't help but think that it might be a blessing.

Vikki recalls her first meeting with me with that type of fuzzy nostalgia usually reserved for a first Christmas or a first kiss. "I pretended I was asleep," she says. "He was rubbing my back and looking me over. He said [to my mother], 'Oh, she has my nose and she has your smile, your lips.'" For years after that initial introduction, she made a mad dash for the television whenever she heard Elvis's name or voice. If it was an old show, she would see me standing behind Elvis, always to his right; if it was new footage, she would wonder where I was.

"If it wasn't him, I would be so disappointed," she says. "We saw each other only once a year—mostly because mother's husband was jealous. He wouldn't allow Elvis albums in the house."

★ 9 ★

MY FIRST ALBUM WITH ROYALTIES

By the time I began working at Sam Phillips's Recording Service, Sun Records had not placed a record in the Top 20 in over two years.[11] The record label was on a downward spiral. The two major talents left in Sam's stable were Jerry Lee Lewis and newcomer Charlie Rich, whose song "Lonely Weekends" had been a regional hit in 1959. Johnny Cash had moved on to greener pastures; Carl Perkins seemingly had dropped out of sight. The reigning Memphis hitmakers were Elvis's former band members, myself with "Tragedy" and Bill Black with his "Smokie (Parts 1 & 2)." Elvis climbed back to the top of the charts that year with "Stuck on You" and "It's Now or Never," but neither song was recorded in Memphis.

As head of production, I presided over a state-of-the-art facility that the *Press-Scimitar* described as "plush" and "futuristic." It boasted a sundeck on the roof and an executive bar. Sam moved from his "no desk" office on Union Avenue to a penthouse office where he had a jukebox-like stereo built into his desk. Seven gold records hung on the wall; none bore Elvis Presley's name. Although Sam didn't come right out and say so, the new studio represented a significant shift in his approach to the music industry. While his efforts previously had been focused on finding new talent for Sun Records, he now was more interested in selling studio time to other labels so that they could record their newly discovered talent. Time was a less temperamental commodity in which to deal. As soon as he had the new studio up and running, he turned his attention to opening a studio in downtown Nashville at the Masonic Building on 7th Avenue North. It was my job to oversee production at both facilities.

With Fernwood Records in disarray, I brought Thomas Wayne over to Sam's studio, where I produced another Nelson-Burch ballad, "The Quiet Look," for Sam's new Phillips label. The record didn't hit, but I stubbornly

---

11. Johnny Cash's "Guess Things Happen That Way"/"Come In Stranger" peaked at No. 14 in July 1958.

continued to work with Thomas Wayne, adhering to the music industry belief that "once a hit, always a threat."

I also engineered several sessions with Jerry Lee Lewis, one of which became a source of contention between the singer and the local musicians union. I don't remember if they actually canceled his card or what, but he got in trouble with them and was suspended. He wasn't allowed to play until it was cleared up. Meanwhile, Sam was desperate for a record. I did the tracks with another piano player and got Jerry Lee to overdub his voice, so that way the union couldn't do anything. I wasn't anti-union; I was trying to help Sam out of a jam. In fact, it was during this period that I became very active in the union, at one point serving on the board of directors. In those days the union was not affiliated with the AFL-CIO; it was strictly a fraternal-type organization. Everyone understood that blacks and hillbillies were not welcome in the union. They couldn't keep either group out legally, but they made it obvious they didn't want them. That pissed me off. I ran for the board of directors—and we got a new president in there. I told all the record companies, "Someday you'll be glad if you just file the contracts and pay your union dues. If a guy wants to work for nothing, that's his business. Just make it legal."

Lewis's problems with the union were indicative of the turn his life had taken in general. Always temperamental, the roasting he took in the media for his marriage to his teenage cousin—and the subsequent nosedive his records took on the charts—made him even more unpredictable. One of the stories making the rounds at that time involved a tour he was on with Chuck Berry. Lewis had been closing the show for several performances, so the story goes, when the promoter informed him that it was Berry's turn to close. After an argument, Lewis finally agreed to go out first. At the end of a thirty-minute set, he whipped out a can of lighter fluid, soaked the piano, and set it afire.

"I'd like to see any son of a bitch top that," he reportedly said as he walked off stage.

In an effort to escape the notoriety and perhaps cash in on the success Bill Black was having, Lewis recorded an instrumental in 1960 titled "In the Mood"/"I Get the Blues When it Rains." He released the song under the name Hawk, but when the record, which was issued on Phillips Records, failed to fly, he dropped the moniker and went back to being plain old Jerry Lee. After several years of near misses on the pop charts, Lewis left Sun Records in 1963 and signed with Smash, a subsidiary of Mercury Records in Nashville. That move signaled more than a change of address, it represented a change in musical direction, nudging him from pop/rock into more of a country sound.

Charlie Rich had been discovered by my A&R predecessor, Bill Justis, who had scored in November 1957 with a gritty Top 20 instrumental titled "Raunchy." Justis felt Rich was a superb pianist. He liked the demo tapes Rich brought him so much that he hired him as a session player in Sam's studio. One day, during lunch at Taylor's cafe with Rich and *Press-Scimitar* reporter Edwin Howard, Justis had some advice for his new piano player: "I keep telling you, Charlie: You're never gonna make it in the record business till you learn to play bad."

Sam released seven Rich singles on Phillips Records—including "Just A Little Sweet" and "School Days"—but the records never got beyond a regional audience. When Rich signed with RCA Records in 1963, Sam sent a telegram to the label stating that Rich still had an unfilled verbal contract with him. As a result of Sam's letter, RCA suspended his contract and Rich sued Sam in chancery court charging him with breach of contract. The lawsuit was settled to Rich's advantage, but his rough new beginning with RCA produced only one minor hit, "Big Boss Man," and it wasn't until he moved on to Smash Records that he got a big hit with "Mohair Sam."

With the talent pool at Sun and Phillips muddied by bad luck, lawsuits, and petty bickering, I focused my attention on the day-to-day operation of the studios. One day while Sam was out of town, I and engineer/consultant John Carroll started rewiring the control room of the Memphis studio. Sam was famous for being tight with his pennies. The best way to get something done, I discovered, was just to go ahead and do it, especially if it involved the expenditure of money. When Sam returned to the studio earlier than expected and saw the mess—wires were strewn about the floor of the control room—he was moderately horrified; but when he saw the finished product a couple of weeks later, he was so pleased he asked us to rewire the studio in Nashville the same way.

What Carroll remembers most about those days were the long hours we put in. "I'd work all day at the television station and radio station and go down there and work all night at Sam's," says Carroll. "Scotty was doing pretty much the same thing, except he was doing it at the studio."

Each day, at one o'clock in the morning, Carroll and I followed the same ritual. "Someone would go to the Krystal downtown and bring back a bushel basket of Krystal [hamburgers]," says Carroll. "It was nothing out of the ordinary for me to eat a dozen at a time."

Carroll always gave me credit for being one of the originators of the isolation technique of recording. "[Sam's] studio was fine as far as its acoustical properties were concerned, except you couldn't keep one instrument out of another instrument's microphone," says Carroll. "Scotty started using baffles. He'd partition areas for different instruments and that worked out real well. The general philosophy was to have a big open room and record it live, like at a concert."

I got the idea of using baffles from the experiment that took place at the Hollywood soundstage when engineers constructed baffled rooms around us. That setup didn't work with Elvis on that day, but it did work in Sam's studio once I got everything set up properly. Sam's studio had a hard tile floor, but there were baffles in the walls that you could open up. If a sound was bouncing, you could arrange the baffles so that it would be absorbed. If you put a full orchestra in the studio, there was no problem. But if you put a small group with a drummer out in the middle of the room, the sound would bounce every which way. I talked Sam into building a drum stand to get it off the floor. Then we added baffles out on the floor. I called them separators. If you had two guys sit beside each other, I would put a baffle between them. They could see each other but the baffles broke up the sound waves from the amplifiers.

Toward the end of 1960, Bill Black scored a monster hit with an instrumental version of "Don't Be Cruel." I talked to Sam about doing some instrumentals of our own. "Yeah, we'll do that," Sam told me. But the weeks stretched out to months and it didn't happen. Sam was quicker at saying yes than he was at giving the final approval. With Sam yes sometimes meant no.

That summer, Robbie Dawson, a young singer with a group called the Carousels, started doing backup work at the studio, backing Ace Cannon and others. I started taking her out on dates. "I remember one club where if you didn't have a tie they would loan you one," says Robbie in an interview for this book. "Once I got to know him, I wanted to be around him. He's jolly, you might say. If you are a person he likes, he lets you know in a hurry."

Sam told Robbie she sang like Kitty Wells, but her singing career never got off the ground. My affair with Robbie in 1960 was brief (she also dated Elvis's cousin, Bobby Smith, around that time), but she was destined to re-enter my life further down the road.

★ ★ ★

In February 1961 I joined Elvis for two performances at Ellis Auditorium in Memphis. Also in the band that night were D. J. Fontana, Floyd Cramer on piano, Boots Randolph on sax, and the Jordanaires. Conspicuously absent was Bill Black, who had continued to put distance between himself and the Presley organization. Bill remained angry over the way he had been treated, and he occasionally expressed those feelings to family and friends, but mostly he kept his hurt feelings to himself.

The shows at Ellis Auditorium marked Elvis's first live performance since the Sinatra television special in March 1960. He had made three movies and recorded three soundtracks during the eleven months since that last performance. For the remainder of the decade, Colonel Parker would push him to complete three movies a year. The way Parker figured it, Elvis's price of $1 million per movie was more lucrative than doing a concert tour.

After the release of *G.I. Blues*, critics accused Elvis of abandoning rock 'n' roll. I found that amusing. We never thought we were playing rock 'n' roll. I considered it pop music. Our music had always been ranked on the pop charts. If my guitar solos were later used to define rock 'n' roll that was fine with me, as long as people realized it represented only one style with which I was experimenting. I never liked the term rock 'n' roll for Elvis and what we were doing. Rock 'n' roll, to me, was strictly more black blues—LaVern Baker, artists of that era. That's what rock 'n' roll came out of. They used that term so much in their lyrics.

What we did was more bop, more out of the old jazz bop thing, with a country-blues feel to it. Like Bill Haley. I consider him more bop. He had a great jazz guitar player. That solo on "Rock Around the Clock" will stand forever. The only thing I came close to with that type feel was the solo on "King Creole." Michael Jackson was considered by some people to be the king of pop, but I don't consider anything he did pop. He was more rock 'n' roll. Is "Don't Be Cruel" rock 'n' roll? No, it's pop. "Heartbreak Hotel"? Go over the later things Elvis did. Are they rock 'n' roll? What he did is not even close to what the Rolling Stones do.

Certainly there was nothing rock 'n' roll about the concerts that day at Ellis Auditorium. Proceeds from the concerts and the $100-a-plate luncheon that preceded them were earmarked for local charities. It was the social event of the year. Tennessee Governor Buford Ellington, who had issued a proclamation celebrating "Elvis Presley Day," was in attendance, along with Memphis Mayor Henry Loeb. RCA used the occasion to honor

Elvis for selling 75 million records. I cringed whenever I heard numbers like that. I was lucky to eke out ten thousand dollars a year.

Happily I was able to put all that out of my head when I was on stage with Elvis. The music was the thing, the reason I endured everything. No matter how much time elapsed between performances, the onstage communication between Elvis and me was always in sync. We possessed a unique, some would say psychic, ability to know where the other was going musically. At times, I felt as though I were reading Elvis's thoughts; it was that intense.

There were plenty of times—when Bobbie needed things or our daughter, Andrea, needed to go to the doctor, or when it was time to file taxes—that I wondered why I bothered to remain on call for Elvis, or why I played my guitar at all, but once we were on stage together and the music was flowing and the crowds were cheering, there was never any question about why I was doing it.

The two shows at Ellis Auditorium were typical Colonel Parker concoctions. They included an impressionist, a comedian, a tap dancer, and a team of acrobats. The music created by the Blue Moon Boys may have spawned a cultural revolution, but for Colonel Parker it was just business as usual. We played seventeen songs that day, beginning with "Heartbreak Hotel" and ending with "Hound Dog," the song we always closed with. It was our most requested song. He'd start out, "You ain't nothin' but a Hound Dog," and they'd just go to pieces. They'd always react the same way. There'd be a riot every time.

I wrote out the playlist for that day on a sheet of stationery I had saved from the Hotel Fontainebleau. There were sixteen songs on the list, along with the key for each song. On the line following "Hound Dog" I scribbled, "Get the hell out!"

After the show Elvis hosted an all-night party at Graceland. Bobbie and I didn't go. We no longer felt comfortable in Elvis's private world. Elvis had flown Priscilla Beaulieu to Memphis from Germany for Christmas, but she left after celebrating New Year's with him and was not there for the celebration that followed the shows at Ellis Auditorium. Elvis had asked her father if she could move to Memphis, but he told Elvis he didn't think that was a good idea. Priscilla made Parker nervous. Jerry Lee Lewis's career was destroyed almost overnight by his marriage to his teenage cousin; Parker urged Elvis to be discreet.

In March, Elvis flew to Honolulu to begin work on his next movie, *Blue Hawaii.* While there he performed in a benefit concert to raise money for a memorial to the U.S.S. *Arizona,* one of the battleships sunk in Pearl Harbor by the Japanese. Performing with him were Floyd Cramer, D. J. Fontana, Boots Randolph, the Jordanaires, Minnie Pearl (who closed the first half of the show), in addition to several other Nashville performers, and myself. Since I had made several stops in Pearl Harbor while serving in the Navy, the concert had a homecoming feel to it. You feel this air of tranquility there. It's restful. It's in the air.

The Hawaiian concert was notable for two reasons: First, it was one of the longest sets Elvis had played in a long time (45 minutes); secondly, it was the last public performance he would give for more than seven years. Wearing the gold jacket he had first worn in 1957, Elvis closed the show with a rocking five-and-a-half minute version of "Hound Dog."

It was the last time I ever saw Hawaii.

★ ★ ★

With Elvis all but invisible as a recording artist, I settled into a new career as a studio manager and technician. The technology of recording had always fascinated me. I wasn't getting rich working for Sam, but it provided me with a steady income, something I had not had since I worked as a hatter. By October 1963 I had obtained a new guitar under my endorsement deal with Gibson: a Gibson Super 400 (Sunburst model). I traded my old guitar—the blond Gibson S 400—to record producer Chips Moman for a set of vibes, a small classical guitar, and eighty dollars in cash. I had been asking Sam for money to buy a set of vibes for the studio, but Sam said he didn't have the money. I sacrificed my guitar.

Memphis was exploding with hit records. Carla Thomas had cracked the Top 20 in 1961 with "Gee Whiz," recorded across town at Satellite, the studio owned by Jim Stewart and Estelle Axton. They followed up that hit later in the year with "Last Night," an instrumental by a young group of studio musicians who recorded under the name the Mar-Keys. "Last Night" peaked at No. 2. The following year, with the name of the studio changed to Stax, they scored with another monster instrumental, "Green Onions," recorded by Booker T. and the MGs.

I told Sam that I really wanted to try my hand at doing instrumentals.

Sam didn't say no; he didn't say yes. He kept putting me off, promising to give it some thought. I couldn't figure it out. The Memphis studio was often booked, but the studio in Nashville was generating more business. I was a guitarist of some renown who wanted to record an album of instrumentals in Sam's studio. Memphis was quickly gaining a reputation as a recording center for instrumentals. Why wouldn't Sam jump at the opportunity?

In November 1963 Stax scored again with "Walking the Dog." You couldn't walk out onto the street in Memphis without stumbling over a hit record, or so it seemed. That same month former Sun Records artist, Roy Orbison, placed high on the charts with his "Mean Woman Blues," recorded in Nashville. I felt extremely frustrated. Memphis studios were gaining a reputation for churning out hit instrumentals: the Bill Black Combo; Booker T. & the MGs; the Mar-Keys. Why wouldn't Sam let me see what I could do? Maybe I could record a hit; maybe I couldn't. All I wanted was the chance to be competitive.

That fall, almost in desperation, I asked Stan Kesler, who worked at the studio as an engineer—and several musicians—to come in on a Sunday morning when the studio was not booked so that we could try our hand at a few instrumentals. We had recorded three or four instrumental demos by the time Sam Phillips showed up unexpectedly at the studio, interrupting the session. I don't remember if he got angry, but it ended up that I paid the studio myself for the use of the facility, even though I was working there.

The tensions from the studio carried over into my marriage. We did what couples often do in those circumstances: We bought a house and moved to Raleigh, a relatively new suburb in northeast Memphis. I was miserable. Bobbie and I were fighting all the time. Sam hadn't shown any interest in me recording instrumentals. I was still being called in to play on Elvis's recording sessions for his albums and movie soundtracks, but that was not very satisfying financially or creatively. By that point, my only direct income from Elvis was a yearly Christmas bonus of $500.

To escape the frustrations I was experiencing with Bobbie and Sam, I spent more time in the Nashville studio, where I met Billy Sherrill. The Alabaman was already working at the studio when Sam bought it; when it changed ownership he stayed on, working for Sam as an engineer. As a result, he and I became close friends. We had a lot in common. Billy was six years younger, but we shared the same Southern heritage and we liked the same type of music.

Billy hadn't worked for Sam long when he attracted the attention of executives at Epic Records in Nashville, who hired him as a producer. One of his first artists was newcomer Tammy Wynette. After leaving Memphis in 1956, she had moved to Birmingham, where she first got her foot in the door of the music industry as a songwriter. During one of my frequent trips to Nashville, Billy asked me why I hadn't done an album of instrumentals. Why indeed? When Billy suggested we do an album together for Epic Records, I jumped at the chance.

"I'd like to take the credit for having the idea," explained Billy in an interview for this book. "I think Scotty was too shy back then to want to be the star of his own album. I had always admired Scotty's style. I think he had the most unique style of any guitar player in the world. He did it before anyone else did it—those rock 'n' roll licks. I wanted to capitalize on the fact that he was the man who played the guitar that changed the world."

Billy Sherrill assembled an all-star cast for the session, which took place in late February or early March 1964. In addition to myself on lead guitar, he had D. J. Fontana and Buddy Harmon on drums; Boots Randolph on sax; Bill Purcell on piano; Jerry Kennedy on second guitar; Bob Moore on bass; and, of course, the Jordanaires.

"We gathered in a studio, and it was like, 'Well, what are we going to do?'" recalled Billy. "Someone said, 'Don't Be Cruel,' so we got Elvis's record out and listened to it and everyone did what they did on the record, except Scotty who would do what the voice did."

We went down the list:

Hound Dog	Milk Cow Blues
Loving You	Don't Money Honey
Mystery Train	My Baby Left Me
Don't Be Cruel	Heartbreak Hotel
Love Me Tender	That's All Right
Mean Woman Blues	

Billy wanted to title the album, *The Guitar That Changed The World*, and I reluctantly went along with that, although privately I feared people would think I was boasting.

"I admire Scotty and I admire his contribution to music," says Billy. "He's in a class by himself. He is the rock 'n' roll player of the century. All those guys that came along, Jimi Hendrix, Eric Clapton, they can play faster, sharper, more compelling licks, but Scotty did it first. I'm sure there are better guitar players than Scotty that are around today. But they fed on his creativity. I don't know where he got his from—God, I guess."

The liner notes on the album, written by Memphis *Press-Scimitar* reporter Robert Johnson, pointed out that I had played lead guitar on all the original recordings, with the exception of "Love Me Tender." Johnson wrote:

> *Scotty was part of the most amazing musical adventure of modern times, the rise from rags to riches and international fame of Elvis Presley. His was the other guitar—the lead guitar! This album grew out of the fantastic experience of being at the side of the man who has sold more millions of records than any other singer in history. And Scotty Moore's guitar has been heard on more million-record sellers than any other guitar.*

The Guitar That Changed The World was one of Billy Sherrill's first projects as a producer, but he went on to become one of the most successful producers and songwriters in country music history. He had hits with Tammy Wynette, George Jones, Charlie Rich, Johnny Paycheck, Patti Page, and dozens of others. Today, when he looks back at the album he did with me, he wishes more had been done to promote it. "The record company at the time didn't see the potential of the album and didn't work on it all that much," he says. "I think Scotty Moore made history. I was glad to be a part of that history."

I was ecstatic over the album. For the first time in my career, I had a project that was my very own. For the first time, I had an album that would pay *me* royalties. When I got back to Memphis, I told Sam Phillips about the project, thinking he would be happy I had a deal with a major record label. Sam didn't say much when he told him; he sort of nodded and mumbled.

A few days later, I received a hand-delivered letter from Sam dated March 17, 1964. "As you know I am real concerned about the events of the past week-end, and feel I must tell you that I feel a real trust has been handled with impropriety," Sam said in the letter. "I think under the circumstance [sic] all purposes, both for you and me, would be best served if you began to seek a new association."

Sam was firing me because I recorded an album. I couldn't believe it. Sam's letter continued:

> *I do not want you to feel that I do not appreciate your real and genuine dedication and concern for the companies you are associated with, but my faith has been severely taken to task, therefore, your continued affiliation with us will not be what I feel is a comfortable*

relationship. I do not, however hold any malice in the matter and shall, and do, hold you in high regard. Also, your presence is welcome at all times and certainly until you make another connection that is satisfactory to you and your family. Further, please do not feel out of pride you have to leave immediately. This is not the case. As a matter of fact, you will be needed to help us avoid another "immediate" departure. I shall be happy to recommend you, both as a person and as an employee, to whomever you approach for employment.

I went home and told Bobbie.

"Aw, he does that all the time," Bobbie said. "He doesn't mean it."

"No, he means it this time," I said. "He put it in writing."

Bobbie doesn't recall me being particularly upset. It gets to a point in the music business, if you stay in it long enough, where you are not surprised by unexpected betrayals or sudden reversals of fortune. The music business was still a toddler. People just made up the rules as they went along. There was no guidebook.

"For Scotty, It was like, 'Well, I have to find another job,'" said Bobbie. "Sam had promised to do an instrumental album with him and he kept putting it off."

Many years later, when Billy was talking to my co-author about the album, he said that he never knew that I got fired for doing the recording. Proud to the core, I had kept it a secret. Said Billy: "That was chicken shit of Sam. He never mentioned that to me. Sam came to my daughter's wedding and never said a word." He paused a minute and then added, "Being fired was probably the best thing that happened to him."

Once Sam gave me my walking papers, I started looking for new opportunities. Stax Records was the hottest enterprise in Memphis, but it had a small staff and was pretty much a closed shop. Same thing with Hi Records, where Willie Mitchell had been put in charge of production. I had worked on some minor projects with Willie, but Hi Records was Bill's gig and the studio really didn't need a veteran guitarist/producer. Chips Moman was in the process of putting together his American Recording Studio, but it would be another year before he had it in full operation, so there was nothing for me there.

I looked toward Nashville. I was motivated to begin a new life in a new city for more reasons than one. Bobbie and I had not been getting along. Not many marriages could have survived what we had experienced. The long separations, the road trips, all the glittery trappings of me being "the man behind" America's reigning sex symbol—all were things that dogged the relationship, but they probably weren't the most difficult to overcome. More damaging to the relationship was the constant stream of work-related betrayals I had experienced during our marriage. At age 32, I needed to try something different, and I needed to do it in new surroundings. I told Bobbie I was moving to Nashville.

"I think Scotty had been wanting to move to Nashville, and that was his opportunity," says Bobbie. "We weren't getting along too well at that time and that was when we separated. I didn't go to Nashville. We had just bought a house at Raleigh about six months before, so it didn't bother me too much either. I thought, 'Well, now we can sell this house.' Sometimes you think something like that—a new house—will make you happy. But it doesn't."

Before leaving Memphis, I sent Colonel Parker an acetate copy of *The Guitar That Changed The World*, along with a letter requesting an endorsement. I wrote:

> *Recently I contracted with Epic Records, a division of Columbia to record instrumentally an album of Elvis' older hits. With the understanding that if it met with any success the project would continue by volumes two, three, etc. I am enclosing herein, a copy of the first album and would deem it an honor if you would write the liner notes for Volume One. Of course, my first thought was liner notes by "Elvis and The Colonel," but realizing label policy knew this would probably be impossible. We have endeavored to present these selections with good taste and with a memorable flavor. Any thoughts you might have would be greatly appreciated. Here's hoping they will be pleasing to your ear.*

Less than a week later, I received a response from Tom Diskin, Parker's assistant. In a letter, dated April 8 on Paramount Pictures letterhead, Diskin wrote:

> *Our hands are pretty well tied on what we can do on other labels, not only in the way of liner notes but there are restrictions that do not permit the use of Elvis' name in conjunction with another commercial record. We receive a great number of requests from the boys in the business and have to go along with the restrictions placed on us because of our association with RCA Victor. For that reason we*

have never done anything along the lines requested. We want to wish you good luck and hope that this LP is a big success, but mostly big royalties for you. KISSIN COUSINS is doing extremely well. We are still on the ROUSTABOUT picture. We are returning this acetate as we felt you may have use for it, and will be looking forward to the release of your album and I personally am going to buy one. You have to admit that is the best kind of endorsement.

It was yet another slap in the face. Of course, I wasn't surprised. I wasn't even offended. Actually, I never expected a response from Parker. If I had offered him $5,000 to write the liner notes, he might have done it. He never did anyone a favor that I knew of where he wasn't paid back tenfold somewhere down the line.

Buoyed by a contract for my first solo album and dreams of royalties for the first time in my recording career, I struck out for Nashville filled with hope, leaving behind Bobbie and our three-year-old daughter, Andrea.

★ ★ ★

When I moved to Nashville in 1964, country music was in a state of flux, a condition perpetuated to no small degree by the revolution in American music brought about by the music recorded a decade earlier by Elvis and the Blue Moon Boys in Memphis. Country music didn't have a carved-in-stone direction in 1964. The biggest selling singles on the country charts were Roger Miller's "Dang Me" and Dottie West's "Here Comes My Baby." The hottest selling single on any chart was Roy Orbison's "Oh, Pretty Woman." None of those hits seemed related to each other, the styles were so diverse.

Former Memphis artists such as Orbison, Johnny Cash, Jerry Lee Lewis, and Charlie Rich were finding new success in Nashville, even as Elvis continued to record his albums and some of his soundtracks in the city; but country music's new wave was already taking shape, making Nashville both a pivotal and an exciting place to set up shop. Two years after I arrived, Waylon Jennings moved to Nashville and ended up sharing an apartment with Johnny Cash. Willie Nelson was already a fixture about town and by 1964 had been made a regular cast member of the *Grand Ole Opry.*

I had made enough contacts in Nashville to start doing sessions, but I didn't want to do that. My playing wasn't tuned in to the way they were doing sessions. I played on a few sessions. But I really didn't care for that.

You were restricted to three hours and had to do four songs and so on. I was too much of a perfectionist to ever fit into the rigid studio system in place in Nashville—at least not as a player—and I knew that. The key to success in Memphis had revolved around unstructured sessions. That was the way I had learned it. I was too stubborn to learn new tricks.

Before I left Memphis, Mort Thomasson, a recording engineer with Columbia Records, talked to me about working for the record label as an engineer. I probably would have taken that job if I had not met studio owner Bill Conner. We discovered that we shared a common goal. Conner wanted a bigger studio. I wanted a studio, period. We found a studio that had gone on the market after its owners had filed for bankruptcy. Since it was in a good location, on Nineteenth Avenue, just off Music Row, we pooled our resources and bought it. It had done business under the name Roi studios. We renamed it Music City Recorders.

As my spirits soared over the purchase of the studio, they sank over the dismal showing my album, *The Guitar That Changed The World*, made on the charts. It became clear to me that the album was going to spawn neither hits nor royalties. Epic never pushed the album, reflecting a long-standing industry aversion to instrumentals. That was one way Memphis and Nashville were different. Memphis built an entire industry on instrumentals. Nashville avoided instrumentals, whenever possible. That was one area where I thought Nashville could learn a thing or two from its neighbor to the west.

The Guitar That Changed The World never charted, dashing my hopes of receiving royalties for the music I helped create. The album didn't sell enough copies to pay production costs and by 1996 five hundred dollars was still owned on the account, which meant that sales did not earn enough to pay for the small advance I had received.

I brushed off that disappointment, as I had done so many others, and went about the business of building a new life. Bobbie and I weren't talking about divorce. Beyond getting a little breathing room, neither of us knew what we wanted from the other. All we knew for certain was that we didn't want to rush into anything.

A little more than a year after I began my new life, tragedy struck.

★ ★ ★

For three successive years, the Bill Black Combo was named "Most Played" group in America by *Billboard* magazine and "No. 1 Combo" by *Cash Box*, a magazine published predominately for jukebox operators. By

1962 the group had four gold records—"Smokie (Parts 1 and 2)," "White Silver Sands," and "Josephine"—and a string of successful albums, including, *Saxy Jazz, Solid & Raunchy,* and *Movin'.* It was reported in the *Press-Scimitar* that anything the combo released was given an automatic first pressing of 250,000.

Bill reveled in the success, but the day-to-day business of looking after the group's interests, which increasingly involved television appearances and a worldwide touring schedule, became a chore. In 1962 he gave up leadership of the group to guitarist Bob Tucker, who already had replaced Reggie Young, who moved on to become a key player in Chips Moman's influential Memphis studio.

For years, Bill had complained of headaches. His wife, Evelyn, thought it was from all the loud music and crowd noise, and the lack of sleep from being out on the road. In April 1965 he complained of pain across his temple and around his upper cheeks. Since he had not been out on the road recently, Evelyn talked him into going to the doctor.

"I thought it was his sinuses, and he did, too," said Evelyn in an interview for this book. "I took him to a doctor we had been going to. He took x-rays of his head and said he would get back in touch with us. About four or five hours later, he called and said he couldn't get a good picture. It was like fog. He wanted him to go downtown to the neurological floor at Baptist Hospital."

Evelyn took him to the hospital, but the admitting nurse mistakenly assigned him to the psychiatric floor. "He's not crazy," Evelyn told the nurse when she discovered the error. "I told her the doctor did not say psychiatric ward—he said neurological ward," says Evelyn. "She threw a fit and charged me $100 for the time we stayed there. I got the doctor's secretary to call her. I said I wasn't going to pay the $100."

Finally, Evelyn got Bill admitted on the right floor. After running some tests, the doctor took Evelyn aside and told her the news was not good. They had found a tumor on the left side of his brain. The doctor said, "We're going to have to open his head to see."

After the surgery, the doctor came out into the waiting room to talk to Evelyn. The prognosis was bleak. He told her the tumor was about the size of a pecan.

"I asked him if he got it all," says Evelyn. "He said they tried, but they had to take quite a bit of his brain to get what they got."

The doctor explained that it would be necessary for him to operate again. For that reason, they weren't going to sew him up. They were going to leave what he called a "floating incision." Before sending Bill home from the hospital, said the doctor, they would wrap his head in bandages. After he told Evelyn the bad news, the doctor broke down and wept.

"What a waste for someone so talented," he said, tears in his eyes.

When Bill had recovered from the effects of the anesthesia, and was able to leave the hospital, Evelyn took him home to recuperate. The doctor told her not to discuss the surgery with him under any circumstances. If she needed to talk to others, he said, be sure to do it in another room where Bill wouldn't hear.

Evelyn was devastated by the news. Bill was only thirty-nine years old. They had three children—Nancy and Louis, both teenagers, and Leigh Ann, who was a little over a year old. Bill had been her lover, best friend, and soul mate since she was sixteen. She could not imagine life without him. Over the next few weeks, Bill seemed to improve. Evelyn nursed him and took care of his bandages. She noticed that when the pressure built up inside his head, the bandages pumped up and down with each beat of his heart. But before long, his behavior became erratic, if only for short periods of time.

One night he awakened and got out of bed while Evelyn was asleep. He leaped down the eight steps from their bedroom to the ground floor—at that time they lived in a tri-level house on Watkins—and ran out the back door. Evelyn awakened when she heard him calling for his father. She ran outside and found Bill in his underwear, standing in the driveway.

"He was trying to find his daddy," she says. "But he had been dead for ten or twelve years." The doctors had told her not to argue with Bill, no matter what he said. With that in mind, she gently nudged him back toward the house.

"'Bill, let's go back to bed,' she said. "It's dark and your daddy's asleep. Let's not wake him up.'

"Well, okay," Bill said, and went back into the house.

When Elvis heard that Bill was ill, he went by the house to visit. He took Evelyn aside. "He said he was sorry about Bill and that if anything happened he would not go to the funeral so it would not turn into a circus," says Evelyn. "He said he'd come back after everything was over with."

As soon as I heard about Bill's surgery, I called D. J. We decided to meet in Memphis, with D. J. driving up from Shreveport and me driving over from Nashville. We met with Bill and had dinner with him. He was his old jovial self and he looked great. We left thinking Bill had everything under control. We later learned that it was all an act. He didn't want his friends to feel sorry for him. He wanted to be brave. Even though neither she nor the doctors talked to Bill about the seriousness of his condition, Evelyn knew he was aware of everything.

One day, during one of his hospital stays, Bill greeted Evelyn with a question when she walked into the room. "Why you losing so much weight?" he asked.

"You know me," she answered. "I watch my weight."

Of course, there was a reason for her weight loss. His illness. "I was worried, that was what it was," she says. But her weight loss wasn't the only thing Bill had on his mind. That day's newspaper contained a story about actor Robert Taylor's death from a brain tumor. Bill showed the newspaper to Evelyn. The story described Taylor's symptoms and how the tumor had made him act.

"That sounds like me," Bill said.

By fall, Bill's condition worsened. The doctors had operated on him twice. They told Evelyn that if they operated a third time, it would leave Bill a vegetable.

"They asked me what I wanted them to do," says Evelyn. "I asked the doctor if he would do it if it was his family. He said, no."

Evelyn told them not to operate.

"The Blacks got upset with me," she says. "They said, 'We've always heard three is lucky.' I said, 'You may have heard everything, but hear this: I'm not going to let them cut on him anymore.'"

The last week of his life, Bill lapsed into a semi-coma. He didn't say much toward the end. He smiled at Evelyn and squeezed her hand. On October 22, 1965, Evelyn and other family members were sitting in the hospital room with Bill when the nurse looked in on them. They had been there about eight hours that day. The nurse suggested they go get something to eat.

"I hate to leave him," Evelyn said.

"He'll be fine," assured the nurse.

After eating, they returned to the room. Bill was dead.

The funeral was held at Bellevue Baptist Church, with burial in Forest Hill Cemetery. Bobbie and I went to the funeral with D. J. Fontana and his wife, Barbara. D. J. and I were pallbearers. Afterward, we went out to Graceland to commiserate with Elvis. Everyone was stunned by Bill's unexpected death. No one knew quite what to say.

"Elvis was sitting out on his motorcycle when we arrived," says Bobbie. "The bodyguards were there. Priscilla came out the door and stood around with the bodyguards, but she didn't come over where we were and Elvis didn't introduce her to us. We didn't stay around too long." When Bobbie said goodbye to Elvis that day, it was for the last time. She never saw him again.

True to his word, Elvis went by to see Evelyn again after the funeral. This time, he took Priscilla with him. By then, Priscilla's father had relented and allowed her to move into Graceland with Elvis.

"I told him how much I appreciated him coming by," says Evelyn. "I always thought a lot of Elvis. He didn't get messed up until after Scotty and Bill got away from him. He was just a young boy who loved music and loved to shake those hips and make the girls scream."

With Bill gone, Evelyn turned her attention to raising their young family. "It was a good marriage," she says. "He was gone a lot, but I took it in stride. I stayed with him through thick and thin. It's just a shame—someone dying that young."

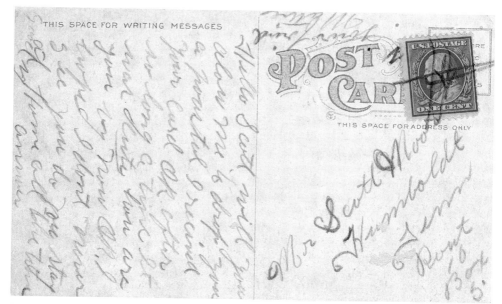

Postcard from Mattie Hefley to Scott Moore, dated April 22, 1910. Courtesy of Scotty Moore.

Undated postcard to Scott Moore from Mattie Hefley. Courtesy of Scotty Moore.

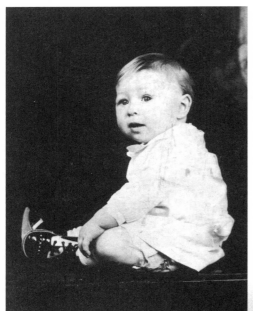

Scotty Moore at three months.
Courtesy of Scotty Moore.

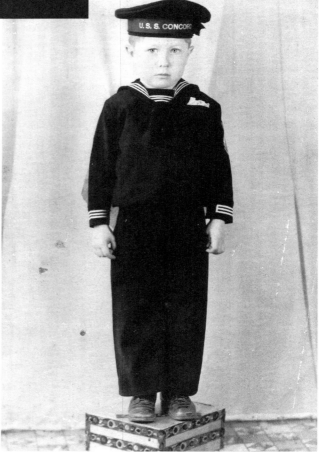

Scotty Moore in the sailor suit
sent to him by his brother, Ralph.
Courtesy of Scotty Moore.

The LST-855, on which Scotty served in China, and its officers. Courtesy of Scotty Moore.

Scotty with Durwood Ramsey on board the *Valley Forge*. Courtesy of Scotty Moore.

Scotty and Bobbie shortly after they were married, circa 1954. Courtesy of Scotty Moore.

Scotty and Bill's first publicity photo, which they sold to fans while touring with Elvis in mid-1950s. Courtesy of Scotty Moore.

WHEREAS, W. S. Moore, III, is a band leader and a booking agent, and Elvis Presley, a minor, age 19 years, is a singer of reputation and renown, and possesses bright promises of large success, it is the desire of both parties to enter into this personal management contract for the best interests of both parties.

This contract is joined in and approved by the Father and Mother of Elvis Presley, *Vernon Presley* and *Mrs. Vernon Presley,* Presley.

IT IS AGREED that W. S. Moore, III, will take over the complete management of the professional affairs of the said Elvis Presley, book him professionally for all appearances that can be secured for him, and to promote him, generally, in his professional endeavors. The said W. S. Moore, III, is to receive, as his compensation for his services, ten (10%) percent of all earnings from engagements, appearances, and bookings made by him for Elvis Presley.

IT IS UNDERSTOOD AND AGREED that this is an exclusive contract and the said Elvis Presley agrees not to sign any other contract pertaining to his professional work nor make any appearances at any time for any other person or manager or booking agent, for a period of one (1) year.

Now, we, *Vernon Presley* and *Mrs. Vernon Presley,* father and mother of Elvis Presley, join in this contract for and in his behalf, confirm and approve all of its terms and his execution of same and our signatures are affixed thereto.

The said W. S. Moore, III, agrees to give his best efforts to the promotion and success of the said Elvis Presley professionally.

SIGNED AND EXECUTED on this 12th day of July 1954.

_____
W. S. Moore, III

_____
Elvis Presley

_____
Father of Elvis Presley

_____
Mother of Elvis Presley

Original management contract between Scotty and Elvis, July 12, 1954. Courtesy of Scotty Moore.

Scotty with Bill Black's children at his home in Memphis. The Chevy in the background was Bobbie's car, which Elvis and the Blue Moon Boys used for their initial tours. Courtesy of Bobbie Moore.

Elvis introduces Bill Black onstage. Scotty is in the right background. Courtesy of Scotty Moore.

"WE COVER THE NATION"

JAMBOREE ATTRACTIONS
INC.

JAMBOREE MUSIC · BMI

P. O. BOX 417 · · · · · · · · MADISON, TENN.
OFFICE PHONE: NASHVILLE 2-6770

Jan. 13, 1955

Mr. Scotty Moore
983 Belz
Memphis, Tenn.

Thank you so much for your letter regarding your
artist and while we are a booking and promotion
agency I don't have anything at present where I
could place your artist. There are few outlets
for hillbilly entertainers in this area around
Chicago.

Kindest regards,

Sincerely,

Tom Diskin

Tom Diskin

Letter from Tom Diskin turning down Elvis Presley, January 13, 1955. Courtesy of Scotty Moore.

Scotty, Elvis, D. J., and Bill on
stage. Photo © 1996 EPE, Inc.

From the Hank Snow souvenir photo album produced for the jamboree tour featuring Elvis, Scotty, and Bill. Courtesy of Scotty Moore.

Scotty and Elvis on stage.
Photo © 1996 EPE, Inc.

Scotty and Bill, Tulsa, OK. Courtesy of Scotty Moore.

On the set of *Love Me Tender*. Left to right: Scotty, Elvis, Neil Matthews, Richard Egan, Bill Black, D. J. Fontana, Gordon Stoker, Hoyt Hawkins, and Hugh Jarrett. Photo © EPE, Inc.

September 18, 1957

Mr. W. S. Moore, III
1716 Tutwiler
Memphis, Tennessee

Dear Scotty:

      This is to advise that, pursuant to your notice
of September 7, 1957, we are accepting your resignation
from our employment effective September 21, 1957, and,
accordingly, enclose herewith notice of separation and
your final salary check in the amount of $86.25, represent-
ing payment in full for all services rendered for us by
you prior to September 21, 1957.

                Yours very truly,

Vernon Presley

Vernon Presley's letter to Scotty, September 18, 1957. Courtesy of Scotty Moore.

Sheet music cover for Thomas Wayne's hit, "Tragedy." Courtesy of Scotty Moore.

Letter from Colonel Tom Parker to Scotty congratulating him on the success of Thomas Wayne Perkins's hit record. Courtesy of Scotty Moore.

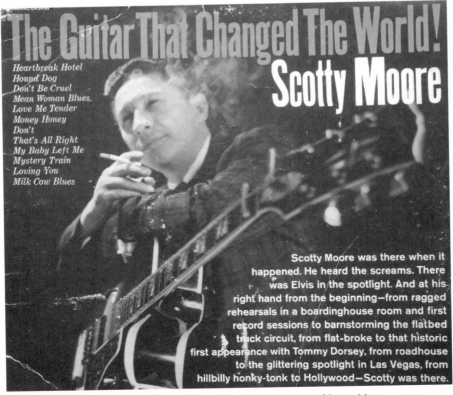

HOTEL Fontainebleau
MIAMI BEACH, FLORIDA

1. HEART BREAK HoTel — (E)
2. All Shook up — (Bb)
3. Fool Such as I — (C) ☆
4. I Got A WomAN — (E)
5. Love me — (F)
6. Such A Night — (E)
7. Reconsider Baby — (E)
8. I Need Your Love Tonight — (G) Boogie
9. ThAT'S All Right — (A)
10. Doing The BesT I CAN — (G)
11. Don'T Be Cruel — (D)
12. ONe Night — (E)
13. Are You Lonesome Tonight — (C)
14. Now or Never — (E)
15. Swing Down — (F)
16. Hound Dog — (C) (GeT The Hell out

Scotty's handwritten playlist for the Ellis Auditorium shows, written on Hotel Fontainebleau stationery from their Miami stay in 1960. Courtesy of Scotty Moore.

The Guitar That Changed The World!
Scotty Moore

Heartbreak Hotel
Hound Dog
Don't Be Cruel
Mean Woman Blues
Love Me Tender
Money Honey
Don't
That's All Right
My Baby Left Me
Mystery Train
Loving You
Milk Cow Blues

Scotty Moore was there when it happened. He heard the screams. There was Elvis in the spotlight. And at his right hand from the beginning—from ragged rehearsals in a boardinghouse room and first record sessions to barnstorming the flatbed truck circuit, from flat-broke to that historic first appearance with Tommy Dorsey, from roadhouse to the glittering spotlight in Las Vegas, from hillbilly honky-tonk to Hollywood—Scotty was there.

Scotty Moore's album, *The Guitar That Changed the World*. Courtesy of Scotty Moore.

SAM PHILLIPS RECORDING STUDIOS OF NASHVILLE & MEMPHIS, INC.

March 17, 1964

Mr. Scott Moore
639 Madison Avenue
Memphis, Tennessee

Dear Scotty:

As you know I am real concerned about the events of the past week-end, and feel I must tell you that I feel a real trust has been handled with impropriety.

I think under the circumstances all purposes, both for you and me, would be best served if you began to seek a new association.

I do not want you to feel that I do not appreciate your real and genuine dedication and concern for the companies you are associated with, but my faith has been severly taken to task, therefore, your continued affiliation with us will not be what I feel is a comfortable relationship.

I do not, however, hold any malice in the matter and shall, and do, hold you in high regard. Also, your presence is welcome at all times and certainly until you make another connection that is satisfactory to you and your family.

Further, please do not feel out of pride you have to leave immediately. This is not the case. As a matter of fact, you will be needed to help us avoid another "immediate" departure.

I shall be happy to recommend you, both as a person and as an employee, to whomever you approach for employment.

With kindest personal regard, I shall remain appreciatively for your association and hard work.

Appreciatively,

SAM PHILLIPS RECORDING SERVICE, INC.

Sam C. Phillips

Sam Phillips's letter of dismissal to Scotty, 1964. Courtesy of Scotty Moore.

Elvis and Scotty: the "comeback special," 1968. Photo © EPE, Inc.

Scotty and Emily on their wedding day. Courtesy of Emily Sanders.

Scotty with Tracy Nelson in the studio. Photo courtesy Scotty Moore.

Thomas Wayne Perkins adjusts microphone for Ringo Starr during the *Beaucoup of Blues* session. Courtesy of Scotty Moore.

Ringo Starr, front row, fourth from left, with the band from the Nashville sessions, photographed at Tracy Nelson's farm. D. J. Fontana sits on Ringo's left. Photo by Marshall Fallwell Jr., courtesy of Rose Drake.

Gail Pollock, arranger Don Tweed, and Scotty in the studio. Courtesy of Scotty Moore.

Carl Perkins, left, with Scotty at Sun Studio in Memphis, circa 1992. Courtesy of Scotty Moore.

Scotty and the Jordanaires at his home near Nashville, 1996. Photo © James L. Dickerson.

Scotty Moore in Nashville, circa 1996.
Photo © James L. Dickerson.

Scotty Moore in Nashville, circa 1996.
Photo © James L. Dickerson.

Scotty and Joe Lewis Walker performing at the Memphis MARAS Heroes Award, 2004. Courtesy of Scotty Moore.

James L. Dickerson and Scotty Moore at his Nashville home. Photo © James L. Dickerson.

Scotty Moore on the train to New York, circa 1997. Photo © James L. Dickerson.

Bill Black Combo: Scotty Moore; left front, D. J. Fontana; back row, left to right: Mike Leech, Reggie Young, Ace Cannon, Jerry "Satch" Arnold, Bobby Woods, and Bobby Emmons. © Rusty Russell.

Scotty with Lee Rocker in Memphis. Courtesy of Scotty Moore.

Scotty with Keith Richards, D. J., and Ron Wood. Photo by Paul Natkin.

Scotty, far right, at New York recording studio with, left to right, D. J., Karen Fontana, Paul McCartney, and Gail Pollock. Courtesy of Scotty Moore.

Scotty and Ronnie McDowell at Horseshoe Casino, Tunica, Mississippi, 2002. Courtesy of Scotty Moore.

Priscilla Presley addressing partygoers at Scotty's 80th birthday celebration. Photo © James L. Dickerson.

Scotty receiving a custom-made guitar from Gibson Guitar president Dave Berryman at Scotty's 80th birthday party in Memphis. Photo © James L. Dickerson.

★ 10 ★

A FAREWELL PERFORMANCE

Not long after Bill Black's funeral, Bobbie and I got back together. Death has a way of nudging people to count their blessings. In 1966, Bobbie and Andrea moved to Nashville to live with me. Andrea turned six in time to start school that year. Bobbie was reluctant to give up a secure job with Sears, but she wanted Andrea to have a live-in father when she entered first grade. Like a lot of people in the music business I had become a workaholic, coming home exhausted from long days. It was nice to hear other voices instead of stone-cold silence when I walked through the door. There is music in a child's voice and in a mother's love.

By the time they got settled in with me, Music City Recorders was up to speed. I had fallen into a routine as an engineer. Instead of playing music, I worked the dials that transferred the music to tape. To me, both aspects—performing and engineering—were equally challenging. As a musician, my job was to make my instrument complement the singer. As an engineer, my job was to transfer the singer's concept of the music to the reality of tape. Ideally, what the singer and producer heard in their heads would be what they heard on the playback in the control room. And I got a kick out of mixing. That way I played *all* the instruments.

In the beginning, I seldom did production work of my own. My main focus was on getting the studio established. However, during this time I continued to work with Thomas Wayne, who had moved to Nashville to help me out in the studio. Eventually, I expanded into production. I released several singles of Thomas Wayne, including "Don't Come Runnin'"/"Kiss Away," distributed on Racer Records, but none of the singles were hits and Thomas Wayne's career continued to flounder. Neither of us wanted to believe that he was a one-hit wonder.

I co-produced with Rayburn Anthony two singles on Jeris Ross, "Brand New Key" and "Old Fashioned Love Song," that made the country charts. When Elvis recorded albums or movie soundtracks in Nashville, I usually was asked to be leader on the sessions. As a diversion from the day-to-day routine of operating a studio, the Elvis sessions were always welcome, but as a source of income they amounted to little more than pocket change.

By 1966 Elvis was churning out three movies a year, but he was making no public appearances and his recording career was almost nonexistent. Between October 1965 (the month of Bill Black's death) and October 1967, Elvis placed only one record in the Top 20, "I'm Yours." Not since March 1962 had he had a chart-topping record.

Dominating the charts in the mid-to-late 1960s were British groups such as the Beatles and the Rolling Stones, and a motley crew of young white and black teenagers under the direction of Jim Stewart, Chips Moman, and Willie Mitchell, who collectively made Memphis the center of the American soul and pop universe with hits such as the Box Tops' "The Letter," Sam & Dave's "Soul Man," and Otis Redding's "(Sittin' On) The Dock of the Bay." Sam Phillips's studio got in one last hit with "Lil Red Riding Hood," recorded by Sam The Sham & The Pharaohs and produced by Stan Kesler.

As the Memphis studios exploded with talent, Elvis sank further into the protective environment of Graceland. For the first time in his career, newspaper and magazine stories about Elvis focused on what he was not doing with his life. Had he given up on rock 'n' roll? An Associated Press article accused him of hiding from the public.

By the end of 1966, Elvis decided to marry Priscilla. She'd been living at Graceland since 1961 and the rising tide of negative publicity about their relationship presented a potential threat to his career. Elvis proposed to Priscilla in December and they were married on May 1, 1967, at a private ceremony in Las Vegas.

I had seen Priscilla from a distance on the day of Bill Black's funeral, but I had never met her. All I knew about her was what I had heard from mutual friends and what I had read in the newspapers. By then Elvis's love life wasn't a major concern for me. Once again, my marriage to Bobbie was falling apart. The Nashville experiment wasn't working out the way we had hoped.

In 1967, after less than a year in Nashville, Bobbie took Andrea and moved back to Memphis, where she was able to get her old job back at Sears. The following year, after fifteen years of marriage, we called it quits and filed for divorce. Bobbie worked for Sears until they closed their Crosstown branch and forced her into early retirement. She never remarried.

★ ★ ★

By the spring of 1968 I was again headed toward a serious relation-ship. Emily Hastings was a 25-year-old hairdresser who was no stranger to the record business. Her sister, Charlene, was married to record producer Billy Sherrill. By the age of twenty-five, Emily had dated Phil Everly and Johnny Rivers, two of the most successful entertainers in Nashville.

Emily had run into me at Sherrill's house over the years, but she never thought about me as a potential mate. I was a 37-year-old studio owner, a quiet, behind-the-scenes player in the music business; she was a striking, vivacious redhead in her prime, well known to the movers and shakers in Nashville. She liked the excitement that accompanied the music business and she liked the glitter and the fine things that usually went with it. She had stars in her eyes. I was a sideman, sometimes a star-maker, but defi-nitely not her type.

One day in early spring, during one of our chance encounters, Emily told me that she was having problems with her television. It was brand new, but she couldn't get it to work. I offered to take a look at it. While there I asked her if she was involved in a serious relationship. She had been dating Freddy Bienstock, an executive with Hill and Range Songs, but it wasn't anything serious. Hill and Range was Elvis's publisher and, in recent years, Bienstock had taken on many of the responsibilities previ-ously assumed by Steve Sholes. Bienstock wasn't one of my favorite peo-ple. I thought he used poor judgment in the songs he offered to Elvis. To my way of thinking, Bienstock and Parker were a matching pair of book-ends. Neither seemed to have Elvis's best interests at heart.

To my surprise, Emily agreed to go out with me. She remembered me from Memphis, where, as a child, she had passed the dry cleaners and saw me standing in the doorway. "The first date we had, we went to a concert," she said in an interview for this book. "We went to see a Spanish guitarist who was very famous. Scotty was absolutely in a trance. I didn't like it, be-cause I didn't like that kind of guitar. Scotty kept looking at the guitarist's fingers. I've never seen anyone so excited. He talked about going back-stage, but for some reason he didn't. I think it was because I didn't like it."

When she listened to *The Guitar That Changed The World*, the album produced by Billy Sherrill, she thought it was wonderful. But she thought it odd that she never saw me pick up a guitar. "He never mentioned Elvis," she explains. "When we were dating, we would go places and musicians on stage would know him and they would introduce him and ask him up on stage. But that didn't impress me." What apparently impressed Emily was the way I kept the conversation focused on her. The other men she had dated spent most of the time talking about themselves. I didn't want to talk about myself. I was genuinely interested in what she thought about things. By May she had moved in with me. I was living in Bellevue then, a fresh-air suburb on the western tip of Nashville.

Late one night the telephone rang. I was at the studio and Emily was at home alone.

"Hello," she said.

"I'm trying to reach Scotty Moore," the caller said.

"Well, you've reached his home, but he's not here. Can I take a message? Who's calling, please?"

"Well, this is ... ah ... Elvis Presley."

"OK, fine. This is Elizabeth Taylor."

Emily thought someone was playing a joke on her.

The caller paused.

Finally, uneasy with the silence, Emily said, "Scotty is at a session. Why don't you call back later?"

Later, when I got home, the telephone rang again. The caller said that Elvis was trying to get in touch with me. When would be a convenient time to call back?

Finally, Elvis called again.

"I left the room," says Emily. "I always thought people were entitled to personal conversations."

Elvis told me that he had been asked to do a television special for NBC. The show would be taped, but he would be singing live in front of a studio audience. He hadn't done a live concert in seven years, not since the 1961 benefit concert in Hawaii. Would I be able to perform on stage with him? I said yes, though not without some trepidation: I had not performed live since February 1961, when I had backed Elvis at Ellis Auditorium in Memphis.

I hadn't seen Elvis since January 1968, when we recorded "U.S. Male" for RCA. On that session Jerry Reed had played lead guitar and I played rhythm. By that time, I had pretty much given up hope of ever again participating in a big way in Elvis's career. I was pleased to be invited to the sessions (pocket money was pocket money) and I didn't begrudge Elvis his success, but I never really expected to ever again share a stage with him.

At the session Elvis talked about his favorite 78 records from his teenage years, about how he had just about worn them out on the phonograph.

He asked me if my studio had the capability to transfer the records to tape. Sure, I said. Elvis asked if I would mind doing that for him. He said he would get the records together when he returned to Graceland.

Sometime that fall I received a small briefcase from Elvis. It was filled with 78-rpm records, many of them showing obvious wear. When I saw them, I remembered them from when I first went to his house. He played them on one of those wind-up record players. Included were Ray Charles's "I've Got a Woman"/"Come Back." Roy Hamilton's "Hurt"/"Star Of Love," Fats Domino's "Ain't It A Shame"/"La-La," and Carl Perkins's "Matchbox"/"Your True Love." I made two copies. I sent one copy to him and filed the other one in the studio. I didn't want to ship the 78s because they were already in such bad shape, so I kept them with the intention of handing them back to Elvis at our next meeting.

★ ★ ★

When Emily came back into the room, I told her about the telephone conversation. We had planned on getting married in June, but since that was the month the television show would be taped we decided to postpone our marriage until August. I asked Emily if she could get off work at the hairdressing salon to go with me to California.

"Scotty was excited about it," says Emily. "He was excited for Elvis because he knew it would be important for him. Elvis hadn't done a show before a live audience in a while. He was scared. We all were. I was scared for them."

Emily was in a whirlwind. She had only dated me for three months, but I had proposed to her—and she had accepted—and now we were flying off to Los Angeles to do a television show with Elvis Presley. It was one hell of a romantic way to begin a marriage.

★ ★ ★

By 1968 Elvis's films were no longer as popular as they once had been. Perhaps because of that, NBC-TV approached Colonel Parker about doing a television special to be broadcast during the Christmas holidays. Parker agreed to let Elvis do the show, but made it clear he wanted it to follow the same format used by the movies. In addition, he said he thought the show should be built around Christmas songs.

Steve Binder, hired by NBC to produce and direct the special, had other ideas. He wanted to do something with an edge: Something a little more rock 'n' roll than Elvis had tackled in recent years. Perhaps Elvis could talk to the audience and his musicians—initiate a dialogue with his fans. Binder didn't mind sparring with Parker. Recently he had produced and directed a television special starring Petula Clark. During the show, guest star Harry Belafonte had touched Petula on the arm, generating a firestorm of protest from racist viewers angered over what they perceived to be a violation of interracial etiquette. Binder weathered that controversy to no ill effect. Perhaps because of that he hung tough with Parker, getting the Christmas playlist cut to one song, then, finally, to none. Then a battle arose over the band. NBC wanted to use its large orchestra. Binder had been talking to Elvis about his vision for the show. He knew Elvis wasn't happy about the direction his music had taken in recent years. For the show to capture the magic of the past, he knew he would have to take Elvis back to his roots.

Binder convinced NBC to allow him to add D. J. and me. When Binder told Elvis he had NBC's approval, Elvis got so excited he called me himself. But there was more to it than excitement. According to Elvis confidant Billy Smith, Elvis was scared to death about doing the show. In a way, D. J. and I were Elvis's security blanket.

★ ★ ★

The last week in June, Emily and I flew to Los Angeles. I created a stir when I refused to check my guitar and amplifier into baggage; I carried both onto the plane. When we arrived at NBC's Burbank studios, we were held up in the hallway outside Elvis's dressing room. Once we got inside, Elvis took Emily aside and explained the delay: Her old boyfriend Freddy Bienstock had been in the dressing room.

"I didn't know what to do," Elvis whispered to Emily. "I knew you went with Freddy."

"Now I know how you feel," she told him.

To avoid a scene, Elvis had Bienstock unceremoniously ushered out a back door. "When I think about it, that was a nice thing for him to do," says Emily. "We would have walked in there and Freddy would have been sitting there. Elvis threw him out."

When Elvis saw me, he fell into conversation with me immediately. There were no handshakes. No phony greetings. We just started talking. To Emily, it looked as if was as if we resumed a conversation we had started years before.

Elvis looked great. He was in good physical condition. Once we started talking, it was like old times. He joked and talked about things we had done.

Emily sat next to Elvis, with me at her side. D. J. sat across the room. The Jordanaires had been invited, but they were so heavily booked in Nashville they could not get away. Elvis's entourage filled the room, watching his every move. Says Emily: "Elvis picked up a guitar. I noticed he had on one of those wide things around his wrists. I asked, 'What are those?'"

"Well, I do karate, and they are from that," he said.

"Well, they are stupid," said Emily. "They look like something from a concentration camp."

The room grew quiet. You could have heard a pin drop. Everyone looked at Emily. Finally, out of self-defense, she said, "Well, they do!"

"Hmmm," said Elvis.

"Elvis kept playing and he talked a while, but I could tell he was angry," says Emily. "Scotty didn't care one way or another. He just laughed. After that, they always put me next to Elvis. They were waiting for the next thing. I didn't know any better. Whether it was Elvis or the President, it didn't matter to me."

We talked about the show, about the songs we could do. Then the subject of dinner arose. "We talked about going out to eat, but you can't do that with Elvis," says Emily. "You have to bring it in or go to his house. As we were getting ready to leave for his house, someone—I think it was Lamar [Fike], kept saying, 'We can't go yet, the car is not ready.'

"Elvis got flustered. He said, 'What do you mean we aren't ready yet?'

"Lamar kept saying, 'The car is not around yet.'

"I kept thinking, what is the big deal?

"Finally, one of the guys leaned over and said to me, 'We can't reach Priscilla.' I thought, what does that mean, you can't reach Priscilla? By then, it must have been right at twelve midnight or maybe one."

In the limo, they kept calling over and over again.

When we arrived at the house, Elvis proudly pointed out that Debbie Reynolds lived next door. Once we went inside the first thing he did was ask for Priscilla. Everyone looked at each other, no one knowing quite what to say.

"She'll be here," someone said. "I guess she's on her way."

"Uh-huh," said Elvis.

Everyone in Elvis's entourage was solicitous of him, but he was clearly irritated by that turn of events. We sat in a large circular room and tried to carry on a conversation. It was difficult to talk because everyone was so ill at ease.

Soon someone announced that dinner was ready. As we were being seated Priscilla entered the room and sat in the empty chair next to Elvis. Emily sat in the chair on the other side of Elvis. "There was no hello, good-bye, go to hell, where have you been?" said Emily. "There was just this cold stare."

Midway through dinner, Elvis turned to Priscilla, really looking at her for the first time.

"Where were you?" he asked.

"Dance lessons," she said.

After dinner Elvis showed Emily, D. J., and me around the house. We went into a sunken den that had a large fireplace with a mantel. Emily noticed a beautiful carved stone chariot on the mantel and commented on it, just making small talk.

"I know absolutely nothing about it," said Elvis.

"It's beautiful. I don't think I've ever seen anything like it."

"I'm sorry I can't give it to you because I don't own it. We're just renting this house."

"I wasn't asking for it," said Emily, slightly offended. "I was just admiring it."

Later, Emily asked me about the incident.

Elvis felt if you said you liked something, he was supposed to give it to you, I explained. At first, that bothered Emily. Then, the more she thought about it, the more it embarrassed her to think that Elvis thought she was asking for a gift. When we returned to the living room, Emily asked Elvis for directions to the restroom. He told her he had no idea where it was located.

"Well, could you ask someone?" Emily said.

"Sure," Elvis said. From the look on his face, Emily could tell that he was embarrassed.

"When he found out, he got up and took me around to where we had been before and he pointed to the door," said Emily.

He said, "It's in there." I went into the bathroom and it was mirrored and I just knew there were cameras behind those mirrors. I had heard the stories. I said to myself, "No, I'm not going to go." I held it.

When I got back with Priscilla again, we went back to the bedroom. I told her I had rather go to the one back there. She said that was fine. She was very nice—a tiny, petite woman, very small.

Priscilla had wonderful things to say about Scotty. She said Elvis talked about Scotty a lot and he represented an important part of Elvis's life and he had helped Elvis through some tough times and had never belittled him. She was so pretty, even with all that make-up on. She was like a little china doll. I must have weighed 120 pounds at the time. I would have made three of her. She was so much smaller than I was. It was like she had a child's body, but she was very, very pretty and very nice.

When Emily and Priscilla returned to the living room, Elvis started talking about their daughter, Lisa Marie. She had been born on February 1 at Baptist Memorial Hospital in Memphis, which would have made her five months at the time. Elvis asked the nurse to wake her and bring her out to the living room. Not surprisingly, Lisa Marie was unhappy about being awakened in the middle of the night. She cried when the nurse brought her out into the living room. Elvis bragged about Lisa Marie, obviously the proud father, but he made no effort to hold her. After a few minutes, the screaming baby was taken back to bed. It was an awkward moment for Elvis. He had asked for the baby without being really sure what to do with her.

Elvis, D. J., and I went into another room to talk in private.

Emily and Priscilla went into the bedroom.

"She showed me her closets," says Emily. "She had a makeup counter that must have been six feet long. I had never seen so much makeup."

I thought it was unusual that Elvis wanted to talk to us in private. He usually felt free to talk in front of his bodyguards. When we were alone, Elvis asked if we would be interested in doing a European tour with him. We both said we would love to do it. He had talked about it when he got out of the Army, but he hadn't mentioned it again since then. He turned to me and asked if I still had the studio in Nashville. I said, yeah, and if we are going to do the European tour let me know ahead of time so I can get someone to fill in for me. He asked me what would be the chances of us going into the studio and just locking the doors for a couple of weeks to see what we could come up with. I told him sure, to just let me know when.

He didn't say what was on his mind. I know he was tired of the movie songs. He might have wanted to go back to where we were in the early years. Knowing his mindset at that point in time, it gave me renewed hope. He just wanted to try something without somebody saying, "That song fits this scene in the movie."

After we talked for a while, Elvis took us all out to the garage to see his cars. By that time, it was approaching dawn. With a wake-up call at 5:30 a.m., Emily and I returned to the hotel to freshen up before reporting to the NBC studios at Burbank.

Emily wanted to talk to me about Elvis and Priscilla, but I wasn't interested and changed the subject every time she brought it up. It wasn't any of my business any more than my relationship with Emily was any of his business. That was the code we lived by in the early years and it still seemed valid to me. Relationships and music were separate sides of the same coin. You could look at them separately but not at the same time.

★ ★ ★

On Thursday, June 27, we started taping at 7 a.m. in Studio Four. We began with the amusement-pier segment, and then moved on to the "Little Egypt Club" and the discotheque segments. Elvis did well on the vocals, nailing them on first takes, but he sometimes floundered on the dance steps. Once he was supposed to break a bottle over an extra's head, but it wouldn't break. Elvis cracked up and everyone on the set laughed. During one of the dance segments, a female dancer was supposed to slide her arms down his leg, but she was a little off target and ran her hand along his crotch. Elvis broke out into laughter.

"I really like this," he said, beaming.

Except for a constant stream of women coming into the dressing room to see Elvis, Emily was the only woman allowed backstage. "At first there weren't any women in the room with him, but then he got used to me being around, and I started to see one woman after another," says Emily.

I didn't object to that, but they were kissing all over each other with other people in the room. It was more the women doing it than Elvis. Maybe that was the girls' way of letting me know they were with Elvis. Later, when I saw Priscilla again, I felt uneasy. I felt like I had betrayed her because I knew something she didn't know. I felt sorry for her, but I didn't know what to do. Scotty's reaction was that it was none of my business. He said, "What you see is what I lived and this is why I don't want to be part of it anymore." Then I began to understand.

When Elvis laughed, everyone laughed. If something funny happened—and he did not laugh—no one else in the room laughed. Says Emily: "Elvis said things to people I would not have liked if I had been one of them. Things like talking down to them, being sarcastic, treating them with total disrespect. He never did that with Scotty. He never said to Scotty, 'Go get me this or that.' He treated Scotty entirely different than the way he treated the others."

At one point, Emily said she wished she had a Coca-Cola.

One of the bodyguards looked at her in horror, saying sternly, "Elvis drinks Pepsi."

"I can't help what Elvis drinks," said Emily. "I drink Coca-Cola. That's what I want."

Suddenly, the room sank into a stone cold silence.

"You," said Elvis, motioning to one of the bodyguards. "Go get her a Coke."

The bodyguard hurried down the hall to get the Coke.

"There was a line he wouldn't cross with Scotty, and that was obvious," says Emily. "He would watch Scotty, and before he said something to Scotty he would think about it, whereas with someone else he would mouth off. He always had something to say about someone who left the room and I always felt like he never did that with Scotty. I think Scotty knew everything there was to know about Elvis, but he never brought up his faults. They had this mutual respect for each other and there was a line neither one of them would cross."

★ ★ ★

One of the best ideas Steve Binder had was to place Elvis on a small stage in the round. With him on the stage were D. J., Charlie Hodge, Alan Fortas, and myself. Off-camera was an electric bass player. Although Hodge was an accomplished rhythm guitarist who had been with Elvis since he got out of the Army, he was there primarily to offer moral support, along with Fortas, a member in good standing of the "Memphis Mafia."

Fortas—the nephew of Supreme Court Justice Abe Fortas, who resigned from the Court in 1969 under scandalous circumstances—sat on the stage with his back to the camera and never attempted to play a musical instrument. A Memphis high-school football hero, Fortas had joined Elvis's entourage in 1958 and served primarily as a bodyguard, although for a time he managed Elvis's Circle G Ranch located south of Memphis.

Before going on stage, Elvis, D. J., and I rehearsed in the dressing room, picking, jamming, singing, cutting up. It was like the old days. Binder told us to play anything we wanted to play when we got in front of the audience. By the time we hit the stage at six o'clock that evening, we were ready for anything. Elvis wore a black leather outfit that had been chosen especially for him by a costume designer who mistakenly thought Elvis was famous for wearing black leather. The outfit was uncomfortable, but Elvis liked the way he looked in it.

"I was really surprised at how good looking Elvis was," says Emily. "His photographs did not do him justice. He was absolutely gorgeous. There isn't another human being who looked like Elvis. He had charisma and he was destined to be who he was. I thought, what a magnificent looking man, just gorgeous. But he wasn't a man I would have personally been attracted to. I admired him more than anything else."

The nearer they came to show time, the more anxious Elvis became.

He kept saying, "I'm nervous. I won't be able to do this. What if they don't like me?" At one point he said, "Scotty, don't let me come in too soon."

"Don't worry about it," I said, assuring him that everything would be all right.

When we walked out on stage, our guitars were already in place. I had my Gibson 400 Sunburst and Elvis had his Gibson J200, a natural grain flattop model I had obtained for him from the manufacturer. We began the show with some of our early material—"That's All Right, Mama" and "Are You Lonesome Tonight."

At one point, I suggested a song title. Elvis looked shocked.

"That's the first words you've said onstage in fourteen years," he said, smiling.

It was the best Elvis had sounded in years. The music was lean, sparse, just like it had been that first week in Sun Studio fourteen years before. During the first couple of songs, Elvis kept glancing at me. My brightly colored guitar shone in the camera lights. It was bigger than Elvis's guitar, it was better looking, and it sounded better than his. Elvis decided he just had to have it.

"Scotty was playing lead for a while and all of a sudden Elvis wanted to play lead," says D. J. Fontana. "So he goes over and grabs Scotty's guitar."

D. J. was horrified. He knew how meticulous I was about my guitar. "I thought, 'What are we going to do here.' Scotty wasn't very happy about that. Elvis was a flogger and I knew he was afraid he'd scar up the guitar. It worked out, but, oh boy, he doesn't like anyone to touch that guitar."

Elvis played my guitar for the remainder of the show. It is the guitar with which he was most often photographed in promotion photos for the show. It is the guitar on the cover of the videocassette. At one point, Elvis said, "I think I'm gonna put a strap on this and stand up."

He looked over at me. "Got a strap?" he asked.

I didn't have a strap.

Elvis stood, balancing the guitar on his thigh as the strummed and sang, "One Night With You." I wasn't happy about the situation because I knew he was trying to get my goat, as we say in the South; but I never showed my displeasure. I kept going, never missing a beat, playing Elvis's guitar with the same determination and skill I had done with my own. Since Elvis was the star, he wanted the biggest, flashiest guitar, but there was more to it than that. Elvis, above anyone else, knew how I was about my guitars. By taking my guitar from me on stage, Elvis was subjecting me to a test of our friendship. We both knew what the gesture meant.

We did two hour-long shows in the round that night. Critics later were unanimous in their praise of the performance. People who had not been around in the early years to hear us together were amazed at the stark power of the music. When the show aired on December 3, 1968, it was the highest-rated program of the week. Writing in the *New York Times*, John Landau said: "There is something magical about watching a man who has lost himself, find his way home." From that point on, the show was referred to as Elvis's "Comeback Special."

★ ★ ★

On the plane back to Nashville Emily and I sat in silence, more tired than anything else. We didn't talk about the show. We didn't talk about Elvis. We viewed the trip as sort of a midsummer outing. For Emily, it was also a lesson in Elvis Presley economics. The trip ended up costing us money. Despite her young age, she was savvy to the ways of the music business.

The "Comeback Special" was more than just a seminal event for Elvis; it was a potential turning point for me. A part of me wanted to be excited about the European tour Elvis discussed with us and the talk of a behind-closed-doors recording session at my studio in Nashville. Another part of me was afraid to be excited about it. At thirty-six, I didn't want to be disappointed yet again. The music business is bipolar by nature. You're up one minute, down the next. After a while the ups and down take a toll, both physically and emotionally.

On August 28, 1968, less than a month after we returned from Los Angeles, Emily and I were married. In many ways, Emily was my exact opposite. She was outgoing, vivacious, a risk-taker who encouraged me to push the envelope. I fell hard for Emily. In the throes of middle age, I was mesmerized by her vitality and her youthful optimism. For the first time in my life, I awakened each morning as excited about the woman lying next to me as I was about my music. It wasn't so much that Emily made me feel younger as it was that she made me feel alive.

We purchased a small, A-frame house on one of the highest hilltops in Nashville. It was a gingerbread house, warm and rustic, a romantic enclave for two people starting out on an adventure. I pushed myself at the studio, working 14- and 16-hour days. I wanted to give Emily everything she wanted (and deserved). With my income from the studio hovering around the $12,000-a-year mark, I knew that would be difficult. For that reason, I looked with growing anticipation to touring with Elvis. It was just the financial infusion I needed.

I waited patiently for word from Elvis.

When the television special aired, I received a letter from Jim Beedle, a disc jockey at WXCL in Peoria, Illinois. "I watched the 1956 gang totally wipe out NBC a couple of weeks ago, and the nostalgia was great," he wrote. "I have always been a fan of the great Elvis, and it was so good to see him back in action again. I really think what I dug about his records at the beginning was that knocked out lead man, and then found out it was you. I play the Epic LP *The Guitar That Changed The World* quite often on my shows, and it never fails, someone will call and wonder who that was." Beedle ended his letter by thanking me "for bringing back 1956—the original happening."

I waited for word from Elvis. The year was drawing to a close. The few times I tried to contact Elvis directly my calls were shunted aside, lost in the underling shuffle. I wasn't surprised. I figured it was Parker's doing.

When I finally heard something, it wasn't the news I expected. Word came that Elvis was going to record a new album in Memphis. It would be produced by Chips Moman at American Recording Studios. It would be the first time Elvis had recorded in a Memphis studio since the early days at Sun. I thought that maybe the new album would be used as a send-off vehicle for the European tour. At last, something was happening. I waited with anticipation for a call to report to the studio. That call never came.

Unknown to me at the time, Chips Moman refused to record with anyone except his house band. He had an obsessive commitment to the musicians that had given him a string of more than one hundred hits. He wasn't about to change his way of doing things, not even for Elvis Presley. As a tribute to me, Moman took my blond Gibson to the studio and gave it to Reggie Young to play on the session.

"That's what I thought of Scotty," Moman told my co-author. "His music changed my life. If I had it all to do over again, he would have been invited to that session."

Early on, Moman had a run-in with Parker over publishing rights to the songs Moman brought to the session. Parker called him aside and told him the publishing would have to be assigned to Elvis. Moman bristled at that suggestion.

"I'll tell you what," he told Parker, "if you feel that way we'll just wrap this session up right now and consider these songs very expensive demos."

Parker backed down and the session continued.

The Memphis session gave Elvis his first No. 1 hit since 1962. "Suspicious Minds" was praised by critics, who said it was Elvis's best work since the early days at Sun. I was used to disappointments, but Emily was not. It was one thing to be let down by Elvis—I was used to that—but it was something else to feel that he was letting down the woman that I loved.

I took the exclusion as a personal affront. What I did not know at the time was that it was not Elvis's or Parker's decision to exclude me from the session. It was not even Moman's decision, since using musicians other than his own house band was never a consideration for him. Moman could no more have used other musicians than I could have upended my sock drawer. The 827 Thomas Street Band was at the core of Moman's belief system.

Unknown to me, Moman was one of my biggest supporters.

"One of the things I missed with Elvis was his old band," says Moman. "I always liked Scotty and Bill and D. J. Fontana. I thought they were really unique. In my opinion, up until the 827 Thomas Street Band cut him, no one took an interest in his music after Scotty and Bill were gone. It was just a job for him. You could hear it on his records. Everything was rushed. I always thought it was sad that Scotty and Bill didn't stay their whole career with Elvis. They were unique together."

If the January 1969 Memphis recording session was a disappointment, news that same month that Elvis was planning a Las Vegas engagement was an even bigger blow. I was told flat out there would be no European tour. I met with D. J. and the Jordanaires to discuss the Las Vegas job. For them to all drop everything they were doing in Nashville to go there for two weeks would amount to a significant loss of income.

We got together and did an estimate. I don't remember the figure, but we told them we would have to have "x" amount to make it worthwhile. Says Gordon Stoker of the Jordanaires: "We would have had to get out of 34 scheduled sessions. It wasn't financially feasible for us to do it." When they received our fee they hit the ceiling, I'm sure. If we had known they were going on the road, it might have changed the picture. We might have sacrificed on the chance that the other things would happen, but no one told us anything about going out on the road after wrapping up the Vegas performance.

When Parker refused to pay us what we would have lost by giving up our work in Nashville, we said we would have to decline the offer. Parker responded by hiring James Burton, a respected session guitarist in Los Angeles, to put together a band for the engagement. Reportedly, Burton was paid $5,000 a week as the band leader.

The Vegas thing was the crowning blow.

I washed my hands of the entire affair.

Then I put my guitar in its case and didn't take it out again for a live performance for 24 years, limiting my guitar playing to the occasional recording session.

RINGO, TRACY, AND A CAST OF THOUSANDS

Tracy Nelson was never one to mince words. When asked where she lived, she said, "I live way the fuck out in Crib Death, Tennessee—my nearest neighbor is three-quarters of a mile away." The blues singer explained that her farm was west of Nashville. There are many ways to get to that farm, but the road that led her there began in 1969 at Music City Recorders.

That year Tracy and her group, Mother Earth, were out promoting their self-titled debut album, when the tour ended and they looked up from the road haze to get their bearings—and found themselves in Nashville. Since their record label wanted a new album, they decided to record it in Nashville. They rented a farm outside town and, working with producer Pete Drake, recorded a complete album at a studio named Bradley's Barn.

One day Drake took Tracy by Music City Recorders to meet me.

"Of course, I knew who he was," says Tracy. "I was mystified by *this* Scotty Moore."

She asked me about my guitar.

I said, "Oh, I never play anymore."

It had only been a few months since I had retired my guitar, but—like the Wild West gunfighters who hung up their guns—the gesture represented a serious commitment to abstention. Once I made up my mind to put my career as a performer behind me, I devoted the same meticulous attention to detail when I started setting up a studio. Working with a Memphis carpenter, I rebuilt the interior of the studio, designing it with sound quality in mind.

I kept thinking about wood. Why is there wood in a Stradivarius violin and in guitars? There must be a damn good reason. I asked the carpenter about different types of wood. The carpenter suggested balsa, but that didn't sound right to me. Too light. The carpenter then suggested pecky cypress, a coniferous evergreen that thrives in the lowlands of Louisiana and Mississippi. It is more porous and rougher than regular cypress. One of its most common uses in the South is for fishing boats. It can absorb water without losing its structural integrity.

We started checking around and found we couldn't get it in Nashville. It would cost an arm and a leg to have it shipped in, so the carpenter went back to Memphis and checked with a couple of places and found a place where he could get the raw stuff right out of a mill. He brought back some samples. When I saw the samples, I knew that was it.

The pecky cypress was cut into one-by-twelve planks and installed untreated on the studio walls. The raw, rough appearance of the pecky cypress looked great and absorbed sound. It was perfect. Well, almost perfect. A couple of weeks later, when the soft, absorbent wood dried, it shrank, leaving half-inch cracks between the planks.

I thought, "Well, I'll be damned." I got me a fruit tree sprayer and filled it up with water. Every few weeks, I wet the suckers down. It worked—and it also helped re-cycle the air in there. It took out the cigarette smell and made it seem fresh.

I had no problem keeping the studio booked. To keep up with demand—and to support my new wife—I worked as an engineer, pulling 12- and 14-hour days. One of my regular clients for over five years was the Air Force, which used the studio to record its syndicated radio program, *Country Music Time*. The program was produced quarterly by the Air Force recruiting branch and distributed to radio stations across the nation. It was hosted by Technical Sergeant Perry Bullard and featured a wide selection of recording artists, including Ferlin Husky, Jimmy Dickens, Stonewall Jackson, and Charlie McCoy. The program was taped in the studio and transferred to vinyl discs and mailed out in six-disc sets to radio stations. In between the banter and the music were commercials designed to lure new recruits into the Air Force.

★ ★ ★

After our meeting, Tracy and Drake decided to book Music City Recorders for a session with Mother Earth. Unlike the sessions with the Air Force, which were staid and well-heeled, the sessions with Tracy were wild and woolly, totally unpredictable.

At age twenty-two, fresh from the hippie and rock scene in Los Angeles, where Tracy was labeled the "new Janis Joplin" by the music press, a comparison Tracy despised—"I'm a better singer than she could have ever been," she was fond of saying—she reveled in shocking the

Nashville musicians who gathered around her in the studio. She talked like a man, cussed a blue streak, and used her simmering sexuality to her advantage. Occasionally, she showed up at the studio flashing a stash of marijuana.

Pete Drake's wife, Rose, laughs when she thinks about it today. At the time she was Pete's girlfriend. "We had never heard women use four-letter words like that," she said in an interview with my co-author.

When Tracy got around those country guys, she was so polite. Then, when she found out it embarrassed them, she just would not hush. She loved it. Scotty blushed, everyone did. Hippies hadn't really hit Nashville yet. They had the hippie look here but not the hippie ways. Pete took her into the front office and told her that women didn't talk like that—and that just set her off. Some days she'd come in and say, "Well, I'll be good tonight," or she'd say, "You guys have had it tonight." They were afraid to bring people into the studio because they didn't know what Tracy was going to do next.

I might have blushed a time or two; so much of what she said was unexpected and totally off-the-wall, but I loved every minute of it. We just hit it off from the beginning. If I hadn't been married to Emily, Tracy and I might have gotten together.

With me as their engineer, Mother Earth recorded a second album at Music City Recorders. When the album, *Make A Joyous Noise*, was released, it contained two discs: a "city" side and a "country" side. Playing on the country side, which was recorded at Music City Recorders, were D. J. Fontana on drums, Larry Butler on piano, Boz Scaggs on rhythm guitar, and the Jordanaires. A couple of times, I brought out my guitar to play on some of the tracks.

"We were just flabbergasted to have him on the session," Tracy says.

What was amazing was to sit around with Scotty every day. I'd think, "Jesus, look at this. I'm shooting the shit with Scotty Moore." If you got to be holed up in a room with someone, Scotty's the type of person you would want to do it with. He's very witty and has an appreciation of irony. I was curious about why he put his guitar away and on occasion I would ask him about it. He would say, without saying it, that he didn't want to talk about it. He felt really burned by how

*things went. He just decided the music business sucked and he didn't
want to be in the middle of something like that. The studio was sort
of a haven for him.*

★ ★ ★

Ringo Starr and I had something in common. One had recently gone
through a professional divorce; the other was in the process of getting
one. By June 1970, when Ringo arrived in Nashville, the Beatles had announced their breakup. No one was surprised. Any fool could see that
there was trouble in Beatleland.

When "Let It Be" topped the charts in April, No. 3 on the charts was
John Lennon's "Instant Karma (We All Shine On)." Ringo had already released a solo album, *Sentimental Journey*, a collection of standards produced by George Martin. Although there would be more chart toppers
from the Beatles—"The Long and Winding Road" went to No. 1 on June
13, the week before Ringo arrived in Nashville—the Beatles clearly were
pursuing separate careers.

Pete Drake met Ringo in England, where he had gone to do session
work. George Harrison had introduced them. Pete was the premier ped-
al-steel guitarist in America. A native of Atlanta, Georgia, he moved to
Nashville in 1959, where his innovative guitar work made him a legend
among studio musicians. Although his work pushed numerous singles to
the top of the country charts—including Roy Drusky's "I Don't Believe
You Love Me Any More" and George Hamilton IV's "Before This Day
Ends"—it was not until he released a solo single, "Forever," that the public
discovered his talents. By the time he met Ringo, he had recorded with
Bob Dylan, Joan Baez, and Elvis Presley. For George Harrison, who had
been experimenting with slide guitar, Pete was the real thing, someone he
wanted to recruit for an album.

"Come on over to Nashville, and we'll do an album," Pete told Ringo.
It was sort of an off-handed comment, the sort of thing you say to be
friendly. It never occurred to him that Ringo would say yes.

"Well, OK," Ringo said, not needing a hard sell. "Why not!"

When Pete returned to Nashville, he booked time at Music City
Recorders for the latter part of June and asked me if I would engineer the
session. Pete did most of his work for his label at my studio, so he was
comfortable working there. With my help, he put together twelve of the
city's finest session players, including D. J. Fontana on drums, Jerry Reed
on guitar, Charlie Daniels on acoustic guitar, Charlie McCoy on harp and

electric bass, Jerry Kennedy on dobro and electric guitar, Buddy Harmon on percussion, Shorty Lavender and Jim Buchanan on fiddle—and, of course, the Jordanaires.

All of the players were well known to me. I especially liked Jerry Reed, with whom I had worked on sessions with Elvis. Jerry was the only man besides myself and Chips Moman who had ever stood up to Colonel Parker. That, in itself, was enough to endear him to me.

The first thing Ringo did when he arrived in Nashville was to go to Ernest Tubb's Record Shop to get a stack of genuine country albums. Then he went to Sears Roebuck to buy toys to ship back to his children in England. Pete registered Ringo at two hotels. At the hotel where he did not stay, he was registered under his own name. It was an attempt to side-track the fans and reporters who had gotten word of the session. Ringo actually stayed on the fourth floor of the downtown Ramada Inn, where he checked in under an assumed name. The hotel no longer exists, but, at the time, it was popular with celebrities who came to town to record on Music Row.

When Ringo arrived at the studio the next day, he was greeted outside the door by an off-duty policeman with a clipboard. Pete had hired him to keep out the curious and to provide protection for the ex-Beatle. Standing next to the cop was Emily Moore.

"Name, please," said the burly cop.

"Ringo Starr."

The cop ran his finger down the list on the clipboard.

"Ringo, Ringo, Ringo," he mumbled. Then he looked the "funny" Beatle squarely in the face and gave him the bad news. "Don't see it. You can't come in."

Emily was dumbfounded.

"That's Ringo Starr," she said. "He's the reason you're here."

"Oh, yeah," the cop muttered. "Ringo Starr—you can go in."

What little ego Ringo still possessed—the press was already wondering aloud what poor Ringo would do without the other Beatles—was deflated as he entered the studio to face a roomful of Southern boys, most of whom bore a healthy skepticism of Ringo's ability to do justice to country music. Emily walked in behind Ringo and told me about the incident. I fell out laughing, but didn't tell the others. I kept that delicious tidbit to myself.

"Ringo was real quiet, but he was like one of the guys—a super nice guy, real laid back," recalls Rose Drake. "With Scotty being real quiet and

Ringo being real quiet, there didn't seem to be a whole lot of extra conversation in the studio."

For D. J. Fontana, it was the first session he had ever played on in which the singer was a drummer. Ringo played on a couple of songs, but he was there to sing, not to play drums. "I have to give Ringo credit," says D. J. "Had it not been for him, that band would have fallen apart. He was such a stickler for tempo. The guys would say Ringo wasn't a drummer. I'd say, 'The hell he isn't!'"

The sessions lasted three days, going from about six o'clock in the evening to one o'clock in the morning. The studio was always packed. To satisfy public demand for information, Pete and I allowed reporters from the Nashville *Tennessean* and the *Nashville Banner* into the studio for brief glimpses of the session. Incredibly, the reporters got Ringo mixed up with songwriter Sorrells Pickard, who wrote four of the twelve songs used on the album. When Ringo read the newspaper stories the next day, describing him as a heavy-set, goateed man in a red shirt, he couldn't believe it. "They didn't even know who Ringo was," says Rose. "They kept describing Sorrells. Every move he made, the newspaper got it totally confused with Ringo."

After reading the newspaper story, Ringo protested to everyone around him: "But I didn't do that. I didn't do that!" To everyone's surprise, Ringo blended in exceptionally well with the other musicians. If every once in a while they had a little fun with him, it wasn't because they didn't like him. Southern boys only fun around with people they like, or people they think they might be *about to like*. Sometimes Pete or I would conclude a playback of a vocal with a comment that maybe it needed a little more echo.

Laughing good-naturedly, Ringo would respond, "Yeah, I guess we do."

One time we kept moving him away from the microphone until he was all the way out of the studio and down the hall and almost out the back door.

"Just a little bit further," we told him each time he moved.

"But you can't hear me," Ringo protested.

"We know, we know," we said, laughing.

Ringo took the joke in stride. He worked like a real trouper. We were using head arrangements that we made up on the spot. He only had the three days to learn the songs. He would start singing, and all the pickers would put it together.

"Whatever we wanted to do was fine with him," says D. J. "Sure, he struggled with the vocals, but I thought he did a good job. He's not a bad singer at all. He has that little English accent—yeah, I'd buy that album, sure would."

The day after they wrapped the session, they all piled into Pete's bus and lumbered out to Tracy Nelson's farm to take photographs for the album cover. Nashville photographer Marshall Fallwell, who was friends with both Pete and myself, was hired to take the pictures. He had been allowed into the studio for the entire session and did an admirable job of documenting the madness. As surprised as anyone was Tracy Nelson. "We were sitting around the house one day and Pete or Rose—I forget which one—called and said, 'We're on our way out with Ringo Starr to take some pictures.' They didn't want to give us any warning so no one would know where he was. When they pulled up, I, of course, was trying to throw together some lunch. Ringo was a vegetarian and all I had in the house was bacon."

Tracy, who had never met Ringo, was impressed by his shyness. "He was very sweet," she says. "We had these horses and cows, and they would come right up to the house. They wanted to take pictures of him with a horse and it scared the hell out of him. I had to coax him to put his hand out to give the horse sugar, but he ended up making friends with the colt."

Before leaving Nashville, Ringo gave Pete one of his silk shirts. Pete had kidded him throughout the session about his wild clothes, which, in the land of rhinestone shirts and over-sized cowboy hats, took more than a little gall on Pete's part. Ringo may not have had a deep appreciation of Southern humor, but he knew a good heart when he saw one. The shirt was an acknowledgment of that.

The album was titled *Beaucoups of Blues* (after the lead cut) and was released by Apple Records. Pete did the project without anything in writing from Apple. People told him he was a fool to work that way, but he had faith it would work out. "I think the world will be shocked when his record comes out," Pete told a Nashville writer. "[Ringo] worked his tail off. This should be the thing that puts Nashville music on Top 40 stations." Also expressing confidence in the album was Tommy Hill, manager of Window Music Publishers, which held American publishing rights to the songs: "I believe this is one of the best things to ever happen to Nashville."

When the first single, "Beaucoups of Blues," was released in October, *Cash Box* selected it as one of its "Picks of the Week." Said the review: "This is a fine country single that because of Ringo's name and the pop overtones of the song itself should be going well on the pop side in short order." The song also was praised by *Billboard* and *Record World*.

Unfortunately, the single never made it out of the eighties on the charts, but it did open the door for other hit singles by Ringo. Today the album, which was re-released in 1995 by Capitol Records, is regarded as a landmark work by the ex-Beatle.

For my part, I chalked up another "first," becoming the only person to work for the two most influential independent labels in record history— Sun Records and Apple Records.

★ ★ ★

Inexplicably speeding down the entrance ramp to Interstate 240 in Memphis, Thomas Wayne Perkins crossed four lanes of traffic, picked up even more speed, and then shot across the median into incoming traffic, slamming flush into a car driven by Vance Simelton of Little Rock.

Seven hours later, Thomas Wayne was dead.

Police determined his death to be an accident, although there were indications he had floored his accelerator as he came off the ramp. Since they couldn't prove what he was thinking when his car went out of control—only that it did go out of control—they wrote it up as an accident. Vance Simelton was simply in the wrong place at the wrong time.

Thomas Wayne was buried on August 17, 1971, at Madison Heights Baptist Church in Hendersonville, Tennessee. Those who attended the funeral couldn't help but think how tragic it all was—and how ironic that his only success bore the name "Tragedy."

For more than a decade, Thomas Wayne had struggled to re-create the success of that 1959 hit. I recorded countless sessions with him, released singles on my Belle Meade label, which I had begun shortly after moving to Nashville, and promoted him at every opportunity. Nothing worked. The public had decided Thomas Wayne's place in history was as a one-hit wonder. In the end, the best I could do for Thomas Wayne was to offer him work in Music City Recorders. I understood what Thomas Wayne did not understand: Hit records are a flirtation from the public, not a promise of a long-term relationship. Some artists feel that a hit record entitles them to a lifetime of hit records. I have always known better.

I wasn't surprised when I heard about Thomas Wayne's death. His behavior had grown more and more erratic over the years. Every once in a while he would tend to get high and flip out on me. I think some of his problems were due to an ongoing and long-running dispute with his ex-wife, Charlene. In fact, he had gone to Memphis on the weekend of his death to resolve a conflict with Charlene over their daughter, Maria Elena.

Hugh Hickerson was also among those not surprised at Thomas Wayne's death. Hugh was an audio technician who often did work at my studio. After Thomas Wayne left Music City Recorders to work for Pro-Sound Productions, then for a recording studio named NAR, where he was employed at the time of his death, Hugh continued to have contact with him on a professional level. They became friends, according to Hickerson, but were not what you would call "drinking buddies."

Shortly before he died, Thomas Wayne made a startling confession to Hickerson. He confided that he had once parked his car across both lanes of the interstate one night—and turned off his lights. He did it at a blind curve that would have made it impossible for traffic coming at a high rate of speed to stop. Fortunately, the highway patrol arrived on the scene before an accident occurred. They found him sitting in the car, waiting for whatever was going to happen.

"He said he was arrested and they were going to send him for psychological evaluation, but he got an attorney who got him out of it," Hickerson says. "We talked about it. The impression I had was that he was doing it in order to achieve a violent end to his life."

The last time Hickerson saw Thomas Wayne was at the NAR facility on Division Street when he went to the studio late one night to repair some equipment. He didn't see Thomas Wayne when he first walked in, but since he knew his way around the studio, he went to the back room where the equipment was located. Later, when he finished, he walked back out into the studio. He saw someone at the piano, but in the dim light he couldn't tell who it was. As he walked closer, he saw that it was Thomas Wayne. From the look on his face—and the weird sounds he was making—it seemed like he might be in trouble.

"Is anything wrong?" asked Hickerson, walking around the piano.

Thomas Wayne didn't respond, just kept making funny sounds.

Once Hickerson was close enough to see what was happening he was taken aback.

Thomas Wayne was having sex with a woman on the piano bench. Neither Thomas Wayne nor the woman was fully undressed, but they displayed no embarrassment at being interrupted. They just kept doing what they were doing.

"Excuse me," Hickerson said, and left. He never saw Thomas Wayne again.

"I sensed that he was very distraught with his life," says Hickerson. "Thomas Wayne wanted to regain that part of his life that he had lost. He was a nice guy, but he was one of those guys that, if you were around him, you could sense that he was suffering. There was some pain he was feeling. If he had not avoided that psychological evaluation, that might have enabled him to see it through. His death was such a tragedy, not only for himself but for the other man involved in the accident."

★ ★ ★

By 1971 two of the three people with whom I was most closely identified, both personally and professionally—Bill Black and Thomas Wayne—were gone, felled under tragic circumstances. At least Elvis was still going strong. Not going strong was my marriage. The harder I worked to provide for Emily, the longer the hours I put in at the studio, the more we seemed to argue about me never being at home. The more neglected Emily felt, the harder I worked to make her happy. The faster that circle spun, the more I drank to dull the pain. Then the drinking itself became an issue between us.

By late 1971, Robbie Dawson had returned into my life. She had married a military man and moved to Japan. When she began having problems with her husband, she returned to the States and called me, initiating an affair that lasted well into 1972. One result of the affair was a daughter, Tasha, born on July 19, 1973. After the affair ended, Robbie moved to Mississippi, where she died of cancer in 2007. "I never asked Scotty for anything," said Robbie. "Just him knowing that he has a daughter is enough for me. I loved him from day one—and, to the day I die, I will love him."

Emily never knew about my affair with Robbie. It was the drinking that got to her. One night, I came home from the studio, maneuvered around the three sharp turns that made the drive up to my mountaintop home an interesting exercise in motor vehicle dexterity, only to be greeted by an empty house and a locked door. When I couldn't find my keys, I smashed in the door with a sledgehammer and went upstairs and went to sleep.

Emily moved out of the house and filed for divorce. It was granted on November 22, 1972. "Scotty is not a person I ever thought I would marry, but I really fell in love with him," she said in an interview for this book. "I will always love Scotty; we will always be close. I never doubted that Scotty loved me. I'm sure a lot of what happened was the pressure of him trying to do things for me. He pushed himself to the limit in a lot of ways."

In 1973, within months of the divorce, I sold Music City Recorders and started working as a freelance engineer: Have ear, will travel. Mostly I worked out of Monument Studios. I worked nights and slept days. Mort

Thomasson, one of the owners, preferred to work days, so that arrangement worked out well for everyone. I had my own key, and I came and went as I pleased.

Gail Pollock was working for Monument when we first met. She had no idea that I had an association with Elvis. She knew nothing about my background. That may have been because I never talked about my past. One day Gail was in her office talking to a man who had dropped by to book studio time. While they were talking, I came in to book some time for myself. Gail introduced us. We exchanged pleasantries and then I left.

"Is that the real Scotty Moore?" the man asked, his face showing disbelief.

"Well, that's his name," Gail answered.

"You mean, *the* Scotty Moore, the one who played with Elvis?"

Gail had no idea what he was talking about.

"No," she said. "He's an engineer."

Thomasson, who was sitting there when the conversation took place, laughed when the man left. "Scotty will dance at your next two or three weddings," he said.

"Why?" she asked, still not getting it.

"For not telling that guy he played with Elvis."

"Did he, really?"

"Hell, yes," Thomasson said.

Gail was speechless. "I didn't even know Scotty played guitar," she says. "I saw him several times a week—probably just about every day—and it never came up. He never mentioned it and no one else did either. I asked him about it, and he said, 'Yes, I'm guilty.' That was all that was said."

★ ★ ★

Fiercely independent, my mother Mattie Moore lived alone on the farm for twelve years after the death of my father. As a teenager, she had promised to spend all her days with Scott—and she kept her word. She never remarried. She never built a new life to replace the one she had lived with her one and only husband. Of course, living alone on a farm in Crockett County was not like living alone in a city. She had neighbors who cared about her. She never felt isolated because help was only a phone call away.

By February 1975 her health was failing, and she was admitted to a Jackson hospital for surgery. She wanted to go home to recuperate, but there was no one there to take care of her, so she was persuaded to enter a nursing home where she could receive 24-hour-a-day care.

Mary Ann Coscarelli, a dark-haired, brown-eyed schoolteacher who had met me shortly after my divorce from Emily, volunteered to go to Jackson to look in on Mattie. She and I dated off and on, and she lived with me briefly, but our relationship was volatile, punctuated by frequent arguments, which I attributed to her hot-blooded Italian ancestry.

Mattie was grateful for the visits. "She and I got on quite well," recalled Mary Ann in an interview for this book. "She was a very feisty lady, a very strong lady. I was concerned about her, as I would be for any human being going through that type of problem. I went to serve as a liaison, to keep the family members informed as to her condition."

Mary Ann's visits didn't extend past February. Mattie didn't recuperate well after her surgery, and, at age 83, she passed away before the month was out, only days away from the anniversary of my father's death. Mary Ann and I went to the funeral together. Afterward, we gathered at Mother's house with the rest of the family to reminisce about old times. For me, it was a hurtful time, for it reminded me of the isolation I felt growing up on the farm. I had learned that it was possible to feel loved by one's family and isolated from them at the same instant. It presented an emotional dichotomy that would trouble me for the remainder of my life. What I felt in my heart and what I was able to express to other people were not always identical.

After Mother's death I threw himself into my work at Monument. I had lost my mother and father, my musical alter ego (Bill Black), the symbol of my musical independence (Thomas Wayne)—and I had endured three divorces, the last of which had left me emotionally drained. Studio work is a notoriously effective salve for bruised spirits. The rooms are usually dim, almost dark, purposefully built to provide a womblike environment. Because music has a life of its own, it is easy to get lost in the mechanics of transferring it to tape; the process offers a unique opportunity to control and manipulate emotions with a flick of a switch or a turn of a dial.

I thrived in that environment. If anything, I worked too hard. I engineered demo sessions for would-be singers and songwriters. I engineered sessions for established artists. Just about every country singer in town came through at one time or another. Sometimes I engineered sessions just for the hell of it, or just to help someone that I felt had talent.

Harpist Cindy Reynolds falls into the latter category.

"[Scotty] made a tape of me with D. J. Fontana on drums and Bill Humble on bass," she told a reporter for the Nashville *Tennessean.* "[He] played it for producers in town just to get work for me—for no other reason."

Others I worked with during that time were saxophonist Norm Ray and harmonica player Terry McMillan. Gail Pollock recalls me working so hard I looked "like a turtle" because of back and neck strain I received hunched over the soundboard.

"It was set up so he had to look to his side," she says. "He would sit for hours with his head turned to the right. He started walking stiffly and couldn't unbend his neck. You could feel a knot on his shoulder. He had to go to a chiropractor."

It was during this time that I renewed my friendship with Carl Perkins. For the past decade, Perkins had toured with the Johnny Cash band. He was a regular on Cash's network television show that ran from 1969 to 1971, and often was spotlighted with solos. The exposure brought him a contract with Columbia Records that led to several albums, including *On Top* in 1969 and *Boppin' the Blues* in 1970. But by the mid-1970s, Carl's career was once again in a down cycle. I had always liked Carl and respected his work, so in 1975 when Carl asked me to play on "EP Express," a song he was recording for Mercury Records, I took my guitar out of storage and did the session with him. The lyrics of "EP Express," which was written by Carl, consisted of song titles from Elvis's recordings. Despite our shared musical ancestry at Sun Records, it was the first time that Carl and I had ever recorded together. I enjoyed his music. He was a good ole country boy like I thought I was. We considered ourselves friends.

★ ★ ★

One day I bumped into another Sun Records alumnus, Jerry Lee Lewis, at a disc jockey convention. We met in Mercury Records' hospitality suite and sat around talking, having a few drinks, going over old times. Of course, that was a mistake. Jerry and I didn't have any *good* old times. One thing led to another, and the subject of my guitar playing came up. Jerry told me that I wasn't good enough to play guitar in his band. Those were fighting words.

D. J. Fontana, who was there with his wife Barbara, remembers what happened next. "Chairs were going every which way, and Scotty and Jerry were rolling out in the floor," he says. "I thought, 'Damn, what are they doing?' Scotty was just beating the fire out of him, really. They were fighting to kill each other."

The sight of two forty-something-year-old men slugging it out in public is not a pretty sight in the best of circumstances. In this case, D. J. was friends with both men, so it wasn't a sight he wanted to witness. He hurriedly got Barbara to her feet and led her to the door.

"I didn't want to get in the middle," D. J. says. "I knew Scotty could take Jerry. I don't think they have ever really gotten along. They like each other, I think, but they just have different attitudes. When I saw them out there wrestling, I thought, 'Shit, I'm going home.'"

So did I. Things like that really grated on me. As the months went by, I seemed to withdraw more into myself. I rented office space in the building at 1609 McGavock that housed Monument's warehouse. With my mind made up about never performing again, I settled in for the long haul. Working as an engineer was about as far away from the music business as you could go and still stay in it. It was where I wanted to be.

★ ★ ★

On August 16, 1977, I was at the studio when I received a telephone call from Emily. I was surprised to hear from her. There was a breathless urgency to her voice.

"Have you heard about it?" she asked, her voice rising. "About Elvis—he's dead. It's on the news."

All the things that I thought and felt that day are a blur to me today. I recall that it came as a total surprise, a lightning bolt. At least the timing of it struck me that way. At a deeper level, that psychic part of me that always knew what Elvis was thinking before he even thought it was not surprised that he had met a premature death. I always said he would never grow old gracefully. I don't think he could handle it. Maybe in the back of his mind that was part of it—that he had a death wish. We'll never know. I look at pictures of him taken the last year and I can see the drugs. When he started putting on weight, he looked like he could be on anything. He looked loose—like he was coming unglued, falling apart.

When Emily hung up the telephone after talking to me, she felt sorry for me. Just because we were divorced did not mean she did not feel my pain. "I never saw Scotty cry, but that was the only time I ever heard his voice break and I knew it was great turmoil for him," she says. "He was truly crushed. That was a part of his life—and a friend for life, someone he cared about. There was real sadness in his voice."

The Memphis Police Department initially reported Elvis's cause of death as either heart failure or an accidental overdose of drugs. Before the day was over, spokesmen for the police department denied that a drug overdose was a suspected cause of death. In the years following his death, countless theories evolved about his final days, each more spectacular than the other.

I have no special insight into Elvis's death. We had not spoken since the "Comeback" special televised in 1968. When I think of Elvis, I think of the man I knew in the early years, when he was young and vibrant and ready to set the world on fire. I never met the bloated, awkward Elvis I saw in photographs in later years. That Elvis was a stranger to me.

With Elvis's death, I lost more than a friend. I lost the hope that our "misunderstanding" would ever be resolved. That wasn't something that I thought about all the time. But it was something that was always in the back of my mind—the possibility that, at any given moment, the telephone could ring and it would be Elvis and everything would be like it was in the old days and we would be off and running again. Now I knew that the telephone would never ring again. The waiting was over.

★ ★ ★

Three days before Elvis died, Memphis songwriter Sharri Paullus, whose physician husband had once treated Gladys, called Vernon to tell him that she had written two songs for Elvis. One of the songs, "Heartbreak Avenue," was perfect for him, she said. Vernon told her to send the demos over to Graceland. "I can't promise he'll do them, but he will listen," he told her.

When Elvis came in that night, he listened to the songs. Vernon called Sharri back the next day. He told her Elvis loved "Heartbreak Avenue."

"He said he could do the same thing with it that he did with 'Heartbreak Hotel,'" he said. "We'll send over a car for you tomorrow."

The next day, as she waited for the car to arrive, Sharri turned on the radio.

That's how she learned that Elvis was dead. There would be no car for her that day, nor any other day. "I couldn't believe it," she said. "That's what you call getting close."

T. G. Sheppard was at Graceland the day before Elvis died. The following day J. D. Sumner called him and asked if he was sitting down. "The first words out of my mouth were, 'It's Elvis, isn't it?'" recalls Sheppard. "It was scary to see him go down the way he did, especially when you were there in the lean years and saw him lean, mean and sharp looking. Then to see him change, it was very depressing." One of Sheppard's memories was of being in the den at Graceland when everyone began scrambling after they'd received word that someone had climbed over the wall and had something in their hand that they were pointing at the house. "Elvis was freaking. He grabbed his gun and there was a fear in him that I'd never seen before."

On August 18, 1977, Elvis's funeral was held at Graceland, followed by a brief ceremony and burial at Forest Hill Cemetery.[12] Pallbearers included Joe Esposito, Lamar Fike, George Klein, Charlie Hodge, Billy Smith, Jerry Schilling, and his personal physician, Dr. George Nicholopoulos. Producer Felton Jarvis was scheduled to be a pallbearer, but he was unable to attend. I did not attend the funeral. I remained in Nashville.

Minutes after he heard about the death, Colonel Parker booked a flight to Memphis for the purpose of meeting with Vernon over merchandising rights to Elvis's name. The King might be dead, but that was no reason for the kingdom to suffer. The way Parker saw it, Elvis was worth as much dead as he was alive, maybe more. At the funeral Parker wore a bright blue shirt, opened at the collar, and a baseball cap, looking like he was decked out for a summer barbecue. If he had any feelings for the man he called "son," he kept them to himself.

---

12. On October 2, 1977, Elvis's body was removed from Forest Hill Cemetery, along with that of his mother, and both were reburied side by side at Graceland. The relocation was spurred by a bizarre incident earlier in the year when three men wearing dark jumpsuits were arrested and charged with trespassing on cemetery property.

★ 12 ★

ON THE ROAD AGAIN

Carol Burnett and Dolly Parton could not have been more different. Dolly was bubbly, effervescent, and charmingly democratic in her approach to those with whom she worked. She'd just as soon hug you as look at you. By contrast, Carol was intense and standoffish, someone who avoided eye contact and conversation, preferring the solitude of her own company.

None of that matters to me. Just an observation.

Carol and Dolly were in Nashville to tape a television special at Opryland, *Carol and Dolly Together Again for the First Time*. Before they taped the show, they gathered at Monument to record the music. I was the engineer. When they moved over to Opryland for the actual taping, I went there, too, pulling duty on the soundboard as a freelance engineer.

At the studio, Carol sat with her husband and daughter on one side of the control room. They talked among themselves, but avoided conversation with the staff. It was almost as if they had pulled their wagons into a circle as a means of self-protection. Carol didn't feel entirely comfortable in Nashville and her discomfort showed.

Of course, Dolly felt right at home in the studio. Over the years I had engineered a number of her demo sessions—back before she became famous, when she was Dolly Parton, the wannabe—so I was used to her gregarious, down-home ways. Unlike Carol, Dolly has the same engaging personality off stage as she does on stage.

When Dolly walked into the studio, she was wearing an oversized sweater that hung down to her knees. The massive sleeves were wadded up to her elbows. The baggy sweater belonged to her husband, Carl, a large man who would have filled it out nicely. As she entered the control room where I was seated, she whirled about in a modelesque manner with her arms extended as if to say without actually saying it, "Here I am!"

Dolly made eye contact with me and said, "Scotty, I knew you wanted to see me in a sweater."

I did but maybe not that particular sweater.

From the mid-seventies to the early eighties, I engineered a number of television shows, often working with Hugh Hickerson at Opryland Productions. "I don't think a lot of people knew about Scotty's background," says Hickerson. "A lot of the artists he worked with probably didn't know. I don't think Ann-Margret or Carol Burnett knew. I think a lot of the country artists would have known." The anonymity suited me just fine. Talking about Elvis—or guitar picking—weren't high on my list of things to do.

Ann-Margret's show, which was taped at the Opry House in February 1977, was titled *Ann-Margret . . . Rhinestone Cowgirl*. Her guests were Bob Hope, Perry Como, and Minnie Pearl. With Hope and Minnie Pearl on the set, I was pretty much kept in stitches. Told they would have to run through a number one more time, Hope grinned and said, "Want to take it from where we got off the plane?"

Producer Gary Smith told reporters for the *Tennessean* they were doing the show in Nashville because they thought a country flavor would result in higher ratings. Leaving Los Angeles to do the show, he said, had cost them about $75,000 extra, but he thought the added expense would be worth it in the long run. Smith was impressed with the facilities.

What he didn't know was that, technically, it was still a work in progress. For several years, Hickerson and I had struggled with the Opry House management to make changes to improve the acoustics and technical capabilities of the facility. When I first started working there, Mort Thomasson saved my butt by coming up with a solution to a technical problem.

They had an orchestra pit—well, it wasn't actually a pit; it was built flush with the floor that came down from the audience—and we were having problems with the bottom end of the strings. On the way home one night, I stopped by Monument. It was seven or eight o'clock and Mort was still there. We started chit-chatting and I explained the problem to him. He had never been out there, so he asked me to explain how it was set up.

I explained how the orchestra pit was about two feet below floor level and had open space between it and the basement floor.

"That's the problem," Mort said. "It's like a big bass drum."

Armed with that perception, I went back to the theater and dropped in eighty-cycle cutoffs on the strings and boosted it to a level where the strings could be heard. I didn't know it at the time, but Mort had firsthand knowledge of that problem from when he worked at Columbia, where their Studio A was built on coils. The whole floor had coils under it. It was the same thing I was dealing with at the Opry House.

When I recorded the orchestra in the studio at Monument, Ann-Margret came by to do scratch vocals. She would sing the actual vocals live when the show was taped, but the music itself would be prerecorded when the program aired. I enjoyed working with Ann-Margret, but apparently she was unaware of my long association with Elvis because she never brought it up. Of course, I knew about her longtime romance with Elvis; but I saw no reason to say anything.

Gail Pollock was in the studio when Ann-Margret did her vocals. "She is such a beautiful creature," she says. "At that point, country music was not big like it is now. She was of a larger magnitude star than what we normally dealt with. She was so perfect it hurt your eyes to look at her—but she's not that great a singer."

I did so many television shows during that time—often sharing engineering duties with my friend, Conrad Jones—they have since all blurred in my memory. I did three remote shows called *Nashville on the Road*, and a series of thirteen hourlong programs called *Music Hall America*, which featured a cast of kids who sang and danced in Opryland Park. One show I did with Conrad was the Joey Heatherton special. Working with us in the control room was Conrad's cousin Terry. During a rehearsal, Heatherton wandered about in the audience, singing on a riser. She kept yelling up at the control room for more fold-back because she couldn't hear herself. Terry pushed the talk back that went into the auditorium and said, 'Hell, the commodes are white capping up here now it's so loud."

When he was interviewed for this book, Conrad described me as a perfectionist who was a "fanatic" about little things. "He would not accept the fact that we were using [lightweight] 10 KC telephone lines," he explained. "We would have to tweak and twist every knob there trying to get a little more high and low end, which the telephone lines just lost. Gosh, he would hound Hugh Hickerson and myself into oblivion. He had been a session musician. He really had trouble accepting [the limitations of our technology]."

Whenever musicians from my past showed up to do a television show I made it a point not to leave the control room to talk to them. "I don't know how many Johnny Cash shows we did with Carl Perkins, Jerry Lee Lewis—people who would have loved to talk to him—but unless it was sound related, he stayed in the control room," said Conrad. "He was not Scotty Moore, the picker. For years, we tried to get him [to perform again], but he would just look at you and grin and say, 'Elvis is dead.'"

One of the things Conrad remembers best is the way he and I watched the clock. As the second hand moved toward the clock-out time, we would look at each other and grin. In my briefcase, which I carried with me wherever I went, was a bottle of Johnny Walker (Red). The instant the big hand hit the mark, the briefcase snapped open and Johnny Walker became the star.

★ ★ ★

It was while I was working as a freelance engineer that I became a businessman. In 1976, when Monument decided not to renew its lease for the building it was using as a warehouse, I was approached by the building's owner about purchasing it. The owner said he would make me a good deal on the building. Tommy Hill, an employee of Gusto Records, told me where some equipment could be picked up at auction for a good price. If I wanted to bid on the equipment and open a tape-duplication business, he would be happy to put up money as a partner.

I bought the building and the equipment, and then opened a business under the name Independent Producers Corporation (IPC). The business made copies of tapes in large quantities for studio owners, songwriters, and musicians who needed cassettes to distribute or sell to potential clients and customers. I hired two young women to operate the plant, and I allowed my nephew, Jerry, to oversee the accounts payable and receivable. I supervised the overall operation of the business, but continued to work as a freelance engineer.

Soon after I started the tape-duplication business, my daughter, Andrea, came to Nashville to live with me. She enrolled in classes at Nashville Tech and worked part-time at the tape plant for about six months. When she became homesick, she went back to Memphis to live with her mother. The following year, when she was nineteen, she returned to Nashville to live with me once again. For the previous eight years, Andrea had only visited me once a year, usually at Thanksgiving, so living with me full-time required some adjustment on her part.

"It was kinda tough," she admitted. "I've always been real picky and didn't date too much. The first thing he told me was that I needed to be on the pill. That way he didn't have to worry."

Although re-establishing parent-child bonds with me proved more difficult than she imagined, Andrea enjoyed working at the tape plant.

"He's a good boss," she says. "My mother always said he paid people well. He treats his employees like family." Her best memory of those years, she says, was "just sitting around drinking" with her father. "Once I got to be an adult, I think he could relate to me better."

★ ★ ★

For me, the eighties offered an opportunity to put my past behind me. I became Scotty Moore, the engineer, the businessman; many people I worked with had no idea I even played a musical instrument. It was like I entered the Witness Protection program. Scotty Moore, the guitar legend, ceased to exist.

In 1982, IPC bought a print shop, which we named Villa Printing. Located on Edgehill and Villa Place, it specialized in small-order jobs. As the demand for cassettes increased at the tape plant, so did the difficulty in obtaining cassette inserts from local printers. Owning my own print shop allowed me to do faster and better work at the tape plant. Within a couple of years, the name of the print shop was changed to IPC Graphics and it was relocated downtown. At that point, both businesses were incorporated into the same company.

By 1980, Gail Pollock, who had been helping me part-time at the tape plant—"I was like unpaid help whenever they needed it because Scotty and I were friends," she says—learned that I wanted to hire someone to handle the graphics and do the layouts on the eight-track labels.

"I said, 'Scotty, why don't you just hire me?'"

As a result, Gail left Monument to work full-time for me. People joked that she was to me what Della was to Perry Mason: My right hand, my shoulder to cry on, my business advisor.

Occasionally, an enterprising writer tracked me down and asked for an interview, but with a few exceptions I begged off, saying I really didn't have anything to say. Elvis was dead.

Just because I gave up performing did not mean that I had lost interest in guitars. In March 1987 Allan Cartee, with whom I had worked on previous occasions, called and told me that he was leaving town and wanted to sell his guitar. He had a Gibson Super 400. Would I be interested in buying it? I told him I wasn't playing any longer. But he brought it by to show me. He had bought it for a session with the Stray Cats and it only had been played one time, by Brian Setzer.

I bought the guitar for $1,500. I saw it as an investment, if nothing else. The guitar sold for about $5,000 new. I didn't know if I would ever again play it in public, but, as an investment, I thought I couldn't go wrong.[13] I added the guitar to my collection, which still included the original Ray Butts amplifier I bought in 1955. For years people had been collecting my castoffs; I decided to become a collector myself.

★ ★ ★

In September 1989 I ran into Carl Perkins at a Music Row party honoring Carl for a No. 1 song he had co-written for the Judds. Carl and I drifted away from the others and stood out on the porch for more than an hour talking. We had grown up about twenty miles from each other in West Tennessee. I had always liked his records. A few times, while he still was recording for Sun Records, I sat in with him at a club in Jackson.

We talked about the old days a lot. Finally, the conversation took a sharp turn into the present. Carl looked at me, a broad smile creeping across his face.

"We never did do an album together," Carl said.

"Hell, I haven't played in years. I wouldn't know what to do with a guitar."

"It's just like falling off a bicycle—you never forget how," Carl said, laughing.

"I'll think about it."

It was shortly after that meeting that Carl was diagnosed with throat cancer. I kept in touch with him. Carl told me that he didn't think he would ever again be able to sing. The radiation treatment had destroyed his saliva glands, making it impossible for him to do vocals.

I told him that we would do the album as soon as he whipped the cancer.

Carl said he didn't know if he wanted to whip it if he could not sing again.

In 1989 ABC-TV accepted a proposal from Priscilla Presley and Jerry Schilling for a weekly series titled *Elvis*. The thirty-minute program focused on Presley's early years with Bill and me. The idea was to show the teenage Elvis, as he was in the beginning of his career, not the slick, seasoned performer that he became in later years.

Jerry, who had met Elvis while playing football in Memphis, ended up working for the entertainer. He was on Elvis's staff from 1964 to 1976, and subsequently became a manager for the Beach Boys and the Sweet

---

13. In 1992 Scotty asked Gibson the price of a Super 400. They said they only made them on special order. They had a price tag of $17,500.

Inspirations. After Elvis's death, Priscilla hired him to be the creative affairs director of the Presley estate.

Priscilla and Jerry, along with a third investor, produced the television series themselves. Actor Michael St. Gerard, then twenty-five, was chosen to play Elvis; Jesse Dabney was picked to play me, and Blake Gibbons to play Bill Black. Chosen to be the singing voice of the young Elvis was country singer Ronnie McDowell.

Immediately after Elvis's death in 1977, Ronnie co-wrote a song about the entertainer titled "The King Is Gone." Partly as a result of the success of that song, Dick Clark Productions asked him to do soundtrack vocals for a 1979 television movie about Elvis. Ronnie scored several hit singles on the country charts in the late seventies and eighties, including "Wandering Eyes," "Older Women," "Unchained Melody," and "Watchin' Girls Go By." When time came for Priscilla and Jerry to choose a vocalist for their series, Priscilla requested Ronnie. His voice was so close to Elvis's, she sometimes could not tell them apart.

Jerry Schilling had met me several times over the years, but by the time he became a salaried employee, my contacts with Elvis were limited to occasional recording sessions. As a result, Jerry didn't have a strong personal relationship with me. When he asked me to be a consultant for the TV series, he wasn't sure what to expect. He had heard the stories about me shunning the spotlight. I surprised everyone, myself included, by saying yes.

"Knowing Elvis the way I did, I knew the support system he needed," says Jerry. "Scotty was like the rock in the foundation that Elvis depended on. That is why Scotty was his manager in the beginning. Scotty was low key, strong, honest, certainly a talented musician—and he gave Elvis a lot of strength. They were out there on the road and there wasn't anyone else. Scotty was the rock, sort of like the pope is the rock of the church. Knowing Elvis and Scotty the way I do, I can see why Elvis depended on him."

To my surprise, I enjoyed being a consultant for the show. I especially liked the actor who played me in the series. When it aired in February 1990 most critics were unanimous in their praise of its authenticity. Robert Oermann, music critic for the Nashville *Tennessean*, wrote: "By any measure, *Elvis* is extraordinary television . . . when you're dealing with the most famous entertainer in world history the truth is more fascinating than any fiction could ever be." To hammer home the point, Oermann's article bore a headline that said: NEW PRIME-TIME PRESLEY SERIES EXHIBITS ASTONISHING AUTHENTICITY. Unfortunately, television viewers were not as receptive of the series and it was not renewed for a second season.

★ ★ ★

By 1989 I had grown accustomed to being a "former" guitarist. It had a comfortable feel to it, like a pair of old shoes. Over the years, countless requests for information, artifacts, guitar-playing tips, and personal appearances arrived at my tape-duplication business. Gail answered the letters and screened the calls, but I turned down all requests for personal appearances.

One day Jerry Schilling received a telephone call from someone in the Rolling Stones organization. They wanted to know if he knew how to get in touch with me. If so, would he mind asking me if I would meet the Rolling Stones? They were in the middle of their Steel Wheels tour and would be happy to fly me to one of their concerts.

"I called him, and he was at the tape factory," says Jerry, who told him about the request from the Stones. "He said, 'That might be a kick.'"

Jerry relayed the message to the Stones, with the admonition that he was certain that I would not want to perform. A few days later, the Stones business manager called Jerry back.

"Did you talk to Scotty?" Jerry asked.

"Sure did," said the business manager.

"What'd he say?"

"He said, 'Why don't you call me back in a week?'"

Obviously flustered by his conversation with me, he asked Jerry what he should do next.

"Call him back in a week," said Jerry.

Eventually, I agreed to go to St. Louis to meet the Stones. It was an all-expenses-paid trip. They had offered to take care of everything. When I boarded the plane in Nashville, I carried only an overnight case—no guitar case. I was serious about not performing. I wasn't playing guitar during that period.

I arrived at the St. Louis airport early in the afternoon and took an airport van to the hotel. I didn't try to contact any of them—I figured they would get me up on the game plan. Later on that afternoon, someone called me and told me what time we would leave the hotel for the stadium. That evening we all piled into a caravan of vans. To my surprise, Emmylou Harris also had been invited to the concert. I was a big fan of hers, but had never met her. That was a double dip for me—the Stones *and* Emmylou.

After attending a press party at the stadium, I went backstage to watch the show. I stood on the right side facing the audience. Johnny Johnson, Chuck Berry's piano player, was there. Chuck wrote "Johnny B. Goode" about him. He went out and played a number with them. They did a hell of a show. I was not a big fan, but after they did that show, I became a fan. I timed them. They did two hours and forty minutes nonstop. After the concert, we returned to the hotel, where we had dinner in a private room that had been closed off for us. Then we went up to Keith's room— and him and me got plastered. He had several guitars there. He wanted to learn the lick to "Mystery Train," so we played until four-thirty or five o'clock that morning. I got up the next morning, and, with two hours' sleep, flew back to Nashville. Man, I was hurtin' bad.

For Keith Richards, the encounter with me was a dream come true. "For a few brief hours, it was like sitting at the feet of the master . . . digging the cat himself," he said in an interview for this book. "Scotty—what a gent!"

When I arrived in Nashville after my visit with the Stones, I called Jerry Schilling and told him about the trip. To my surprise, I had become an instant celebrity among my own employees, all of whom seemed shocked that *their* Scotty Moore had palled around with the Rolling Stones. About thirty people at the factory wanted one of those T-shirts. I told Jerry that I didn't want them to give me any, but if they could give me a good deal on them I'd like about thirty of the shirts for my employees.

"We were so surprised he went," says Gail Pollock, who still has her Steel Wheels T-shirt. "For years, we had been trying to get Scotty to crawl out from beneath the rock."

★ ★ ★

One day in 1990 Chet Atkins called and asked if he could bring someone over to meet me. Guitarist Mark Knopfler with Dire Straits was in town doing an album, *Neck and Neck*, with Chet and had asked if he could meet me. As the three of us sat in the back office of the tape plant and talked, Chet noticed that I had an old RCA 77DX microphone on my desk. It was practically an antique, a holdover from Music City Recorders.

"Does it work?" Chet asked.

"It did until I cut the cable off."

I was using the microphone as a paperweight. When Chet showed an interest in it, I gave it to him as a gift. The gesture had unexpected results. Sometime later, Chet showed up at the office carrying a guitar case.

When Gail told him that I wasn't there, he opened the case on the counter to show her what was inside. It was a Chet Atkins Gibson Country Gentleman guitar.

"It was a real dark mahogany instrument," says Gail. "It was gorgeous—it was one he had used himself."

Chet left the guitar for me as a gift.

★ ★ ★

By 1992, I felt like I had been hit by a rock, a big one, at that.

The printing shop wasn't getting enough orders to stay afloat. The economy took a nosedive that year. The big companies were already running three shifts a day. They cut prices and ran them on their third shifts just to keep their employees.

In an effort to keep the printing shop afloat, I sold the tape plant to Gail Pollock. She changed its name to We Make Tapes. Unfortunately, that transaction was not enough to save the printing business. With each passing day, it plummeted ever deeper into debt. To make matters worse, the tape plant was one of its biggest clients.

"What we did print-wise was nowhere enough to keep the print shop running," says Gail. "It didn't do well because it didn't have enough work from just us to keep it going."

Early in 1992, while I was agonizing over my failing business interests, I received a phone call from Carl Perkins.

"You're not going to believe this but I just came back from the doctor and he said the cancer was all gone."

"You ready to do that record?"

"Let's get at it."

"Carl, I haven't picked up a guitar in 24 years."

"You can do it—I know you can."

I had grave doubts about my ability to pick up where I'd left off, but I was not about to let an old friend down, especially one who had licked cancer.

In March, Gail Pollock and I drove to Carl's home in Jackson to talk to him about recording again. We met in his studio, which was at the rear of the house next to the swimming pool. Carl suggested that we do the album in Memphis at the old Sun Studio, which had been reopened in recent years for recording sessions.

"Scotty was sitting there, thinking 'I can't play a guitar—no way,'" recalls Gail. "Carl was singing and practically doing a show for us right there. Scotty kept thinking, 'I can't do this.'" But Carl was convincing. We agreed to book time in April at Sun Studio.

As we stood in Carl's carport before leaving, I suggested Carl write a song about Sam Phillips for the session. "Remember how he kept making us do it over and over?"

Carl grinned. "'Damn, Sam.'"

The next day after church Carl called me and read me the lyrics to the song he had written overnight. He had titled it "Damn Sam."

"Do I have to sing this song again?"

Carl had worked in Sun Studio several times since the fifties, so he was more familiar with it than I was. I'd not set foot in the studio in nearly thirty years. When I saw it, I was surprised at how little it had changed. It was the same old room with acoustic tile on the wall and ceiling. Of course, it didn't have the same equipment. It needed a little paint and cleaning up.

In addition to Carl and me, the lineup for the session included Carl's sons Stan and Greg, D. J. Fontana, Paul Burlison, James Lott, Donnie Baer, Johnny Black, Willie Rainsford, Joe Schenk, and Marcus Van Storey.

"It was so neat to watch those old guys," says Gail. "Marcus told me he was supposed to be in the hospital that week.

"I said, 'what for?'

"He said, 'Oh, they wanted to check my heart, but I wouldn't miss this for the world.'"

We did three sessions at Sun, with each lasting about five hours. Among the songs we recorded were "Blue Suede Shoes," "Mystery Train," and "Damn Sam." Since Carl was still recuperating, he couldn't sing for long periods at a time.

"He was very, very skinny—and his shoulder was hurting real bad," says Gail. "I had some stuff I used to rub on Scotty's shoulder sometimes, so I went and got it and rubbed his shoulders with it. He was not well, but he did a great job on the session."

When I returned to Nashville and listened to the tapes, I wasn't happy with the quality of the recording. I thought we had enough material, but some of the tapes were garbled and weren't usable. So I hired a remote audio truck and took it to Carl's house. His wife graciously let us move some furniture out of the den to get the drums in there and we recorded half a dozen songs there in his den. Tracy Nelson came down and did two songs with us.

I titled the album *706 ReUnion: A Sentimental Journey*, released it on Belle Meade Records, and sold it by mail order. A glowing review by

Michael Price in the *Fort Worth Star-Telegram* said the Moore-Perkins alliance had "yielded the richest roots-rock album since Fort Worth's Ray Sharpe delivered his 'Texas Boogie Blues' collection in 1980 . . . Moore's playing—though he has claimed to be rusty from inactivity—packs as much brisk authority as it did those nearly forty years ago, and Perkins's voice soars."

In May 1992, a few weeks after I returned from Memphis, I filed for bankruptcy. The printing shop stopped production in June and vacated its offices in August. I was both embarrassed and angered by the bankruptcy. Embarrassed because I didn't like to feel that I'd let other people down. Angry, because bankruptcy makes you feel like a criminal or something even worse, though I'm not sure what that could be.

I cleaned out my desk and took my things home. I live in a rural area northwest of Nashville in a two-story house that sits off the road in a clump of tall trees. I have a large kitchen that is heated by a wood-burning stove. It is the room where I spend the most time. I converted the actual living room into a studio. A second room, located just off the living room, was converted into a sound booth. I have a small soundboard and an assortment of equipment I use to edit both sound and videotape.

The bankruptcy forced me, at age sixty-one, into an early retirement. I no longer had a studio or a tape plant or a printing shop. I did have a guitar or two. Two weeks after the session in Memphis with Carl, I received word that Marcus Van Storey had died of a heart attack.

Gail, who recalled her conversation with Marcus, felt he "died a happy man" because of his participation in the session. She wondered if it would have made any difference if he had gone to the hospital instead of playing in the session.

★ ★ ★

Early in the summer of 1992, Memphis writer James L. Dickerson met me at the tape duplicating plant to interview me for a national newspaper magazine, *CoverStory*. I had not done an interview in many years and probably would not have done that one except that my daughter Vikki knew him because of mutual friends and because her husband, Emmo Hein, once worked for Dickerson at a radio syndication, *Pulsebeat—Voice of the Heartland*. To my surprise, I enjoyed the interview and posed for photographs with my guitar. We talked briefly about doing a book someday, but it was another four years before that became a reality.

While I was deciding what to do next, whether to look for an engineering job or consider performing again on a regular basis, I accepted a booking with Carl Perkins at Ellis Auditorium in Memphis. The concert, scheduled for August, was part of the "Good Rockin' Tonight" show, a festivity of the annual Elvis Week celebration. By 1992, Graceland had become Memphis's leading tourist attraction. The previous year, 670,000 people had passed through the front gates, with the number increasing each year. Also appearing on the "Good Rockin' Tonight" show were the Sun Rhythm Section—minus Paul Burlison, whose wife, Rose, was ill—guitarist James Burton, D. J. Fontana, Ronnie McDowell, and the Jordanaires. I was nervous about performing again. My last performance had been the 1968 "Comeback" special—*24 years* ago. Anyone would have been nervous under those circumstances.

Ronnie McDowell had met me, but had never talked to me at length. Between sets at the auditorium we got to know each other. When I told him I was scared to death about performing again after so many years, Ronnie reassured me, and then suggested I go out on the road with him and his band as a means of getting my chops back in shape. I did and had a great time. It is a little like getting back on a bicycle after several years absence. You are a little wobbly at first, but then everything comes back to you and before you know it you are peddling at full speed.

By the time "Good Rockin' Tonight" rolled around I was as ready as I ever would be. Gail watched the show from the rear of the auditorium. "It was one of those, 'You have to be there' performances—it was electric," she says. "It was a great show. But it was very difficult on Carl. The doctors told him he could do twenty minutes—and he did an hour and twenty minutes. He could hardly talk afterward."

I was hooked. Again. There is something addictive about music. A week after the Memphis performance, I went to England with the Jordanaires for performances at more than a dozen venues. Carl was booked as the headliner, but had to cancel at his doctor's insistence and was unable to make the trip.

"I'll never forget the first show," says Ray Walker of The Jordanaires. "Scotty was uptight. He looked a little pale—and he had this quizzical look in his eye, almost like he wasn't going to walk on stage. But when he did, those people came unglued. They recognized him, and when he hit that guitar lick, it happened again. They absolutely came unglued."

I couldn't believe it. We'd do those shows and people my age and older would come through the lines, their hands absolutely shaking, with tears rolling down their faces—and the majority of them would have their little grandkids with them carrying Elvis records to get signed.

The following year, D. J. and I went to Jackson to appear on a telethon with and for Carl Perkins. When it came to public performances, there weren't many people who could get me to say yes. Carl was among the few who could.

Unknown to me, my childhood friend, James Lewis, was watching the telethon at his home a short distance away in Crockett County. As a joke, he called in a one-hundred-dollar pledge if the telethon sponsors would get me to sing.

"Of course, I had never heard him sing a note in his life," says James, laughing.

I didn't sing that day—and I didn't find out about the pledge until three years later.

★ ★ ★

When Lee Rocker, the former bassist with the Stray Cats, first started playing rockabilly in the late 1970s, disco audiences looked at him like he was crazy. Didn't he know Elvis was dead? Over the next several years, the Stray Cats—with singer/guitarist Brian Setzer and drummer Slim Jim Phantom—almost single-handedly introduced a new generation to the music created in Memphis. After the Stray Cats split up in 1993, Rocker joined with guitarist Mike Eldred and formed a new group named Big Blue. They went to Memphis to record their debut, self-titled album. Long before they booked the session, Eldred wrote me a letter, telling me how much he had been influenced by my playing. To his utter surprise, I answered his letter.

The end result was that I agreed to sit in on their Memphis session.

"Scotty, you want me to send a limo to Nashville to pick you up?" asked Rocker.

"No, I've got a car."

"Is there anything I can do?"

"No, I'll just put my guitar in the car and drive to Memphis."

Rocker was amazed once the session began. For years, the Stray Cats had emulated the early work I had done at Sun—and not just the picking. They moved microphones around, trying them at different distances. They experimented with analog delays on the tape. They did everything they could think of to get that magical sound. When I walked into the studio, Rocker thought, finally, he would discover the secret.

To his surprise, there was no hoodoo magic involved. "Scotty came in and put a microphone in front of his amp—and that was it," he says, laughing. "I realized we had wasted a lot of time trying to get that sound. It's *his* sound."

I played on two of the album's cuts: Jimmy Reed's "Shame, Shame, Shame" and "Little Buster," a song written by Rocker and Eldred. "I didn't want to go back and cut Elvis stuff," says Rocker. "I think he enjoyed playing on something that was new."

In 1994 Gary Tallent, bassist in Bruce Springsteen's E Street Band, asked me if I would play on a session he was producing with Sonny Burgess. "The funny thing about it was that I was trying to direct him to play like he played thirty years ago," says Tallent. "He would look at me, like 'that's thirty years ago.' In some ways it's like he's starting fresh again."

Tallent was amazed that he remembered my old licks better than I did. "We have studied what he did more than he has—and I guess that's true for anyone in this [business]. Basically what he does is instinctive. He doesn't rely on a bag of tricks. He just plays and figures it out as he goes along. Rock 'n' roll is improvised music—and that's how he goes about it. It took that situation for me to realize—of course, that's rock 'n' roll."

★ ★ ★

For most of the summer of 1994, the media was swamped with stories of a massive Elvis tribute that was going to be held at the Pyramid arena in Memphis. The event would be offered to the public on pay-per-view television. Mercury Records would subsequently release an album of material recorded live at the concert. The list of performers signed up for the concert was impressive: Tony Bennett, Melissa Etheridge, Chris Isaak, Michael Bolton, Carl Perkins, Bryan Adams, Aaron Neville, Dwight Yoakam, Tanya Tucker, and Travis Tritt. It would be the biggest Elvis tribute *ever*.

In late September, two weeks before the event was scheduled to take place, I received a call from one of the producers. Would I be interested in putting together a band and performing at the concert? I was taken aback. The concert was only two weeks away. D. J. and I were already booked with Ronnie McDowell in Indiana on that same date with the Jordanaires, so I told him we couldn't do it. I said I wasn't going to cancel on them and I didn't think any of the others would either. The producers called back and said they would be willing to add Ronnie to the program. That would be fine, I told them, except that they were booked at the other venue.

Finally, they said they would buy out the show for us—whatever the promoter thought he would lose by rescheduling the show, they would pay it.

With everyone agreed to those terms, Ronnie's date in Indiana was rescheduled. As I got ready to go to Memphis with D. J., the Jordanaires, Ronnie, and the members of his band, faxes started arriving from the producers on a daily basis. Unfortunately, they would not be able to use Ronnie's band. I persuaded them to use two members of the band—Kevin Woods, the guitarist, and Steve Shepherd, the keyboard player.

We arrived in Memphis the day before the concert. When we went to rehearsal, we discovered that most of the singers we were supposed to perform with had not yet shown up. To help the producers, Ronnie offered to fill in for them. Before the rehearsal began Don Was, the musical director, committed two major gaffes. First, when the Jordanaires were mentioned, he said, "Oh, are they still alive?" Second, he told me what key he would be playing *his* songs in. I set Was straight on the Jordanaires in quick order; then I told him he would have to do Elvis's songs in the same key I had always done them.

"Scotty actually saved the show," says Ray Walker of the Jordanaires. Gordon Stoker agrees: "If it hadn't have been for Scotty, [the show] would have been in serious trouble."

A few hours before showtime, what had thus far been merely unpleasant suddenly became a nightmare. I had been going through this hassle with them—it was horrible—then we broke to go back to the hotel to get dressed and eat. It was then that one of those honchos came around and said they were running low on time. Ronnie had been bumped and would have to do his song on the pay-per-view pre-show teaser. If there was still time during the main show, he could do his number then.

I thought I had covered every crack, but someone outsmarted me. We had rehearsed with all those other guys and we would have looked like assholes if we hadn't played. I called Ronnie's manager, Joe, and he did the worst thing a manager could do—he told Ronnie, who just slipped out of the hotel and went back to Nashville. He was *that* hurt.

I felt horrible about what happened to Ronnie. They had a right to cut acts, but it was the way they did it. I went ahead and did the show. We backed Chris Isaak on "Blue Moon," Michael Bolton on "Jailhouse Rock," Carl Perkins on "Blue Suede Shoes," and Bryan Adams on "Hound Dog." As I participated in the excitement of the packed arena, halfway across the country my old Navy buddy, Frank Parise, watched on television.

★ ★ ★

On July 4, 1995, D. J., Carl, and I performed at the third annual American Roots concert at the Washington Monument. The event was organized by the National Park Service and the National Council for the Traditional Arts. It rained that day, and what I remember most about the concert was how hard the stagehands had to work to keep the equipment dry.

"In the wings stood Scotty Moore, looking as stoic as ever, cradling the kind of Gibson guitar that helped launch countless rock careers," wrote Mike Joyce for the *Washington Post*. "When he and Fontana joined Perkins on-stage, it was strictly 'go cat go.'" The reporter wrote that I was still laying down "sparkling solos."

At 63 I still had the fire, still had the burning desire to perform. It's not the sort of fire that grows cold with age. Throughout 1995 and 1996, I toured with Ronnie McDowell. Typically, Ronnie did his regular show, performing the country hits he racked up over the years, and then concluded with a 45-minute tribute to Elvis, which featured D. J., the Jordanaires, and me. "The people react great to Scotty," Ronnie said in an interview for this book. "We were in Laurel, Mississippi, doing a little show at a fair. The young girls just screamed every time I mentioned their names. Scotty leaned over to me and said, 'Man, this is just like 1955.'"

We did autographs and people made comments like, 'You don't realize how many memories you brought back. We close our eyes and we're young again."

One of the things I'm famous for, at least among fellow musicians, is my reluctance to deviate from the playlist. I like for things to go as planned. Sometimes Ronnie will say "This isn't on the list" and go into a song he hasn't told me about. I just laugh it off and say, "There you go again."

Ronnie knows it drives me crazy when he improvises. "He hates the way I do my show because I don't stick to a format," says Ronnie. "Everything I do is off the cuff, and my band is used to that. Scotty would like for me to stick to a format. When he complains, I say, 'You mean to tell me Elvis stuck to a list?'

"He says, 'We never veered off of it—what we wrote down is what we did.'"

But I know it's all in fun. And the fun doesn't stop on stage. Musicians are notorious practical jokers. One night, after engaging in a serious conversation with Johnnie Walker (Red), I dropped off to sleep on the bus. While I was asleep, slumped over in one of the plush chairs, the boys in the band decorated me with fruit—a banana in my pocket, grapes in my lap and in my hand. When I awoke and rubbed my face, I was a mess.

But I didn't get angry. That's life on the road.

"Outside of us, Ronnie was the first person outside Scotty's [immediate circle] that had a personal appreciation of him," says Ray Walker. "Scotty could see that he was safe with him. That was really a good marriage for Scotty."

In mid-1995 I partnered with James L. Dickerson to write my autobiography for the Simon & Schuster music imprint, Schirmer Books. After all those years, it took a little bit of arm twisting for me to agree to tell my story, but my Memphis daughter Vikki was insistent that I do it and I finally agreed. I found it ironic that the advance on the book was for more than my total income from Elvis during all those years of hard living on the road.

We chose a title for the book, *That's Alright, Elvis*, and I began the physical, emotional, and mental search for the artifacts of my life. I examined photographs I had not looked at in many years. I sat for many hours of recorded interviews with James as the memories of my life were brought into focus and dissected like specimens in a biology lab. He wanted to write the book in the first person, but I preferred the third person because a lot of the first-person books I'd read came across to me as too self-serving. James said he needed to interview my ex-wives and other from my past to obtain a rounded view and wondered how he should handle statements that might come across as critical. I told him to let them have their say. They had earned it.

Spliced between continuing performances with Ronnie, I worked on the book and spent much of 1996 working on a compilation CD. The purpose of the CD, which was titled *All the King's Men*, was to celebrate the contributions that Bill Black, D. J. Fontana, Elvis, and I had made to American music. In addition to scheduling a session later in the year with Keith Richards, Levon Helm, and the Band at Helms's Woodstock, New York, studio, we went into the studio to record songs with the BoDeans, the Mavericks, Cheap Trick, Ronnie McDowell, Tracy Nelson, Steve Earle with Lee Rocker, Joe Ely with Lee Rocker, Joe Louis Walker, and some of the surviving members of the Bill Black Combo. We also traveled to Ireland to record a song titled "Unsung Heroes," with Ron Wood and Jeff Beck.

D. J. and I hadn't actually heard of the BoDeans but when we met them we found out they had grown up on Elvis music. Turned out, they were real easy to work with.

Following the session with Cheap Trick, Bun E. Carlos, the drummer, asked D. J. and me to sign his snare drums. Later, as I was walking past, Carlos asked D. J. to sign his sticks. Overhearing the request, I could not help myself, and quipped, "You must have a wood-burning stove."

Of course, 1996 wasn't all work and no play. Early in the year, I received an invitation to guitarist Les Paul's 81st birthday celebration. I had met him in the mid-1970s when he traveled to Nashville to work on an album with Chet Atkins. Some of the most popular recordings of his that I recall are "The World's Waiting for the Sunrise" and "How High the Moon," both recorded with Mary Ford.

I had not been to New York City since the mid-1970s, but Paul was an early hero of mine and I broke with tradition in this instance and boarded a plane, party-bound for the Iridium, a jazz club on West 63rd Street. I slipped into the club and was seated at a table without anyone knowing that I was there. Les was more than an hour into his set when someone told him that I was in the audience. He dragged me up onto the stage and put a guitar into my hands before I even had time to protest. We played some jazz tunes and I had a great time. If it hadn't been for Les Paul, we guitar players might be playing harpsichords. He always played what I call "in between" tunes; those fall between small jazz band numbers and dance music. He invented the electric guitar. Every guitar player there is should bow down at his feet. I know I do.

Later, when we had time to talk, I told him that the first thing I ever heard him play was a tune on Peacock Records called "Okey Dokey Stomp." He turned to his manager and said, "Did you hear that? He knows 'Okey Dokey Stomp.'" He just grinned.

★ ★ ★

I had begun my professional life out on the road—and now, in the twilight of my career, I was back on the road again. By the time I went to New York, I had emerged from my bankruptcy and I had accepted that I would probably have to perform for the rest of my life to put food on the table. I feel no bitterness about the way things worked out. I believe in Elvis as much today as I did in 1954. It is scandalous that my total take from fourteen years with Elvis amounted to only $30,123.72; but never will you hear me blame Elvis for that, not even on my darkest days.

"Scotty truly respected Elvis for his abilities and he cared about him as a human being," recalls ex-wife Emily Sanders. "He never said an unkind word about Elvis. If there was something that troubled Scotty, it was something that saddened him because Elvis didn't come through on something—but he never cursed him."

Why would I? He was like a brother to me.

One night in 1996, I called co-author James L. Dickerson following a storm that left eight inches of snow around my house. My electricity had gone out, but my telephone worked just fine. I was home alone, as usual. Unfazed by the darkness—and below-freezing temperatures—I assured my co-author, who expressed concern about my safety, that I was doing just fine. On my wood cook stove simmered a can of beans, which I planned to wash down with my favorite scotch. Once I finished the beans, I planned to use a candle to make my way up the dark stairway to the bedroom. The world would look different after a good night's sleep. It always had.

A few weeks later, the week after Christmas 1996, James accompanied Gail and me to a Nashville nightclub to listen to Tracy Nelson perform. I don't often go to nightclubs, but I was a staunch Tracy Nelson fan—and I wanted to show James why I enjoy her music so much. We met James in the parking lot of the tape plant, located just off Music Row. James left his car—a Miata convertible—in the parking lot of the tape plant and rode in the car with us to the nightclub. "Do you think my car will be safe here?" he asked.

"As safe as it would be anywhere," I said.

Later that night—it was after midnight—we drove James back to his car. The downtown streets were deserted at that time of the night and no one was seen in the vicinity of the parking lot. After talking a few minutes, James got out of the car and we drove away. When he got in his car, he discovered that someone had cut a hole in the roof and stolen several items, including a .44 Magnum revolver. As he pulled out of the parking lot and drove onto Music Row, a late-model car with mismatched headlights pulled up close behind him, pursuing him through the deserted city streets past the old RCA building and the current address for Mercury Records. The chase lasted for several blocks and James was able to lose his pursuers only because his smaller, faster car was more maneuverable than the land barge that stayed on his tail. He said at one point he pushed it to 100 miles per hour hoping a cop would get in pursuit.

When the crime was reported to Nashville police, they said it sounded like a carjacking attempt. They had his gun and planned to use it to get his house keys and everything he owned. After making certain that he was all right, I asked the obvious question.

"They didn't get the manuscript, did they?"

James laughed. "No, never got close to the manuscript. But I feel sort of naked without my .44. Hope they don't kill anybody with it."

"Did you report it to the police?"

"Sure."

"When they wipe their fingerprints off the murder weapon, they will probably wipe yours off, too."

"Gee, thanks."

★ 13 ★

JAMMING WITH A ROLLING STONE

The way Rolling Stones guitarist Keith Richards tells it, he was thirteen the first time he heard me play guitar. It was late at night and—stubbornly against his parents' explicit orders to go to sleep—he was in his bedroom behind closed doors listening to Radio Luxembourg on a transistor radio. One minute the reception was fine, the next it was riddled with nerve-shattering static. Back and forth it went. Suddenly, from the bottomless depths of a sonic wave of ever-changing white noise, emerged the heart-stopping music of "Heartbreak Hotel."

Keith literally chased the song about his room as he ran from one corner to the other, holding the radio up over his head to snare a few additional uninterrupted moments of music. In an instant, "Heartbreak Hotel" had energized him and forever changed his life.

"I had been playing guitar, but not knowing what to play . . . without any direction," Keith said in an interview for this book. "When I heard 'Heartbreak Hotel,' I knew that was what I wanted to do in life. It was as plain as day. I no longer wanted to be a train driver or a Van Gogh or a rocket scientist. All I wanted to do in the world was to be able to play and sound like that. Those early records were incredible. Everyone else wanted to be Elvis. I wanted to be Scotty."

For 40 years Keith dreamed of playing on a record with his hero. On July 9, 1996—40 years, 2 months, and 18 days after "Heartbreak Hotel" first topped the charts—that dream came true when Keith went to Woodstock, New York, to meet up with D. J. and me for a recording session at a studio owned by Levon Helm, who had made his own indelible mark on music history as a member of the Band. We had no way of knowing it at the time, but Levon was only a couple of years away from being diagnosed with throat cancer. Just looking at him, there was no hint of trouble.

D. J. and I went to the Woodstock studio to record a new song, "Deuce and a Quarter," with the three surviving members of the Band: Levon on drums, Garth Hudson on keyboards, and Rick Danko on bass. Also joining in the session were more recent Band members Richard Bell on piano, Randy Ciarlante on drums, and Jim Weider on guitar. Producer Stan Lynch, for more than two decades the drummer with Tom Petty's Heartbreakers, was there to supervise the session. The song, which was written by two Nashville songwriters, Gwil Owen and Kevin Gordon, was recorded for the album *All the King's Men.*

D. J. was ailing somewhat when we arrived at Woodstock, but after a short stay in the hospital he was ready to get down to work. We laid the track the first night. On the second night Levon arrived and sang, after which we did the overdubs. The Band was great to work with. They reminded me of the early days when we started bringing extra musicians into the band during the recording sessions. Nobody was there to try to be a star or show someone else up. Everyone wanted to do it right and make it work.

At around 6:30 of the third day, Keith Richards arrived at the studio, accompanied by a rather large bottle of vodka, a generous supply of orange soda, and his 82-year-old father, Bert. I greeted Keith in the center of the crowded studio, and Keith introduced me to his father, a diminutive man with bushy white hair set off by a jaunty red cap. I took to Bert right away. I don't know if he is Scottish or not, but he looks like he is. He looks like you'd expect a bunch of sheep to fall in behind him. Right away I noticed that Bert was very interested in the session, watching every detail from a choice spot in the balcony of the studio, but I didn't find out why he was so interested until later. Keith said that when he first told his father about the session, he insisted on attending, explaining that he just had to meet the man who had kept his son glued to the radio 40 years ago.

Some six months before the Woodstock session, Keith spent an entire day revisiting my early work with Elvis. "It was the same feeling I got the first time," he explained. "I've been listening all day. Such tasteful licks and so ominous . . . such delicate finger picking. It was just a guitar and an upright bass and an acoustic. The use of space . . . silence is our canvas, which a lot of cats don't realize, but Scotty certainly does."

During rehearsal at Woodstock, Keith and I sat in chairs facing each other: Keith with his vodka and orange soda, and me with a jug of Johnnie Walker (Red). "Deuce and a Quarter" is one of those bluesy, old-time rock 'n' roll songs that march to a rockabilly cadence, and Keith and I faced off on the floor of the studio, rocking to the groove of the music, our graying hair adding an unexpected dash of dignity to the song.

ALL THE KING'S MEN

Scotty Moore and D. J. Fontana

Featured Guest Artists

Keith Richards and The Band . . . . "Deuce and a Quarter"
The Mavericks. . . . . "I Told You So"
The BoDeans . . . . "Locked Up in the State of Illinois"
Bill Black Combo . . . . "Goin' Back to Memphis"
Joe Ely with Lee Rocker . . . . "I'm Gonna Strangle You Shorty"
Cheap Trick . . . ."Bad Little Girl"
Ronnie McDowell & the Jordanaires . . . . "Soulmates"
Steve Earle with Lee Rocker . . . ."Hot Enough for Ya"
Joe Louis Walker . . . . "Strange Love"
Tracy Nelson . . . . "Is All of This For Me?"
Ron Wood & Jeff Beck . . . . "Unsung Heroes"

When time came to do the vocals, Keith asked me to stand next to him and give him direction. Levon sang the first verse. Keith did the second and they shared the third. Also observing were Marshall Crenshaw and Memphis rockabilly pioneer Paul Burlison, both of whom had been invited to the session.

At around 3 a.m., after the session was done, Keith, D. J., and I sat around and talked a while longer. For Keith, it was "the final cycle" of a lifelong ambition. He explained that the two people that he most he wanted to work were Chuck Berry and me. What a compliment that was. Having said that, he paused, looking at me for a long moment. Finally he said he didn't know why I had started playing guitar, but he knew why he had started—and it was because of me. Then, becoming the interviewer, he asked me who had influenced me.

"Everyone who played, especially jazz guitarists," I answered.

Surprised, Keith looked at me, another newfound bond uniting us. He, too, had been influenced by jazz, although he confessed, somewhat apologetically, he had since become a "hillbilly cat." Keith said that while Elvis

Presley had knocked him out as a performer, it was the band behind him that first had attracted him to the music.

"Everything that goes around, comes around," I said. "Like you and Charlie and Ron and that singer in front."

Keith pointed out that while we both had worked with front men our entire careers, *his* front man was still alive.

"What's his name?" I joked.

"I don't remember," deadpanned Keith. Then, after a pause, he shook his head and added with a hint of resignation in his voice: "We all need one, man."

By the end of the session, some eight hours later, I had finished off a jug of scotch and Keith had dipped well into his second. Keith came to have a good time, that's all that was. He and Levon hung out until daylight. He was still there when I left. I had met my match—and I can hang in there with the best of them.

Four months later, in December 1996, D. J. and I went to Ireland to add another musical notch to our CD: this time a song with guitarists Jeff Beck and Ron Wood. We went to Wood's home at Digby Bridge in County Kildare to record a Beck/Wood–penned song, "Unsung Heroes," written as a tribute to D. J., Bill Black, and myself.

I had met Ron before, but I'd never met Jeff. The session started out slow, with everyone sort of randomly picking out melodies on their guitars. There were notes scattered here and there, punctuated by occasional periods of silence. Everyone, myself included, was hesitant to step up and say let's go down this road. After a while we took a break and I retreated to a corner, where I worked on a lick I was hearing inside my head.

"What's that?" asked Ron, curious about my musical doodling.

"I don't know. Just something I started fooling around with a week or two ago."

Suddenly, Ron's eyes brightened. "That's it! Keep going!"

Ron picked up a 1954 Fender Strat and began experimenting with rhythms, spitting out lyrics about coming face to face with his heroes. Beck picked up on that and tossed in a magical string of filler lines as only he can do. "Unsung Heroes" suddenly became a song, screeching out for air the way a newborn baby screams after being birthed on the backseat of a cab.

I was glad it happened that way. That was the way it happened in the beginning with Elvis, Bill, and me: just a bunch of guys sitting around playing music, encouraging each other when it felt right, a spontaneous combustion of raw energy. We stayed up until daylight for three days in a row. It was a party. D. J. played his fanny off. He had a ball. The boy was up for it, let's put it that way.

At one point during the session, Mick Jagger called and spoke to Ron for a while. Then I got on the line. Mick was upset that he had not been invited to the session.

"I had a feeling that something was going on over there. I didn't even know that you guys were in the country. How come you didn't ask me?"

I told him that I felt we had pushed our luck getting Keith and Ron.

"Well, if you do another one, I want to be on it."

I told him he could count on it.

Later, as we listened to a mix of "Unsung Heroes," the room grew quiet and Ron's eyes seemed to mist over. I told Ron and Jeff that Elvis, Bill, D. J., and I had done our part. It was time for them to take the torch and move it further on down the road.

★ 14 ★

I'M PRETTY MUCH STILL HERE, I GUESS

One of the first things that I did after my autobiography, *That's Alright, Elvis*, was published in the fall of 1997 was to hit the road with my co-author to promote the book. We began our book tour with a train ride to New York City, a re-creation of the ride that Elvis, Bill, and I made on our first trip to New York, only this time around, there were two major differences: The first was that because I lived in Nashville, and Memphis no longer had direct train service to New York, we had to drive all the way to Birmingham, Alabama, to board the train—and the second was that nearly fifty years after my first trip, train service had gotten worse. I thought the modern trains, especially the Pullman cars, would really be knockouts, but the old ones that I travelled in the 1950s were much better.

On the first leg of our trip, from Birmingham to Atlanta, a TNN camera crew accompanied us on the train, taping everything we did. That wasn't too bad. The interviewer, Lisa Young, asked me why I had waited so long to write a book. I told her that I swore I never would do one because there were so many Elvis books out there. When I told my co-author that it had all been said, he answered, "Well, you just don't know." So we did a book.

We stayed in the club car for most of the trip to Atlanta but said good-bye to camera crew when we arrived. It was fun being interviewed as the scenery zipped past and the train wheels made their trademark traveling music. I must admit the journey was not without flashbacks. On the first trip we were just a bunch of Memphis boys on an adventure. We didn't know what to expect in New York. On the train we were pretty much ignored by the other passengers. There were no attractive female reporters holding microphones in our faces, hanging on our every word. This time people paused to shake my hand and to tell me how much the music meant to them. The conductor pulled up a chair to talk. The first trip the conductor gave us stern, watch-your-step looks.

We stayed in Atlanta a day or two doing interviews and a book signing that attracted an Elvis impersonator or two. I·can live with that, just barely, when they wear the wigs and dress like Elvis during the Vegas years; but when they curl their lips and try to talk like Elvis I want to let out a rebel yell and run out the back door.

From Atlanta we went to Washington, D.C., where we did more interviews and book signings, and then on to Philadelphia for more of the same. The best part about Washington was a black cab driver from Alabama who talked about how much he missed soul food from the South. He was a real trip and seemed genuinely happy to see someone from the South. I felt fine, but I kept breaking out in a cold sweat whenever I had to walk more than a few steps at a time. James noticed my sweating and kept asking me if I felt all right, and I told him I did, which was the truth as I saw it, except for maybe feeling more tired than usual. I told him that I felt better than I looked. "If you say so," he said, unconvinced.

We had book signings planned for New York, but they had to be canceled because the publisher ran out of books before we arrived and there was nothing for me to sign. If a bestseller is a book that sells out before everyone that wants one can get one then we had a bestseller. What I enjoyed most about the trip was playing a concert in Central Park with Ike Turner, Joe Louis Walker, and Matt "Guitar" Murphy. The fans were disappointed that I didn't have books to sign, but they were very enthusiastic about the concert.

Before we went on stage I hung out in one of the air-conditioned trailers with Ike and his wife. Ike and I have some of the same memories of recording for Sun Records and performing in the racially segregated Mid-South, but our interpretations of those memories differed somewhat. I attribute that to the social restrictions of that era. Our audiences were almost entirely white and his were almost entirely black. When he recorded "Rocket 88" in 1951 with Sam Phillips, a song most critics consider a precursor of rock 'n' roll, the audience for the record was perceived to be black. As time went by, his audiences became whiter and ours became blacker. That acknowledgment was at the heart of the cracks that we exchanged in the trailer that day, comments that seemed to leave his wife mystified. For us it was one of those "you had to be there" moments.

After the show, we were all standing around backstage, talking and posing for pictures, with me on one end, when Ike said, "Scotty, you've got to stand in the middle—you're the fly in the buttermilk with this one."

That cracked me up. It was hard to believe that it had been nearly half a century since Ike and I had started out in Memphis.

We ended the tour back in Birmingham, but had to cancel a scheduled book signing there, too, because the store was unable to get books. Gail Pollock picked us up at the train station and drove us back to Nashville. We had dinner along the way and Gail said that she was shocked that we sat at the same table. "I figured you two wouldn't be speaking after that trip," she laughed. I guess she thinks I don't travel too well. She should know. She's been my faithful traveling companion for almost thirty years.

Not long after the book tour ended, I learned that a song from *All the King's Men* was nominated for a Grammy. "Goin' Back to Memphis" (the title was borrowed from James's book of the same name) was an instrumental recorded by the Bill Black Combo. D. J. and I wanted to play tribute to Bill Black on the album, so we asked Reggie Young, who had been one of the founding members of the Bill Black Combo, to re-organize a group to do the recording. He brought in five other Memphis music veterans: Mike Leech, Ace Cannon, Jerry "Satch" Arnold, Bobby Woods, and Bobby Emmons.

We didn't win the Grammy, but it was an honor to be nominated.

★ ★ ★

The year after the release of the book and the CD, it seemed like I was always on the go, whether to promote the book and CD or simply to perform. I continued to travel a lot with my friend Ronnie McDowell. He got a booking in October 1998 in Paducah, Kentucky, that I initially turned down. But the day of the performance I had second thoughts about not going and decided to drive up there with Gail and surprise him.

I arrived at the venue early and set up my amplifier on the stage. Then I left, knowing that Ronnie wouldn't see my amplifier until he walked out on stage. Once Ronnie and the band arrived, I returned to the venue and went backstage without anyone in the band seeing me. Gail took a seat in the audience to watch the show. It was while I was alone backstage that I started sweating all of a sudden. It was sort of like what happened on the trip to New York. My skin felt like it was on fire. I thought it was because they hadn't turned on the air conditioning. I took off my coat, but that didn't help. Then I took off my tie. I was burning up like I had a high fever, but I felt fine otherwise. No chest pains. No headaches. Finally I got Steve Shepherd's attention on stage. He is the keyboardist and he was positioned so that he could see backstage. He saw that I was in trouble and he got Gail's attention in the audience. When she came backstage, I told her that something was wrong. I couldn't explain exactly what was wrong, but I felt like hell. When we returned to Nashville, I was so weak that I couldn't walk up the stairs. Two weeks later, I underwent a triple-bypass heart surgery that was followed with bouts of anemia, kidney failure, and the loss of hearing in my left ear.

All that sounds pretty grim, but less than five months after having that heart surgery, I flew to Europe and did thirteen shows. That was when I joined up with Pete Pritchard, a bass player that had played with me on my first English tour in 1992. He's been a good friend ever since. He helped me put together a band that has stuck with me for several return engagements in the United Kingdom, France, Belgium, the Netherlands, Finland, Norway, Denmark, Sweden, Switzerland, and Germany. Jimmy Russell is the drummer. He's tasteful and he doesn't pound the bass drum all night long like some do. Liam Grundy plays keyboards and David Briggs plays second guitar. Paul Ansel does the vocals. When they're not performing with me, they play with other bands. The fact that they have other gigs makes me appreciate them even more when they drop what they're doing so that they can tour with me.

I love to go to Europe because there I am looked on more as an influence to their guitar heroes than as Elvis's lead guitarist. I have a great time there seeing fans not only my age, but younger fans that seem to get younger with each trip. At one show at the Mean Fiddler in London, there was a young man about twenty who stood right in front of the stage and sang every word to every song. When it was time for me to take my solo, he pointed to me, and when it was time for D. J. to do something special on the drums, the young man pointed at just the right moment. I laughed all through the show.

While I'm talking about new friends, I should tell you about Jacques Vroom. At the tail end of the book tour in 1998, I went to Arlington, Texas, in a Winnebago to sign books and do as many radio interviews as possible. It was a miserable ride. The only time I could get any sleep was when the vehicle was parked. At any rate, Jacques showed up at one of the signings and introduced himself. At that time, he published a rock 'n' roll memorabilia catalog and he asked me about items that he could obtain for his collection. You couldn't say enough nice things about him, really. We hit it off right away and he's traveled with me on many occasions, often using his airline connections to get my tickets upgraded to first class.

In Los Angeles I was doing some shows with ex–Stray Cat Lee Rocker, when his former bandmate Brian Setzer called him and asked if it were true that I was performing with him. Lee told him that I was, and he invited him and former Stray Cat Slim Jim Phantom to the show. Veteran session drummer Earl Palmer (who recorded with Fats Domino, Little Richard, and Ray Charles, to name a few) also showed up, so when the time came to do "Mystery Train," Lee invited them all up on the stage to play along with us. That was a great night. It was the first time that all three Stray Cats had played together since 1992.

On another night with Lee, we went to San Francisco to do a show. My good friend Tracy Nelson was at the show, as was Jacques, who had flown there with me. Before we went on stage, we gathered in one of the tiny backstage dressing rooms. Tracy made herself comfortable on the couch, stretching out the full length of her body, and Jacques sat in one of the chairs. They watched me powder my hands, something I always to do to keep them from getting wet and sticky when I play guitar. Unable to contain his curiosity, Jacques asked, "By the way, Scotty, what are you using the powder for?" I smiled, and said, without missing a beat, "To powder the crack of my ass." Tracy laughed so hard that she rolled off the couch onto the floor.

★ ★ ★

In March 2000 I was inducted into the Rock 'n' Roll Hall of Fame in the sideman category. I had mixed feelings about that. I was happy to be recognized for my contributions to music, but saddened that they felt they had to rewrite history to do it. When Elvis, Bill, and I made those first recordings, it wasn't as Elvis Presley and his sidemen. We were a band, just like the Beatles or the Rolling Stones. We were called either Elvis, Scotty and Bill or the Blue Moon Boys. There were no sidemen making the music we recorded. We were partners.

For the Rock and Roll Hall of Fame to ignore that is tantamount to giving the Beatles an award inscribed, "To John and Paul, but not to their sidemen, Ringo and George." I'm not upset about it, just frustrated that people would use an award to rewrite history. Giving me an award under those conditions was a slap in the face to Bill Black and D. J. Fontana. How can you ignore Bill and D. J. and still honor rock 'n' roll?

The best part about going to New York for the ceremonies was that it provided me with an opportunity to make a record with Paul McCartney. Two days after the ceremony at the Waldorf-Astoria, D. J. and I went to

Sear Sound studio to re-record "That's Alright," with Paul replacing Bill on bass and Elvis on vocals. D. J. was happy to go to New York for the session, but he didn't go to the Hall of Fame ceremony because he was too pissed off. I don't blame him.

The session was the brainchild of Atlantic Records head Ahmet Ertegun. The idea, as he explained it, was to do a television documentary and a CD, with D. J. and me doing a series of sessions with guest artists. It didn't turn out exactly that way. D. J. and I did the session with Paul, and we did a few sessions at Abbey Road Studio in London, but not all of them were used on the CD or on the television special.

I expected Paul to come into the studio with an entourage, but he arrived with a man he had gone to school with as a youngster. Paul was a nice, everyday good guy. It felt like we had known each other forever. The studio was filled with people carrying clipboards and pens, but none of them had any business being there. They didn't fool me, and I'm sure they didn't fool Paul, either. Paul is a vegetarian, so they had all the snacks laid out, vegetarian-style, and he made the rounds, quietly doing his dips, totally unbothered by the fluttering clipboards. He is used to that sort of thing, I guess.

Paul told D. J. and me that he was a fan of our early work, and we told him that we were big Beatles fans—and we are. What I didn't tell him was that when the Beatles were at their peak, from the mid-sixties to the early seventies, I was working as a studio engineer in Nashville and I didn't have much time to listen to the radio. I got turned on to the Beatles' music because of all the people that came into the studio to record sound-alike songs. And, of course, I later engineered Ringo's Nashville album.

When time came to start the session, Paul said that he would have brought Bill's bass to the session, but he was concerned about transporting it to the United States in an unpressurized cabin. I laughed and told him the story about when we were traveling with the equipment strapped to the roof, and hit another car, sending the bass skidding out onto the road. As we inspected the damage to the cars, we heard Bill in the distance testing the bass . . . thumpty thump, thumpty thump. Paul got a good laugh out of that, as did Elvis and I at the time. I'm pretty sure that tough old bass would have survived the flight.

Finally, we got down to business. We recorded "That's Alright" live, with Paul singing and playing bass. We played it live, which is to say that we didn't put down the track first and then sing over it. It was a different experience from the original recording with Elvis because we didn't have to wear earphones in Sam Phillips's studio and we did in the modern, new studio. The only overdubs we made were when the song was played back so that Paul could add "slap back" to the recording by sitting down and slapping his hands against his legs in time with the music. Afterward we went into the control room to listen to what we had done. After two playbacks Paul asked, "Well, Scotty, do you have anything else you want to do here?"

I laughed. "I've done more here today than I did the first time."

Paul laughed and said, "Well, as soon as we get the orchestra and the girl singers, we'll be through." It was a joke, of course, because when we first recorded "That's Alright," Elvis was years away from adding orchestras and girl singers to his records.

After the session, when we posed for photographs, Paul saw Gail and Karen Fontana enter the room, and he playfully said, "Here come the girl singers!"

Paul, D. J., and I posed for a photograph with Gail and Karen, after which Gail returned to the control room just as a young woman entered and sat down. My friend Jerry Schilling introduced her by simply saying, "This is Heather."

At that time no one knew that Paul was dating someone named Heather. We did know that Paul had a stepdaughter named Heather, so we naturally assumed that she was the late Linda Eastman's daughter. About ten days later he had a press conference to announce their engagement. We were all mildly horrified, quickly searching our memories for everything that was said, wondering if anyone had referred to Paul as her "daddy."

There have been more brilliant recording sessions ruined by careless words than anything else I can think of. Technical mistakes can be remedied. The spoken word, if hurtful, even if uttered accidentally, lingers like a poison that can taint the best of music.

Later, Paul told *Pulse* magazine: "I love the early Elvis stuff, and it was such an honor to work with those guys. I mean, Scotty, to me, some of those early solos were just mind-blowing. Where some of them came from, I don't think he knows. You talk to some of those guys—'Well, I was just goofin' around, Paul.' They're so self-effacing."

★ ★ ★

One of the things in recent years that gave me a lot of enjoyment was my home studio. It has been dismantled now, but for years it allowed me to do my own recording projects without leaving the comfort of home. To build the studio, I added a room onto my house and constructed a stone wall out from the base of the addition. The studio also enabled me to engineer and produce other projects. I did an album with Ronnie McDowell at my home that I am particularly proud of, and I'm proud of my part in Alvin Lee's album *Alvin Lee in Tennessee*. D. J. played drums, Pete Pritchard played bass, and I played on a couple of tracks, in addition to making production suggestions. Stan Dacus engineered the album, which was interesting since both Alvin and I had connections with him that went back to the 1970s. At my suggestion, an old friend of mine, Willie Rainsford, played keyboards. Later, Alvin told BlueSpeak.com: "[Scotty] was the original raw sound . . . A lot of his runs are based on jazz notes but played with rock 'n' roll energy. He transcends all styles and every solo he plays is a singable tune in its own right. If anyone has ever done more for the guitar than Scotty Moore, I don't know who it is."

★ ★ ★

In November 2003 I was driving my tractor, mowing the grass out behind my house, when my right leg started hurting. I didn't think too much about it. Aches and pains seem to go along with operating a tractor, mainly because pumping the pedals you're using muscles that you normally wouldn't use. The next day I was sore and stiff when I awoke, so I went to an osteopath. He injected my hand with the medication that he usually used to take out the stiffness, but he didn't seem concerned about the leg pain.

A couple of weeks later, Gail brought me a stack of photographs to autograph. When I tried to write out the dedications, I got the letters all wrong. I would think one thing and my hand would write something else. I had a hard time making the letters. Instead of writing "again," I would write "agian." We had to throw away a lot of photographs because I ruined them. It was then that Gail noticed that I was clinching my hand and holding it close against my chest. She encouraged me to go to a doctor and get a checkup, but I didn't see any reason to do that. Other than the problems with my hand and leg, I felt fine. Besides, two ailments out of a possible thousand that could affect a man my age didn't seem so bad.

"I thought he might have had a stroke," says Gail. "For two weeks, he wouldn't go to the doctor. On December 2, three days before a party that Gibson Guitars put together to celebrate his birthday and his 50-year association with them, he went into town to sign papers for the production company that was going to film the party—and he couldn't sign his check! It was darnedest scrawl you've ever seen. I fussed with him all the way home, giving him hell about not seeing a doctor."

Late that afternoon I received a call from Ira Padnos, a New Orleans anesthesiologist who organizes a music festival each year, the Ponderosa Stomp, to feature the old timers of rock 'n' roll, jazz, and rhythm and blues. He had come to Nashville for my party and had called Gail to get directions. I felt comfortable talking to him because I knew him and trusted his judgment. I gave him my symptoms and he told me that it sounded like a bleeding problem, not a stroke. He told me to go to a hospital right away. I didn't, mainly because of the party. I didn't want to ruin it for everyone. I postponed making a decision until the next day, hoping that the problem would go away. When I awoke the next morning, the problem was worse, so later that afternoon I called Gail and asked her to take me to the hospital.

When we pulled up at Baptist Hospital, the valet attendants were nowhere to be found, so Gail let me out of the car and left to find a parking place. While she was gone I went to the admitting office and checked myself into the hospital. My primary doctor, Bryce Dixon, was there and sent me up to intensive care, where they gave me a CAT scan. Later, they told me that I had a two-inch-thick hematoma on my brain. They said they needed to operate immediately, but they couldn't because of the anticoagulation medication I was on. Instead, they gave me packed platelets all day to build up my blood. Two days later, they took me into surgery and operated on my brain. The next several weeks are still a blur to me.

After the surgery, the surgeon, Dr. Harold Smith, told Gail that he was amazed that I had been able to walk into the hospital. "He shouldn't have been able to walk with something that size inside his head," explained the doctor. "I am even more amazed that there was absolutely no damage to the brain waves. For the past two or three weeks, his brain was jammed against the other side of his skull and when we took out the hematoma, the pressure that had been there was suddenly released and caused his brain to flop back against the other side. Essentially, we rattled his brain."

I am told that they kept me in a drug-induced coma for nine days because I was having seizures. Once the seizures stopped showing up on the CAT scan they brought me out of the coma. I was in the hospital for 33 days, but I don't have any memory of the first three weeks. My memory begins in the hospital room, after they moved me from intensive care, and basically all I remember about my stay is how bad the food was.

When I was released from the hospital on January 8, they told me not to drive my car since my motor skills were not up to par. They seemed to know what they were talking about, so I didn't drive my car; but they didn't say anything about not driving my lawn mower. The grass was so high in my backyard that I didn't see any harm in taking a spin on the mower. Everything was fine until I drove too close to a ditch that ran alongside the house. The mower toppled over into the ditch, with me on it. It took me a while to get out from under the mower. I wasn't hurt, but it put a pretty good scare into me.

I called Gail and told her I had a problem.

"What kind of problem?"

"You'll see when you get here."

When she saw the mower, Gail asked, "How'd that happen?"

"Don't ask," I told her.

Gail was amazed that I wasn't hurt. We got the tractor out of the barn and wrapped a rope around the tractor and the mower and pulled the mower back up out of the ditch. It wasn't a big deal. I just got too close to the edge. Getting too close to the edge is an occupational hazard for guitarists.

Every morning when I awake, all my bones crack. It didn't do that before the surgery. I don't know whether things will ever get back like they were before the surgery. I don't know why I was chosen to survive Elvis and Bill. I did everything they did. I spent all that time on the road, eating bad food, getting no sleep, just enjoying what we were doing. Why I made it this far and they didn't, I'll never understand.

★ ★ ★

When Johnny Cash died, it was another chink out of the wall. I knew Johnny when we were all just starting out. We weren't close, but we followed each other's careers. I don't think we miss Johnny as much as we thought we would because he was ready to go at that point in his life. It was his wife, June, who kept him going. When she died, he apparently didn't see any reason to continue without her. I hope they remember him from the old days . . . "I Walk the Line," and that sort of thing.

One friend that Johnny and I had in common is Marty Stuart, who played in Johnny's band for a while and married one of his daughters. I got to know Marty when Johnny went to the facilities at Opryland Productions to record his television specials. Marty spent so much time with me in the control room, asking questions about the machinery, that the director had to look for him when he was needed on stage.

I never realized I had an impact on Marty until the week of my brain surgery, when he told my co-author a story about going to Memphis when he was at low ebb in his life. It was foggy that day, and he took a wrong turn downtown and ended up on the Mississippi River Bridge. After he crossed the river into Arkansas, he pulled off the road to turn around and it was then that he heard a train coming. He slapped my version of "Mystery Train" into his CD player and listened as the train cut through the fog.

"It was one of the highlights of my life," Marty explained.

Scotty is one of the most eloquent guitar players that ever picked up a guitar. He is the personification of soul in guitar playing. When John [Cash] died, the only other death in my life, musically speaking, was when Elvis Presley died. When John died, there was a lot of media around the event and a lot of folks calling me and I said no to most of it. I took my cue from Scotty. Of all the people that worked around Elvis, the one who handled it with the most dignity was Scotty. When Scotty talked about Elvis, it was for the right reasons, and when he showed up on behalf of Elvis, I felt like Scotty was still representing the man and not the cartoon figure. And when he didn't show up, it was for all the right reasons. I want Scotty to know that he has always been a beacon to me. He is a man of purpose.

I am moved by stories like that because it goes to the heart of why I play the guitar. Lord knows, it was never to get rich. No, for me, it's all about doing something with a guitar that affects people in a positive way. It's a way to leave a mark that fellow travelers can follow: *Scotty was here!*

★ ★ ★

In March 2004 I went to Europe on my first tour after the brain surgery. While I was on the plane coming back, my oldest friend James Lewis died. You met him in the first chapter of this book. We didn't see much of each other in later years, but he was still a big part of my life at an important time in my life and I miss him.

That summer I went to Memphis to help celebrate the 50th anniversary of the recording of "That's Alright" at Sun Studio. On July 5, 2004,

I pressed a button that started a simultaneous playing of the record on 1,500 radio stations around the world. When we went in for Elvis's audition in 1954, I never would have expected the 50th anniversary to be remembered, much less played on radio stations around the world. It gives me a great feeling to think that what we did will last for later generations.

★ ★ ★

It took a while, too long if you ask me, but in April 2009 D. J. Fontana and Bill Black were inducted into the Rock and Roll Hall of Fame as sidemen. I received word of the honor in January 2009 from Bill's son, Lewis Black, who was pleased that his father finally had been recognized for his contribution to American music. I attended the ceremony and no one applauded more enthusiastically than I. No one ever plays music for the purpose of winning awards. But recognition for a lifetime of work, whatever it may be, is always welcome. We are still waiting for the Hall to recognize the Bill Black Combo.

★ 15 ★

HAPPY BIRTHDAY TO ME

2011, I must admit, gave me pause.

It was the year I turned 80.

At 20 or 30 or 40 years of age no one ever thinks about turning 80. It just seems too far away. Besides, I'm convinced that most people live their lives with the expectation that they never will make it to 80. The odds are against you.

The worst part about surviving to 80 is not the aches and pains, or the frequent trips to the doctor, or even the realization that physically you can't do the things that you used to do. The worst part is the memories you carry of those who did not make it. It is almost always a long list.

Do I ever wonder what Elvis would have been like at 80? Of course I do. He died at 42, but he remains a playful, cocky 20-year-old in my memory. And what about Bill Black? He died at 39, but he will always be a lovable twenty-something character in my mind. If the truth is told I doubt that Elvis would have become what he did without Bill's overpowering personality on stage, always nudging Elvis into the limelight where he belonged. Elvis resisted at first, but then he got so caught up in Bill's exuberance that he actually began competing with Bill for audience attention. Then there's Carl Perkins who was only 66 when he passed away. He went through a lot in his life, including public neglect, but I can well imagine him at 80 singing "Blue Suede Shoes" to an appreciative audience.

Sometimes I walk in and out of those memories like a ghost exploring an empty house. I can tell you what I see and hear in those empty rooms, but you will never see and hear what I do because you were not there in the beginning to experience it. You can only imagine it. It saddens me that I can't share those visual memories with you. What I can do is write another book, this time a first-person account of my life, which gives my co-author James the opportunity to do what he wanted to do in the beginning: make my life more accessible. It is hard to believe that James and I have been talking about my life for twenty years. You'd think he'd be tired of it by now, but he keeps coming back for more.

I was pretty far into the year of my 79th when I received word that Memphis wanted to help me celebrate my 80th birthday. My first reaction was, hell no! I'm much too old to be celebrating birthdays. To me a happy birthday is one that comes and goes without me noticing it. I changed my mind after Kevin Kane, president of the Memphis Convention and Visitors Bureau, convinced Gail that it would be something I would enjoy. Kevin and Gail partnered with Dave Berryman, president of Gibson Guitar Corporation, to throw an invitation-only birthday party at the Gibson facility in Memphis on December 10, 2011, two weeks before my actual birthday, which comes at an awkward time between Christmas and the New Year.

Dave Berryman is an interesting person in his own right. With a background in business (he has a MBA from Harvard), he does not have a musical bone in his body and yet he and a couple of business partners saved Gibson from going under in 1986 by acquiring the company and restoring its prestige. He generously offered the Gibson Café in Memphis as the venue for my birthday celebration and served barbecued ribs prepared by the Blues City Café, which is owned by Kevin Kane. Once they had a time and a place, Gail compiled a guest list and helped prepare a keepsake invitation that included a CD of the 1998 Grammy-nominated instrumental "Goin' Back to Memphis," recorded by myself and several survivors of the Bill Black Combo, especially guitarist Reggie Young, who is a Memphis/ Nashville guitar legend in his own right.

Two days before the event we drove to Memphis so that we could settle in and be relaxed, and so that I could attend a recording session at Sun Studio, where my English band had booked time to record. The following day, Saturday, was meant to be a time to visit with a few friends in the hotel lobby, but there were so many well-wishers who came into town for the celebration and dropped by my hotel room to visit that I ended up never going downstairs.

I spent hours, it seemed, on the telephone.

Robin Zander of Cheap Trick called to wish me a happy birthday.

Paul McCartney called from Copenhagen, where he was performing with his band. To my surprise, he sang "Happy Birthday" over the telephone as only he can do.

Shortly before 7 p.m. Gail and I left the hotel and walked over to the Gibson building, where I decided to stand at the entrance, just inside the door, to greet each and every guest. I saw people I had not seen in many years and to a person they were shocked to see me being a standup host. Judging by the guest book, I ended up shaking more than 400 hands, including those of Billy Swan, Ronnie McDowell, Jerry Schilling, and Priscilla Presley.

The entertainment portion of the party was kicked off by Sonny Burgess and the Pacers, an Arkansas-based band that recorded five singles on Sun Records, including "Red Headed Woman" and "My Bucket's Got a Hole in It." I have known Sonny since the mid-1950s, when he traveled with Johnny Cash, Elvis Presley, Roy Orbison, Carl Perkins, and Jerry Lee Lewis. The band that night was impressively tight musically, especially when you consider that some of the members had been on the road for more than half a century, and Sonny's vocals were as raw and energetic as they were in 1955, though perhaps a tad hoarser. Also performing that night were my German band, John Barron and his band from Hamburg (with whom I tour when I am in Germany), Lee Rocker, and Tracy Nelson, who sang "Careless Love," a song she had recorded with me in 1971 at Music City Recorders, accompanied at the party by my friend Bucky Barrett.

When the time came for speeches, George Klein kicked things off and soon passed the microphone off to Priscilla Presley, who shocked everyone by taking the stage to wish me a happy birthday. After all these years she is still a beautiful woman, someone who can hush conversations simply by stepping into the room. I was greatly moved when she tearfully recounted her conversations with Elvis about his friendship with me. By the time she finished there was not a dry eye in the house.

Of course, Gail dragged me up on stage to say a few words. I'm comfortable on stage with a guitar in my hand. Not so much when I have to talk. I was genuinely moved that so many people had come to my party, so speaking from the heart that night was not a problem. I was also moved when Dave Berryman joined me on stage and presented me with a magnificent replica of the original Gibson ES 295 guitar that I had started out with in 1953. Gibson craftsmen had re-created it to exact specifications and just holding it brought back memories.

Priscilla and my good friend Jerry Schilling stayed at the party almost to the very end, as did most of the guests. When I left that night and returned to the hotel it was difficult to fall asleep because of a constant stream of memories, some involving family, others recapturing moments from the past with Elvis, Bill, and D. J. It was a grand event and I can't wait to see what they come up with for my 100th birthday.

Sam Phillips.

Elvis Presley.

Bill Black.

Carl Perkins.

To a man all gone.

I salute you gentlemen—and hope to see most of you on the other side.

POSTSCRIPT

When it comes to Scotty's place in rock 'n' roll history, the Rolling Stones' Keith Richards is emphatic with his opinion: Scotty is Number One.

First of all, he was laying the licks down for my generation. He gave us the grounding. If you are my age, he was the beacon. You heard a lot of other cats later, but Scotty is the one who turned you on. To me, and it's a sad thing to say, but without Scotty, Elvis wouldn't have been as big. It was Scotty and Bill Black's rapport—and Scotty's ability to understand the space he was working in. Elvis got big so quick, he overshadowed the band. Parker, the beloved Colonel, being the man he was, saw no percentage in the band. It is really scandalous what Parker did to Elvis. I'm sure the Colonel told him that Scotty and Bill were being paid a fortune. Knowing this business— and knowing the Colonel—I would put money on it.

For his part, Scotty takes praise today much as he took it in the beginning: with a grain of salt. To his way of thinking, some 50 years after he helped lay the foundation for a multi-million-dollar music industry, it still has a surreal quality to it—not the music, but the history of it, the way it happened as he lived it day to day. When he says "walk a mile in my shoes" if you want to understand the music, he does so with both conviction and humility.

Scotty has finally accepted his role in American music. In doing so he has realized that what he for so long fancied as a magical interlude in his life was instead history in the making that ultimately affected every facet of American society.

—James L. Dickerson

ACKNOWLEDGMENTS

Scotty Moore would like to thank the following for their help in putting this project together: Ed Frank and Cathy Evans of the Mississippi Valley Collection at the University of Memphis, John Bakke for authorizing use of the Jerry Hopkins Collection at the University of Memphis, Craig Gill, our editor at University Press of Mississippi, the late James Lewis, Bobbie Moore, Andrea Weil, Lee Rocker, David Briggs, Mary Frawley, Emily Sanders, Evelyn Black Tuverville, Gail Pollock, Tracy Nelson, Hugh Hickerson, Reggie Young, Ronnie McDowell, Rose Drake, the late Robbie Dawson, Gary Tallent, Ralph Moore, Jerry Schilling, John Carroll, Fred Burch, the late Marshall Grant, Keith Richards, Paul McCartney, Ron Wood, Conrad Jones, Chips Moman, the late Tammy Wynette, D. J. Fontana, Billy Sherrill, Mary Ann Coscarelli, Sherri Paullus, Robert Dye at Graceland for his most helpful cooperation (Elvis, Elvis Presley, and Graceland are registered trademarks of Elvis Presley Enterprises), the Naval Historical Center, Analee Bankson, the Jordanaires (Gordon Stoker, Ray Walter, Neal Matthews, and Duane West), Frank Parise, Merle Parise, the Memphis/Shelby County Public Library and Information Center, the Jean and Alexander Heard Library at Vanderbilt University Library, the Public Library of Nashville & Davidson County, Edwin Moore, Evelyn Lewis, Louise Moore, and Gerald Nelson.

For giving the reason to undertake the original biography, *That's Alright, Elvis*, James L. Dickerson would like to give special thanks to Vikki and Emmo Hein.

GUITARS OWNED BY SCOTTY MOORE

DESCRIPTION	DATE PURCHASED	DATE SOLD/TRADED
1) Fender Esquire	1952	1953
2) Gibson ES 295	1953	July 7, 1955
3) Gibson L5 CES (blond) (serial number A-18195)	July 7, 1955	January 1957[14]
4) Gibson Super 400 CESN (serial number A-24672)	January 1957	1963[15]
5) Gibson Super 400 (Sunburst) (serial number 62713)	October 1963	February 1986[16]
6) Gibson Super 400 CESN (serial number 080253002)	March 1987	destroyed[17]
7) Gibson Chet Atkins Country Gentleman, a gift from Chet Atkins	1988	donated[18]
8) Gibson Chet Atkins Country Gentleman	October 1999	still in use

---

14. Now owned by Larry Moss, Memphis.

15. Chips Moman sold this guitar to Heather Mozart for $108,000.

16. Now on display at Hard Rock Café, Memphis.

17. Destroyed in Nashville flood of 2010 while on loan to International Musicians Hall of Fame.

18. Donated to Chet Atkins Appreciation Society in July 2010.

SCOTTY MOORE'S INCOME DURING HIS YEARS WITH ELVIS

YEAR	GROSS	INCOME FROM MUSIC	INCOME FROM ELVIS
1954	$2,249.49	$379.49	$139.25
1955	$11,265.03	$8,052.24	$8,052.24
1956	$9,166.63	$9,001.13	$8,193.58
1957	$10,251.65	$10,251.65	$6,656.65
1958	$2,322.00	$2,322.00	0
1959	$13,547.64	$13,547.64	0
1960	$8,339.38	$8,255.38	$1,582.00
1961	$12,482.10	$12,482.10	$2,500.00
1962	$11,066.90	$11,066.90	$500.00*
1963	$14,932.74	$14,932.74	$500.00*
1964	$13,311.30	$13,311.30	$500.00*
1965	$11,549.07	$11,549.07	$500.00*
1966	$15,702.17	$15,702.17	$500.00*
1967	$13,327.44	$13,327.44	$500.00*
1968	$12,040.27	$12,040.27	$250.00*

The column of figures labeled "Income From Music" includes "Elvis-related" income from motion picture companies and recording companies; the column labeled "From Elvis" represents income received directly from the entertainer for performances and bonuses.

* Christmas bonuses

SCOTTY MOORE DISCOGRAPHY

Elvis Presley records on which Scotty Moore played lead guitar, rhythm guitar, six-string bass, or acted as session leader

1954–55

Baby, Let's Play House
Blue Moon
Blue Moon of Kentucky
Good Rockin' Tonight
Harbor Lights
I Don't Care If the Sun Don't Shine
I Forgot to Remember to Forget
I'll Never Let You Go (Little Darlin')
I Love You Because
I'm Left, You're Right, She's Gone
Just Because
Milkcow Boogie
Mystery Train
That's All Right
Tomorrow Night
Trying to Get to You
When It Rains, It Really Pours
You're a Heartbreaker
I Got a Woman

1956–57

Money Honey
Heartbreak Hotel
I'm Counting On You
I Was the One
Blue Suede Shoes

My Baby Left Me
One Sided Love Affair
So Glad You're Mine
I'm Gonna Sit Right Down and Cry
   (Over You)
Tutti Frutti
Lawdy, Miss Clawdy
Shake, Rattle and Roll
I Want You, I Need You, I Love You
Hound Dog
Don't Be Cruel
Anyway You Want Me
Playing for Keeps
Love Me
How Do You Think I Feel
How's the World Treating You
Paralyzed
When My Blue Moon Turns to Gold
   Again
Long Tall Sally
Old Shep
Too Much
Anyplace Is Paradise
Ready Teddy
First in Line
Rip It Up
I Believe
Tell Me Why
All Shook Up
Peace in the Valley

I Beg of You
That's When Your Heartaches Begin
Take My Hand, Precious Lord
Got a Lot O' Living to Do
Mean Woman Blues
(Let Me Be Your) Teddy Bear
Party
Hot Dog
Lonesome Cowboy
One Night (of Sin)
Loving You
It Is No Secret
Blueberry Hill
Have I Told You Lately That I Love You
Is It So Strange
Don't Leave Me Now
I Beg of You
One Night
True Love
I Need You So
Loving You
When It Rains It Really Pours
Jailhouse Rock
Young and Beautiful
Treat Me Nice
I Want to Be Free
(You're So Square) Baby I Don't Care
Don't Leave Me Now
Treat Me Nice
Blue Christmas
My Wish Came True
White Christmas
Here Comes Santa Claus
Silent Night
Don't
O Little Town of Bethlehem
Santa Bring My Baby Back (to Me)
Santa Claus Is Back in Town
I'll Be Home for Christmas

1958–59

Hard Headed Woman
Trouble
New Orleans
King Creole
Crawfish
Dixieland Rock
Lover Doll
Don't Ask Me Why
As Long As I Have You
Young Dreams
Steadfast, Loyal and True
Doncha' Think It's Time
Your Cheatin' Heart
Wear My Ring Around Your Neck

1960–61

Make Me Know It
Stuck On You
Fame and Fortune
A Mess of Blues
It Feels So Right
Soldier Boy
Fever
Like a Baby
It's Now or Never
The Girl of My Best Friend
Dirty, Dirty Feeling
The Thrill of Your Love
I Gotta Know
Such a Night
Are You Lonesome Tonight?
Girl Next Door Went a Walkin'
I Will Be Home Again
Reconsider Baby
Shoppin' Around

Didja' Ever

Doin' the Best I Can

G.I. Blues

Frankfort Special

Tonight Is So Right for Love

What's She Really Like

Big Boots

Pocketful of Rainbows

Wooden Heart

Tonight's All Right for Love

Milky White Way

His Hand in Mine

I Believe in the Man in the Sky

He Knows Just What I Need

Surrender

Mansion Over the Hilltop

In My Father's House

Joshua Fit the Battle

Swing Down Sweet Chariot

I'm Gonna Walk Dem Golden Stairs

If We Never Meet Again

Known Only to Him

Crying in the Chapel

Working on the Building

Lonely Man

In My Way

Wild in the Country

Forget Me Never

I Slipped, I Stumbled, I Fell

I'm Comin' Home

Gently

In Your Arms

Give Me the Right

I Feel So Bad

It's a Sin

I Want You With Me

There's Always Me

Starting Today

Sentimental Me

Judy

Put the Blame on Me

Hawaiian Sunset

Aloha Oe

Ku-U-I-Po

No More

Slicin' Sand

Blue Hawaii

Ito Eats

Hawaiian Wedding Song

Island of Love

Steppin' Out of Line

Almost Always True

Moonlight Swim

Can't Help Falling in Love

Beach Boy Blues

Rock-A-Hula Baby

Kiss Me Quick

That's Someone You Never Forget

I'm Yours

His Latest Flame

Little Sister

Follow That Dream

What a Wonderful Life

I'm Not the Marrying Kind

A Whistling Tune

Sound Advice

For the Millionth and the Last Time

Good Luck Charm

Anything That's Part of You

I Met Her Today

Night Rider

Home Is Where the Heart Is

Riding the Rainbow

I Got Lucky

This Is Living

King of the Whole Wide World

1962–63

Something Blue
Gonna Get Back Home Somehow
(Such An) Easy Question
Fountain of Love
Just for Old Time's Sake
Night Rider [unreleased]
You'll Be Gone
I Feel That I've Known You Forever
Just Tell Her Jim Said Hello
Suspicion
She's Not You
I Don't Want To
We're Comin' In Loaded
Thanks to the Rolling Sea
Where Do You Come From
Girls, Girls, Girls
Return to Sender
Because of Love
The Walls Have Ears
Song of the Shrimp
A Boy Like Me, A Girl Like You
Mama
Earth Boy
Dainty Little Moon Beams
I Don't Want to Be Tied
Plantation Rock
We'll Be Together
Happy Ending
Relax
I'm Falling in Love Tonight
They Remind Me Too Much of You
Cotton Candy Land
A World of Our Own
How Would You Like to Be
One Broken Heart for Sale
Beyond the Bend

Take Me to the Fair
Bossa Nova Baby
I Think I'm Gonna Like It Here
Mexico
The Bullfighter Was a Lady
Marguerita
Vino, Dinero y Amor
(There's) No Room to Rhumba in a
    Sports Car
Fun in Acapulco
El Toro
You Can't Say No in Acapulco
Guadalajara [track only]
Malaguena [track only]
Echoes of Love
Please Don't Drag That String Around
(You're the) Devil in Disguise
Never Ending
What Now, What Next, Where To
Witchcraft
Finders Keepers, Losers Weepers
Love Me Tonight
(It's a) Long Lonely Highway
Ask Me
Western Union
Slowly But Surely
Blue River
Night Life
C'mon Everybody
If You Think I Don't Need You
Viva Las Vegas
I Need Somebody to Lean On
Do the Vega
Yellow Rose of Texas
The Eyes of Texas
Santa Lucia
The Lady Loves Me
You're the Boss

Today, Tomorrow, and Forever [unreleased duet with Ann-Margret]
What'd I Say
There's Gold in the Mountains
One Boy, Two Little Girls
Once Is Enough
Tender Feeling
Kissin' Cousins
Smokey Mountain Boy
Catchin' On Fast
Barefoot Ballad
Anyone (Could Fall in Love With You)

1964–65

Memphis, Tennessee
Ask Me
It Hurts Me
Girl Happy
The Meanest Girl in Town
Puppet on a String
Roustabout
Wheels on My Heels
There's a Brand New Day on the Horizon
Carny Town
It's Carnival Time
One Track Heart
Big Love Big Heartache
Hard Knocks
It's a Wonderful World
Poison Ivy League
Little Egypt
Cross My Heart and Hope to Die
Spring Fever
Do Not Disturb
I've Got to Find My Baby

Fort Lauderdale Chamber of Commerce
Startin' Tonight
Do the Clam
Wolf Call
Go East, Young Man
Shake That Tambourine
Golden Coins
So Close, Yet So Far
Harem Holiday
Mirage
Animal Instinct
Kismet
Hey Little Girl
Wisdom of the Ages
My Desert Serenade
Come Along
Petunia, the Gardener's Daughter
Chesay
What Every Woman Lives For
Frankie and Johnny
Look Out, Broadway
Beginner's Luck
Down by the Riverside
When the Saints Go Marchin' In
Shout It Out
Hard Luck
Please Don't Stop Loving Me
Everybody Come Aboard
Frankie and Johnny #2 [unreleased]
Drums of the Islands
Datin'
Scratch My Back
Stop Where You Are
A Dog's Life
This Is My Heaven
Paradise "Hawaiian" Style
A House of Sand

Queenie Wahine's Papaya

Sand Castles

1966–67

Leave My Woman Alone [soundtrack
    only]

You Gotta Stop

Yoga Is As Yoga Does

The Love Machine

She's a Machine

Sing You Children

I'll Take Love

Easy Come, Easy Go

City by Night

It Won't Be Long

Old McDonald

I Love Only One Girl

Baby If You'll Give Me Your Love

Double Trouble

Long Legged Girl (With the Short
    Dress On)

There's So Much World to See

Could I Fall in Love

Come What May

Where Could I Go But to the Lord

If the Lord Wasn't Walking by My Side

Without Him

Somebody Bigger Than You and I

Beyond the Reef

In the Garden

By and By

Farther Along

So High

Love Letters

Tomorrow Is a Long Time

Down in the Alley

Where No One Stands Alone

Stand by Me

How Great Thou Art

Run On

Adam and Evil

All That I Am

Spinout

Never Say Yes

Beach Shack

Am I Ready

Stop Look and Listen

Smorgasbord

Stay Away Joe

Dominic [unreleased]

All I Needed Was the Rain

You'll Never Walk Alone

We Call on Him

High Heel Sneakers

Just Call Me Lonesome

Singing Tree [unreleased]

Big Boss Man

Guitar Man

Suppose [unreleased]

Clambake

Hey, Hey, Hey

Confidence

Who Needs Money

A House That Has Everything

You Don't Know Me [unreleased movie
    version]

How Can You Lose What You Never Had

The Girl I Never Loved

1968

Stay Away

Goin' Home

Too Much Monkey Business

U.S. Male

NOTES

CHAPTER 1

The postcards exchanged by Scott and Mattie Moore are in Scotty Moore's possession.

James L. Dickerson visited the old Moore homestead in 1996. It was then owned by James Lewis, who generously took time from his schedule to give Dickerson a tour of the house. Lewis's daughter lived in the house at that time. Lewis has since passed away.

CHAPTER 2

All of the letters and telegrams referred to in this chapter can be found in *Foreign Relations, 1948-1950, volumes VIII, IX and X*. These volumes, which are made available to select university libraries by the government, contain State Department communications no longer considered classified. In a telegram to the Secretary of State on October 14, 1948, Ambassador Stuart, who was assigned to the embassy in Nanking, complained that the naval command was interfering with his efforts to organize an orderly evacuation.

Facts On File contains excellent week-to-week summaries of developments in China during the months referred to in this book in its annual publications.

CHAPTER 3

All of the quotes from Marion Keisker in this book, not otherwise identified, were taken from interviews in the Jerry Hopkins Collection at the University of Memphis. Also in the collection is the letter to Hopkins from Keisker that challenges Sam Phillips's version of early events at the studio.

In response to his query, Tammy Wynette called James L. Dickerson to talk about her memories of Scotty. At the time she called, she was out on the road in her tour bus. An earlier conversation between Dickerson and her husband had been disconnected when the mobile phone on the tour bus entered a different cell area. This time, Tammy pulled the bus off the road to make the call on a land line. She said she was in the middle of nowhere. To Dickerson, it sounded like she was calling from a pay-phone booth.

CHAPTERS 4-8

Unless otherwise stated, all quotes in this book attributed to Bob Neal were taken from interviews in the Jerry Hopkins Collection at the University of Memphis. A financial statement made out by Bob Neal for Scotty Moore and Bill Black is still in Scotty's possession.

Comments from Jack Clement were taken from interviews done by Dickerson in 1986 and 1995.

Comments from Frank Page were taken from an interview done by Dickerson in 1995 and from interviews in the Jerry Hopkins Collection at the University of Memphis.

Comments from D. J. Fontana were taken from an interview done with Dickerson in 1995. He was most cooperative and offered to assist with the project in any way possible.

Comments from June Carter Cash were taken from interviews done with her in 1985.

Bobbie Moore was interviewed in 1995.

Evelyn Black Tuverville was interviewed in 1995.

Carl Perkins's account of the hospital visit was taken from the *706 ReUnion* album recorded by Scotty Moore and Perkins in 1992 at Sun Studio in Memphis. In addition to music, the album contains conversations between Scotty and Carl.

All comments from the Jordanaires, unless otherwise identified, were taken from a 1995 interview with Dickerson at Scotty Moore's house, where the singers had gathered to do overdubs on a tape in Scotty's home studio.

The account of Elvis Presley's fight at the service station was taken from published press reports.

Fred Burch was interviewed in 1995 and Gerald Nelson was interviewed in 1996.

Comments from Reggie Young were taken from interviews done by Dickerson in 1985, 1986, and 1995.

Sharri Paullus was interviewed in 1995.

The account of Elvis's meeting with Marion Keisker was taken from interviews on file in the Jerry Hopkins Collection at the University of Memphis.

Hal Kanter was interviewed in 2000.

Vikki Hein was interviewed in 1995.

CHAPTER 9

Dickerson came across Scotty's blond Gibson in 1985 when Chips Moman moved back to Memphis after living in Nashville for a number of years. Dickerson wrote a story for *The Commercial Appeal* about Moman's ownership of the guitar and arranged for Moman to be photographed with it. Herb O. Mell, Moman's assistant, told Dickerson the Smithsonian Institution had asked if it could display the guitar and had appraised it at $400,000. When the story was published, and

Moman saw the price tag that Mell had attached to the guitar, he was annoyed. He didn't mind showing off Scotty's guitar; he just didn't want the whole world to know how valuable it was. In November 1992 Moman asked Scotty for written authentication of the guitar's history. In 1996 Moman told Dickerson he would never sell the guitar, "not even for a million dollars." He subsequently sold the guitar for $108,000 to Heather Mozart, an Elvis memorabilia collector.

John Carroll was interviewed in 1995.

Billy Sherrill was interviewed in 1996.

All comments from Sam Phillips were taken from interviews with Dickerson in 1985 and 1986, published press accounts, and interviews on file at the University of Memphis. All letters from Sam Phillips referred to in this book were in the possession of Scotty Moore until donated to the Rock 'n' Roll Hall of Fame Library and Archives, a new project of the Hall of Fame opened in 2012.

CHAPTER 10

Emily Moore Sanders was interviewed in 1995.

Chips Moman was interviewed in 1996, 1985, and 1986.

CHAPTER 11

Tracy Nelson, Rose Drake, and Hugh Hickerson were interviewed in 1996.

Gail Pollock and Mary Ann Cosarelli were interviewed in 1995.

CHAPTER 12

Conrad Jones and Ronnie McDowell were interviewed in 1996.

Andrea Weil, Jerry Schilling, Gary Tallent, and Lee Rocker were interviewed in 1995.

Keith Richards was interviewed in 1996.

CHAPTER 13

Gail Pollock was interviewed in 1997 and 1998.

CHAPTER 14

Gail Pollock was interviewed in 2004.

Marty Stuart was interviewed in 2004.

CHAPTER 15

Gail Pollock was interviewed in 2011 and 2012.

INDEX